Strickland

Strickland

A ROMANCE

Hilary Masters

St. Martin's Press • New York

DESIGN BY FEARN CUTLER

Library of Congress Cataloging-in-Publication Data

Masters, Hilary.
  Strickland.
    p.   cm.
    ISBN 0-312-03484-9
    I. Title.
PS3563.A82S77   1989   813'.54—dc20   89-34901

First Edition

10 9 8 7 6 5 4 3 2 1

PART
I

Chapter

I

Gunfire in the woods all morning. Strickland cannot concentrate; the old account sprawled upon his desk like a thick hedge. He cannot penetrate the rhetoric, and the explosions to the north of the house distracted him, kept him outside the events though it was a history he had announced.

"It's the last inning," T.D. had said last fall. "You're the only one that can lay down a hit." Then the blood began pouring out. Hunting season, early November, and there had been this print above the old professor's bed—*First Light Kill*—which Strickland had noticed only as he turned to call for a nurse. Hunter in a blind pats a retriever holding the limp body of a mallard in its jaws.

"I don't mind telling you, I'm a little afraid of them," the game warden says yesterday. A fresh-faced boy in forest green with a huge Magnum buckled tight to his right hip and high up. Strickland wondered how fast he could draw strapped like that, and what was there in the woods around Silvernales that required such heavy armament? No matter, the soft, round blondness in the face would question the moment anyway and become the target, so it was irrelevant how he carried his weapon. Taking aim could be fatal, sometimes.

"Well, what did they say?" The name tag fastened over the left breast pocket of the game warden's tunic said R. Van Deusen. A local name, a big family from around Copake. Robert or Richard or maybe he's just called Van.

Hey, here's Van, voices call out on a big Saturday night at Strang's Hotel in Copake Falls. Or maybe his wife, one of those unobtrusively pretty women making change at church bake sales, would place a small hand, nails clear-polished and trimmed, upon the lapel of his jacket. *Oh, Van, you don't mean it?*

Strickland and the officer talked by the latter's dark green cruiser parked in the gravel turnaround by the barn. The tulips Nancy had planted were just poking up around the foundation. Mostly red. Van Deusen had let the motor idle and kept one booted leg inside the open door, ready to pull out of there quickly and on to a genuine breach of the New York State Fish and Game Law where he could draw his revolver, thoughtfully.

"First off, there's no law says they can't shoot anytime they want. There's no season on that."

"It's intolerable," Strickland said. "I'm engaged in some very important work—some of it related to our national defense." He let his voice glide into a deeper register, a thunderous vibrato that always made sound engineers frantic. The game warden regarded him with an impartial blankness. "They start shooting at daybreak and it goes on to mid-afternoon. And not just on weekends. Some of them can't even speak English."

"You have talked to them, then?" Van Deusen made a motion as if he were about to get out a notepad, make out a report. Now Strickland was being investigated.

"Only last fall when they drove up here to ask permission to hunt on my land. Their car license was from White Plains." The game warden's nod was welcomed—an ally at least on this point. "One of them did all the talking for the others. He was a translator, but I had trouble even understanding him. Of course they ignored the signs I posted all around the property."

"They think differently about these things. I've talked to their like before. They say that in the old country, if the landowner doesn't personally hunt on his land, then anyone can hunt on it." The young man smiled, pumped up by his own information.

"What is this? This is the U.S. of A., not Sicily."

"Well, they haven't trespassed yet, have they? I can't do nothing about their target practice. It's on their property. Why don't you talk to them, Mr. Strickland? They're your neighbors."

"Neighbors?" A large red-tailed hawk scribed ciphers overhead. "See that hawk? I used to have a lot more of them flying around. That would be illegal, wouldn't it?"

"Yessir, strictly illegal. Do you have evidence they have been shooting hawks?"

"Now how can I get that sort of evidence?" He walked around to the front of the car's hood. He was the same height as the game warden; it was the uniform that made the younger man seem larger. "I just know they've been knocking them down. Another thing. You know they shoot songbirds too. And that's illegal. They put them into sauces."

"Into sauces," Van Deusen said carefully. He was taking it all down somewhere.

"That's right—spaghetti sauces." A volley of rifle fire crazed the clear air. "Hear that?"

"Sounds like the 32.40 and a 30-30. Yes, that's what that was." Van Deusen nodded, satisfied with his identification. He turned back to Strickland with a grave expression. "You're telling me that Louie's spaghetti joint over in Green River puts orioles into his tomato sauce?"

"No, not him. He uses commercial stuff from cans. But these guys . . ." Strickland watched the puzzlement darken the sunny features. All alike. Take any farm boy and put a badge on him, wrap

•5•

an MP band around his left arm, and his perception of the possibilities of the world is reduced to one-on-one.

"That your telephone?" the game warden was saying. It had been ringing for a little, then it shut off.

"It's plugged into a recorder. Okay, can you file some sort of a report? A complaint? Just for the record?"

"I'll file a report—certainly. But they're your neighbors, Mr. Strickland. Why don't you talk to them?"

"They're not neighbors. They have no intention to live on that property. They only bought it to set up their hunting camps. Trailers," Strickland added significantly. "I've heard they live in trailers." He regrets he's said this. Van Deusen probably has relatives living in trailers all over the county.

In fact, all of Silvernales was a trailer park. Even the post office was a trailer. Rectangular plastic containers drawn up nose to flank like the boxcars Strickland could remember in the staging yard of the Santa Fe Railroad in Salina, Kansas. *This is Carrol Strickland of the Voice of America, speaking to you from downtown Silvernales, New York, where the residents have formed a unique community. As we listen in, we hear . . .*

—Here's Van. How nice to see you. What brings you here?

—Hello, Aunt Martha. Just thought I'd drop by on my way back from talking to that fella up on the hill. He's made disparaging words about the way you and the rest of my relatives in the county have chosen to live.

—We try to keep a clean, wholesome community; nothing fancy.

—You do the best you can with what you have.

—Amen to that, says Aunt Martha, pouring a long, cool glass of Lipton's iced tea.

The best of the day to you. (Music up and out.)

Oh, brother. Strickland shook his head clear of the script. The air was full of such scenes, old radio interludes. *All right, Federman; who are our next contestants?* Now the air had gone soundless but for the diminishing purr of R. Van Deusen's heavy-tired LTD as it rounded the bottom of the driveway. The three emergency lights on its roof caught the light and resembled small turrets ready to fire. Strickland ran toward his house, resolved that if he made it through the back screen door before the gunners above the house started up, his day would be saved. Bang-Bang! He didn't make it.

"Such hazards are the fleas that come with that dog we call civilization," T.D. Moon used to say. "Stand up straight and you can be sure some bozo in the bushes is going to take a potshot at you." Mooney's boys would nod, sip his scotch and stretch out their legs as if to compare scuff marks on their buckskins. What good days they were. "But we got to stand up straight. We're the only ones, boys."

"This is Mooney's novel," a newcomer would be told. "Malcom Cowley included it in that famous piece of his in the old *Vanity Fair*." The sophomore's eyes gleamed in the reflected elegance of the professor's study. Then, to pull the hook deeper. "You roomed with Dos Passos in Greenwich Village, didn't you, Mooney?"

"Oh, gosh, Carrol." That wonderful laugh dismissed any claim to fame. "That was so long ago. But old Dos and I did share rooms for a spell but he moved out since I kept interfering with his love life. He was holding afternoon seminars with a little lady from Barnard. I still remember her dark eyes—among other things."

Even the fire in the hearth had chuckled.

Those Thursdays at Prof. Moon's made a special fraternity. Everyone took off his honors at the door when he entered that paneled study layered with latakia and the spicy smoke of Moon's Gauloise cigarettes. They breathed a commonality, whether All American, class grind or class president. They became Mooney's Boys. "Hiya, Bub," he'd say at the door with that cigarette stuck in the corner of his mouth, left eye narrowed behind the heavy, black frames. Bub, he called all of them; all the same name. He had given them new names as well. Years later, someone would say, You were one of Mooney's Boys, and it squared the shoulders.

Several months ago, Strickland had been blinded by the whiteness of the room, the bed and the mound of white upon it, as if all color had been drained or pushed out by the colorless liquid being pumped into one of Mooney's arms. "Hiya, Bub."

"Funny thing, hearing you the other night did make me think of that stuff in Saigon," Moon had said in November. The professor's features looked the same but shrunken; the disease made him a caricature of his former self. Strickland recalled trophies swinging in pawnshop windows in Bangkok. Headhunter's barter. "Was it all that terrific?" Moon had rambled. "So childlike, maybe that was the reason. Young and tart. You can imagine, Bub, how these thoughts made me feel in my present condition." The private laugh cheered Strickland, numbed as he was by the horror of the hospital room. This was the side of Moon only a few of them knew—not the public, sardonic professor.

"Defend the Reverend Donne, Mr. Strickland, against Mr. Dryden's charge that he played at metaphysics—affected them I think he said; more wit than intellect, not unlike our late, lamented Democratic candidate for the Chief Executive, Mr. Stevenson—more affected than effective."

The nose looked more like a beak without glasses, denuded and bony—had he ever seen Moon without those heavy, black framed glasses?—which made the smile vulnerable. Almost sweetly turned as he continued to speak. "All your fault, Carrol Mellifluous Strickland. I first heard you on the campus radio. You had a program late at night."

"'Music to Study By,' I believe it was called."

"Sure, 'Music to Study By.' Sure." Once more the private laughter. "That's the voice of America, I remember saying to myself. Deep. Manly but sensitive. Doesn't know it all but smart enough to catch on. No pretensions. Also a bit of a dreamer, but a practical edge. Sold—American. If it works, it must be okay. You were a natural. That voice will be important, I said to myself."

"To sell soup."

"I don't want to hear that kind of talk—not now, not from one of my boys. You did good, Bub. Real good. It wasn't your fault.

None of us were to blame. The front office didn't want us to win the pennant. Too many trades in mid-season."

The free hand near Strickland tightened on the sheet and the mass beneath the covers hardened, like sudden stone. The small head turned away. The skull was baby smooth.

"Should I get someone?" The body rocked, a sign Strickland took as negative. "What can I do?"

A sound like air coming from a ruptured inner tube, and Strickland looked away quickly but there was no odor. The fingers relaxed, the body seemed to settle and the head turned back. Moon's sunken cheeks were wet as if he had been crying, but it was perspiration. "I'd give my left nut for a Lucky, I don't care what the surgeon general says. What's his habit, do you suppose—brass buttons? Whew! That one went out of the park. Naw, those fucking nurses are too damn eager to give you happiness with their needles. *Dicique beatus ante obitum nemo* and so forth. Remember your Ovid?"

"I never took Latin."

"Well, why the hell should you? Nobody talks it anymore. Which reminds me of such things. Carrol, I was just sorry as hell about Nancy. Damn bad luck, Bub."

"Thank you, T.D. I appreciated your letter."

"But she left you a daughter . . ."

"Leslie."

"Yes, Leslie who is the spitting image of her good-looking ma, I bet." The smile, more naked without the eyeglasses, called for a positive response, one last reason for optimism. Boys, he used to say, we may not be perfect but there's none better, none even close, so it's our duty to share this near-perfection with others. Like the actress says to the bishop, spread it around, he'd chuckle and look over his glasses.

So Carrol Strickland replies, "Yes, she's very much like her. Even to Nancy's procrastination. Actually, I would have been here sooner but . . ."

"Cut the shit." One frail hand had lifted in the air. "I got no time for that. Now listen. Emerson Caldwell, a crypto asshole. Right?"

"Sure."

"That's not convincing."

"Well, he meant a lot to some of us, T.D. No one talked to the Russians the way he did."

"He meant a lot to his mother too. He meant a lot to his wife too. I've been hearing from her. You'd think he was George Washington and Adlai Stevenson rolled into one. She's been writing me about some papers of his. He was like Adlai and that was his problem. Now, listen." The voice stopped and Strickland could almost hear the effort summoned in the silence.

"You remember Caldwell said he had delivered this order from Kennedy to call off the hit on Diem. Lodge denied such a note. You get the picture? A direct presidential order signed by JFK is a lot different from the phone call that—who was it—"

"Bundy, I believe."

"Right. Bundy . . . that Bundy is supposed to have made to Lodge. Comprenez?"

"Sure, the phone call disappears into the air, a matter of conjecture to be denied—as Lodge did deny getting it—whereas the Presidential order with JFK on the margin puts several curious footnotes into the history, not the least of which is that the President of the United States was a party to the assassination of the leader of another government—and an ally to boot."

"Oh, Golden Throat—if I had anything left to get hard, it would do so just to hear you talk like that. Jack was okay. He could play the hardball but it was that little twerp of a brother who was the problem. They had that meeting toward the end of October."

"That was '63, I believe."

"Thank you, Dr. IQ. I have a lady in the balcony. A box of Milky Ways to that little lady. I think Harriman was at the meeting. McCone and Bundy. Bobby talked Jack out of it. They called in Caldwell and he drafted the order. He made a pretty good secretary. Kennedy signed it and our man took the red-eye. The order said, call off the hit."

"But he never delivered it."

"He delivered it. Lodge slipped it into his back pocket. He was told to. We had to get Diem. We had every right to knock him off, especially his brother. For Christ's sake, there was a monk burning on every street corner. Remember? They never had to turn on the streetlights that summer in Saigon. Ouch!"

The covers poked up as Moon's knees lifted with the pain. Strickland stared into the snowlike counterpane before him until he became blind. He wanted to become deaf as well. He wanted to speak no more of these matters. Did anyone care about them anymore? The old phrases, the tired words. Sometimes he would hear his voice pronounce them as it must have sounded coming out of speakers all over the world: confident, genial, and substantial. And he would bite his lips.

"Oh, Daddy, what have you done?" Leslie would say. "You're bleeding. You've cut your mouth."

But their cause had been just. He had to come back to that. It was easy to turn to a history book to see who had prepared the mess, starting with Dulles—well, go back to the French. But their cause was just. They had tried to make it work, bring sanity to that circus. Stand up straight in the bushes. Permit decency and freedom to flourish. That's what Moon had said.

"Let's say our man stopped off at State and got someone to make an official copy of that order before he got on the Saigon Clipper. Say he had someone like George Williams witness. Caldwell might have done that. He wanted his place in history too, and he knew this game. So, maybe there's an official copy of this order with Kennedy's initials on it somewhere in his papers right now. Maybe the Widow Caldwell doesn't know about it. She sounds like she doesn't."

"Remove and disperse, you mean."

"It neatens the file, Strick. We owe it to a lot of good men. We owe it to history. The widow is looking for an official biography— Parsifal in a Brooks Brothers suit. I put her on to you. She remembers your book. You had some nice things to say about Caldwell."

"I meant them."

"Well, you can mean this too. But you have to total that stop order. Diem has to stay knocked off the way we say it happened. Trigger-happy gooks made a mistake. Right?"

"Why am I the lucky one?"

"Listen, Bub, I'm doing you a favor. You need another book. For tenure."

"I thought I already had tenure."

"Nobody gets tenure." Moon had started to laugh at his own joke and the laughter turned to coughing, a curious hiccupping sort of laugh that shook his body more and more violently as the eyes held Strickland, who was already on his feet and looking for the bell cord. The expression in those tired-looking, wasted eyes changed from entreaty to frustration to fear. Moon had more to say but he couldn't say it, couldn't get the words out through the blood coming in a great rush, staining the white sheets and counterpane like a revenge held back too long. Then Strickland saw the picture over the bed.

First Light Kill was the sort of print Nancy collected; scenes of fellowship in russet-toned fields with dog and gun, or the bejeweled eruption of a trout coming to surface on a taut line. Her father had taught her all that and their kitchen still offered a gallery of such scenes, matted and discretely framed in black with gold shadow, which Strickland always reviewed when he passed through that room, thinking then—just yesterday, just as the screen door slams behind him too late to escape the gunfire, thinking then that it was time to take the pictures down. He had always thought them corny anyway, sentimental calumets that masked a betrayal of sorts. Even with the windows open, and he tried to keep them open as much as possible, aromas of rosemary and nutmeg and thyme stubbornly permeated the air. In the cupboards beneath the bar counter were pots and colanders that hadn't been used in a long time, and they ought to be cleaned out also, put into the next rummage sale at the Presbyterian Union Church in Irondale.

—That fella up on the hill has contributed all these strange-looking contraptions.

—What in tarnation is that thing there supposed to do?

—Says it's for to press a duck.
—Press a duck! Well, I guess that beats all, don't it?

The voices in Strickland's mind were almost a daily meditation. But the voice on the phone record had come through the air also, over the airwaves, they used to say, and all these voices began to sound the same to him, his included. The magnetic particles of sound arranged themselves on a special ribbon, no different from the tape of the phone machine, and they were played upon arbitrarily like the set of glass chimes still hanging under the eaves of the dining room porch that was tinkled by any breeze. Something Nancy had liked to sit under of a summer evening, nestling one last nightcap of bourbon in her lap. He would hear these voices like the sounds of old radio shows coming from the distant, different apartments of his life.

—Oh Don? Don Wilson?
—Yes, Jack.
—(Applause.) And more gunfire. Gunfire.

He tries the sentence once again. *Dear Mrs. Caldwell, The manuscript you have so generously forwarded contains a most impressive amount of pertinent information. If I may be so bold to suggest a meeting at your convenience that I might review the entire collection of papers* which would then do something to something for something—this sentence has no subject. *If I may be so bold, I suggest a meeting at your convenience at which time I could*—apologize for being bold. Be bold.

"You can only suggest being bold," Nancy would say. "What do you have to be bold about? Certainly not what comes out of your mouth. Have you ever spoken anything that was your own—in your own words? Or that isn't some sort of interview pap? In truth. If I may be so bold. The truth of the matter. The point to be made here. Jeezus, Carrol, that golden throat of yours has deformed you. Some people are born with a hump and some with a short leg—you have that goddamn voice."

"Oh, Daddy," Leslie asked him one day. "Why did it happen? Why did it happen to us?"

"It was like a mandarin puzzle, the more you took it apart the more there was to solve. Men like Dulles, Lodge, Kennedy, even Johnson, all had the best of intentions. To help out. A complex situation. Ho's threat misunderstood from the beginning. Diem arrogant, not able to rule. It wasn't another Korea. Everyone thought it was another Korea. Wrong assumptions from the beginning."

"Oh, Daddy, that's not what I mean. Why us?"

Strickland kept trying to find the words. A phrase would slip into his mouth like a worn lozenge, something he had sucked thin over the years, turning it over and over and over. "You mean us, the U.S. of Americans? That why?"

Leslie nodded and pulled her legs—why did he always have to notice her heavy legs—up beneath her on the sofa. They had been in the library. Not even the books were his but had mostly come from Father Endicott's library at Furness Academy. Why did he always look at his daughter's legs? If the truth be known, his eyes automatically went to a woman's legs first—even if the woman was his daughter, Leslie; about twenty at the time of this question in the library, though she had asked him similar questions in other rooms, other times, until something went flat behind her eyes. She had waited too long for the answer, he knew that. He had made her wait too long. Any answer composed of sounds—vowels and consonants and diphthongs that he had put together on his own. But this is to digress. He was sorry her legs were so heavy. Sorry that she had not taken her mother's slimness. Since puberty, she was forever going on diets or saying that she was. Nancy was almost boyish and her legs had been elegant. Her ankles fragile and birdlike, but strong. Sexy.

"What is this? You want me to wear this on my ankle?" She had held up the slim gold chain. It was eighteen karat, an antique chain, made over by a jeweler in Saigon. Meticulous craftsman. "Like one of those French whores left over from the old regime? Is that what you want me to be?"

Dear Mrs. Caldwell, Your confidence in me is most flattering, which emboldens me to prevail upon your patience to make a further request. Without question, Ambassador Caldwell's memoir constitutes an important component to the history of our involvement in Vietnam and it would be a distinct honor for me to prepare the manuscript for publication. To do him justice, the whole panoply of his thought and observations should be put into the perspective of this memoir, for I fear your husband's innate and noble modesty has eliminated from his account numerous occasions when his contributions were of such significance that their recognition must not go unnoticed.

May I come to the point on this spring day—as gunfire renovates the woods? Truly, the American people and history are entitled to a fuller account of his importance than what the man himself gives. I would like the opportunity to review all of his papers.

*I recognize and applaud your hesitancy—*gunfire. His language is peppered, blown to smithereens. Gunfire. GUNFIRE. Strickland stares at the words on the page of paper in the typewriter. He sees the phrases, the blocks of paragraphs become targets, like the NO HUNTING signs he had spent two days posting around the boundaries of his property last fall. A week later the cards hung in shreds from the trees and fence posts, blasted by shotgun and rifle fire.

Send for Officer Van Deusen of the New York State Conservation Department. *Roaming the wilds of Van Buren County, his trusty Magnum at his side, the trim, eager, and always alert game warden has been called into his superior's office—the crusty but affable Captain Slake. As our story opens we hear—*
—Sit down, Van—I have an important assignment for you.
—Yes sir. It's that fella up on the hill, I bet.

In his files, Strickland has an index card on Mrs. Caldwell, part of his research for *Saigon, Signing Off: Carrol Strickland's Last Report.* Caldwell, Virginia—née Cameron. Born Pittsburgh, 1910. Father a protégé of Frick. Wealth from patents for safety devices for coal mining. Protect the workers and make a tidy profit too. The

American success story. Typical story, T.D. would say. Idealistic young man out of Princeton joins hands with rich doobie-do out of Miss Choate's. It takes money to support ideals, or is that only in America? How come Liberals always have such big wallets? Where did all that dough come from, do you suppose?

But would this older doobie-do go for it? She seemed to have the widow's syndrome, keeping all the bones to herself, holding back the one last joint. The memoir she had sent was ordinary stuff, something the Ambassador must have dashed off when he began to hear wings around his head. The diaries, the journals—all of Caldwell's erratum; that would be different, and in that pile of memos would be the one memo that might clean the slate. How would it read?

> *Dear Henry . . . Tell Don we are no longer in the ball game.*
>
> *JFK*

or

> *Lodge—President negative. Stop operation.—Bundy.*

or

> *Mr. Ambassador—The responsibility you last cable outweighed by considerations here and abroad. French neutral idea has picked up support on both sides. Tell Conein to discourage his generals. Caldwell delivers this and has my confidence.*
>
> *President*

From the time he steps over the broken stone wall and into the second field, Strickland knows he is being watched. Just off his right shoulder, up in the woods along the brow of the hill, he can feel a surveillance set up that makes him straighten his posture. To the left and behind, his house roof beckons above the fall of the meadow, but he would not turn back. He would not give those who watched him from the woods the satisfaction of thinking they had driven him out of his own fields, out of his own property. His boots dig into the soft earth and his hands slip casually into his corduroy trousers—it is fine weather—football weather as Scott Fitzgerald used to say, or as T.D. Moon said Scott Fitzgerald used to say. But it is April.

The stump of a huge tree is a favorite destination. Peeled of its bark and silvered by the elements, the hard wood had stayed there many seasons, like a bench waiting for him and Nancy, he would think; set on this small rise in the middle of the field and the weeds kept close as a lawn by the shale shelf that lay beneath the sod. The stump had beckoned on that first glorious walk. Their property. Every seedpod and stone, every crumbling husk left behind by animal or vegetable had been carefully turned over and inspected to be made part of the luminous patchwork that composed that day. They had surveyed more than their property.

The view from this old tree stump had been the best discovery. The freshness of that perspective seemed imperishable. Even as Strickland sits down on the roundish bench of the stump, careful to turn his back squarely to the woods behind him, the range of the Berkshire hills to the northeast compels his gaze and then his breath seems to catch and lift as always. To the south, the whole Harlem Valley undulates into the distance. It would not be so bad, he thinks, if a shot from the woods took him right now—he could almost feel the cross hairs coming to rest on the red plaid of his wool mackinaw. Few last looks at the earth could surpass this one.

This view had charged Nancy that first day. He had never seen her so caught up with anything like this before. —Forget about her. She meant Leslie, whose chubby legs stuck out from the tree trunk like a midget's on an elephant. —Don't worry about protecting her; we're the ones this is for. This is ours. Ours. And Nancy had twirled like a dancer on top of the moss-covered knoll, arms out and the same look of exhilaration he was to see later that night in the moonlit bedroom of the old farmhouse, almost bare of furniture and musty with a history that had been deeded to them only that afternoon in the lawyer's office in Green River. She had frightened him a little. "For

Christ's sake, Carrol, take hold of me. Don't fiddle around. Grab me! Here! Here! Goddamn it, do it! Yes."

Nor had there been any need to protect Leslie. Nancy had been right. The girl's preteen plumpness did not stretch out into slimness, had not developed those womanly configurations that this society, Strickland lately understood, makes both shameful and hazardous to their possessors. The girl's thickness became intransient, compounded itself. Her own heaviness became her best defense against the danger from which Strickland had thought to protect her on this tract of sixty remote acres in southern New York with beautiful views of the Harlem Valley.

Gunfire. By instinct, Strickland almost throws himself to the ground, behind the old tree trunk. Coming in, they used to say. But they would say it at La Pagode or on the terrace of The Continental and usually in response to one of those little motorized rickshaws bratting down Hai Ba Trung. Coming in. A false fluency, Strickland finally admitted, like that summer he spent in Paris just before he met Nancy. He spent so much time at the American Express office speaking with the French girls in English that he began to think he was speaking French, until he stepped out the door onto the Place de l'Opéra. Coming in at the bar of The Continental.

Well, maybe he might just turn around and walk up to the line of the property above. Just stare into the woods where all the firing was coming from, dare them to throw one his way. He would confront them head-on, show them the quiet, purposeful manner— the real stuff—so he stands up, turns to face the woods and takes up a measured stride across the field. The forest has fallen silent. A hawk circles overhead, screeching—not a warning, but maybe more of a vengeful proclamation; no quarter. Yes, he would avenge the hawk's slain kin, just by his very presence; challenge them with a meaningful target. Himself. Strickland inspects the ground for evidence; a mite-smitten wing, a rotted skull. The day was holding back and time had become stuck. Step by step he walks directly up the rise toward the line of trees. Pickett and his men must have felt the same way, he thinks, must have experienced the same stillness in the soul just before all hell broke loose.

But he makes the line and stops at the old barbed-wire fence gone awry, its strands rusted through, but which yet fairly marks the division of properties. On his side is a meadow of heavy grasses with insurgent burdock poking up to suggest all is not well in the earth below. A dense forest lies on the other side of the fence, composed of birch and maple; oaks that seem to grow tumors rather than branches. The different trees are almost woven together by thick ropes of wild grape and other vines Strickland cannot identify, tying them all together, as it were, into one amorphous species.

His eyes adjust to the dimness. The morning sun barely limns the vertical and slanted lines of the forest and birds flit silently through the intervals, catching this minimal light on their wings so they resemble flakes from a dying fire. Strickland senses he is seeing something for the first or the last time—would there be any difference?—and thinks it is not a privilege so much as a demonstration of something that should always be remembered.

Walking westward along the boundary, he counts a half dozen No Hunting signs he had posted, all of them shot full of holes, some marked with obscenities. The anger these renderings express amazes more than it alarms him; something even amusing in the anger's abstraction from its cause. What provoked such hate, he would never understand.

"They all want what we got," T.D. Moon used to say. "We can't make many friends from the top of the heap. On the other hand, we can't very well go around the world, crying Here 'tis, Here 'tis."

At the corner of his acreage, a junction made by an old stone wall and the wire fence and from which he could see the blue silos of the Schuyler farm, Strickland came upon the poster he had hammered into the smooth surface of an ancient sycamore. This sign looked almost new, except for the drawing made with a marker pen just below the legend that warned trespassers of their punishment.

The white space was large enough for the anonymous, primitive

Raffaello to draw the complete figure of the female but only the penis of the male could be sketched into the space, lofted and detached, but firmly held between her lips. The usual fantasy to be found on the walls of lavatories since Pompeii, Strickland muses, or even before. In fact, he sometimes checked the different stalls of a public facility, providing the place was empty, just to review the sketches left behind by unknown artists. It amused him that he would sometimes have to put on his reading glasses to study these sketches; often the light was very dim. So he had become a connoisseur and by this earlier criteria, hurriedly formed of course, he judged the meticulous detail given to this female form, as well as its position and placement within the space, to be above average.

WE FACK YOU DAUHTR

The picture had taken his interest, so he had not noticed the crude lettering. The statement had been printed just above the block letters that proclaim NO HUNTING. It was ambiguous, not to mention ungrammatical. They couldn't even spell *daughter*; he whistled. Threat or statement, it does not matter, and Strickland is about to rip the sign from the tree, then stops. It might be better to let it stay, to show imperviousness to such insult and, at the same time, to give a lesson in cool command. Show no response to the slight so the slight turns back upon them. Decorum at all times, gentlemen, Mooney would laugh. Decorum at all times.

In any event, the figure on the poster does not at all resemble Leslie—the face, distorted by the act, features a long nose that comes straight down from the brow, quite different from Leslie's pert little button. The body, the legs especially, is very slim.

How long have the two men been watching him?

Strickland congratulates himself on his self-control, that he had not touched the poster on the tree, reacted to it—only looked. Both were short, pudgy and wore the same baggy jumpsuits of camouflage material. Both were dark-complexioned and one sported a thin black moustache, similar to one a barber at the Waldorf Astoria Strickland remembered. The other wore a narrow-brimmed hat with a leopard-skin band. Three long feathers are stuck into the hat band. Hawk feathers, Strickland thinks as he continues to look at the men from across the boundary line. Bandoliers of cartridge belts crisscross their chests, and each carries a high-powered rifle. A breeze from the northwest carries the stench of liquid fertilizer up from the Schuyler farm.

The tableau suddenly breaks. The man in the Alpine hat hands his rifle to his companion and walks toward Strickland. He stumbles awkwardly over the uneven ground, unaccustomed to such terrain, Strickland notes with amusement, despite the Great White Hunter garb. As he nears the wire fence the fellow removes his hat, almost sweeps it low before him in a courtly fashion so that the tips of the feathers brush through the wild grasses. Strickland is fairly certain they are hawk feathers.

"*Favore* . . . *senor,* mister . . . *buon giorno* . . . happy days." The man's smile is so earnest, so contrary to the sadness bottomed in his large dark eyes, that Strickland is taken back.

"*Buon giorno.*"

"Ah, Mister." Even the eyes almost smile. "*Parla lei?*"

"*Un poco* . . . *un poco,*" Strickland replies casually. They stare at each other, one waiting for the other to continue. The hunter holding the guns observes them impassively.

"Please . . . *favore* . . . Mister Streecken-len . . . please. *Café?*" Again the hat sweeps down and around as a motion with the other arm makes way for him, as if the same bit of business were to sweep the barbed wire fence apart. The distant fanfare of a milk truck's air horn barreling down Route 22 to the north salutes the invitation. The moment was too good to miss, Strickland thinks, and steps neatly over the top strand of wire, showing them how it is done without catching one's clothing.

He would say later that he had not been afraid, walking between the two of them, single file through the underbrush, through whips of young sumac. "Actually, there was something very comical," he would say, "about the three of us—these two little guys on either side of me—though to be truthful, I had a moment's worry that the

Strickland identifies the shapes of the Berkshires to the north and this perspective gives him an idea of where he is. Several years ago a developer had come to Silvernales, bought this top of the hill, subdivided the land, cut roads through the woods, and then declared bankruptcy, leaving the lots to grow over and this unfinished road to the care and maintenance of the town. Strickland remembers local taxpayers were outraged by the inadequacy of the bond put up by the developer to complete this road. Some asked Strickland to address the town board on their behalf, thinking his professional delivery of their grievance might give it more success. The town fathers, rural Solomons, decided not to finish the road and used the bond money for a small park. His hosts on this fair spring morning must have been the only buyers of the subdivision. The door of the trailer has opened.

A portly man about his age appears in the doorway, then steps carefully down onto the step, then onto the ground. He is wearing a crisp white shirt, whipcords and black jackboots. His face is long with a morose expression and his eyes repeat both the form and the aspect. His hair is almost flat white and his face looks freshly shaved, even moist. With a little sigh, the man sits down rather grandly in the other chair and leans forward to stretch his hands toward the fire. Heavy rings present gems the size of marbles stuck between the knuckles of each hand.

Strickland was to say later that it was the strangest interview he had ever had. The man in the white shirt had begun talking in long, elliptical sentences—he could tell they were elliptical in content because of their rhythm, the way they paused in the center, like a caesura, as though another thought was introduced, then all the parts brought back to the same point. Very formal and with a certain elegance. The conclusion of each thought, essay, was definite and unmistakable and signified by a curious gesture of the ringed hands—the right one turned over the left and both brought together like that, back to back, so that the small globes crashed and scraped.

"What he talked about, I couldn't know, though the sense of his discourse was fairly clear, of course," he was to tell his audience later.

"I got the feeling that he was explaining some sort of procedure to me, a way of doing things or a set of customs. Yes, that's the word I want, *custom*. His manner was patient, almost diplomatic. But to be truthful, I had that in mind, especially after having talked to the game warden the day before. I remembered what he had told me. It was rather one-sided, you might imagine, and this fellow was making a very persuasive case for whatever it was he was making."

Oddly, it had been like a dialogue, even with only one side speaking; maybe like a discussion or a polite argument that he had somehow lost without saying a word. Seeing the two of them from a distance, say from across the clearing where the marksmen were taking their turns, they would appear to be intimates conferring on some personal problem. Perhaps a younger brother—Strickland—with only the flecks of gray in his black hair, has dropped by on this fine spring morning for a talk with his older sibling. They did seem related somehow. And, indeed, Strickland gets the feeling that the man beside him is passing along confidential and critical information. This is a family matter, its importance momentarily clothed by elegant phrases he cannot understand. He is listening to a history that will never be set down on paper. How would Moon handle this? Strickland feels awkward and blind to the truths being told but held tantalizingly secret within the speaker's elegant diction in the same way the brilliant sunshine makes the flames of the small fire before him invisible.

The door of the trailer opens and the guide steps down carefully, carrying a steaming mug in each hand. His timing was perfect for the discussion on the bench was clearly over and the coffee, freshly made, was to be a cup of friendship, an alliance to be drunk to the two worlds that had miraculously joined to make peace. He could see all this in the man's expression. To disappoint the hope on that face, this happy expectation, would be a crime against mankind, Strickland thinks. World peace seemed to hang in the balance. He takes the hot mug in both hands. The hunter in the feathered cap stands to one side, his eyes dazzled by the glorious significance of the two men on the bench sipping coffee together. A miracle—certainly a communion of sorts—and he had been the intermediary.

Would he be handed over, Strickland wonders, to representatives of the UN or the Red Cross when the two of them accompanied him to the border? He has chosen to return by way of the unfinished road now that he has his bearings. The two walk with him through a thick hedge of hawthorn and raspberry gone wild, and into a parking lot that had also been scraped out by heavy machinery. At least a couple dozen cars were parked, but how they got there Strickland could not immediately understand; a large tree lay across the dirt road about fifty yards down. In the crotch of a great oak, about twenty feet off the ground, a man in a camouflage suit stood on a scaffold. He held a small carbine.

"This is very much against the law," Strickland says. "You can't block this road. This is a town road. It has to be kept open for emergencies." Also for game warden Van Deusen, he thinks to himself. The officer had mentioned he had tried to investigate the camp but couldn't get past a tree across the road and by the time he walked in on foot, whatever evidence there may have been had been put under cover. The scaffold of kills had been taken down, folded up and put away somewhere.

"Di cosa si tratta?" The man in the white shirt steps forward, his brow heavy. *"Cosa è?"*

His aide speaks rapidly, eyes first on Strickland then on his superior—going from one to the other, concern gaining momentum in his expression. The pink face of the older man deepens to red.

"Tell your leader," Strickland says, "that tree will have to be removed. This is a town road and must be kept open at all times. I have spoken to the town board about the road before and I can speak to them again." Did he sound as ponderous as he thought?

The translator's efforts pick up, his voice rattles, and he seems anxious he will not be able to say all that is necessary, all that can be said to prevent a catastrophe. He begins to run out of words, he slows down, and Strickland recognizes a couple of phrases used several times, mere verbiage thrown up like a levee against the rage that gathers in the other's face. He holds his hat before him to implore their reconsideration, to distract them perhaps from this dangerous confrontation by the fanciful jiggle of hawk feathers.

Then the older man starts to speak. Judicious, almost half-humorous sounds come from his lips. His gestures are rhetorically correct. One arm sweeps down, one bejeweled hand majestically lays a path through the air. The two hands come together, back to back, and the clink of glass on agate seals the decree.

"There. You see, Mister." All smiles once again, the guide puts on his hat to have both hands free to better imitate his master's gestures. "This cannot be the town road . . . you make mistake . . . where are the signs for the No Parking and the speed . . . and . . ."—here Strickland has to stand up to give his own audience his version of the courtly pantomime—". . . there is no yellow line painted down the middle."

But he does not tell Cora Endicott and her grand-niece everything. Just as he is escorted through the hedge of raspberries gone wild, he spies a ribbon hanging from the thorny branch of a hawthorn, much like those markers used by land surveyors, though this material was not tied to the branch as those are but lay around it loosely as if it had fallen onto the branch from the sky above. Nor was it the Day-Glo orange used for that purpose but a light blue, the same color of ribbon he watched Leslie tie about the long fall of her hair that morning, pulling it up and off her plump neck.

"Where are you off to?" he remembered asking her.

"I promised to do some work for the Heart Fund this morning. North of here. There." She pulled out the loops of the blue ribbon and looked satisfied with the effect.

Chapter

2

Returning to the telephone answering machine, Strickland plays back the message left on it two days ago as he talked with the game warden. ". . . about fiveish. You'll meet my lovely niece, little Robin. Ciao." He better call Van Deusen, come to think of it, to tell him what he saw at that hunting camp. Around five would mean he'd have to drive down to the city tomorrow, for he has an interview, and then was supposed to meet Mrs. Caldwell, and the train service from Dover Plains could not return him in time for the dinner date. "Good morning. May I speak to Officer Van Deusen, please."

"Ray is out in the field." Her voice is almost without inflection, probably speaking while standing at the kitchen sink, the phone on the adjoining wall. "May I take a message?"

"This is Carrol Strickland."

"Of course, Mr. Strickland. I should have recognized your voice." He can see her laying down the apple and paring knife. Taking up his concern.

—*Oh, Ray, guess who called just as I was making the apple pie.*
—*Honey, whoever it was didn't spoil your cooking. This pie is dee-licious.*

—That's because I only use pure ingredients and the purest ingredients to be found are in Crispo Pie Crust Mix.

LOOK FOR IT AT MARKET TODAY. CRISPO PIE CRUST MIX—IT'S A DARN SIGHT BETTER.

"May I take a message?"

Strickland is not specific. He has some information that might be useful. Perhaps the game warden could call him. Mornings are best. He keeps it simple. "I'll be sure to tell him," young Mrs. Van Deusen says.

"Daddy . . ." Leslie's cheerful voice speaks to him off the tape. "Daddy, I'm staying with friends in Chatham. You remember the Smiths? I'll be home Friday." He doesn't remember the Smiths. How is she wearing her hair, down and loose? Tied up with a ribbon? What sort and what color?

Strickland rewinds the answering machine and goes to the shower. Lately he's been worried about himself. Such thoughts— snippets as they are—accumulate, begin to weigh heavy on his mind. Sometimes he thinks his head has become an archive of junk, scraps cut out of important statements, memorable phrases, which if the truth be known, go on to be important and memorable only because of the extraneous material left behind in his clutter. He has performed some service, then. He has been useful.

He bends his head under the pummeling water of the shower. It isn't the body. That hasn't changed—still the same ordinary, stocky piece of equipment that has carried him around since his twenties, nor does it look all that different. So it is up here, on top of the shoulders, where it is happening. Where it has happened. No surprise there. Last fall, at Mooney's death bed, he felt something rise in his head and turn over tiredly—like an animal in a zoo on a hot summer's day. He wanted nothing to do with Emerson Caldwell's memoir, nothing to do with any of that anymore. Too many questions that couldn't be answered, beginning with the one his daughter threw at him a while back—why us?

But he had been shanghaied, you might say. The old professor was calling in an IOU that Strickland had forgot about nor had he even had a chance to say yes or no—to turn down the assignment. Moon had died just like that, before he could say anything. He lets the water run down his arms and over his hands, following the course of his own blood as Moon's blood had run in rivulets down the white counterpane. Had he staged the whole thing, his gory death? Strickland laughs and chokes on warm water.

Funny business, Nancy called it.—You're in on some of this funny business, aren't you? They were driving up to Leslie's graduation at Furness. He had just got in the night before—the whole way from the Philippines and another day before that from Saigon. Nancy drove as he tried to nap in the corner of the passenger seat. Everything was going up for grabs. Thieu had started the war all over again and was asking for more money. Watergate. The crew had jumped ship. The House was holding hearings on Nixon's impeachment. That had been on the car radio.

"Mr. Chairman."

"The Chair recognizes the Honorable Hamilton Fish of New York."

"If the truth be known, sweetheart, you're in on this funny business, aren't you?" Strickland feigned sleep, not too difficult to do, and did not answer. He remembers observing through nearly closed eyes Nancy's knees and the way the tendons behind the knees framed the smooth flesh between them, for it was a hot June that year and Nancy drove with the cotton skirt pulled up high. Her legs already golden. Looking down, Strickland sees that the memory has stiffened some response in him, which makes him turn front to the shower for self-chastening. Nancy had been dead several years.

The weather is not so warm on this particular April morning as he drives down the Taconic Parkway through Westchester, on his way to the city. A mist lies in some of the hollows beside the road and the world looks quite beautiful. He has tuned the car radio to a classical music station, so Mozart tests the seams of the Volvo.

* * *

Good morning, this is Carrol Strickland with the news. Good morning, this is Carrol Strickland and here is the news. . . . with the news. Carrol Strickland with the news. Carrol Strickland—and here is the news.

Most of the old-timers had been singers, some even with operatic training, so the voice just floated up from the diaphragm with such ease that it gave you the impression they could talk, tie their shoes, and turn a somersault all at once. Breathless. They seemed to have no breath. Goddamn, remember Graham Mc-Namee? Now there was a spokesman. But Strickland has to practice all the time, keep the instrument in shape. He couldn't fall back on any training or method. He was a primitive. An original. The sound came out of his head, came out the way he imagined others heard him. That was all he had to go on, this impression of how he must sound to others.—*Good morning. This is the news and I am Carrol Strickland.*

"Why don't you say, sometime, just for the hell of it, here's the bad news." Nancy had turned off the impeachment proceedings—the process was so boring.

"Because that would be a redundancy." He remembers speaking through the haze of his fatigue. "News is always bad. When it's not is when you hear someone say, 'Here's good news.' No need to announce the other." Then he drifted off, rocked to sleep by the road joints as they passed up through Connecticut and into Massachusetts.

He was amused by the way they were treated at Furness Academy. For the first time since they had begun showing up for parents' days and the usual functions, he was the one sought after, waylaid for a chat, some scrap of inside talk that could be bartered at a subsequent supper table. *Carrol Strickland—he's just back from there, you know—he told me that . . .* Surely Nancy was still the daughter of Everett Hale Endicott, was still remembered as her father's brilliant tennis partner when they took the amateur doubles crown four or five years in a row. The headmaster's daughter, clever and doing fun things; a trifle arch some would say but so often her comments really hit the mark. Punctured pomposity. Her brilliant smile, the wide mouth and perfect teeth, sharpening the edge of her sarcasm. But at Leslie's graduation it had been different.

"Why are we holding off on Hanoi? Why not bomb those bastards and get it over with?"

"The feeling is that it would only stiffen resistance, England and even Germany during World War II, for example."

"How about the dikes? I've seen estimates that say it would take care of several hundred thousand of them."

"That's probably true, but there's a sense that it too would have an adverse effect."

"But why, Carrol, is this taking so fucking long?" (Leslie's English teacher and his too when he went to Furness. Still the pipe in the mouth, the bony forehead. The thin jaw had a hard time with the language, getting the word *fucking* out without breaking the bones. Trying to be casually profane with one of the upperclassmen.) "For God's sake, this has been going on for ten years now. More. We're the most powerful force in the world. We are pouring everything into it. Why?"

"This may sound frivolous but, in truth, it's like the old joke. They all look alike." He had waited for the laugh but got only a bulging eye as when he hadn't done his homework. "It's not like Furness playing Kent or Wilberham. There's no one side of the field and we're the only ones wearing uniforms. This old lady you talk to, an old granny, may be the one who set up the ambush you walk into. The kid with the big eyes and Charlie Brown grin is packing enough nitrate around his waist to blow field headquarters sky-high and probably will."

"There they are. How lovely." The teacher quickly changed the subject. He didn't want to hear about the complexities and turned toward Endicott Hall just as the graduates came out on the porch, gowns blowing in spring winds. They did all look alike, except for Leslie. He could spot her immediately. The faces around her were Oriental, also a good number of black ones, and all of them smiling, nodding, skylarking within the classic colonnade of the hall's portico. Yes, a few ordinary white faces peered out from beneath the mortarboards, but they seemed to melt away, become inconsequential within this pool of darker faces. It looked to Strickland like the noon-hour rush around Lam Son Square, which he had only just left. They spilled out of the building's huge doors and down the graceful steps onto the green lawn, a surge of adolescent energy that somehow had not cracked the walls nor upset the Palladian balance that had just contained them.

"What was it he said again?" Nancy had called from the bathroom of the motel room. "Old Barnes always tapping the pipe stem against his teeth and trying to get a peek up your skirt." Her voice was already whiskey thickened and the sound of it stirred him.

Strickland had just come from a hot shower and felt wonderfully complete. "I had been looking at Leslie up there on the steps of your father's hall and I heard him tap the stem, like a small gavel calling my attention to order and, come to think of it, I bet he had been saving up this little bon mot for . . ."

"Oh, for Christ's sake, Carrol." She flushed the toilet. "Just spit it out, can't you?"

"You might say, then, this war was lost on the playing fields of Phillips Andover, Exeter and St. Paul's. That's what he said." How cool the sheets had felt against his shower-hot flesh, and the contrast expanded the arousal Nancy's voice had started so his bone-tired condition was pulled into a miraculous hardness that poked up with every suggestion of the eternal. He had been surprised, had thought himself too worn out with the day and night on the plane, but there it was.

—This is Carrol Strickland reporting to you from the monument erected on Iwo Jima—Cut two: These massive redwoods predate Man and will probably survive him—Or cut three: I can see the Hindenburg slowly coming toward us like a feather; toward its tall mooring mast, which rises some one hundred feet into the air. It is practically standing still now . . . the back motors are holding it just enough—it's bursting into flame! This is terrible . . . one of the worst . . .

Nancy saw him when she came out of the bathroom. "I didn't know you still went in for white women? Then she fell on the bed with that familiar abandonment, coming apart in a stupor of booze which never failed to excite him for her collapse appeared to make her completely vulnerable though it was she who often possessed him, as she did this afternoon taking and using his hard cock for her own purposes with a self-absorbed lubricity and her climax was so devastatingly complete that he was both grateful and, at the same time, left to wonder what she did when he was in Vietnam. Then he thought about something else.

Even on that spring afternoon in the Walden Arms Motel, there was something particularly exciting about being in bed with the headmaster's daughter. Despite the stretch marks on the taut belly that roiled above him, Nancy Strickland had gone back to being Nancy Endicott who had come into his dorm room and pulled down her tennis whites and hopped into bed. This never happened, though it had been every boy's fantasy at Furness Academy when he was there and the accumulated charge of that student body's fantasy about her—the school had not gone coeducational yet—rose and hung over the campus like a cloud loaded with electricity, awaiting the slightest contact for release.

The sight of Nancy Endicott returning her father's serve, arching her compact body, turning and running and shaking her head, the glossy black ponytail flagging disgust with herself when she made an error, became almost a vesper reverie for several classes of Furness Academy.

The short skirts, sleeveless tops and coy panties of tennis attire seemed designed for her tight little figure and, in fact, she never looked better in other clothes—even as a grown woman, wife and the mother of his daughter, lying beside him on that motel bed and put into a snoring sleep by their quick, forceful sex, her body still had an adolescent quality about its firmness as if it were not quite fully developed but had been halted in its growth, kept fresh—if not virginal—by an athletic tone.

In good weather, the sounds of the matches between the headmaster and his daughter could be heard from every part of campus. The pong and snap of each hit sent vibrations through the collective undergraduate spine. Sometimes Endicott's clipped voice would be heard: "too good," and looks would be exchanged, for the picture of Nancy Endicott sending a passing shot down the line behind her father was reproduced fifty times or more in evening study hall.

She had a way of making a shot crosscourt that sent her ponytail straight out, all the energy that propelled the ball from her racket coming back through her slim, muscled arm by some rule of physics the boys in study hall were trying to memorize right then, to course down her torso, over her tensed behind and to follow the smoothness of her right thigh and calf of leg; then, the charge released into the air, harmlessly, as the right leg lifted straight out like a ballerina's and the toe of the foot touched some invisible button in the air. "Dee-luscious," one of the senior fellows used to say and make a gesture.

Her father had been ferocious at the net but little Nancy skipped and played around him, lobbing the ball over his head or sending a backhand that caught him going the other way and then she would giggle, one hand covering her large, perfect teeth as if someone, sometime, had told her they were a little too prominent. The headmaster looked the same way in class—at the net. He had a way of looming, though he wasn't a very large man. It was the long, wide face topped by the thick pompadour of iron gray hair that made him seem ominous. Endicott's grim countenance seemed to rise above them in European History like one of those line storms that would come up over the Kansas prairie suddenly and without warning and with the sun still shining but the birds falling silent and then Strickland, the boy, would look up from where he was sitting on his bike in downtown Salina and see this towering thunderhead had silently moved in right on top of everything, quietly tethered over the town by some awful presence that meant to destroy them in a single explosion. "When you get up to the university, Strickland, look up an old chum of mine, Professor T. D. Moon. He'll help you along. I've dropped him a note about you." Thank you, Mr. Endicott. Thank you for everything. Thank you for your daughter, too. Yes, thank you for her especially.

"Good morning, my name is Carrol Strickland." The receptionist has looked up. The whites of her eyes are spun sugar within a
creamy chocolate face. High cheekbones, straight nose, small
mouth—beautiful, he thinks. Only the color is different. "I guess I'm
a little early. Made all the lights." The walls of the place are decorated
with the three-sheets of the pictures the outfit has produced.

But in truth, Strickland was always a little early for appointments in the city because he had never got used to the metropolitan
tempo, and he always confused the city's dense uproar with physical
impenetrability. The distances were not all that great. His professional rounds encompassed about a dozen square blocks—agencies,
recording studios, and restaurants where menu items bore names like
the Edward R. Murrow Deluxe or the Bill Stern Special. Even when
they had lived in New York, the few minutes it took to get from their
apartment in the East Eighties down to Madison and Fifty-fourth
Street had always surprised him.

The eternal hick, Nancy used to say. On the other hand, he
would wonder how long had it really taken to bike out to his folk's
farm outside of Salina, pedaling west and therefore uphill. Maybe it
had only been as far as, say, from Grand Central to Penn Station.
Memory adds mileage to such routes, perhaps.

"But it's all uphill. People don't realize that Kansas is not really
flat. Actually, there's a slight grade rising from east to west all across
the state."

Nancy Endicott had stared at him over the punch bowl. He
couldn't tell if she was impressed or if he had made a fool of himself.
Probably both. She was just back from Europe and was about to start
at Northampton and this was the Headmaster's Smoker for boys. She
was helping out. The only female in the place and her father's hostess.
New boys had already heard the dark rumors about Mrs. Endicott, a
shadow sometimes seen passing the second-floor windows. A drug
addict, the rumors went.

"Is that so." Nancy Endicott's mouth went wide. The smile

glistened, the crystal cup in her hand glistened, the firelight in the hearth of the headmaster's library glistened—the leather and polished wood. It was like a set from some movie with Ronald Colman that Strickland had seen in Salina. He had felt giddy and pressed himself against a wingback chair to ease the sudden urgency he felt in his bladder. But it turned out that the young girl had been even more dazzled, which was difficult for him to believe.

"Kansas. You talked to me about Kansas and it sounded like Timbuktu. Then the way you sounded, even then. You looked like a tadpole, all eyes and a big head, but your voice was gangbusters. I got hot just hearing you say it. Kan-saz-z-z."

"Carrol, I'm Cindy Block." She stands poised and slim before him, one hand thrust out. The nails are polished red and very long. He almost makes a wide sweep of his hand before taking hers, to avoid the points. He follows her down the narrow hallway to her cubicle. Not much of an office for a producer, but everything is disposable, transitory these days—even producers. One window looking south; he sees the Brooklyn Bridge.

"This is a real turn-on for me, meeting you." She sits so her profile is turned toward the window light, hardened by it.

Cinder block, Strickland thinks, but says, "Why is that?" He is smiling, a recognition in his expression, for he knows what she is about to say, his fame already a conspiracy between them. It has happened many times before.

"My dad used to watch the "Friday Night Fights" all the time. I grew up hearing your voice! You sold that beer like it was going out of style."

"Thank you," Strickland says, always grateful for a compliment though she has confused him with another announcer—in truth a much older man, for a program that aired about the time he himself was still in school. "Music to Study By" was his program then, but Cindy Block never heard of that one.

In any event she has grown serious, the misinformation does well enough, fills in the allotted space in the protocol—and Strickland's stomach tightens. He crosses his legs and looks down at his boots. If there was time he would go by the shoemaker on Forty-sixth Street and order a new pair. These Wellingtons show cracks across the instep though the leather still took a good shine.

"I'm certainly not going to ask you to audition for me," she is saying. A furrow knifes her forehead into two parts. Like an old phrenology diagram, Strickland thinks, and the right half is supposed to be reason and the left intuition—or was it the other way around? What was there behind those two parts, if you could part that line in the middle of the brow and look inside? You'd see all the ticktocks learned at a couple of good schools, all the ticking and tocking a good-looking woman learns in this business to become a producer of a thirteen-part series on Antarctica—all the right responses in there, but nothing original enough to tell someone like him that he was too well known, too recognizable, that he had been around too long. He and his deformity had played the clown too many times.

"We have some fabulous footage," she's saying, crossing her legs so that one slim foot, barely sheathed in an open network of leather, grazes one of his boots. "I'd like you to see it while you're in town . . . let me set up a screening for you." And she almost reaches for the phone. Funny shoes for a TV producer, he thinks.

"No, listen—thanks but I have an appointment to get to. I seem to be the official biographer of Emerson Caldwell and I'm meeting with his widow."

"Fabulous," Cinder Block says and her insouciance makes him feel silly. She hasn't the slightest idea who Emerson Caldwell was. "You're just too good for us on this one," she is saying. "Your voice would become a—a persona, you know what I mean? We need someone who is more background. I'm really sorry because it would be a kick to work with you. I'd really love to work with you sometime."

"I'd like to work with you sometime," Strickland replies and stands. Maybe over this neat desk with the Snoopy pencil holder— something leftover from Mount Holyoke days?—or maybe up against the wall over there underneath the bookshelves. That would set those bric-a-brac a jiggling. My goodness, that's an Emmy! The wundertwat has got herself an Emmy. However, so, she must have something, but whether Strickland feels shamed by this recognition or depressed by it is not clear to him right now. She does walk him to the elevator, borrows a Kleenex from the café-au-lait receptionist, daintily wipes her nose and sticks out the other crimson-tipped hand. "Take care."

Somehow the day has become brighter and Strickland stands on the sidewalk of Madison Avenue blinking like a groundhog that's just come out of hibernation. How many groundhogs does he have left up in his back fields? Not many, he figures, because the merry marksmen of Palermo have been popping them off since the first warm days in March. He is suddenly very angry. Not that they mean all that much—they were, after all, only groundhogs, but they were his groundhogs. His clients, to use the old term.

Nor was he all that sure that someone was not taking aim at him right now, lining in the sights as he stands in the sunlight on Madison Avenue surrounded by the noontime swirl of traffic and office workers. Not even lunch, he thinks—Cinder Block didn't even take him to lunch.

Crazier things have happened. He feels targeted, set up by the failed interview and wheeled into position by the appointment with the Widow Caldwell this afternoon. We'll have tea, she had said on the phone, and he could hear in those three words all the sorry souvenirs of her life as a diplomat's wife. He would enter a foyer of fans and comment on a mantel of ivory pieces.

Something more to pin on the wall, something to pull out for company. Strickland knows that even Cinder Block would probably trade his name at lunch. Guess who I had to turn down this morning, she might say. Carrol Strickland, remember him? Mrs. Emerson, even as he turns down Forty-sixth Street, is clearing a page for him in her album.

The shoe store is comfortably aromatic, leather and polish and the sharp seasoning of resin glue. Machinery whines. Small nails are tapped by several cobblers in the back. They hold more brads between their lips, moving them from mouth to shoe with almost a perpetual motion of the left hand as the right keeps time with a small hammer. Strickland appreciates this professionalism and enjoys watching their industry. He stands beside racks of ready-made moccasins and sneakers.

No, Angelo is not here. He's still in Florida. Florida? Sure, why not. The man rolls up his sleeves another notch and hitches the blue apron. He's a cobbler, a nephew taking a turn running the front of the store. Strickland remembers him from before.

"It's these boots," he says, slipping the right one up and holding it up. "I need another pair made."

"Look, that's Angelo's work, okay? Come back when he's here."

"But can't you just put the order in? Surely the shape is on record somewhere. He's done several pair for me. I'm an old customer, I go way back." Strickland searches the opposite wall for his picture. It used to hang in fly-specked celebrity with others who had dropped over from Rockefeller Center for new heels or a pair of hand-made brogues.

"Hey, mister. What I tell you? Angelo is not here. Come back one week, two. Okay?" The man has turned on his own good heels and gone back to attend other customers, leaving Strickland to browse the informal portrait gallery on the shop's wall. He wants to find himself but he also wants to delay his exit. He has noticed one of the customers, a stunningly beautiful young woman, about twenty-five. He can't blame the clerk for dismissing him.

But she isn't the customer; it's the much older man she accompanies. He looks like a prosperous accountant—well-heeled Strickland thinks, just as he finds his own photograph on the wall. The picture of himself hasn't been moved but looks down at him from between Arthur Godfrey and Tony Martin. He wonders if that's the reason he came into the store: to see his own image. The accountant looks like he's run out of black ink and sits in stockinged feet, smoothing a patch of his bald head with one hand and holding a blue leather pump with a gold monogram in the other. The girl seems to prance with annoyance, turning this way and that before a wall of shoe boxes.

"Well, what should I get?" the old guy says.

"You don't want my opinion," she says, looking away and replacing a shoe on a display rack. The reach arches her back, thrusts out her hips.

"Yes, I do."

"No, you don't. You've rejected my suggestions all morning."

"Tell me, Shirley. What should I get?"

Strickland, the clerk—even the cobblers in the back seem to have laid down their hammers—the whole store waits for her response. "Here," she says finally.

She has grabbed a moccasin-style loafer in white leather with a dark maroon heel. Her choice seems arbitrary, a random choice from a promiscuous selection. He watches the man slip on one and then the other and then stand to look at his feet in the floor-level mirror. The footwear has a curious funereal look, something that might be slipped upon the cold feet of a thoroughly dead bishop.

"Hey, very nice. Very nice," Angelo's nephew says. He nods at the girl and she smiles and also nods. They seem familiar.

Strickland doesn't think he's changed all that much from the photograph on the wall. The moustache is a little different and that's all, he decides as he heads toward Fifth Avenue.—*Good morning, Arthur.—Good morning, Carrol. It is so good to have you with us on this fine morning. Carrol Strickland, ladies and gentlemen, who has joined our Chesterfield Club for a few weeks while our own dear Tony Marvin goes after some tarpon down in the Florida Keys. I wish you folks out there in Radio Land could see this good-looking fellow with a big black moustache; how long have you had that, Carrol?*

The moustache had been Nancy's idea. The one in the picture at the shoe shop was fuller, a square bar of black like a hyphen above his lips. "Your mouth is much too sensitive looking," she said. "It doesn't go with your voice, nor your face. Who can take that poet's face seriously, especially when you open it to speak, as the song says, and you sound like the *Queen Mary* coming into harbor."

This was true. He had learned to speak softly in public, to

waiters and room clerks and sales people. Once, in Brooks Brothers, he forgot and asked for help in a normal voice and the whole floor came to a standstill, everyone smiling, looking away to smile more at the skinny pollywog with the bullfrog voice. He learned to control it, but the moustache helped for it gave him a sober, important look that went with the voice so he could let it out.

—*It's nice to be here, Arthur.*

Strickland notices her walk first, that long lope of a stride some New York women affect, he always supposed, to proclaim their independence and success, for she does not look like the usual secretary out for a lunchtime stroll, and indeed she was looking right at him, has even changed her course and was bearing down on him. He is taken back and tries to place her quickly—someone he's met somewhere. She smiles and is surely about to speak. Where would they have lunch? He tries to think of a suitable restaurant nearby.

"Your pants leg is outside your boot," she says and passes on. Strickland bends down and adjusts the clothing.

The Kodak panorama in Grand Central spreads part of Hong Kong harbor over the station's huge concourse and Strickland stops at the top of the marble balustrade to view it. He feels a twinge of something he decides is curiosity and lets people pass around him; some jostle him, for he seems not to be there at all. The details in the enormous transparency are phenomenally realized. He can almost count the petals of the flowers on the sun-splashed balconies of the apartment buildings and hotels that rise like spectacular stalagmites around the seaport. On one balcony, a woman leans on her folded arms and looks down at the scene below her on the floor of the railroad station. Her pose is calm, at rest, and though her face is turned to one side so its expression cannot be seen, the impression she gives is that she is slightly amused by what she is watching.

"It's a late call, Skip, I know but I just happened to be down here at Grand Central, around the corner from you and I thought you might like to have some sushi."

"Boy, would I, but I got this damn deadline on another one of these cops-and-robbers pieces. Hold on a minute, Strick. I've got someone on the other line."

Strickland sits back in the phone booth and waits. Across the marble floor from him is a newsstand with two attendants who continuously make change for a steady stream of commuters. The face and nude torso of a beautiful woman hangs like a valence around the stand's perimeter, repeated over and over on a magazine's cover. The headline on the late edition of the *News* has the word TERRORISTS in it. Strickland cannot see the rest.

"There we are, Strick." The voice in his ear gets comfortable. "That's taken care of. Now we can talk."

"I was with Mooney last fall."

"I heard you were. Damn it, Strick, I couldn't make it. I had this boring piece to do for the magazine. I can never seem to get away from deadlines. But you and the other guys made it. It meant more to him to have you there than anyone."

"I don't know about that."

"I would have loved to have been there to say good-bye to that old Ahab. He gave it a good chase. All those good old days."

"And right to the very end, Skip. He was thinking and working." Working me over, Strickland adds to himself.

"Oh yeah, on what?"

"Just some research." TERRORISTS BOMB. The paper is folded too quickly for him to see what. "Nothing important. I was right there with him when he died, Skip."

"Ah, my . . . think of that."

"Quite a mess."

"Yes . . . yes . . . Strick, can you hold for just a minute? This other line is heating up."

Strickland makes a survey of the newsstand. Paper buyers greatly outnumber magazine buyers. Does anyone buy the big glossy magazines? Covers with pictures of yachts under full sail in Caribbean waters, and others with plates of food that resemble the mythical atolls to be visited by those sparkling vessels, and still others with the nymphs that inhabit such islands. In fact, as Strickland has been talking to his old classmate, two or three men, the same two or three men, have stood before the magazine display looking at the nude torsos like farm animals bemused by the view of a distant pasture. TERRORISTS BOMB ENGLISH something.

"Skip, I've caught you at a bad time I guess."

"Oh, it's just the usual rat race, Strick—nine ways to make a buck. You know how it is. I heard you the other night on some program I just happened to turn on. Something about elks migrating in Canada."

"I made that a few years back," Strickland says. Nancy was alive then. They had become part of the community of Silvernales. One evening, Leslie got stung by bees while sitting on the back stoop. "I had no chance to say no. He died on me, Skip."

"My, my."

"He asked me to do this one thing—to neaten the file, he called it—and then he dies."

"Think of that. Still working the old rice paddies and the numbers. That all seems like a bad dream doesn't it, Strick? Were we all doped up or what? A bad trip."

The conversation becomes like pasteboard in Strickland's mouth and he finally hangs up. He stays in the phone booth and reviews the figures scrawled on its metal wall. Many use this complex of pay phones as offices; right now, he is surrounded by men and women worriedly giving orders, taking directions; anxiously reading from long lists of items that seem to be out of stock. When will the shipment arrive? Has the position been filled? What's the list price?

Maybe if he were to call one of the numbers written next to the phone, he would be plugged into a current exchange, a human bartering that was ongoing and vital. For if he were to leave the booth and walk out of the Forty-second Street entrance to Grand Central, he could look up at the glass wall of the building opposite where his old colleague's office was located. On the twenty-third floor, Skip lounged back of his desk, casually going from one phone to another, putting the different incoming calls on hold to answer others, confident of a history he had left behind because he knew the part he had played in that history. Regrettable or not, he had had a part in that history.

But Strickland had been only another call coming in from that history, a curiosa that Skip was always pleased to turn over in his ear, to stir his memory pleasantly, for the resonant voice was full of the ingredients of a time past, pleasurable to stir like the martinis Skip would stir at the Hotel Duc on those hot, muggy nights in 1975. In the same way—Strickland has one hand on the telephone receiver— that program he made on the elk still held Nancy alive in the light of those stunning first mornings in Silvernales when they would awake with the sun pouring through the uncurtained windows. Somehow, whenever that program was aired, his voice carried those moments; did not bring them back to life but carried them; even the sudden stab of pain in a little girl's tender flesh. "It hurts awful, Daddy."

He had always been the voice-over, never on camera, but the voice giving the account, relating an event, a history made by others—such as the man on the twenty-third floor in the building across the street who, perhaps even as Strickland still sits in the phone booth like one of those realistic statues whose lifelike quality startle people in museums, meets his deadline confident that his place in history has been verified by the phone call he's just received. Which of these numbers on the wall of the booth would verify him, Strickland muses.

So, instead of walking out of Grand Central, he only walks across to the newsstand and looks down at the headlines. TERROR-ISTS BOMB BRITISH BUS. Quickly he picks up and pays for another tabloid. Cheaply printed, its front page pictures two naked women embracing. As he returns to the telephone carrels, he flips through to the classified section. An old lady has taken his booth and is already speaking intently into the mouthpiece. She has neat stacks of coins lined up on the small shelf beside her and several shopping bags around her feet. The other phones are all taken. Strickland looks over the ads, considers their different offerings while he waits.

"How funny—they think a line painted on a road makes it official. Come. Give me a lift, Robin is waiting supper for us." That evening Cora Endicott raises her arms to him from the chaise lounge, her fingers crooked and brittle looking, and Strickland bends down to raise Nancy's elderly cousin in his arms.

The ailment that was slowly wasting her seemed to flood her bosom and hips with a plumpness drained from her legs and arms so that Strickland felt as if he were carrying a child, a child in a peach chiffon gown that trailed down and wrapped around his legs so that he had to be careful where he stepped when he stepped up from the sun porch and through the French doors and into the dining room. Cora Endicott weighed no more than the young prostitute he had visited earlier in the day.

Carefully, he placed his hostess into the large armchair at the head of the table and took his own place across the table from her grand niece. He had been trying to get a good look at Robin Endicott since he had arrived, only a little after five-thirty, but she had been so busy serving them in the garden, passing a tray of snacks, renewing their drinks and fixing fresh cigarettes into Cora's ebony holder that it had been like trying to observe a hummingbird.

"This is my niece who is staying with me." Cora had introduced them. "Or grand niece, I should say," the old woman added dryly.

But her movements between them, coming and going, had been graceful; smooth as the way she draws the napkin across her lap and fixes him with an attentive stare, attuned to his narrative with a rhythm he noticed on the patio. During his long account of the hunters, his morning's interview with their leader in the white shirt, she seemed to know instinctively when to pause in her ministries— when to drop ice cubes into a glass as he made a point, when to wait upon a turn in his story, and he appreciated this gift. He even found himself speaking to these several parentheses, to fill them with more elaboration or even with a joke.

"Oh, Carrol, you don't mean it." Cora lays down the smoking cigarette in its holder upon the large ashtray by her plate, and it tumbles onto the tablecloth. The young woman quickly puts it back into the ashtray. Cora would smoke throughout the meal.

"Truly. The place was like a shrine. Emerson Caldwell's portrait over the mantel. The tea set presented by Marcos. Screens from Sukarno. A sideboard from Borneo. Silk throws from Taiwan. And on the mantel—"

"Erotic ivory miniatures. I don't believe it." Cora shifts in her chair and cuts at the meat on her plate, holding knife and fork in her fists as a child might, but she lifts the morsel to her mouth with a cramped elegance. The Endicott teeth, which had given Nancy a winning, forthright smile, give her cousin a grotesque look, a relic of a more youthful expression perhaps considered gamine at one time—Strickland had seen family photographs—but that now resembled crude artifacts uncovered by the skin's shrinkage.

Meanwhile, the girl Robin has started to talk of the ruins of Angkor Wat and the sculptures on the temple of Konarak, using terms like *Indravarman style.* "You know something about this," he says, trying to catch her face against the light. He's seen her before somewhere.

"Robin majored in art history at Vassar," Cora says, clenching the cigarette holder between her teeth.

"Yes." She gives a small laugh. "A good major to be a waitress." She has lifted her shoulders slightly to shrug and sways to one side. Strickland thinks the gesture is charming.

"Basta, I won't have that." Cora puffs quickly. "You were much more than the hostess. She practically ran the Black Oak Inn over in Sharon."

"Not really," she murmurs and sways once again, to the opposite side. She sits with her back to the doors that open into the garden so the light forms a nimbus around her heavy hair, leaving her face obscured, and his eyes cannot adjust to see her clearly but Strickland has remembered now. The cinnamon-color hair, set ablaze by the late sun, is the same that kept falling dangerously close to the candles on the table as she served him and Leslie at the country inn several months ago. And dangerously close to their soup as well.

"What exactly does an art history major look for?" he asks.

"Museum work. Curating. Cataloging private collections. But I'm afraid it's a cul-de-sac at the moment." She gives the French phrase a special elegance.

"Even in New York? I thought there was an art boom going on." He can see her face more clearly now—a wide brow and long nose set within a heart shape.

She has shrugged once again. "I'm afraid I just don't have the connections for that."

"It's perfectly awful," Cora says to him. "Who one knows is everything these days. Genuine talent, ability is no longer considered." Robin has stood up and is clearing plates from the table, taking them through a swinging door into the kitchen. "She's been a godsend for me," the invalid continues quickly and slightly under her breath. "I let her use the apartment over the garage and she looks after me. She sketches," Cora adds quickly. "My dopey nephew messed up his marriage and this poor girl has been on her own almost since high school."

Strickland has wryly noted Cora Endicott's impatience with "connections" for she was a product of such linkages; her whole life had been supported by connections. The family had prospered because of this kind of chain that stretched from these trim Connecticut estates back across to the stony fields of the Massachusetts Bay Colony. Entries and couplings, he thinks, growing more amused by his own associations; for indeed it seems to him, in a flash of wisdom induced by several daiquiris and some ripe Moulin au Vent, that the formula for most of the world's success is the simple geometric proposition presented by the male and female sex organs.

"What makes you smile?" Cora asks, leaning toward him.

"The beautiful arrangement," he says automatically. Robin has just served them a delicious-looking compote of sherbet and fresh fruit, with a sportive madeleine cocked into one side of the dessert. A wreath of fresh mint encircles each crystal dish. "This is just beautiful."

"You see what a perfect treasure she is," Cora Endicott says.

"Well, it's not exactly Cordon Bleu or even L'Ecole des Trois Gourmandes," Robin shrugs, redoing that attractive shift of shoulder as she takes her place opposite him. He can see her eyes now. They are dark and set elliptically beneath a rather heavy brow. Her French accent seemed impeccable to him; the words have rolled off her tongue with a sensual ease.

Why did you pick me, the girl today had asked him. The massage parlor had turned out to be only a couple of blocks from Grand Central. It was located in the vacant penthouse of a new apartment condominium. The receptionist resembled a suburban housewife who had only just set down her shopping bags to answer the phone and take the money. Three prostitutes, one of them black, sat in a row on a padded bench against the balcony windows. They looked like three women waiting for job interviews. You took me because I'm the youngest, right?

You also look very neat, he said and undressed in the corner of the small room. While he folded his clothes over a wrought-iron chair, she had turned on a small lamp with a red bulb and fiddled with a tiny transistor radio, finally choosing a Top Forty station.

What will it be today? Naked, she seemed thinner, even younger than he had supposed. These are off limits. Her hand went to one breast. You can touch but no kissing, I save them for my boyfriend. Oh, I get it, she said, as she permitted him to arrange her on the cot, kneeling.

No, Strickland said, you don't touch either. Leave your hands in your lap. Yes, like that. She licked her lips and regarded him expectantly. He was in a forest, the red light in the room made the trees grow at a fantastic rate. Their leaves brushed against his face and body, covering him except for that part that floated toward the girl on the poster. No trespassing. Violators will be punished. To the limit of the law. Take it, he told her. Yes, like that.

The huge white leaves that patterned the slipcovers of Cora Endicott's living-room furniture usually blossomed on the divans and heavy chairs by the first of June. He wondered if Robin's efficient housekeeping was responsible for this early appearance. The linen is unseasonably cool to the touch as Strickland places the invalid upon one of the thick cushions before he himself sinks down into one corner of the sofa. They were having coffee and drinks.

"I think this night air is a little chilly yet," Robin was saying as she closes several windows.

"Thank you, dear," Cora says and looks toward Strickland with a significant lift of one eyebrow. He has been watching Robin. She moves quickly, not so much gracefully as without gratuitous motion, and he notes her hands and arms are without jewelry. In profile her face has the same economy—clean-lined and a firm jaw, the lips thin but rather sensuous by contrast. Not a beautiful face, he thinks, but original.

"Now then," the young woman continues, "if you don't need me further, I'll say good night." She had already set out ice, glasses, and whiskey on the sideboard.

"Oh stay with us, Robin," her aunt says.

"Thank you, but I have some work to finish. The scribblings of an apprentice," she laughs and looks down. "But nonetheless, something I want to finish." Her hand were clasped together and held at her waist. Strickland notices her legs are slim and shapely, one canted in toward the other in a classic pose—something from a frieze or the picture of one. Then she was gone, the sound of her high-heeled sandals making a quick tattoo on the terrazzo before she stepped onto the lawn and was absorbed by the night's silence.

"Isn't she charming?" Cora asks and returns to the task that his arrival interrupted. A wastebasket beside her chair spilled over with torn and frazzled papers; envelopes, brochures, printed letters. On the bamboo tray set across the arms of her chair was a large checkbook and several unopened envelopes that Cora took up, one by one, to open, review, and then write out a check for enclosure in the accompanying self-addressed, stamped envelope.

At the same time she begins the young woman's history. But Strickland only listens partly. If she recognized him, she gave no sign and he was relieved because he had been embarrassed by his behavior that evening when he and Leslie had dined at the Black Oak Inn. Once or twice he had considered returning to the place and apologizing to the waitress, but the service had been so terrible—no spoons for the soup and the wine not decanted until they were nearly through the entrée—that he felt justified in leaving her a very small tip, a gratuity that censored her service by its token nature. It had been Leslie's birthday, after all.

On the other hand, why hadn't she recognized him? He was a little put out that she had not and his pique amused him as he listens to Cora Endicott's narrative, punctuated by puffs on the ebony holder. The story had taken on the details of a Daphne du Maurier novel. The chef at the Black Oak was an older man, a cruel but brilliant master of classic cuisine and perhaps—Strickland laughs—punishing the help in his frustration with the new fads in raw vegetables.

—*Oh, Chef Beurrier, I am only a poor working girl enslaved in your evil kitchen.*

—*Hey, hey, hey. I shall train you to do things my way, but first you will be chained to this steam table. But wait! What's that noise? Who is that laughing in the corner?*

—*It is the Shadow . . . put down that whisk, Chef Beurrier . . . the Shadow knows . . .*

"Bruises? You say bruises?" Strickland asks. Peepers have begun to sound outside.

"Yes, bruises on her arms and thighs. She tried to hide them from me and I forced her to tell me about them. The bastard." Cora stamps out her cigarette, ejects the stub from her holder and promptly arms it with a fresh one. "I wanted to call the police but Robin convinced me it would only cause her trouble. She would have to bring charges. Anyway, she was safe with me by then."

Perhaps Robin Endicott did not recognize him because she was used to being tipped so meagerly by the diners at the Black Oak. Her poor performance—she had even spilled some of his soup into its serving plate—had almost asked for it. "You're going to stiff her,

Daddy?" Leslie had asked. But what puzzles Strickland, as he sips bourbon and listens to Cora, is the great difference in the girl's manner this evening. From cocktails on the terrace on through dinner and then preparing coffee and drinks for them here in the library, her performance had been a paradigm of service; not obsequious but in the background, thoughtful and elegant all at once.

Cora's monologue carries through the night by the weight of its own minutiae; she talks like some old social arbiter out of a James novel, one of those he had never read in school but knew the outline and characters well enough from studying crib notes. Recently, as if in a strange retribution, he had had to read all of *Wings of the Dove*. Strickland sinks into the sofa and sips the bourbon, letting the day's fatigue take over to numb his sensibilities. The Endicott family history is all very familiar but he no longer resents hearing it.

"My family has a history too," he yelled at Nancy after one of these evenings with Cora in Connecticut. "Oh, I know all about them," she replied. "The honest wheat farmers of the plains. Noblemen of the soil. I can see them setting up the family organ and opening up the treasured copy of *Pilgrim's Progress* on the stump of a cottonwood. Cozy nights in the sod hut. Don't be such a snob, Carrol. It's not Cora's fault, it's not my fault, that our people started this place," and she held out her glass for a refill. If he wanted to make up this quarrel in bed later on, he'd better refill it. That was the understanding that passed between them.

Nor can Strickland's impatience be provoked when Cora insinuates the centerpiece of her soliloquy, a topic that always interested her because she did not have the facts, but he rises, instead, to fix them more drinks, a nightcap for him. Nancy's relationship with her father was no longer his concern. So he made the usual sounds of mystification, pretending to share his hostess's ignorance as he placed the glass of bourbon and water in her hand. The fingers that grasped the glass seemed to have been broken and reset at unnatural angles to give the most ordinary tasks, like holding a glass or raising a cigarette holder to her mouth, a curiously exotic quality—spiky.

Yet she receives the glass not without grace, Strickland notes, for to be so served by him—or by someone like her grand niece—was a custom that had long ago given the awkwardness of her infirmities a kind of dignity. So he joins the impoverished art student in making the same contribution to this woman's style, and Strickland reflects that his service of "the thing," as Nancy called the war in Vietnam, was cut on the same pattern too. Even in the hospitable air of this sumptuous living room, he rankles with the memory of his former colleague's arrogant usage of him that morning.

It was not the first time he had been made to feel outside a community that he felt he had served well, placed outside a history that he had spoken for and that had been rewritten all the while to leave him out of it altogether. It had never been his to begin with. That history, the casual, unspoken familiarity men like Skip had with each other, all within the fabric of certain events, had no more been his than had the ornate roast duckling at the Black Oak Inn been Robin's creation. She had only served it.

At last he lifts Cora Endicott out of the scrap-page rubble of her funding and into the wheelchair parked by the piano and sees her up the slight ramp into the bedroom wing across the foyer. The gravel of the driveway under his boots reflects the moon's pale, platinum surface. It is not a full moon, he cannot remember which side of it wanes or waxes, yet it is full enough to illuminate the garden. The pagoda-like roof line of the coach house is clearly outlined, and he stands for a moment by his car to observe the three lighted windows beneath the long, slanting eave. He tries to imagine what Robin Endicott may be doing in there. A young woman's chores—he was familiar with some of Leslie's preparations for bed—or she had talked of a sketch; a still life perhaps, a pastel of spring flowers whose blooms were slightly withered around the edge and with a figurine beside the vase. He pictures her collecting small, pretty things for her borrowed table top. The gravel crunches behind him.

"Oh, Mr. Strickland." She has stopped abruptly. Her pose is stiff with the sense of her intrusion. "I'm sorry to startle you. I was just out for a walk."

"And a perfect night for a walk it is too, Robin."

"Yes, it is lovely here. Aunt Cora has been very good to me. She has literally saved my life."

Chapter

3

Earlier that day he had called his home number from a pay phone in New York and listened to himself. He had hoped Leslie would answer. *Hi, Dad. We were real busy at the Heart Association* . . .

But the recorded message rolled into his ear: *"I'm sorry not to be in but if you will just leave your* . . *."* But why aren't you in? Who's in charge? How many hawks have those hoodlums blown to pieces? Where's your daughter? Where are you, Golden Throat?

He had been on a corner of Madison and Eighty-third, curiously, a block away from where he and Nancy and Leslie had lived before they moved to Silvernales. Was all of America a small town, he wondered, even New York City, even this part of New York City that seemed so glossy and slick with know-how, expensive tastes decorating both sides of the streets with shop windows that looked like the open bureau drawers of a French courtesan? Among these shops he spotted a dry cleaner they had used, the newsstand, the pharmacist, the green grocer—all of them could be picked up and put down in any village near Silvernales, business continuing without pause. Well, maybe not the green grocer. It seemed to have been taken over by some kind of Orientals—Koreans probably. They seemed to have taken over all the fruit stands in New York.

Dead air in his ear. He almost speaks into the mouthpiece to print his voice onto the tape slowly winding round itself ninety miles away, to complete the loop of his own voice answering itself on and on into infinity. His mother had used a kitchen cleanser with a label showing a Dutch girl, sleeves rolled up, bare legged and feet in wooden shoes—the image repeated over and over, getting smaller and smaller until the figure of the girl with her white cap and rosy arms, her business-like stride across the face of the label had been reduced to only a gray dot. One summer afternoon, sitting on the back porch and away from the Kansas sun, he found himself staring at an empty can of this cleanser on top of a bag of trash. His eyes and then his mind, his whole person drawn into the infinity of the figures, into a rapidly diminishing world where oblivion was not to be feared as it was feared in his dreams, waking to nightmares to sob against his mother's hard breast. She had been patently consoling, mostly.

But there were all kinds of infinities, Strickland reminded himself and stepped from the telephone booth. Like those two East Side matrons who strolled ahead of him as he walked toward Virginia Caldwell's apartment. They moved with the same purposeful stride as the figure on the can of cleanser, their skirts moved side to side—they could have been skating down Eighty-third Street, blades fixed to their wooden shoes, save they were wearing soft leather boots of a roguish character, probably Italian—but this infinite fascination all came down to the same point, he thought. The Dutch girl on the label, all of them. Everything was reducible to the same point.

Thirty minutes earlier and about forty blocks south, he had slowly stripped a young woman, and the result was the same—incredibly the same and he was always surprised by the sameness and surprised that he was surprised. He had taken his time with the prostitute, unfastening hooks and slipping down a shoulder strap, not so much to get his fifty dollars' worth as to slow down his fall through the trance, to delay the collision with the infinite point, a gray dot where oblivion ended.

Only later would it occur to Strickland that the same impulse to clothe this fancy also led him to reduce the object of it to its lowest denominator. "You're a dangerous man," Nancy had said one time. They had gone for an evening walk in the meadow and had made love on the polished surface of the tree stump, right in the middle of the field as it got dark. "You're a lot more dangerous than those Steve Canyon types you hang out with."

"Me, dangerous?" He was flattered as much as mystified by her words. She seemed flustered herself and had been readjusting her clothes in a distracted fashion as if what had just occurred between them had been somehow unaccountable, aberrant. "How am I dangerous?"

"Because you don't really care, I think. You are indifferent. It used to turn me on. Still has a sting to it—as you see." She laughed dryly. He could not see her expression in the darkness around them.

Virginia Cameron Caldwell wore what used to be called a morning coat though it was early afternoon, and she had been waiting for him in the open doorway of her apartment near the elevator with the good-humored patience of the well born. "So nice, Mr. Strickland." She greeted him with a quick handshake, then led him through a narrow hall. The apartment looked like one of those cramped shops on Lexington Avenue that specialize in Eastern objets d'art, and Strickland wondered if he was expected to stand through the whole interview, for the chairs and ottoman, two divans, were occupied by bolts of silk, porcelains, bowls, figurines, framed pictures and some kind of jigsaw work in dark wood like a puzzle whose complication had got beyond the control of its maker. *If you break it, you buy it.* Strickland half expected to see such a sign, a discretely lettered card perhaps resting up against the glazed belly of a Chinese god.

"Heah we are," the diplomat's widow said. She was by the room's one large window and lowered herself upon its padded seat. With the window behind her and enclosed, as it were, by the framed memorabilia of her husband's career—photographs and citations—she had deftly made herself part of the display.

"Here?" Strickland asked, questioning the chair she had indicated. It seemed to be made of thin tubes of black lacquer.

"Heah. Oh it is quite sturdy, I assure you. A warlord in the late Manchu period had it made for himself and he weighed close to three hundred pounds. Now, Mr. Strickland," her voice floated out from the bulk of her silhouette in the window light, a Buddha speaking with the gentle accent of Tidewater Virginia, "I'm afraid I must disappoint you. I have decided you cannot have mah husband's papers." But from Pittsburgh, he reminded himself, yet speaking like one of the FFV. A fortune in elocution lessons, probably. Maybe she had never lived in Pittsburgh.

What he would really like to have said, Strickland thought later, was *fine, okay* and then he would have stood up, knocking over the tier of porcelain behind him, maybe. Instead he said nothing, and found himself staring at one of the framed photographs that made a kind of diadem around the figure of this career matron.

The photograph showed Emerson Caldwell standing with Jack Kennedy, Sorensen, Maxwell Taylor, in civvies, and two other aides he couldn't identify. Caldwell stood between the president and one of these unknown assistants. Kennedy had his right hand partially tucked into the pocket of his suit jacket and the aide had his left hand similarly clipped into the pocket of his coat pocket. Caldwell, so bracketed, had the expression of a man who had just been told the single answer to everything; an answer at once so exhilarating and so terrifying as to make him fresh faced, the lines and creases of all previous misinformation erased. It was a picture of the mob in action. He bet they were talking out of the side of their mouths when the camera shutter clicked. *Okeh, sweetheart, now you're gonna get it.*

Strickland had not known this bunch. His class, so to speak, enrolled with a second generation, but they talked the same way; a preppie infatuation with movie tough guys. *We gotta ice the slant. Knock off that little cocksucker. Deliver the goods. Pound his ass. Rub him out.* The phrases were quaint in the Eastern Seaboard mouths, humorously antiquated, and—more times than not—accompanied innocent endeavors. But there were the other times too, and these orders came down to men like Carrol Strickland from Salina, Kansas, who always looked a little uncomfortable in a Brooks Brothers suit, who could never slip half a hand into its jacket pocket without feeling unbalanced. The lingo made no difference between knocking off Dartmouth the coming weekend or rubbing out a few villages in the morning.

"You make a persuasive case, Mr. Strickland," Virginia Caldwell had been saying. "Your voice . . . excuse me, but have you ever done any acting? I would think you'd be very good at that sort of thing." Her vowels and consonants sounded like small collisions underwater.

Strickland had to laugh, but continued his pursuit of the Widow Caldwell's vanity, letting his muffled good-fellow heartiness play chorus to a quick anecdote about a role he played in a college production of *He Who Gets Slapped*—he had been the strongman, just another hunk smitten by the beautiful bareback rider, Consuela. If he could only find that vein in this DAR Grande Dame, he could tap it and walk out with the papers. Meanwhile, his verbal soft shoe had had some effect. He caught a different accent in her look, not quite mothering—maybe house mothering. Maybe that was it. The old family silver gone with the Yankees but the manners and genteel bearing marketable at the nearest chapter of Kappa Sigma.

"How amusing," she said and leaned forward as if to hear more. More what? He had to keep her listening, lead her away from the subject, her decision, until she was far enough away from that decision and on new ground where she could make a new decision. Come now, Virginia Cameron Caldwell, where's the little button that will let loose the papers like wheat coming down the chutes of the grain elevators into the hopper cars of the Atchison, Topeka & Santa Fe—a whispery avalanche that used to clog his nose and eyes with gritty fiber? He culled up more college high-jinks. The old broad seemed to have a racy appetite for such stories. Yuck yuck.

"Oh, my, I don't think I've ever heard of such doings before," she said and patted her top-heavy figure. For a split-second, Strickland had a picture of the ambassador climbing on top of this monument to Southern manners by way of the Monangahela Valley, perhaps a little distracted still from his recent words with the Thieu family, but climbing on with all the Caldwell determination of his Midwestern Christian Endeavor—hot times at the High-Y—to raise a flag to erotic rectitude.

"But that wasn't all," Strickland pursued Mrs. Caldwell's aroused fascination, not letting her catch her breath, you might say. She was almost walking away from her refusal to give him the papers on her own now. He supposed the large file boxes stacked in front of an ornate screen were the documents she had decided not to let him have, maybe this morning, or even just before he rang the bell, she had turned to herself in the mirror, humming some old plantation tune probably, and then saying to herself Virginia, you will betray the trust of the nation, the ideals of Mr. Jefferson not to mention Mr. Madison or even Massa Robert himself if you allow these valuable papers out of your possession. A sacred trust. The screen was of several panels, each with an exquisite Chinese painting. The center one was of a lone figure in a small boat that seemed to be suspended in a mist rather than floating on a body of water.

"I guess you could say I was a loner," Strickland said.

"Yes, I can see that you might have been," Virginia Caldwell nodded. "Shall we have some sherry?"

"That would be fine. You know, the first time I tasted sherry was when I came to the university—at one of Professor Moon's get-togethers. I thought it was only a girl's name up until then. Back in Salina, Kansas, we didn't have much of a choice what with the dry's keeping any kind of liquor from our innocent gullets."

"Oh, I know that territory all too well." Mrs. Caldwell handed him the wine in Wexford crystal. "The ambassador was from southern Illinois, I guess you know, and he had many stories of that barbarous place . . ." *where a white man couldn't get a decent shave on a Saturday morning not even from a colored barber,* Strickland finished her sentence in his mind, though she did not say that directly. He let her take up some of the conversation, let her contribute corners and blind paths to the maze he had led her into and bided his time.

"I must say, I greatly admire your book on the last days in Saigon," she continued, fiddling with some sort of jewelry around her neck. "Your appraisal of the ambassador's part was imminently fair, I thought."

For the last several minutes, Strickland had been watching the window of an apartment across the street in a high rise that blanked the view as the brick walls had walled up Melville's Bartleby. But in one window the figure of a young woman moved through what seemed to be an elaborate and frenzied ritual. He could only see her from the waist up, and at this distance it was impossible to tell whether she was wearing a flesh-colored body stocking though the effect was the same as if she were nude: her poses and turns had a freedom to them, a self-absorbed ecstasy that convinced him she was nude. Yet she was not alone, for she seemed to be directing her movements toward one point of the room, bending over from the waist and rolling her shoulders in such a way that would make pendants of her breasts, presenting them like ornaments for an audience to examine. Perhaps reach out to assay. Strickland allowed his fancy to drift on the languid recollections of Mrs. Emerson Caldwell, talking affectionately of her husband's dirt-poor beginnings, tolerantly taking account of his background, its shallows and snags, from the high ground of her own distinguished heritage. There must be prostitutes in every building of New York, Strickland thought.

"Well, then you can imagine how I must have felt when I first came to the university and met that fantastic crowd around T. D. Moon." It was time to take back the conversation, to take the widow by the hand and up to the counter where she could change her ticket. *Oh, Trailways and Travelers' Aid, we are entrusting this daughter of steel barons to your care—may she arrive at her destination unchanged and unchallenged but with a certain lightness of luggage.*

Nancy used to call it his Poor Little Carrol number. "I'm sick of it. What's all this feigned inferiority? You almost shuffle when you get into it. I bet you do a mean Step-and-Fetch-It imitation. My God, Carrol, what happened to you? What awful snobbery did you suffer that makes you manipulate everybody with this phony rube act?"

Manipulate had been a favorite word for Nancy then; she had been reading a lot of popular psychology and even had packed a volume called *Love and Addiction* in with her nightgowns and tennis outfits. What had brought this outburst from her he could never remember, but the words were part of a familiar harangue and he was always sorry about that particular argument, whatever its cause, for it was to be their last one as she packed her bags for her retreat to that resort where she dried out, slimmed down and put an edge on her tennis game, and, as he was to learn later, attend to other matters. When he had been finally able to clean out her closet and bureau drawers, he'd discovered she had also packed her diaphragm on that last trip.

Mrs. Caldwell had been nodding sympathetically. His account of how the dean had passed him over for some jerk from Tuxedo Park—he had to make up the what-for—raised a watery heat in her eyes. "But to tell you the truth," he let his voice glide into a *basso serioso*, "it was Professor Moon who made me see how your husband and I share a similar heritage and even, if I may be so bold, the same sort of principles. Believe me, Mrs. Caldwell, I am a very busy man with . . ."

"Oh, I know you must be."

". . . many commitments. I'm supposed to narrate a series on the Antarctica for PBS but I would put that aside because I am convinced—more like compelled—to believe that Ambassador Caldwell's account of these terrible events has to be installed in this nation's history."

"Oh yes . . . oh yes . . . we met Professor Moon in Saigon, first," she said almost dreamily. "He was a Fulbright professor at the University of Saigon when we met."

"Funnily enough, I may have been his Boswell all along."

"Poor Emerson. He was a man being pulled apart by asses. He would sometimes weep . . . I tell you, Mr. Strickland, weep at my knees. 'What are we to do, Virginia?' he would say and we would talk long into the night."

"There, you see how important that you must give history this account—your account."

"Oh my, not . . . my part."

"Oh yes, the time for modesty is past, Mrs. Caldwell. At some point in those early hours before dawn, I'm convinced you said something to the ambassador that inspired him, freshened that native integrity nurtured in the rich soil of Illinois. I will have to ask you to dig down deep for that." Too far, Strickland thought, he'd gone too far, but the woman had rolled her eyes.

"Emerson did confide in me," the widow said, drawing herself together. Across the way, the girl in the window swayed langorously, arms above her head. "Yes, I could tell you things that might surprise you, Mr. Strickland."

"America's honor. Did absolute power corrupt? One man stood up. His name was . . . Caldwell." Strickland stopped abruptly. A voice from control. *Okay, Strick, but you need to shave half a second. One more time. Here we go.* He leaned toward her, hoping the chair wouldn't disintegrate into Manchu dust. "Think of the families in this country that need to read this man's wisdom. Can we deny them a view of his conscience? Think of the empty places at those dinner tables of a Sunday, the empty chairs and—yes, the empty beds. How can we deny them this man's story? Dare we keep from them the paradigm of his integrity? His courage?"

Were those darkies singing on the levee? Music coming up through her head like mist rising off the backwater? Her mouth had gone loose, an old scrap of the last drapery rescued from the Yankees. Oh, massa been brought home, sing him sweet and low—mostly low, because most of them empty chairs at the table, and the empty beds and them empty dreams are in the houses across the "ribber" from you, Mrs. Caldwell.

Say like Roger Wilson of Silvernales, New York, the son of Georgia Wilson. But is that fair? Georgia Wilson who was hired by Nancy, mostly just to talk to, still keeps showing up every Saturday morning, whether there's cleaning to be done or not—as if she hopes to find Nancy there in the kitchen ready for some village gossip, or maybe expects to find some word about Roger. Even if Strickland were to take off, abandon the house, Georgia would still show up, probably, not even freed by his absence but eternally bound by the same sort of fiction that he had just been holding against Mrs. Caldwell. Strickland stood up and his teeth ached. The girl across the way had disappeared.

"The paradigm of his integrity," she'd been saying. "Yes, I like that. Oh dear, Mr. Strickland. What a dilemma you present me." She pronounced it dee-lumma like, the name of some new fruit growing on her patio, say a cross between a lemon and a honeydew. "What am I to do?" She looked toward him for the answer.

When the doorman helped him load the cardboard files into the backseat of the taxi, he had almost asked the cabbie to wait so that he could walk across the street to check the call list in the apartment building's foyer. The very impossibility of picking her name out from the dozens of other tenants pricked the impulse. It might be a name so simple, so homespun one might say, that it would stand out in the directory as if illuminated.

Because, as Mrs. Caldwell had turned to gather the last boxes of her husband's papers, the girl in the window had reached down to pick up and hug the audience for her solitary dance. Two large, fluffy cats. She had been dancing for her cats.

"So what's in the boxes?" Leslie asks, the same question the girl Robin had asked but now the cardboard cases were stacked on the dining-room table.

"You turned your lights off just as I drove up last night." Leslie shrugs and pours milk into her coffee. "How come? You heard me?"

"I didn't feel like saying good night," she says. "I had had a long day."

"At the Heart Fund business?"

"What is this, some sort of an interrogation?" She looks up at him with a little anger and he wants to go to her, to put his arm around her and say it was all right. Her face is puffy and sullen and he wants to wipe it fresh and pretty as he used to wipe away the sticky traces of caramel and sandwich mayonnaise. Her mother's eyes— amused and a little scornful—turn away. She reaches for the sugar.

"Whoa, there, pardner." Three quick spoonfuls are shoveled into her cup.

"Lay off, Dad. I'm a food junkie."

"Don't say such things."

"It's true." His daughter stirs her coffee and looks out the window beside the breakfast table. Morning breezes lift the edges of paper napkins and furl the lace edging of her housecoat.

"So tell me what you did yesterday?" Strickland sits down across from her. The red-checkered tablecloth is between them. "I'm really interested."

"We talked about the campaign in the fall. By the way, I volunteered you to make some radio commercials for the county chapter. Okay?"

"Sure, fine." Anything, Strickland thinks, to give you, my darling, an advantage—no, not an advantage, but just to even things up for you. Use this voice, this deformity as your mother used to call it, to give you a place, a role. But do you need that second roll with butter and jam?

But is that the extent of it, why he had played the fool, the mouthpiece, for tyrants so that this greedy post-adolescent with all her baby fat saturated with more fat could sit around all day on volunteer committees with other cast-offs who had nothing better or who can find nothing better to do? Was that the end of it?

"Christ, let's close that." He leans across the table abruptly, so the cloth is pulled awry and the salt cellar falls over as he reaches up to slam down the window.

"What's the matter with you?" Leslie pulls away, her expression worried.

"Don't you smell it? Can't you smell it? The Schuylers are using too much of that liquid fertilizer on the fields. I've told them to be careful. They're going to leach that shit into the springs and there goes the water supply."

"Take it easy, Dad." She speaks with her mouth almost full, tucks a piece of bread back into one corner and then blots her lips with a paper napkin. "Think of it as one of the smells of spring."

"You know what it is, don't you? They take the manure from their cows and liquefy it, let it cook for a little in those big tanks, then they spray on our fields. Inject it into the ground. They're pumping shit into our land."

"So why rent the fields out then?"

"Well, your mother and I wanted them to be used, to maintain the balance of the place. To keep it in farming like it always had been. For you, Leslie." But that wasn't entirely true. It was the same with the old farmer they had displaced—a peculiar status quo phobia— something about getting out of Salina, Kansas made him feel guilty about changing things. Striding about these fields in his hand-made Wellington boots made him hesitant, for some reason, to control their cultivation, even though he instinctively knew the soil was being misused, as the old man's cows had been mistreated. "You should have been here yesterday." He starts to tell her about all the gunfire in the woods and his strange interview but then he remembers the ribbon caught on the bush.

"What about yesterday?" She holds her mug firmly and sips the coffee.

"Oh it was just more of the same. Those guys up in the woods firing their weapons." He is watching her closely. She looks down into her mug, then out through the closed window.

"Dick Schuyler says that they can milk their cows four times a day now."

"Who is Dick Schuyler?"

"He's your tenant's oldest son." She looks at him levelly across the rim of the cup. "Take it easy. The nerve in your forehead is jumping."

"Is he on the Heart Fund committee?"

"Don't be silly." She gets up and goes to the sink. Only about ten, maybe fifteen pounds off would make a real difference, Strickland thinks. A rifle shot cracks the stillness and then two more, in quick succession. "Oh," Leslie says quickly and rinses out her cup. "I better get dressed. Here's Georgia."

Blue smoke and a twitter of fenders, a loose rear bumper with the faded MIA sticker just above the exhaust, the Cadillac carries its rusted dilapidation up past the house and onto the parking area by the barn. So many times he had to get out on a cold morning to rescue its driver from its obstinate decrepitude, and even now the old car pulls up beside his Volvo and groans to a stop, everything letting down in the traces by Fisher Body like a Conestoga that has come all the way across the country and has reached the Pacific and can go no farther. Couldn't even if there were farther to go. The phone calls always started the same way.

"Hey, Mr. Stricklan'—how're you doin'?"

"Where are you?"

"I'm here down at Mrs. Robert T. Murphy's. It's another predicament."

The Cadillac always seemed to stop a mile or two from his house, so there was never enough time for the Volvo's heater to get warm and some mornings were near zero. "For God's sake, Georgia—get a new car. I'll help you get a new car."

"That car's good enough. Jimmy's got to fix it on the weekend, that's all."

And Jimmy, her youngest son, would fix it on the weekend; tearing down the engine or taking apart the transmission in the front yard of their house on Clover Lane, a white frame farm house with a side garden and, in good weather, morning glories growing up the chimney wall which also was this kind of open-air garage, on the one side of it with a shed of rusted parts and small cranes, pulleys and chains. It was as if Georgia had her side of the house with its neatness and pretty flowers, and her menfolk had the other side of the yard for their messy deconstructions.

Jimmy's weekly repairs did not seem to keep pace with the car's disintegration, an unforeseen failure of a gasket or hose line always occurring a mile or two from their house, always as Georgia was either coming or leaving the house, causing a predicament. "It don't look like much," Georgia would say about its rusted shell, "but it still runs good. Running better than ever."

Strickland at last understood what she meant was that the parts Jimmy had fixed on the weekends were running better than ever but that it was a big car, this Cadillac, so there were a lot of other parts, mysterious and obscurely placed, which hadn't yet been fixed and that could go at any time. And did. Even now, as he watches her get out of the car, the heavy door seems ready to pull itself off its hinges so it takes all of her strength to push it back shut against the grease and rust and dirt that have formed an entirely new compound in the crevices and moldings, almost as strong as the original metal casting.

She leans her tall body into it, thin legs braced and levering, to walk the door closed like a balky turnstile; turns to adjust the front of her dress and fixes the large ceramic beads around her throat. They catch the sunlight. Nancy had given her those.

The gunfire doesn't phase her. Several shots from the woods just now, but Georgia continues toward the house with the serenity of the truly saved. Not that she ignored the noise, didn't hear it, but had somehow assimilated the Italian marksmen and their "sport" into the way things were, the way things are bound to happen so why not get used to it. A faith almost, Strickland thinks. Like that bumper sticker on the Cadillac. "Look here what I got," she had said one morning a while back. *BRING 'EM BACK—MIA.* Sticking that strip of paper to the tarnished chrome of the bumper could magically bring Roger Wilson back from Vietnam—some part of him that maybe his younger brother could work on over the weekend and maybe fix up.

Can't you do something, Nancy had written him? He did take a run up the delta to the perimeter where Roger's unit had set up their volleyball court and maintenance depot. Come to think of it, it didn't look a whole lot different from the Wilson side yard on Clover Lane except that the vehicles were all painted drab and had gun mounts on them and the trees dripped latex when cut. What a civilization, leaving its junked machinery all over the map to rust.

Sure, they remembered Roger Wilson—he was one crazy dude. All of their faces sunny and glazed with a concern practiced out of deviltry and their own blend of Oolong. Ol' Roger, he just walked off one afternoon, just started walking off, going north one afternoon after the monsoons had let up. *Hey, Rog, you dumb fucker, you're going the wrong way, the pussy express stops on this side of the road,* but he just kept walking, shaking his head like he's listening to some meanness from Jimi Hendrix, like he's answering some kind of music that only he could hear. Would you say serene? The word would take a while to work through the hard matter in their ears, the scar tissue left inside their heads by the junked dreams of a mobile generation. Yeah, like serene—calm like his mama walking toward the house from that old Cadillac not even caring about the gunfire sounding in the woods above her and because she doesn't worry about it; it has nothing to do with her so it's not going to touch her. Like that.

"Mornin'."

"Good morning, Georgia."

"Nice out there." She hangs up her purse in the back room and slips on the blue cotton smock; her uniform. Next comes the exchange of her shoes for the low-cut sneakers kept in the corner by the washing machine. A dark blue bandana folded into a tricorner and pulled up and around her hair completes her ensemble—the professional domestic in an upper-middle-class exurban household. But there is little for her to do.

"Have some coffee?" But she has already poured a cup for herself and sits down in the chair that Leslie used.

"Them tulips look nice. They're coming up good."

"Yes." Yes, the tulips Nancy had planted with Georgia standing to one side helping, holding out one bulb at a time from the paper sack. It had been a family chore and she calls it up now to assert some claim on the place, on this time of the year showing itself on these grounds. She is a handsome woman, like an older Billie Holiday, if Billie Holiday had become old. This house and the care of it meant a good deal to her, but why it did had always puzzled Strickland. She had her own family and it wasn't a matter of forsaking them or even dividing her loyalties, or even changing from one world into another as she changed into her working clothes in the back room.

No, the more he thought about it, it was as if there was no division at all to her—or maybe the division was all from his side. He could remember coming on Nancy and Georgia laughing over something, side-holding gusts of ha-ha-ha's in the middle of house-cleaning, like sisters talking over old boyfriends they had shared and when he would try to ask about it later, Nancy would look at him dumbly—one of those none-of-your-business looks.

"I have some shirts to do and I guess the upstairs needs to be looked at."

"The spring covers need changing," Georgia says. She puts down her cup in a prim sort of manner. Then starts to laugh at his ignorance of these things. "All the draperies and the sofa covers has got to be changed over."

Was there ever a chance of saving Roger Wilson, son of Georgia Wilson and the late Wallace C. Wilson, carpenter and housepainter? *This is Carrol Strickland, speaking to you from a breakfast nook overlooking downtown Silvernales, New York, where we are about to hear from that eminent folk artist Georgia Wilson who is ready to ask the musical question, Why do I love you?* Why oh why?

All those papers on the dining-room table, the collected wisdom of Emerson Caldwell, and not one mention of Roger Wilson in any of them. They lay silently as the woods above the house are at the moment, the energy of the explosions within them long ago expended and all that lost energy rising like smoke, drifting over Silvernales, drifting over all the towns like Silvernales, all the cities. Talk about sulphur rain? The whole country slowly frying to a mindless crisp—tasty but you can starve to death eating it. What was it Moon had said about mushrooms?

"You see that program last night on the pond?" Georgia is asking. She looks wisely toward him and he knows she's talking about some program that she especially watched just to talk with him about it this morning—his type of program, she would think. "It was about a year in this pond, all the little animals and things in it growing." She stopped and looks at Strickland as if she hopes he will give the specifics: name the species of plants and pond life. Identify the pond.

"No I missed it. On public television was it?"

"Uh-huh . . . that station from Albany. My, it was beautiful. All those plants just dancing in the water and the little bugs—did you know they came from eggs, like a whole cluster of them on a stick? I didn't know that. But that snake . . ." she shivers and drinks her coffee. "I could just likely do without that snake. He swallowed this big frog all at once with just this little ol' frog leg sticking out of his mouth and twitching." And she starts to laugh at the comical aspect of the food cycle. Her teeth are very white and even.

"It sounds like an interesting program. I'm sorry I missed it," Strickland says and leans back in his chair. The morning sun warms his chest but he shivers a little too. The mockery of those programs was no different from the contrived accounts he used to announce: life and death in the rice paddies, which also sometimes had its comical aspects—a whole company higher than kites playing tag football under fire. A poker game where the chips were the dried ears of yellow-brown men. That sort of thing never made it into the programs, just like the awful truths that lay in wait in the ooze of that pond's bottom could never be filmed. You spoke around them in belling, mellifluous tones that sent ripples out into the brain and lulled the gullible.

The good faith in Georgia Wilson's face made him turn aside—he could not explain to her the techniques of film editing, of cutting a voice into a frame at the right split second so that the viewer would be distracted, would not see the actual horror taking place or recognize it for what it was: one being consuming another, the humorous incongruity of severed ears. And all the while the yellow rain fell on everything.

"There's good programs," Georgia says tentatively. And why don't you watch them, she's probably thinking? Everybody in Silvernales thinks you watch good programs like this one on the pond and you don't do it, and I'm the one that ends up watching them instead of the ones I'm supposed to watch—isn't that something? She laughs to herself, hugging her deep bosom, and she could be laughing at this contradiction, which may or may not have occurred to her. Strickland gives her the benefit of the doubt and laughs too.

He looks into the sensible, good-natured face across from him and tries to find words to return her care, her interest. She had made an effort to speak with him, had upset her family's nightly addiction to some sitcom to find something the two of them could share this morning, to clear a small space for them in the overgrowth of their histories where they could chat for a few minutes in the sun, over coffee, like two plain, ordinary human beings. Like friends, almost. He could see all this in her calm, assured expression—an acknowledgment of their sameness—as she waits for him to answer. Waits for him to fill in the blanks of this program she came across, switching through the channel selector.

If we could only do without desire, Strickland is thinking as he looks into Georgia Wilson's trusting face. It is the source of all falsehood, all anger and mockery.—Yesterday, Georgia. No, don't look away. There's nothing out there. She's not out there puttering about with those long canvas gloves; they're in the back room with the trowel. Now listen to me, though you can't hear me, but yesterday for a few dollars, about what I'm paid to read only a word or two for a program like you watched last night . . . "The ever-present poetry of the marsh exerts its ageless metaphor" . . . for crap like that, for what I get paid for just saying crap like that, yesterday I took a girl about the age of Leslie, younger maybe, and used her without desire.

"Seems like I almost expects her to just walk up from the hollow sometimes," Georgia is saying. "Like she's only been down there looking at her gladiolas coming up."

Arm in arm with Roger perhaps, Strickland almost says and it would not have bothered Georgia if he had. She might have even laughed at the idea. Ka-POW, POW. The Italians have come closer to the house, perhaps pursuing a herd of chipmunks. The sound of an upright piano coming down the stairs, end over the end, pulled the housekeeper's dark eyes to his.

"Sounds like Leslie is mad about something," he says.

"What have you gone and said to that girl now?" Georgia chides.

Chapter

4

But she always seemed to be angry about something these days. How long had it been since she had been the bouncy, daughter-pal who used to swing on the arm of his ideas. He figured it was a part of growing up and sometimes almost asked Georgia about it—she had raised a daughter too—did this kind of behavior or this sort of sullenness come with maturity? But he had met Georgia's daughter, he couldn't remember her name, and she always regarded him with the same sort of dark, brooding stare he sometimes got from Leslie. He put it down to the fact that he was picking up her mother—the Cadillac on the fritz—to bring her to the house to iron some shirts or dust the mantels, and the daughter must have interpreted this to be some sort of servitude her mother was being driven to, some variation of colonialism she had been made aware of in poli sci at Greenville Central School.

Maybe that was it. Nancy always had a layer of anger just under that cover of civility and brittle brightness—like an old courtyard of brick lying just under a carpet of spring flowers. Maybe all their time as girls and young women had been spent as subjects in a vast colonial empire that had demanded and enforced their good dispositions while permitting them a few silly whims, but freedom came with the menstrual revolution when all the resentments and angers of that repression could be acted out. Even now, as Leslie marched past him in the dining room, she wore a sullen mask, though he guessed it was also worn to ward off any question he might ask, like: Where are you going?

Because he was convinced that once in the barn and settled behind the wheel of her Chevette, her expression would change. This look would be put away as she tuned in the country rock station from Pittsfield and when she turned the key, her expression would also start up, a sunniness that used to warm all of his travels and his homecoming. Nor did he dare turn around when the car passed down the driveway, for to catch even a glimpse of that fleeing happiness would be more than he wanted to see.

Meanwhile Georgia was in the kitchen, adjusting the dial of the radio there to the morning classical music program that accompanied her chores. Nancy had always done this and Georgia continued the custom as she put the tennis trophies, the pictures and knickknacks back exactly on their marks after dusting. The announcer of this program was lugubrious-voiced and spoke chummily of the Bach boys as if they were old pals. Strickland was always amused by the man's cadence, his inflated seriousness, wondering as he carried the Caldwell papers into his study, if the announcer had decided at some point in his career that the sound of his voice was as important as the music he introduced.

That was one of the hazards of the trade. After a while, you began to think the event would not have taken place if you had not been there to describe it, to give it a resonance—to use the modish word—or it would remain unrealized without your help. Sometimes late at night, just to scour himself of this notion, he would put on the old tapes of people like Murrow and Collinwood or the young Cronkite and listen for that quizzical, somewhat bemused tone they all had that made them heroes of a sort because they hadn't been sucked in by the event. They had only come on the accident and just had time, it sounded like, to take a breath before talking about it; a little skeptical about the whole business, about human beings. It was no longer possible to do that.

One of Karl Philipp Emanuel Bach's sonatas for the clavier teases his ear. Georgia has moved the portable radio into the living room across the hall from his study and he hears her humming along with the baroque variations as she slips off draperies, unzips pillow covers. He senses that she wants to work near him this day and he responds to this camaraderie as he lays out the boxes of the diplomat's papers on the floor of his study.

Moreover, the intricate order of the music plays upon the chaos of the Caldwell papers, shames their random confusion within the boxes and folders that are marked off by the year or month. It was like that, Strickland thinks. Every month and year of the whole business segmented and labeled in an orderly fashion, yet within the given envelope, whether for a month or a minute, everything was haywire. Everything going according to plan toward the light at the end of the tunnel—week by week, month by month, year by year. Orderly haywire.

"The whole thing is going to blow up in our face," Nancy would say. But he could never convince her of the ordained order of such things, that they happened bit by bit—several hundred casualties a week, a hamlet taken here, a province lost there. She was the product of that good, solid liberal imagination that hoped for the Apocalypse as both a punishment and a reward and, in its frustration with the prophecy never being fulfilled, always blamed itself for allowing the Vietnams.

That was the problem: the urgency inspired by the revelation. Old Saint John had maybe chewed too many laurel leaves on Patmos Island but there was that phrase, "shortly come to pass," which stuck in the liberal craw like a sour ball of something chewed, a moral principle swallowed too quickly and now giving a little discomfort to righteous digestion. Palliatives were to be found in movies and popular literature—they fulfilled the prophecies at least for an hour or two, soothed the pangs that came from an overindulgence in guilt and gave momentary relief. Even yesterday in New York, bookstore windows were stacked with the latest novel of a writer who practiced these apocalyptic visions. Strickland wondered what sort of plant the man smoked or chewed or inhaled, because his books offered such romances of violence and ponderous malevolence as to be ludicrous to anyone who had been there. But these novels and others like them supplied the retribution that never came to pass, produced the orgasm for a desire created by that ne'er-do-well visonary from Galilee who, after being boiled in oil for a little while, was probably a little more angry at the establishment and more eager for its fiery destruction than most people might be.

But here's something that just occurs to him. He's just come across a folder labeled "Cabot Lodge." What if the Company or some other bureau funded these novels and films that so satisfy the liberal imagination? Not the John Wayne carnivals of revenge; they only excite the knee-jerk response. Everyone knows about certain books being paid for, certain publishers that were on the Company payroll, but most of them had been dry stuff—memoirs and dumb histories. Why not a few novels and even some movies to placate this desire for total destruction, which would satisfy the urge to be punished for being part of a history they happened to share?

"Consider this possibility," he remembers Moon saying. "Those fools and jesters in Shakespeare's courts are not there to tell the truth to tyrants. Whose paying their bills, pal? Whose setting them up with a warm place to sleep and a plate of chow? Old Lear couldn't give a good fuck about the truth. If he had, the story would have had a different ending. Right? No, those boys in the tassled hats are in the company pay just to give the impression that the tyrant is tolerant of such opinions, to play to the decency in the court, and incidentally— in the audience—while the ruler goes about his business cutting the throats of children. They were the original PubRel boys, those jokers."

Strickland has come across some amusing observations of Henry Cabot Lodge; how he wore his belt, his preferences in wines, and his tiresome accounts of his senate campaign against Jack Kennedy are the most noteworthy items in this folder along with a peck of memos, scribbled times and dates of phone calls, appointments. Caldwell had been meticulous; he must have saved everything. Perhaps within that pear-shaped decorum lived an actor looking for a spotlight. A different sort of vanity from his counterpart, Lodge, who seemed to glory in his defeat by Kennedy and allowed himself to be used by the man who showed him, in that senate defeat, which way the bear went through the buckwheat. Even took some pride that he had been one of the backs JFK had stepped on on his way to the White House. But no message from the President to Lodge—call off the dogs. That would have been too easy. Strickland sits down and opens another file.

"I'll wait until you're done in here?" Georgia stands in the doorway, a dust cloth in one hand and a floor mop in the other. Then she leaves without waiting for an answer—the mess around him enough of an answer. Vivaldi cavorts in the living room as she finds something else to do. The music skips and repeats and repeats and repeats. Dust in the record groove. The sound is reduced and the long-suffering voice of the announcer makes excuses for the condition of the record. The engineer gives it another try.

That's the way it happens, Strickland thinks. A little thing like that and without warning—a slight particle of dust in the groove that has been run through countless times. Like those times they drove back from parties by moonlight and without lights: the highway familiar so the handling of the car was almost without thought, the movements made deftly without any thought and unperceived but done nevertheless as they had to be done, as if the curve in the highway made the wheels turn, the pavement directing their passage so that the two of them seemed borne along by the terrain, by inspiration almost, and then something slightly different is felt. Some small change in the rhythm, like the fribbling in a heartbeat suddenly makes the body aware of the heart beating; or, say, a farm truck comes out from a side road for no reason at two in the morning or a deer spooks from the shadows—the unforeseen variation, that particle of dust becomes the final resolution.

Nancy might have known this at last. As the 737 made its approach into San Diego, chairs up and trays returned to their storage position, the routine return to earth worked its way through the familiar checklist. Hundreds of times. Hundreds and hundreds of times the power glide down this groove in the air, the engines and airfoils singing their own mournful harmony. Had she looked out the window, eager to get on the ground, to get into her tennis game or into someone's bed—it didn't matter—the view would be familiar. "The swimming pools look like pieces of turquoise," she told him once. "Like beads from a necklace that have come apart."

So maybe she had been looking at those greenish-blue fragments, thinking about them maybe as Navajo jewelry—the pitiful but beautiful fragments of a people subjected and destroyed by our brand of colonialism, she'd make that kind of an association—when a slight tremor ran through the plane. A little vibration under her feet, something different, so the person next to her might have looked up from the airline catalog offering luggage and barometers and highball glasses. Just a speck of dust in the groove and then the sorrow.

No big deal, Nancy. No big bang, either, before the fire. He often thought of that but not the awfulness of the flames and the scorching smoke but, strangely of the hem of the slip she had put on that morning. Cotton, crispy white with lace around the hem. He remembered how the lace looked against the tanned flesh of her legs; so white and so pretty and clean.

So there's your Apocalypse—a piece of lace turning black, turning into smoke as the flesh becomes charcoal. Better to do without desire, if that desire looks for a Big Finish so as to make a clean start. Because there is no clean start and there never has been. No hope of one, either. Just an orderly procedure, a routine checklist, winding down one groove after another into places like Hué, the craziness of it in the folder he holds in his hands, or places like San Diego, the mockery of that he keeps stored deep, out of the light.

More gunfire again, real this time and not the sounds in his head that have been supplementing Caldwell's reports. "This is intolerable," Strickland says aloud, his voice like the rumble of a line squall. He had meant to call Warden van Deusen. Ray. *Ray, this is Carrol Strickland. We've got to do something about these fellows up here.* He would tell him about all the kills he had seen two days ago. Illegal. Hawks. *Yes, I know you're undermanned, but let's swear in some deputies and organize a sweep. Clearly these people are breaking the law. Can't we enlist the sheriff? Where's the state police?* But as he touches the phone, it rings.

"Yes, hello." He half expects the game warden's voice on the other end. But there is no sound, only the hash of the open line and just before she does speak he knows it is her. Something about the way the silence seems to hang back, almost a sway of deference.

"Carrol, I'm sorry to trouble you. This is Robin Endicott. There's a problem with my aunt and I know no one else who can help me."

Strickland will always remember the look of her apartment that first morning. The rooms above the carriage house on the Endicott place had been painted a flat white like the lime wash on the old horse stalls below though that paint had yellowed and become grimed by the oily exhaust of automobiles. He could still smell hay, the aroma coming up through the floorboards of the apartment to charge the air and combine with the sunlight to make almost a combustible mixture, he thought. And, as if to offer itself as the spark for such combustion, a single red rosebud stuck up from a plain white vase set upon the glossy white surface of what had once been a round dining-room table, its legs cut short; the whole display bracketed on two sides by a sofa and large floor cushions also covered in white. The bud vase was chipped and he could see some of the veneer on the table had peeled away and he was surprised by the way these imperfections moved him. In an instant, as brief as the glance of sunlight against the glossy white moldings of the high transomed windows, he had a picture of the girl, Robin, carefully choosing these treasures at country flea markets, carefully counting out their price and bringing them back to this barn where she would flow white enamel over their imperfections.

He would soon stop referring to her as a girl, but right then Leslie was uppermost in his mind and they seemed not all that different in years, he reminded himself as Robin prepared tea in an alcove behind oatmeal drapes. Could she offer him some tea for his trouble, she had said in the driveway in the tone of the waitress he had first encountered, even pulling on her right arm at the wrist—an anxious pose to wait the customer's desire. Then this high-ceilinged room above the old stables, to which his eyes had to grow accustomed as if all the light outside of it had somehow been concentrated, augmented within the plain white walls.

So unlike the white-washed interior of the Schuyler barns, he had walked through earlier on his way to Cora's, illuminated by rows of low-watt bulbs screwed into porcelain sockets linked by BX cables, and hanging with cobwebs, cardboard tags with peculiar computations, and strangely, the long noose of a string around the neck of a deflated balloon. Also, unlike this airy loft where he now waited for a cup of tea, the aromas of the cow barn were sodden, ammonia-like pungencies of raw manure and rotted straw that cleaned out his sinuses as no drugstore preparation could. The stench was too moist and the light of the bulbs too feeble to threaten any explosion, unlike the single red rose that seemed about to put a fuse to Robin Endicott's modest surroundings.

He had hardly been able to see inside the barn, even after his eyes grew accustomed to the dimness, and this lack of light was not due to any sense of economy in the Schuyler family—the season's new pickups nosed in by the corn crib—but perhaps to accord with what went on in this place: a casual handling of animal parts, a coupling of bizarre implements, hoses and suction tubes to fleshy paps, an activity that probably called for some privacy, some low illumination.

Even the Schuyler hired hand seemed to move blindly down the rows of high haunches, putting out his hand now and then to push at one of the tall, tail-swished sterns as if to find his bearings or maybe only to touch, and so acknowledge one of these machine-laden creatures as another being; perhaps to give encouragement, to urge the surrender of that last drop to the suction that drew the milk into the clear plastic pipes running parallel to the BX cables and into the stainless steel tanks of the spotless creamery located at the end of the barn.

"Hi, Dad," Leslie said cheerfully. Her face flushed, almost the same color of the Schuyler boy's hair. They had both looked up, startled to see him. They looked clean and fresh like the last two pieces of crisp cereal in the bottom of the bowl, as sparkling as the tiles of the creamery where they sat playing a game of cards.

The young farmer stood up, a little awkward in his high rubber boots, which was unusual because Strickland had often seen him, seen him from a distance, to be sure, as he passed on the highway, but he had seen him walk across the barn lot with the same graceful lope of airmen in old movies strolling to their waiting planes. And, in truth, a kind of dawn patrol had taken place here only a few hours earlier—the first day's milking, the first of four: Strickland remembered Leslie telling of the new regimen. Those poor teats behind him were given little rest.

"Mr. Strickland . . ." Dick Schuyler greeted him.

"Just saw your car," he said to his daughter. "Collecting for the Heart Fund?"

"Oh, Daddy." Leslie made a face and turned back to the cards. It looked like a game of double solitaire.

"Actually, I wanted to talk to your father," he looked at Schuyler. The younger man had turned beet red and his ears stuck out even more as if to fan the heat of his face.

"He went into town to get some parts."

"Well, I can talk to you. We have to do something about those guys up on the hill behind us. Do you let them hunt on your land?"

"Pap don't give them any permission at all."

"But they still hunt on it, you're saying."

The young farmer shrugged. "It's hard to keep them off. We got no time to patrol it." He paused, almost sniggered. "We got other things to do."

Like play solitaire with my daughter, Strickland thought, though the innuendo in the younger man's voice had burst in his face. The old attitude of the natives had shown itself: he and Nancy were idlers. His profession was to be questioned: something that didn't come out of the soil, out of animal heat and which couldn't be tasted or give nourishment. Ah, the arrogance of the working class; the peasantry that surrendered themselves to the whims of the seasons, had always charged him with the crime of frivolity, of being unnecessary and working at it! It wasn't always this way, he sometimes wanted to say. He knew about honest work, about the hard pain in the gut that comes from watching a season's labor burn up or rot in the ground.

Dick Schuyler stood expectantly, perhaps waiting to get back to the card game—in fact he held cards in one hand, the jack of diamonds that could release the suit might be the next card. His fingers were stubby and surgically clean as if both hands had been boiled and sterilized, but where this process occurred in this place that reeked of excrement, Strickland could not conjecture. Even the old, cracked radio playing country western on a shelf near the ceiling seemed to have been dipped in something rather awful. For a split second, he had a picture of these pinky clean hands touching his daughter, unfastening Leslie's blouse and freeing the heavy breasts within.

"Well, I'd like to talk to your father," he said quickly. "I think those fellows present a major problem for our community. We need to put together some sort of a petition. Tell him I came by, won't you?"

"Sure." Dick Schuyler grinned. He was no longer blushing. Outside, a truck roared down the highway like a device hastily put together and launched from the center of Silvernales, just over the hill, to slice through the morning's predictable sequence. Probably a milk tanker, Strickland figured, and too full to stop here but its diesel racket failed to shatter the invisible bell that enclosed the milky-sweet luminosity of the creamery. Leslie sat at the table between them and for a little bit offered the only movement in the room: a careful alignment and realignment of the cards laid out before her.

The shock of seeing her there, comfortably in place as if this card game had been going on for some time, every morning perhaps, had dried up his quick, easy language. Somehow he got out of there and into his car without too much awkwardness though his anger stumbled about within him, falling over itself and knocking into his confidence. It was the sense of collusion that upset him the most—the idea that she had probably been meeting with Dick Schuyler for how long?

Collusion was the word. As he drove away from the farm, leaving the ranked blue silos framed in the rear-view mirror, he reminded himself that it had been farm people like the Schuylers, the solid husbands of the earth, who had let in the so-called sportsmen in the first place. Their landowners association had sold non-resident memberships to all those Italians from New Rochelle so they could hunt, and that's how they had discovered the area in the first place. Now they were up there on the hill behind him, property owners themselves, to ransack his peace. Writing obscenities on his boundary markers.

More than his peace. He was driving too fast and took his foot off the accelerator as he crossed the line into Connecticut. Yes, there was more to it than that. Years earlier, he and Nancy had imagined a retreat where the child could grow up away from the city's filth and all the disparagement of the spirit. What a strange exodus, he would often think. It almost required proclamations.

The disparagement of the spirit that hangs like an ominous cloud high above Cayuga's waters.

You are right, of course, Carrol. As always. We must put aside our own ambitions, our own pursuits and conveniences for the sake of the child.

May I tell you that you look especially breathtaking tonight.

Why thank you, darling.

Something like that—their talk had gone something like that. Maybe not exactly. At the Blue Bar of the Algonquin. At least there. The topic was turned over in many places around the city, some of them Nancy's old haunts. Like Bradley's in the Village or some bar near Bloomingdale's. But look what had happened. Strickland smoothed the left part of his moustache, his fingers pressing the bristly hairs into his flesh. The gesture signaled anxiety or thought. They had ended up, delivered Leslie almost into the very hands they had tried to avoid. Gangsters and shit-kicking farmers!

So the whiteness of Robin Endicott's room over the old stable, the light focused through the large casements at either end to spill fountain-like onto the round white table, the whole clean brilliance of the place scoured and freshened his being, leaving him a little light-headed, almost weary but pleasantly so, as if he had just worked through some arduous routine and was being rewarded by the scarlet perfection of the single rose, freshly cut and perhaps just for him. Looking at it made him drowsy, an amulet presented by a hypnotist, and he would say later that the calm he felt at that moment, the tranquillity, became an addiction—instantaneously acquired and never again appeased. He would do almost anything, he promised himself, to experience that tranquillity again.

"I must be surrounded by beauty," Robin is saying from the kitchen alcove. China and flatware faintly sound like wind chimes. "No matter how egregious it may be, I must have some authentic beauty close by. All else can be dispensed."

"Like this rose," Strickland said but she did not hear him.

"This is my refuge," she said, carrying a tray bosom-high and moving across the room toward him with a graceful rhythm so he was briefly reminded of the first time he had seen her, waiting on Leslie and him at the restaurant. Somehow, the more times he saw Robin the more details of that first sighting seemed to occur to him. "Now," she said and placed the tea things down on the table. The note of expectancy in her voice moved him by its childlike anticipation, as if the items on the tray were unknown to her, as if she had not prepared them herself.

The teapot was blue and the cups white. Two linen napkins folded their creamy texture over and around themselves. A small antique plate with a floral design in brilliant greens held seven biscuits, fanned upon each other like fallen dominoes but almond colored. Wedges of lemon on a black saucer. And in the center, as if the purpose of the whole arrangement had been to celebrate this one detail, was a porcelain rice bowl containing five cherry tomatoes. A small dish of sauce sat beside. Even within the mayonnaise there were tiny green accents; chopped chives, he guessed.

In his travels in the Orient, Strickland had seen similar presentations of food, of packaging—mundane items of existence abstracted into near-perfect works of beauty; so he was familiar with the genre, but what took him off-guard, and so made this simple ceremony special, was the sense that Robin had made, out of what he imagined to be a very limited pantry, a repast whose meager sumptuousness appealed to and satisfied far more than physical hunger.

She had not sat beside him but had knelt on one of the large cushions, the material of her skirt spreading out around her. She served him a cup of tea and offered the plate of cookies, and for a split second the impulse to take all seven of them, to grab them by the handful and thrust them into his jacket pocket, pounced on him like a bandit. Where and why this feeling came from he could only guess at, but right then he carefully took one of the cookies and looked down into the thick softness of her hair. The light turned the color of it to bronze and polished the white curve of her slender neck.

Also, he was distracted and flattered by the evidence that she had prepared for his visit to her studio, by the way she would go from cup to plate to the sauce for the tomatoes, folding and refolding the napkin before him; all part of a presentation that she must have rehearsed as he drove over, responded to her call. "Here, try these . . ." or "Now, this . . ." or "Will you have lemon?" all spoken like parts of a script—her part of a script and one spoken for her own benefit, to keep track of the moment as much as to serve him. But of course Cora Endicott's attack had not been planned.

"Thank you for that." Robin looked up at him. Her expression was somber, older than it should be. "Thank you for coming."

"Has she had these often?" Cora Endicott's white and green bedroom had smelled faintly of vomit. He had traced the smell of smoke to the origin of the black cigarette burn on the rug. The bathroom glistened wetly, when he got there—the girl must have mopped it from ceiling to floor—but Strickland was also interested by the sunken marble tub, the luxurious fixtures in gold plate that Cora had implanted for herself in this prim Connecticut village. He noted the lighting—that peculiar peachy hue associated with cheap funeral parlors, which would flatter the older woman's reflection in the mirrored chamber as it did the dead. "What does her doctor say?"

"He was out of town. I tried to call him. I called you. I had no one else to call," Robin finished and looked to one side, as her torso pulled in the opposite direction—that singular pose she had taken at the dinner table the night before. "It's her gall bladder, I guess. The poor dear just loves to eat and drink too much." She turned and laughed at him over her shoulder.

"You're fond of her, aren't you."

"I would have died without her. I would have—" and Strickland was caught with one of the cherry tomatoes halfway to his mouth, some sort of decorum instructing him to wait, not to take a bite until she finished the sentence. But she only shrugged and he bit into the plump, tangy flesh of the fruit. The green flecks in the sauce were chives. "One good thing; she won't know that you were here. She's very taken with you and if she knew you had seen her like this—well, I won't tell her." Robin faced him now, and she smiled. He was delighted with the innocent conspiracy.

In fact, when he had arrived there was nothing for him to do but to admire the way the older woman had been tucked into bed, her hair brushed and her flesh cologned. The rubbish from the morning's funding had been bagged and put to one side. "She's sometimes careless," Robin had said, showing Strickland several folders with burn marks before stashing them in the plastic garbage bag. But cigarettes and holder and a clean ashtray of crystal had been placed on the table beside her, ready for her when she awoke. How everything had been put right! Robin must have worked very hard in the half hour or so after she had called him, and but for the damp darkness on the pink carpet, which she had been spraying with a scented disinfectant—the one last chore—nothing in the room had suggested someone had been sick but a faint, sour smell mixed with a smoldering odor, but even that had almost disappeared. He stood there at the foot of the bed.

Cora breathed easily, eyes closed, her small round head thrust back on the pillow, a strain on the thin neck. Her mouth was partially open so the family grinders glimmered in the curtained light. The girl finished the cleaning up, suddenly looked up into his face and he noted the perspiration above her upper lip; these tiny beads that told of her effort and anxiety. Her tongue curved up and gathered the sweat.

"More tea?" She served him carefully, again, so unlike the almost wanton dispatch of plates and courses he remembered that night at the Black Oak. He wanted to talk to her about that night, about her in that place and how she had come to be working there—obviously unhappy to be working there and so out of place there. Her face in repose, from this angle looking down, seemed plain, and the profile emphasized the jaw line so the heart-shaped winsomeness of the full view was replaced by an angular toughness that could be taken for determination and experience. Strickland was reminded of old paintings, he couldn't remember the artist, that featured working-class women with faces aged to an unhappy sophistication by their menial tasks. European, probably.

Meanwhile, Robin also had become entranced by the single rose in the center of the table. She sipped her tea, broke up a cookie and placed a piece of it into her mouth—slowly and without attention as her gaze turned upon the flower. "You don't realize how much this place means to me no matter how mere or credulous it may be. Sheer material has never been that important to me. I'd rather have one very fine plate than a cupboard full of things that offended me."

"One perfect rose," Strickland heard himself say, impressed by his own seriousness.

"Yes," Robin replied and turned to him. Her smile melted the lead from his remark to give the cliché a fresh value. "Your work must be intensely rewarding. Emerson Caldwell. Was he instrumental to our policy in Vietnam?"

"Yes and no," Strickland started, and then continued to tell her a little about the late diplomat, as part of his mind tried to piece together where she had heard about his project—probably last night he had talked at dinner about his successful interview with the man's widow—while another part of him, somewhere below his intellect, was warmed by her interest and the effort she had taken to inform that interest. She had looked up a few facts—even in the little time she had had since last night—probably in her benefactor's large library. For Cora Endicott, reading, as well as distributing her fortune among particular causes, was the important ingredient of a sedation that eased her infirmities.

"Was Caldwell's midwestern background used as a hedge by the eastern bloc around Kennedy?"

Strickland recognized the source behind her question, Teddy White's book on Kennedy's election, but he was more impressed by

the casualness of her manner, the off-hand display of certain knowledge like that of a colleague, perhaps someone his own age who had
known those times rather than the young woman at his feet who had
not even been born at the time and who just then leaned forward to
give him a clear view of her young woman's breasts as if to certify her
youth even more, to even more amaze him.

So Strickland continued to talk about the diplomat, mouth more
than speak the answer to her question for he also followed her
gesture—the reason for her bending toward him so the loose bodice
of her sundress fell away. One of her hands reached between his boots
and picked up one and then another and finally a third crumb from
the tea biscuit he had just eaten; they had fallen to the grass mat rug
that covered part of the floor. Delicately she had transferred each
particle from floor to the palm of her other hand and from there to the
saucer of her teacup and then—then, as if to grace his carelessness, to
assign it a minute importance in some larger proportion—she smiled
and dusted her hands together.

But this evening the pages of the diplomat's memoranda become
blank as he remembers something else in her look. The propriety of
a proprietor. The grass mat was inexpensive and probably from one of
those import places that sold cheap products from the Far East, but
it was hers and it covered *her* floor. He had been messing up her space
and she had been candidly cleaning up behind him—no, in front of
him; her housekeeping a demonstration of ownership as well as a
congenial demand that he respect what she owned, no matter how
modest it was.

Those furnishings, something about the pretended elegance of
the white table with the single red rose and the blinding simplicity
of her quarters—near-poverty made into a sort of high style—
prompted him to put aside Caldwell's report on Robert McNamara's
first visit to Vietnam in 1962 and go to the large dictionary in the
corner of the library. "We are winning this war," the former president
of the Ford Motor Company had said. It was the first of many times
he was to make this statement as secretary of defense.

E-gre-gious *1. remarkably or extraordinarily flagrant: an egregious lie.* **Obs.** *Distinguished or eminent.*

How had Robin used the word? It had been bothering him ever since he'd heard her say it as she fixed the tea tray. She had to be surrounded by beauty, she had said. *No matter how egregious it may be, I must have some authentic beauty close by.* He heard the full-throated sounds of her voice say it again and now, with the authority of the dictionary, he could verify that her usage was off—not quite right, and he was certain this was the case with several other words he couldn't remember right now but he could remember the slight pause in his perception, a skip in his cognition, when she had said them.

Strickland knows he is smiling over the dictionary, feels himself smiling at this revelation of Robin Endicott's ignorance and he even has, just for a moment, an image of himself that resembles the picture on the wall of the shoe store, the curve of the lip gentling the censorious bar of the black moustache—signaling the idea that much more information is known here than can be spoken, but, at the same time, generously forgiving the unknowing for not knowing.

What Strickland was never to understand about her was that the behavior he determined to be pretentious, an affectation of language in this case, was really the sign of an effort to furnish herself with the inventory of a new life—to move herself out of rooms impoverished in every way, in both body and spirit, and into bare but clean rooms, maybe decorated only by sunlight and with only a single flower for distinction. And, if in her urgency to remake her destiny, she sometimes used words that did not quite fit, put on airs that did not quite go with the furniture, they were her own inventions and far different from the modes that had been forced upon her. His opinion about her, as generously conditioned as he thought it to be, was formed by the image of her in this former life, fixed like a specimen and duly identified, so that what he saw as endearing mannerisms were actually frantic acts of survival.

* * *

I hate to remind you of the old cliché—the inscrutable Orient—but it is mindful, I think, in our current situation. Emerson Caldwell's memo to Averell Harriman: Report on McNamara's first tour of Vietnam. *The secretary's assessment of our resources, the correlations with our allies and the estimates of the costs of supply and maintenance are admirable. More than that. It is clear how he acquired the "can do" title at Ford; however, there is one component missing in all of these calculations—the enemy's motives. We know nothing about the insurgents or even who they are or what they want. If I remember my Clausewitz, one of the basic axioms is to know your enemy. We seem to be making the mistake of arming and supplying ourselves to fight an enemy that only exists in our heads, created by our own ignorance and false assumptions—an enemy created by Young and Rubicam. The strategic hamlet program is a failure—something put together in PubRel. The people the compounds are supposed to protect are taking them apart and disappearing into the jungles. This is not Terry and the Pirates. This conflict is only a small cloud but it could become a devastating hurricane if we continue to operate under forecasts like McNamara's. I believe the other side is fighting a different war from what we believe we are fighting and for reasons we haven't even guessed at yet.*

Strickland's voice in the hurricane had been calm, confident and persuasive. The voice of America, Moon had said. He hears himself now, as if the diplomat's memo had switched on a tape stored somewhere in his head. *President Richard Nixon has announced that Haiphong Harbor has been mined as an effort to convince the Communist aggressors that the prolongation of their war against the free peoples of South Vietnam will be at great risk to their own people and commerce. Meanwhile, National Security Adviser Henry Kissinger continues to . . .*

Hold it a minute, Strick (the voice from the control booth). He could hear them talk among themselves. It was cool and soundless in the studio. Windowless. Like being in a trunk. Outside it was May in Saigon, steamy, noisy, the smell of rotted flowers and hot oil. Blue and yellow taxis raced around like waterbugs on swamp water. Down at Mimi's, little dolls were delicately touching the backs of their ears, the backs of their knees with Chanel No. 5. *Okay, Strick. We're going to put Kissinger into the lead. Hal is bringing you the new copy. Got it? Okay? Here we go. Three . . . two . . . one . . . go.*

National Security Adviser Henry Kissinger has expressed the hope that negotiations will continue to go forward in Paris to reach a peaceful and equitable solution to the struggle against the Communist aggressors while President Nixon has announced a step-up in the bombing of North Vietnam installations and the mining of Haiphong Harbor. The White House confirms these measures are meant to convince the aggressor that further delays in the peace progress will only increase the risk of injury to the economic and cultural fabric of North Vietnam.

The voice of America. The voice of Silvernales: a cricket cheerfully comments on the state of the library hearth. Outside the windows an insurgency of peepers rises and falls on the night air, anonymous and pervasive; their rasp penetrates the perimeter of his consciousness and his attention returns to this dun-colored room and the papers and the boxes of folders with more papers and the two walls of books, most of which have stamped on them somewhere Property of Furness Academy. Or some have a label pasted inside the front board: Ex Libris Everett Hale Endicott. Not even the books are his, Strickland thinks, and not for the first time.

"What is all this?" Leslie says from the doorway as if she were repeating her question of that morning, as if the hours in between had not existed and, in fact, as if he had not really answered her yet. She wore a long cotton nightgown and ate a bowl of cereal. "What are you looking for?"

"Why do you say that?"

"Just the way everything is thrown about. Doesn't seem like your usual Mr. Clean Jeans." She sat down on the arm of the sofa, holding the cereal bowl just below her face and spooning a mouthful. Already she was beginning to look like one of the local farm women, heavy-armed and content.

"You always ask me these questions," Strickland muses. He is thinking of a few years back in this very room. His daughter turns the spoon over in her mouth. "You remember asking me why? Why us, you asked me. About Vietnam."

She shrugs. "I don't remember. What was your answer?"

"I don't think I had one. I'm looking for it now. I'm still looking for that answer. What's the matter?"

Leslie has gone on to something else; she isn't really listening. Maybe she no longer believes he can tell her anything important. He sorts through another file—copies of letters, memos, clippings from *Time* and other journals—at least to give the impression of an orderly task. "What is it, Baby?"

"I miss Mama."

"Yes, so do I." Strickland puts down the papers. Down in the village, wheels screech against pavement as someone peels off from the intersection. He resumes his chair and Leslie puts down her plate and moves to him, climbs into his lap. A child's awkward clambering for comfort, though Leslie is no longer a child and, just for a moment—a moment that shames him by the image—Strickland feels as if one of Schuyler's new calves has climbed up on him, stiff-legged and uncoordinated.

"How's Cora?"

"Oh, fine. No problem. Just a little too much to drink and smoke." He stops, not too abruptly he hopes, and looks sideways at Leslie. She would remember her mother; how the secretive, self-important laughter would begin without warning and then the arrogant slant of shoulders and the dark bite of sarcasm, humorous at the first nibblings but becoming more painful as the mouth stretched wider and wider for screams that never sounded. "Miz Strickland is not feeling well," Georgia used to say, and the house would become strangely quiet, funereal, as they all waited for the dead to return. Tiptoe.

So he holds all these memories as he holds his daughter in his arms, as the wheeze and sighs of the night turn over outside. "What's the matter? Don't let the blues get you down."

"I want to get out of here."

"You mean here? Silvernales?"

"There's nothing for me to do here. Except eat." She shifts her position, sits up. Strickland smells the soap she uses. "I want to do something."

"What do you want to do?"

"What can I do?" She considers the possibilities as she bounces on his knees. Some kind of a punishment, Strickland thinks, for him to have asked the question and he clenches his teeth. "I can marry into the Schuylers. I can take care of you. I can volunteer for a few more boards. Animal Rescue League always needs help. Then there's the Cancer Society."

"Stop it."

"Well, what else is there for me? Let's face it, I don't have the build to be a hooker."

"Be serious."

"Oh, I'm very serious." She rises, rather nimbly, and returns to the sofa, her bare feet stepping on the memoranda scattered across the floor like stones across a stream. "I'm getting out of this place. I want to go someplace and do something. Get into the real world. This place is a trap." The concentric chubbiness has hardened and the cute nose in the center seems turned up even more. Her eyes are dark. "I want to get a job."

"Doing what?"

"Well might you ask."

"No, I'm curious." He ignores her sarcasm, the old charge— they had not sent her to the right schools. "What do you want to do?"

"You say that like you can do something about it, like you have things in one of those folders for me to do and I just say something like . . . I want to learn to repair clocks, and you just reach in there and pull out a slip for a watch store in Great Barrington that's looking for someone like me."

"Be serious."

"You don't get the idea." She has picked up the bowl and spoons the last of the milk, scrapes the dish for more. "I'm very serious. So what's all this about?" She gestures to the Caldwell collection spread out on the floor and furniture. The way she's changed the subject shows her indifference to his reaction. Long after she had gone upstairs and the house became silent, even the uprising at the pond quelled, Strickland remained in the library sifting through the papers, piecing out the history they suggested.

Had Moon been playing a final trick on him, a last painful pinch at his seriousness, his eagerness to be part of the team? That kid from Kansas is just a whole lot of good sport. *Carrol, you take the ball and run this way and we'll all run interference.* But no one ran interference and in fact there was no one else on the field. He had the field to himself, and he was running with the ball all by himself. Seriously and with great purpose. All the others, both sides, had gone to the sidelines to laugh at his earnest, solo performance. He had had dreams like that.

"I could tell you almost anything," Nancy said one evening, "and you'd believe it." They were in this very room and her voice had that sensual slur to it that came from several scotches—a sound that aroused a heat he never questioned. "Those whores in Saigon must love the look in your eyes. Must make them feel like sixteen, though I guess some of them are sixteen. You give them back their innocence. You believe almost everything."

But somewhere in this clutter, there might be a note from Washington to Saigon that called off the old assassination; targets long ago blasted out of the trees. Talk about a conspiracy long enough and it comes true—fiction can be made fact. He had been part of that miracle often enough that it had become almost like a habit— something to be desired, to be attained at any cost. Would there be a similar magic if he found that note?

Chapter

5

The mirror over the counter at Louie's Pizzeria catches Carrol Strickland unawares and, momentarily, he sees a stranger, or rather a distant relative; a family resemblance in a stranger that invites inquiry and possibly a reunion. Natives around Green River still tell the story of a family in the last century going to church for Christmas Eve service, crossing Blue Heron Lake by sleigh, the ice breaking through so they sank and drowned, the ice freezing over thick by the time they were missed and traced, so they had to be left under it until spring. Villagers and relatives walked out to keep a vigil all winter, with the faces that stared up through the opaque wall as if the frozen eyes on the other side could yet register recognition, receive comfort. Even the horse, some said, looked ready to continue the journey.

Strickland had come upon this alter image of himself often enough, say in the blue mirrors of Saigon bars—Nancy's comments about the expression in his eyes come back to him again—and in only the past week, on Thursday, in a studio in New York, he had looked up at the control booth, waiting for the engineers to set up for another take, and there in the black glass of the console had been this person, this guy with a moustache, slightly familiar.

"Okay, Strick." The director's voice came from the dark glass "We need to shave one and a half seconds off the middle. Go back to frame fourteen. Ready. Three . . . two . . . one . . ."

"CALL ATLAS FOR TROUBLE . . . HE'LL MAKE IT."

If he had shifted his eyes from the monitor screen, looked back at the dark glass above him, and in just that fraction of the time he so neatly clipped off the voice-over, he might have caught a wonder in the eyes, a look that was part amusement and part disbelief, which questioned his very presence in those surroundings—talking over film clips of staged mayhem, chatting with a prostitute in Saigon, or even sitting at the counter of a pizza place in Green River, New York. The reflection questioned his presence in all those places.

"So what are you doing, Mister Strickland?"

"Here?"

"Here, there, anywhere." Louie's Neapolitan face assumed a worldly weariness; that he should have to explicate his question only proved the truth and the sadness of a long-held insight into his destiny—he was on the wrong side of the counter and people like Carrol Strickland should be bringing *him* a cup of coffee. "What's new?"

"Tell me, Louie." Strickland reached to his right for the milk container. The customer next to him continues to read a newspaper, undisturbed. "Tell me—these sauces you make, you don't ever use birds in them, do you?"

"Birds?" Louie looks stunned and suspicious. "What you mean, birds?"

"You know, birds. Tweet-tweet. Like robins and finches and grosbeaks."

"Oh, like in the old country." The man smiles but it is not friendly. "Naw, it's too expensive."

"Why do they do that—use those birds?" The customer beside Strickland has put down his paper.

"It's for the flavor." Louie wraps his hands in the clean white apron tied around his waist and bends forward slightly—the gesture for the patron of a grander establishment. "The flesh of the singing birds has a—what-you-know—a spicy flavor. But it is too expensive to use now. Everything costs too much."

"I don't think that's right," the other customer says. As transient as he sometimes feels, Strickland still believes he recognizes most of the faces of Green River, if not the names that go with them, at least a kind of breakdown of generic or ethnic categories, but the man beside him looks strangely new. He looks at him closely.

"You should come up to the woods back of my house and tell that to these guys from New Rochelle who shoot these birds."

"Why don't you call the game warden?"

"I've called the game warden."

"You've called the game warden?" Louie asks. Now Strickland gets cautious; maybe Louie is related to some of the hunters, a family member. A soldier.

"Well, I've talked to him on the phone once or twice. He says he can't do anything about it. It's strictly legal." But the proprietor misses the hard edge in his voice. The phone has been ringing and Louie is alone in the place.

Actually, what has brought Carrol Strickland to Green River this morning will be, he hopes, a lot more effective than talking to the game warden. All the way back from the city on Thursday, the idea of the hunters having the freedom of his property possessed him. The image of them casually stepping over the fence line that was his boundary, pissing against his trees like dogs and defacing his No Trespassing posters maddened him to such a degree that it had been necessary for him to pull off the road at Dover Plains, get out and walk around the car a couple of times. Another motorist had stopped to ask if he needed help. Then he got this idea.

"We don't sell many of these," the clerk in the hardware store had said. "What are you trapping, muskrat?"

"This isn't big enough," Strickland said and turned the heavy metal trap over. The gate pad was about the size of a doughnut. "Got something bigger?"

"How big? For what?"

"Like for bear."

"Bear? You got bears?"

"I don't know what they are. Maybe catamounts. They're big, whatever they are."

"I'll take a look."

The beauty of living in a place like this, Strickland often said, was that you could still find things in stores that hadn't been taken over by conglomerates. Old-time hardware stores where you could get almost anything. The inventories hadn't been reorganized yet to supply a mythic country gentleman dreamed up by some young flake just out of Rensselaer Polytech Communications.

No, there was nothing puny about the set of traps that he had finally lifted into the back seat of the Volvo. Nothing like them could be found anywhere south of the Yukon, except for Hartsman's Lumber and Hardware in Green River, New York.

"You better check with the game warden—Van Deusen," the clerk had said. "You might need some kind of a permit for these babies."

And just then, his ears had been assaulted by the brat-bratting of a motorcycle making the yellow of the town's one traffic light. The black motorcycle leaned into the curve of Route 22 that rose and swept up behind the high school. The operator too was all in black, his helmet as glossy as a hearse, the whole rig making his passenger even more distinctive as she burrowed into his back. She wore a yellow sweatshirt, cut-off jeans and her legs were very white. She wore no helmet and the long, dark hair streamed in the wind. Strickland remembers now—that evening at Cora Endicott's—just after Robin had excused herself to work on her drawings, the night's stillness had been perforated by the staccato of a motorcycle's exhaust. But it had seemed to come from the highway and far away.

"I got this nine-millimeter machine pistol," Louie is saying. His helper has returned and has taken over the phone order. He looks like Louie, Strickland notes, a smaller version and probably a cousin. "Boy, it really bangs. I take it out in the woods and do target practice with birds. The trouble is that with a machine pistol, when I hit a bird it just blows it to pieces. Nothing left for sauce. Not even feathers."

"I shot a bird once," Strickland says and turns to the man next to him. "But it was a mistake. I had this slingshot and I was out in the field. I was just a kid." In Kansas. His memory takes over as he speaks, to run off pictures that illustrate the bare account he gives at the counter. An old corn lot. He may have been hunting for something. He couldn't remember for what. How old was he? Nine or ten, maybe. Mid-morning and the sun already hot and then a sudden whirl behind him. Meadowlarks rising, their song like jewels. He spun about, the sun fierce in his eyes. "I just pulled back and let go. A lucky shot—well, I mean I didn't mean to hit it."

"But you did shoot at it," the man says.

"Well, yes, but not in a million years could I do that again. Not anybody. Shoot a meadowlark on the wing with a slingshot? No way." The bird had staggered and gone sideways, as if blown off course by a sudden, strong wind. He'd found it in the stubble. The lead pellet had smashed the breast. The head was perfect, the eyes open. What had he done with it? "It couldn't happen again."

Louie has listened gravely, his expression like that of a figure in some old fresco, attending a miracle that is only slightly interesting—he'd seen it before. Then he unworks his tongue from whatever has engaged it in the back of his mouth. "There's no mistake with this machine pistol. I can empty a whole clip in seconds—it just blows them away."

"You know a lot of people believe they are coming back as birds," the customer next to Strickland says.

"Whatta you mean by that?" Louie picks up a couple of menus and fits them into a clip behind the stainless steel napkin holder.

"Well, you just ought to think about it," the stranger says and goes back to his paper.

When Strickland leaves the restaurant, he stands for a moment in the parking lot of the small shopping center. The heavy spring air of late morning stings the eyes and nose. Green River is surrounded by large farms and their fields were being prepared for spring planting, same as the Schuylers', and the odor of manure is overwhelming. It was the smell of the local industry, he thinks, like in Pittsburgh where Heinz makes fifty-seven varieties. There it must be catsup. Here it's shit. Is there a difference?

Over at the Goodyear Tire Store, a man in coveralls stands before the display window, studiously reading the broadsheets pasted to the glass and which advertise a tire sale. Winter snow treads were offered. Strickland could distinguish the deep clefts of the cleats in the illustrations even from where he was standing—great slabs of black nylon separated by fissures so wide that each tire resembles the diagram of a geological calamity. With tires like that a man could go anywhere, make progress through any quagmire, traverse any field, no matter how sodden with liquefied manure.

But the man in overalls turns and walks away, and Strickland walks to his car. The three cartons sit innocently on the backseat, unmarked and in no way suggesting the power of the mechanisms they contain. He is eager to get them home so as to study the ingenious design of levers and coiled springs. He was only able to give them a cursory examination in the hardware store because he had not wanted to appear inexperienced. Had instructions come with the traps? He might have to go back.

Say, I seem to have forgot the warranties on these bear traps and while you're at it, these seem to be a different design from what I used up in Saskatchewan with Admiral Byrd. Maybe you could go over them with . . .

Glad you came back. Your name's Strickland, isn't it? Warden Van Deusen was just on the phone and wants you to check in with him.. You need a license for those things, and it's also the wrong season for trapping bear.

No, better to figure it out himself. Instructions might be in one of the other boxes and it would be better to keep this operation undercover. Keep the commotion quotient down at low level, Strick, he tells himself. He starts into the back seat to open a box when he hears the motorcycle again. Black and yellow catch his eye as the bike clatters down the highway, going west toward the Connecticut border.

Quick, Kato, into Black Beauty. The mystery of the moped moll lies before us." STAY TUNED FOR ANOTHER EXCITING EPISODE OF THE . . . GREEN HORNET.

Something releases him; he moves quickly behind the wheel. Works the key, finds the ignition—the whole process of getting the car moving is smooth and unerring, like an assembly set going and he has a picture, a picture with sound, of the Linotype machine in an old-time weekly newspaper. All those gears and awkward steel arms meshing this side of collision—the whole weird gizmo activated by depressing a single lever.

But it is only when he is on the highway, the car picking up speed in high gear, and not until he has located some music on the radio, that he comes to terms with what he is doing. It was as if he had blacked out, back there in the parking lot, as the mind does sometimes in panic or in moments of insupportable terror or shock, so that the self is protected from horror or pain. Now he keeps the couple on the motorcycle comfortably in range, sights them between the swivels of his windshield wipers, and he feels in control of them and of himself. Following the gentle contours, the roll of this countryside, he trails them at a distance of about a quarter of a mile and the black Yamaha and the pair upon it become an extension of the Volvo, part of the machinery he was driving, controlling, even like a target, though it might not occur to Carrol Strickland how the target can become the lure for the marksman; how the hunted may ultimately have power over the hunter.

Was it Robin Endicott on the back of that motorcycle? He could not say. The hair, yes, but others had such coloring and length. Perhaps she had excused herself the other evening to meet with this same man whom she now hugged tightly around the waist and clipped with bare knees as an equestrienne mounts a horse. Perhaps the whole time they were at dinner, the whole time he, Strickland, had been trying to catch the color of her eyes in the candlelight, this other fellow had been waiting for her back of the old carriage house, the engine of his motorcycle cooling. Or perhaps he had waited upstairs in her apartment, confident and in silent arrogance, studying the white furniture, turning over in his hands the small vase with the chipped throat. Waiting.

Strickland has pulled closer but he still cannot see the woman's face. She has pressed close into the leather back of the driver, and her hair swirls about her in the fury of the windstream. The road straightens out and she apparently risks the moment to unclasp her hands, reaches down to scratch the underside of one thigh. More of a caress, he thinks, and just where the skin becomes silk-like and then she shifts slightly in posture, an odalisque slant to one side that surely identifies her—that characteristic oblique pose that conveyed both deference and detachment, submissive yet challenging all at once, as he saw her that first night at her aunt's table.

He lets the car fall back, suddenly aware of the twin mirrors that stick out on either side of the bike's handlebars and, in any event, the idea of keeping her and her motorcycle friend on a line of vision, from a distance, amuses him. The bike turns off the state highway and onto the narrow black asphalt of a county road. Strickland follows. The couple have disappeared. Then they reappear at the top of a hill in a burst of speed. He can almost hear her thrilling cry. The terrain levels out and he sights them once more down the hood of the Volvo.

The fields here lift gentler aromas of more natural decomposition; the scents of moist earth and greenery slip through the car's open windows like sweet scarves. The outcroppings of a large stone ridge pushed through the skin of the soil and these gray blemishes explain why the solutions of modern agriculture had not been applied here. Those early Dutch settlers had worked every inch of these fields in their earnest commercialism; they would have cultivated rocks if possible, at least pried them out of the loam and rolled them into place as foundations for barns and houses, dry walls. Their descendants, like the Schuylers, pass over such fields plows up, and so they go wild with crops of tansy and bouncing bet and chicory while the deeper soil is charged with so much chemical energy that the corn and timothy almost explode from the surface rather than merely grow through it.

Making much of little must, in the end, exact its own expense, Strickland muses as he settles into the leather comfort of his car seat. The couple on the motorcycle seem to be wired to the front of his car, the same accelerator under his foot operating both vehicles. He experiments. He lifts his foot off the gas pedal and they both seem to slow. He speeds up; the distance between them remains the same.

But, he continues to think, the soil itself may eventually give out, become so diminished that more and more chemicals are required until the fields around Silvernales and Green River and elsewhere are turned into nothing but vast pools of fertilizers, inland lakes of rotted waste.

So the green breast has been pumped up into an unrecognizable boob and scary to come across, especially to anyone who has been at sea any time. Old Professor Moon loved to read to them from *The Great Gatsby*—how those Dutch sailors stared at this continent rising before them, their capacity for wonder fulfilled once and for all and maybe that was part of it. With wonder comes respect, devotion, and reverence, but when the wonder of the unicorn lays down its head to become commonplace, dogs grow bold and sacred flesh is torn.

For wasn't this even true in his own case? "You phonius," Nancy used to call him sometimes, emphasis on the *phony*, because of the quirk of his vocal chords that set him apart from others, a simple accident of genes or a gift as some said, that had gained him a certain fame and a very good living. His voice had gained her as well, not so much the mellifluous sounds he made with it but the success those sounds would make for him. She had had the perspicacity to foresee his success. More important, it was a kind of success that insulted all of her father's precepts for "getting ahead"; almost every sound that came out of the Kansas farm boy's mouth had been an affront to the headmaster's special canon for success, and the whole elaborate game plan used by the establishment seemed puny and irrelevant. Nancy Endicott had been excited by this phenomenon. *This is Carrol Strickland reporting*, and the gravity, the substance of that voice made Presidents put down their scorecards; that was a power that had thrilled her. Precisely because he was an outsider who was going to make it, he had delivered her from the orderly bonds of expected—if not always acceptable—behavior that had been slowly winding around her. Even more than that, he was to learn.

"C'mon, Phony, say something to me," she would sometimes ask out of a drunken haze. "Tell me what we're doing. What you're doing to me. Use the words. Announce them."

Like a shaft of sunlight, a sudden heat stabbed his groin so he shifts against the Volvo's smooth upholstery; the skin of an animal, made supple and soft as the flesh he had been remembering under his hands. The intersection is empty. The four roads come together as if they were quietly waiting their turn to be mapped, to be made official, and the surrounding fields are just as undistinguished. Strickland has no idea where he is and the motorcycle is gone, having led him to this place—this maze somehow hidden in the open desolation of Connecticut—the operator and his passenger have disappeared to let him find his own way out. He puts his head outside the window and listens.

"Kato, we seem to have lost the Black Rider who is carrying off our favorite Girl Friday. The Green Hornet has come to a crossroads. One of these is the right road—but which?" Tune in tomorrow when we hear the famous crime fighter say to his trusted manservant, *"Put Black Beauty in high gear and go straight ahead."*

Though Nancy's pleasure and excitement eventually turned to scorn, some of the old class rules coming to the fore as she got older, he was oddly grateful for her ridicule for it made him realize that he was disproportionately rewarded—that he had not really worked very hard, had not perfected a skill or invented a new one, but merely opened his mouth and read words someone else had written. Rather than cow him, the guilt she made him feel almost became a distinction and one that he had never possessed before.

All this would come back to Strickland next week when he met Steve Trent in the recording studio. The movie star was making a movie in New York and had been brought in to re-dub his own voice on a series of commercials for an insurance company, originally filmed on the Coast. The two men quickly located each other in a history they could share between takes. Strickland was recording some promos for a network series, and he reminded Trent of a Thanksgiving camp show in Vietnam.

"Oh sure, I remember that." The actor laughed easily, and that one-sided smile quickly called up all of his films. Even the crooked tooth to the right was there—but smaller than in VistaVision. "We called that the Turkey Act: Twats and Trent." Thin lips curled back in the most genial fashion. The insurance company could start counting their premiums, Strickland would think.

That last November in Saigon, few Americans strolled the streets and nobody bought calendars. Nixon had flown out of the war from the White House lawn and the Communists were coming down Route 14 toward Phuoc Binh. Kissinger had gone to China and Emerson Caldwell had been sent to Moscow but no one had been home at either place. Strickland remembered the atmosphere was like an insane picnic where you come late and the potato salad is covered with flies and they've run out of paper cups and everyone is playing killer softball. He still did laps in the pool at the Cercle Sportif, always expecting to hear a rocket coming in whenever he took a breath, and the girls down at Mimi's Flamboyant asked about Nob Hill and how far was this place called Des Moines from Honolulu.

Into all of this came the Steve Trent show, which might have been embarrassing anyplace else, any other time, but which was so banal, so boring that it seemed just right. Six leggy dancers and the tall movie star who could do nothing more than walk out onstage in that peculiar rolling gait and tell dirty jokes. That's all he could do and it was just right.

By what stroke of fortune, Strickland would think as he had coffee with Trent in the studio, what flash of Hollywood magic had transformed the man's gravelly, Indiana twang—he didn't even talk like a westerner—into a universally accepted voice for all the hoary clichés of the American frontier? The quintessential American hero? Every beer-gutted construction crew chief that hung out along Rue Vo Thanh referred to the thirteen-year-old whores dangling on his knees as "Lit-ul Lay-dies," that familiar, hesitant pronunciation learned from the screens of drive-ins in Tennessee or Georgia. And at the Hotel Duc, where the midnight martinis got drier and drier, the more sophisticated company men would show off their personal arsenals and talk about doing a "Steve Trent" if Washington ever sent the army back.

Even the assistant who brought them coffee at the studio, an intern just out of Sarah Lawrence, smiled at the sound of that voice. She tripped over her own feet as she left them, looking back over her shoulder at Trent as he sprawled in a chair, feet up on the desk so the elegant black boots glistened under the fluorescents like lazy snakes. The Marshal had come to town.

Strickland had caught the act at a maintenance base northwest of Saigon and he had been struck by the rush of hilarity that had seized both the performers and the audience, including the women onstage, who cavorted and laughed at the unfunny jokes, posed and presented themselves in ways their mothers in Kentucky or Texas or Nebraska would not recognize, to form a chorus to Trent's monologue about the disproportionate size of the GI penis and the Indochinese vulva and—"Whatta ya mean, ya got no bottle opener; bend over."

The audience had leaned forward as one, almost hanging by their dog tags that swung like dowsing lines from their necks as their faces shone with a kind of discovery—though of nothing like fresh water, but more of an underground pool of rancidness that they had come upon and that shocked them, even took them by surprise after all the rottenness they had bathed in. More likely they might have come upon the small, clear puddle of their own innocence and that had shocked them. Steve Trent, the man who had single-handedly cleared evil from the streets of El Paso, Tombstone, Dry Creek, and Silver Plume, was standing right there in front of them and saying words like *cunt* and *blowjob* and *asshole*. Could you believe it?

Later that night, as Carrol Strickland was preparing to read the evening script from Saigon—no longer worrying where truth turned bottoms up, because at about that time he had begun to understand that the lies his voice activated were meant for those who knew them to be lies, that there could be something like an addiction to falsehood, and that maybe he had been hooked himself as he delivered the stuff—those faces in that audience who had gagged and laughed at Steve Trent's obscenities looked up at him from the script.

Or rather it was their capacity for innocence—not so much

wonder—that had made him stumble over the evening's euphemisms for Thieu's army going to pieces, so they had to rewind the tape and start over. The GIs that afternoon were part of the minimal service-and-supply contingent allowed by the cease-fire, left behind when Nixon had pulled the troops out. Most of them had been back and forth through the sewer that the war had made of that charming country, so their response to Steve Trent's droll spillage had moved Strickland. That there was yet some part of them still innocent enough, untouched enough by the corrupt seepage around them to be shocked by the performance must be proof of the resiliency of the human spirit—if not an insight into the American character.

What made America great, Strickland thought then as he settled down to announce the evening's falsehood, was not Wheaties nor an implementation of eighteenth century idealism but this capacity for innocence, maybe dumbness might do as well, which could still be surprised by forgeries. That there were such things, even as the deception was craved! He would find himself drawn to Steve Trent this afternoon in New York, understanding that the man's every gesture and mannerism had been perfected to accompany a script, something devised by a Howard Hawks or a William Wyler, designed for a persona called Steve Trent just as a clock maker might perfect a new escapement.

They had gone from the studio to an Irish bar nearby that featured a hot table up front awash in the grease from Tudor-size slabs of corned beef and ham but that offered anonymity for Trent in a back booth. Either the customers did not recognize him or they were too drunk to care, and Strickland would admire the actor's instinct to find a safe place for himself, probably developed over years of escaping his own celebrity. He probably knew places like this in every city. In the fly-specked gloom, Strickland saw something else.

Trent's lower lip was highlighted by the parchment-shaded booth light, a reminder of the bar's better days—a place where Lorelei might have met her boss, Edward G. Robinson, to talk over the bulldog edition of the *Globe*—and Strickland would remember this same petulant lip in the face of boyhood chums, every man he had hoped to make a friend of, and how that petulance could curve into a mischievous, lopsided smile, and how one always endeavored to inspire that smile or act or word. By some gesture of fealty.

He recalled one or two pals at Furness Academy, some at the University, a couple of colleagues in Vietnam, and now here was Steve Trent with the same lip. He had seen it on Oliver North on television and felt himself drawn to the man because of its Peck's Bad Boy configuration even though he knew that such a man as the marine officer, if the occasion arose, would never regard him worthy of friendship, of confidence or anything else, and this was an attraction that had betrayed him over the years. Too many times the roguish nature of that smile had drawn Strickland and misled him, had made him feel he was part of the team, and then he would show up at game time and find the ball already in play and in another field. "Where you been?" the smile would ask with a mocking twist of the lip.

Thus the face across from him in the back room obscurity of Dinty Moore's would make a wry expression as Steve Trent said, "Oh sure, I remember Emerson Caldwell. Hell, I was as good a liberal as they come until I saw the light. So, you're doing a book of his letters."

"Well, to be truthful it's not a total review, but focuses on just a few of the critical years around 1962-3." Strickland would be unable to abbreviate his answer to Trent's perfunctory inquiry as to what he was "doing these days." Not so much a failing as a desire to fill in all the details left out of a script. He knew he became loquacious, answered questions at length that had not really called for answers. Give me twenty-five hundred words or less, Nancy used to say. Even with Trent looking sideways, settling and resetting his vodka and tonic—all familiar signals of impatience—Strickland would find himself unable to edit his narrative but continued to review the old ambassador's relationship with the Kennedys, how he had been manipulated to tell lies for them, while the actor nodded and nodded and looked away.

The actor's attention would be instantly gained, if he told him the real reason for going through the papers; the missing executive order to assassinate Diem. He would deny Trent this morsel of scandal that might subsequently be placed on a table in Hollywood to further polish the star's reputation as someone in touch with things—sometimes even consulted. Strickland would enjoy this idea, this holding back, as he elaborated the familiar, boring history, and he would be curiously exhilarated to recognize that the information he withheld, as his narrative imprisoned the actor, gave him a kind of mastery over the other man.

"All tyrannies are at once boring and repressive because of the information they withhold," he was to say to Robin Endicott.

"I disagree," she would reply with that maddening toss of her head. If only she did not do that, Strickland thought, if only she kept her head still just for a little bit, just long enough to give the idea within his words time to sink in before she shrugged them away.

How is she turning her head now, back and forth within the tyranny of a late morning rush of desire? He has come upon the black motorcycle parked in the raw-hewn, can-studded driveway of a ramshackle split-level set back from the highway and defended, as it were, by several whirling figures of dwarfs and pilgrim fathers stuck into the balding lawn. Another motorcycle leans near the black one and a panel truck noses into the half-open door of the garage where two dogs on chains stretch out in the dirt. So there may be more than just the one man who drove her there, perhaps still in his leather outfit, Strickland thought.

Would he remove the glistening helmet, the helm of an invader from outer space, or an invader of inner space? This thought makes Strickland laugh as he pulls up the Volvo some distance from the house, close enough to see the details of the house—the shade-drawn windows in the rear where the bedroom must be—but not so close as to be noticed if anyone (say, while positions were changed) pulled the shade aside and looked out on the ordinary Connecticut landscape. He didn't really get a good look at the girl on the back of the motorcycle but he's almost sure it was Robin. He wills it so, now that he has found the bike, now that he has tracked them down and revealed their secret.

"I expect," Steve Trent was to say, leaning across the table of the back booth and giving Strickland the baleful look that was part of his visual kit, "that you have a lot of secrets tucked inside that Ivy League dome of yours. Oh, don't look so dumb about it, Strick. I've seen you boys in action. I got to know one of Bill Casey's boys real well when I made *So Long, Saigon*. He was our adviser on the picture and he told me mucho info. Well, not everything." Here the actor mugged and looked around with mock apprehension. "Hell, I'm just a broken-down hambone and I don't want to know everything—I want to have my next drink and a little more pussy, just like everybody else. What I'm saying is, I'm no hero as I suspect you are—Jeezus, but you guys get to me. There you sit in your Brooks Brothers schmatas, cool as rock, and I bet you got ninety-nine ways of being mean." The man winked and Strickland would turn away and say nothing, which probably only corroborated the other's fantasy; one more self-deception, self-generated and self-serving. Even Nancy sometimes did not believe that all he did was read from a script. Funny that Steve Trent, who did about the same thing for a living, believed him to be the kind of character the actor played on the screen. Strickland would not be flattered.

"Course, that's the whole deal about Central America," Trent would continue. "I don't need to tell you. We won all the battles but lost the war in 'Nam but that victory lies hidden somewhere in the jungles of Salvador or Nicaragua. You guys had to leave it behind in Saigon. Jeez, the picture of all of you getting on that Air America chopper on the embassy roof still chokes me up, it's like the statue of the boys putting up that flag on Okinawa—those fucking slants, are we ever gonna be done with them? But somebody told me, don't ask me who," here Trent would wink again, all six foot three of him twisting coyly in the booth like a school girl, "somebody told me that we're going in down there against the commies to get the victory the fifty-some-odd thousand dead Americanos were denied in 'Nam. It's down there somewhere and we're going to get it. And bring it back."

Strickland would look around the bar half expecting a standing ovation from the winos and idlers in the place because if it were a film, the speech would have elicited some such response. Instead he saw the young woman who had brought them coffee in the studio. How long she had been standing there he would not know, but she had appeared like a figure out of an old melodrama, the earnest working girl come to fetch her father from the saloon.

"Well, there's Miss Pilgrim now," Trent would say in his gravelly voice and get up, throwing money on the table. "Enjoyed meeting up with you again, Strick. Ever out on the Coast, look me up. I guess it's got to be your place, little lady." As they walked out, one large arm would fall like a beam across the girl's shoulders and Strickland would have a moment's vision of peasant women in Vietnam walking placidly beneath the heavy yokes of their destiny. "Got any roommates?" he heard the actor say.

So it would be another instance of showing up at the wrong field, though in this case, Strickland would ruefully think; Trent had not only moved to another playing field but had picked up the ball as well. After several minutes in the booth by himself, Strickland would leave and take a taxi to the apartment building he had visited several weeks earlier. The girl from before was visiting her mother in New Jersey. Her mother was sick, the woman at the front desk told him. That's too bad, Strickland would say, but very commendable. Yes, but we have Marylee with us now, the woman continued. And then there's Candy, and he might remember Susie.

He would stand in the large empty room of the stripped apartment, blinded by the light from the wall of windows that looked out over the East River. The three women on the padded bench were the silhouettes of sibyls who waited for him to make a request. He would feel as stripped and as bare as the room he stood in, part of him drawn out through the expanse of glass and across the rooftops, across the river and out beyond Long Island and on up the Harlem Valley toward Silvernales. He felt so far away from it, yet everything was in sight—he could almost make out the details of his village—one trailer in particular with an antique weather vane in the shape of a clipper ship set beside the TV antenna. He felt tethered, unable to come back to earth because of the currents that pushed him aloft, yet held just so high above it and no higher.

"Who pleases you?" the woman asked and then the phone on her desk would ring. She spoke intimately, described the new girl, Marylee. Strickland would leave before she hung up.

* * *

He feels just as foolish sitting in the Volvo parked a half mile
down the road from the purplish shingled split-level with the
motorcycles parked in the driveway. He feels tied to this squat, ugly
dwelling and unable to break loose from the spectacles he imagines
inside.

Robin turning her head from side to side, "I disagree. Tyrannies
are repressive but they may not be boring. The fact of their repression
makes for a kind of excitement," she said and poured him more tea.
The single rose in the white vase on the white table seemed to glow
but it was a trick of the late afternoon sun slanting through the fan
lights above the loft's high casements. He followed the light across
the floor to the edge of the room where draperies of a dun-colored
material masked half the wall.

"Is that your bedroom?" he asked.

"No. You're sitting on the bedroom," she said and laughed, and
then rose gracefully from her knees and went to the drapery and
pulled it back, as if she were uncovering a work of art. Strickland
blinked and, he remembers as he sits in the car, that he felt his head
rock back ever so slightly from the impact of the colors and textures
of the clothing in the closet. Dozens of neatly stacked shoe boxes
looked like the multicolored doors of safety deposit boxes in a trendy
bank and, indeed, the long metal pipe supported a small fortune, it
seemed to him, in dresses and suits and coats. The display drew him
to it for closer inspection, an inspection that Robin seemed to invite
as she stood to one side, one hand still on the drapery and her eyes cast
down almost shyly, anxious and yet a little eager, all at once, for his
response to something she had done—but whether for his approval or
not, he could not say.

He had made a quick tabulation of the wardrobe, each garment
adding to the overall sum of his intuition that she could not have
bought these for herself but had come by them in some other way.
They were stolen. Somehow the understanding caught his guesswork
unawares and closed upon him with a sure knowledge that was nearly

• 115 •

painful in the sweetness of its revelation. Sweet because she had revealed to him her own tyranny, her own addiction, and this exposure joined them somehow in a kind of conspiracy. He could tell her everything about himself and it wouldn't matter, he thought; she wouldn't be turned away or taken back. Like one cripple talking to another.

So not knowing but knowing that Robin Endicott was the girl on the motorcycle, Strickland eases the Volvo into gear and quietly pulls away and down the road. He is released by the thought of the secret he shares with her, by the sense that she had placed this part of herself in his safekeeping as surely as she might be placing herself in some kind of helpless jeopardy within the purple house.

He makes Silvernales by noon and is hungry, but his appetite for revenge is the stronger and he passes on up behind his house and into the first field, pulling up at the stump whose smooth, bark-stripped sides gleam in the direct sunlight like aluminum, like the steel of the traps he carries out of the car. Whether he is being watched from the woods along the top of the fields is unimportant. Let them see the traps; they won't know where he will set them. They will lie hidden, the powerful jaws set, ready to snap shut. Always. It is a challenge and a fair warning, all at once. Strickland likes that idea.

You'll remember, boys and girls, in yesterday's episode. Uncle Fred had taken Betty into the woods to look for rare birds while Jack Armstrong and Billy prepared the ancient snares Jack had learned from the Oombahgee Indians. As we listen in today, we hear Jack say, "These little numbers will do the job. We'll find out just how ghostly these Inca ghosts are, Billy."

Chapter

6

Driving back from Albany, Carrol Strickland has taken the Old Post
Road that follows the east bank of the Hudson River through orchards
and the small mill towns once powered by tributaries the Dutch
called *kills* and which still flow into the river though the mills stand
empty like the gaunt mausoleums of a vain and idle race. Like the
post markers he sees, which still poke up by the side of the road as
gravestones might, or like stone dormers that neither admit air nor
light to the earthen attic below, nor to the relics kept there, yet still
continue to give the distance the traveler may be at that point from
Albany; the same distance on this afternoon for Strickland as it would
have been over two hundred years ago when the mileage was first
chiseled on the stone faces. He thinks of clocks that have stopped,
waiting for their time to come round again.

The clock in the studio at the Albany radio station had been the
same make, the same red sweep hand and large numerals, that have
timed his speaking voice almost all the years of his life, and he
wonders, as he turns around the pocket green in the village of Valatie,
at that sameness which was not unlike the statue of the Union soldier
in this small town's center—this same statue standing at the ready in

town squares all over half the continent, like the sentinels of an army that had long ago made peace but had forgot to call in its sentries. MIAs of another war.

The Volvo takes the highway joints smoothly, passes the road signs and post markers, verifying if not renewing the weather-worn numerals on their tablets by its very passage in the same way that Leslie's presence in the control booth of the Albany studio had refreshed him, given his off-hand performance within the clock's sweep of sixty seconds an excitement that was a joy rediscovered.

"Wow . . . right on the mark." The engineer's voice had been young, awkward with the term. Strickland had been able to see his daughter standing in the background. Leslie seemed to glow in the illumination of the panel lights and he also attributed this to her pride in him, which made him happy that he had agreed to do the spots for the Heart Fund—an extra dividend for this favor rendered. Even more, a replay of their old intimacy when she brought him a drink between cuts. "We'll wind up in a sec. Take a break, Strick," the twenty-year-old voice told him, and he was amused by the easy informality of the kid using his nickname; then Leslie came through the studio door with a paper cup in her hand and a large smile on her face.

"Room service." She handed him the soda water.

"How am I doing?" He switched off the boom mike to give them a certain privacy from those who watched through the glass. He liked the picture they made as viewed from the control booth; father and daughter, daughter and father, talking intimately. Pals. Her hair hung loose—no ribbon. Strickland crossed his legs and looked aside. He recalled his suspicions of a little while ago, in the woods, and felt the heat in his face. Leslie misreads his discomfort.

"He asks how he's doing," she snorts and pulled herself up on the table. "You've got the control room in preorgasmic sweats."

"Well, I'm doing the best I can."

"Now don't get all piffy." Her face had grown sullen. His fault but sometimes her language, the knowledge it implied, took him back. He thought quickly to restore the scene.

"Tonto ride hard, like-a-sappy." And it worked—Leslie became all smiles once again, he leaned forward to fellow her amusement—as it had worked earlier when he had arrived at the studio. All the station staff, the people from the Heart Fund down from Syracuse just for the occasion, Leslie's fellow volunteers—all who were observing the two of them at that very moment had been waiting for him to give a class act. He hadn't disappointed. He had warmed them up with some insider's gossip; like what Johnny Carson had said to him that time he subbed for Ed McMahon. This was before the "Tonight Show" had moved to the Coast. All the while, he could feel his daughter's warmth, her swelling pride in him. Then he had read through the boilerplate given him, sat down at the table in the studio, switched on the mike and read the stuff. He had done it in one take. Perfectly. "This is fun, isn't it?" he said.

"Come on," Leslie replied, wariness slanting her mother's eyes.

"I mean all the gadgets, the routines. Putting together sounds."

"I feel a job coming on," his daughter said. She eased off the table.

"Well why not? It's obvious you have a lot of respect from those people in there."

"Only because I can get Golden Throat for free."

"I don't believe that." So there they had been again, though he had kept smiling, face toward the control booth. As far as anyone in there knew, it was an easy back and forth. "This looks like a good opportunity for you. I do know about these things."

"But you don't know about this thing," Leslie came back, smacking her full bosom. "Just back off, will ya?"

"Okay, okay." He had looked down at the script on the table before him. *Have a heart, Louie—put down that cigarette.* "Where do they get this stuff?"

"Some agency in New York volunteers. I guess they take it off their taxes. Like you will."

"I could. I just recorded an entire Henry James novel, *Wings of the Dove* for 'Reading for the Blind.' Do you know the book?" Leslie shook her head and returned to the control room. He had lost her again.

But he had done this, he believed, as a kind of benefit—this one

encountered the Italians recently, the same area near the huge sycamore where he had just set bear traps. But Leslie lost interest as she got older, and Strickland sometimes felt that if she had been a boy, a son, then the two of them would have been able to put together a neat little cabin or maybe a tree house, because boys liked to do things like that, and no one would know about it but them and it would be just theirs; a place they could go.

But it would be much better constructed than the ramshackle cottages he sees on the sprit of land in the middle of the Hudson River. As he sits in the warm spring sun, he quickly designs and puts together a porch on the front of his cabin. It would face northeast so that of a long summer evening a person could follow the shadow climbing the green wall of the Berkshires. It would have to be screened, of course, but nothing fancy. He could get muslin gauze. Something like that.

A large, ocean-going tanker, empty and therefore high in the water, silently passes down river on the other side of the island like a fortress—the whole side of a building that has unaccountably come loose from its foundations in Albany and is now being swept out to sea. Strickland follows the ship, seeing no sign of life on it but imagining the activities on board; the engine room with all its gauges and levers and the immaculate, small bridge perched high at midship with a clear view of everything, and the ting ting of a ship's clock marking off the half hours. Aft, near the fantail, would be the crew's mess and even right now as he watches, some of them would be in there enjoying the best sort of coffee and perhaps a fresh doughnut as they relaxed and smoked and exchanged stories. He feels a witness to this passage as the ship makes the lower tip of the island and then, as if under remote control and with no hand on the wheel, the tanker bears to port and into the main channel down the middle of the waterway. So, from a greater distance, he thinks, another witness could look down on this bluff above the river and the small park and see neither the park nor the man sitting on one of the benches, arms stretched wide along the back of the seat and tie pulled loose. And if such a witness did not exist, even an uncaring witness, such a witness would have to be created, Strickland thinks.

Just then a figure comes out of the door where he had been thinking of the sailors having coffee, and walks to the rail around the tanker's stern. The ship has moved swiftly downstream to become miniaturized quickly, like that picture of the Dutch girl on his mother's cleaning powder being reduced to a dot, so it is impossible to see what the man is doing. Then the sunlight catches the arcing golden thread like a ridiculously slender mooring line thrown out to halt the huge vessel's progress.

"Taking a piss," Robin Endicott was to say later, reaching high for a canister in the kitchen pantry.

"Well, yes," Strickland said, looking away and wondering at her matter-of-fact usage of the word, somehow enjoying that usage as he had been made uneasy by Leslie that morning at the radio station saying something about orgasms, knowing the reason for the difference. It was part of why he looked away. When he had shown up unannounced at Cora Endicott's, Robin had been mopping down the tile of her aunt's bathroom, the long folds of a cotton skirt pulled up and knotted high on her slender thighs, her legs attenuated even more by wedge-heeled clogs, and when she led him into the kitchen he noticed the almost graceless, loose-kneed lope of her walk. It was a frank stride. On the butcher-block table the ingredients for a pie had been set out and she began to mix them industriously and with her skirt still hiked up, so he was reminded of peasant women. Or women in Vietnam working and bending low in the rice paddies, their legs bare and their black gowns tied around their loins—and he looked away as she went on tiptoe to pull down a canister of flour.

Cora sat outside in the rose garden. Through the kitchen windows, her round, puckered face was a child's parody of pleasure as she opened her day's mail and reviewed the different pleas for money. She resembled one of the roses around her, nodding and rocking; crisply fresh and sweet smelling, which was quite different from how she had been only shortly before—before the girl had cleaned her up and wheeled her out into the patio.

Robin's legs seem more tanned than those he remembered that had gripped the whirring mechanism of the motorcycle, if that had been her on the motorcycle. He had been trying to figure out a way to confirm his suspicions without giving away the fact of his surveillance. The very domesticity of her present activity confronted the other image. She had even fastened a long apron around herself—it hung from her neck to her knees—before she laid out mixing bowl, sticks of butter, flour, and the rest of what she needed for the pie. Bon Appetit was embroidered across the top between where her breasts might be. With her hair swept high on her head and her arms bare, a purposeful thrust to her jaw, she looked not unlike some commercial for the good life.

Well, it's goodie time with Goody's Shortening! Goodie-good because it's Goody's.

It was her ease with her own body that made the difference, he felt; a sense of freedom in the way she moved her arms and limbs that communicated the idea that he might be as free with them as well, given the opportunity. All at once, even as he sat in this sunlit kitchen in Connecticut, permeated with aromas of nutmeg and scrubbed tile, the smell of roses in the air like a bridal veil, the dark sweat of that other place where anything went, oozed into his consciousness like a flow of scum with its own sweet addiction.

"Is that a family name?" She looked at him over the edge of a measuring cup. "Carrol?"

"No. Actually my mother was devoted to *Alice in Wonderland* and she named me from Lewis Carroll."

"But that's not the way he spelled it."

"My mother wasn't all that fussy about those things."

"More of a generalist." Robin laughed and began to cut the butter into the flour.

"Well, I guess so," Strickland replied. He wasn't so sure his mother deserved the title nor even if Robin knew its meaning. "She identified with girls who became transformed. Dorothy in *The Wizard of Oz*—that kind of thing."

"Well, after all,"—the dough was pummeled and shaped and then re-shaped—"all that took place in Kansas too, didn't it. I mean, it must have been pretty hermetical out there."

Strickland attempted to cram the "out there" of those gaping prairies into the word. Meanwhile, Robin swept with a professional economy around the kitchen, wrapping the dough ball in waxed paper and putting it to chill in the refrigerator. She clip-clopped to the screen door. "How you doing, Aunt Cora?"

"Just fine, thank you, Robin."

She had raised up on her toes, as if to speak through the screen required extra effort, and the pose lengthened her legs and thrust out her hips. She caught him looking and untied her dress, let it fall around her with an ambiguous expression that said he had seen enough or that her legs had had enough air—or both.

"How often does she have these attacks?"

"Well, she will have her toddies and she likes her mousse au chocolat and she won't listen to what I say. The Endicotts have strong wills, though you know that well enough." She laughed and looked him full in the face, not her usual demure sidelong glance, and the force of her eyes was like the blue glass pupils of ancient statues, the energy of life unexpectedly come across. She shrugged and began preparing the pie filling. It was to be a mixture of apricots, walnuts, and honey.

"Is this your recipe?" Strickland resumed his perch on a kitchen stool, observing her preparations. Robin had just set the dried apricots to simmer in dark rum.

"No . . . well, yes, I guess I've made enough variations on it to call it mine."

"From the restaurant—the Black Oak? Is that where you learned?"

She had begun to pick through walnuts on the large table in the center of the room but seemed to be considering his question as well, turning over its many possible responses as she selected the best nut meats. Several coils of her hair had shaken loose and they softly bandied her face like shadows. "Yes . . . from Max," she finally said. "He was very patient with me and taught me a lot." She scooped the nut meats into a bowl. Then she looked up, once again catching him with that level, direct gaze. "No matter what Cora may have told you, he saved my life. I remember you, of course." Strickland could only look. "That night you and your daughter came for dinner. You had the duckling with the green peppercorn sauce and you stiffed me on the tip."

"The service was terrible." Strickland tried to laugh. But her face had remained very grave.

"Who worries about matching up the tip with the service?" She gestured with an egg in each hand, and her small figure seemed to unravel like a string doll. "What are you, some kind of a high inquisitor who goes around judging service?"

"People should automatically leave fifteen percent regardless of the service, is that it?"

"Try twenty percent and yes. Why not?" She smiled ruefully as she put eggs, walnuts, and a cup of honey into the bowl of a food processor. "Jeez, talk about pity the poor working girl. What if your daughter—I guess that was your daughter with you that night—what if she was waiting on table, how would you like it . . . don't tell me. I can see it in your face—she would get what she deserved. I can see it." She shook her head in wonder and exasperation.

Strickland was amused by her criticism—its spirit—largely because it was made with such good humor, almost as if she were listing the quaint characteristics in a favorite friend, nothing so very serious that needed correction and that might even be endearing. He wanted to think so, anyway. Also, her tone implied an intimacy that pleased him and a forthrightness that impressed him; to freely admit the circumstances of their first encounter—she waiting on table— suggested a frankness that almost amounted to honesty and that, in any event, surprised him.

All those clothes in the closet of the loft in the carriage house arrayed themselves in his mind as he watched her add sugar, butter, and vanilla to the mixture in the bowl. Her matter-of-fact disclosure was part of the same frankness that had brought him here, had brought him to sit on this kitchen stool at this very moment. He could assume anything he wished. He could suspect anything; it didn't matter. However he thought she had acquired the wardrobe was irrelevant to her. However she *had* acquired the wardrobe was irrelevant; what was important was the act of exposure, her admission that she had acquired and possessed all those dresses and shoes and parcels of lingerie. A strange honesty, he thought, like a confession of guilt or a misdeed that did not seek absolution or forgiveness but rather recognition, and the voluntary disclosure somehow made it okay.

Robin had gone out on the terrace to answer her aunt's call as Strickland sifted through different patterns of wrong and right. Earlier that afternoon, he had come across similar cutouts in his own experience and these had aligned themselves like the see-through pages of a home medical volume that shows the skeleton first, then the vascular arrangement, then the muscle structure, and so on; page after page laying up the composition of the human body, save that his diagram became more of a map that guided him from Warren Street in Hudson, east along county back roads into Connecticut and to this kitchen where Robin Endicott was making a pie and probably wondering when he would make a move on her.

When she had pulled back that drapery to reveal her wardrobe, he felt she had also revealed herself to him; both an act of trust and a perverse invitation. Or was it an invitation to behave perversely? The sailor on the tanker had just polluted the moment—even the distant Catskills had looked reduced, eroded—and Strickland had felt doused and dissipated as well. Some years before, after one of those Rotary luncheons in Hudson, a city booster had taken him on a tour of the city, its historical and architectural sites, including the old red-light district for which the river town had been famous. Even up to recent times the houses had been in business and Strickland had wished for them right then, as he stood up from the park bench and stretched in the sunlight, not for the mere sexual satisfaction but for the haven of lawlessness such places afforded. The kind of lawlessness he had known in Vietnam that had stripped off the different social contracts worn like wool shirts in summer to put on an awful freedom—the freedom of a whorehouse. To pig out, as Leslie might say.

"Anyway, we had a waitress sick that night." Robin had returned. "My job was more the management of the place, not waiting on table. But then you would not have known that." As she spoke she advanced upon him directly and squatted low to the floor to pull and adjust one of his pants legs over the top of his boot. She looked up. "This has been bothering me since you arrived. There. I expect your name gave you trouble?"

She gave him no chance to comment, to pull back from her or even to ask why she did him this particular service. It had all been smoothly done like part of a dramatic scene in a larger play; her entrance from the patio, her dialogue, the business with his pants and then back to the pie making when she asked about his name. "I expect people thought it was a girl's name. I've always hated my name."

"Not until I came East," Strickland said. He watched as she took the chilled pie dough from the fridge and began to roll it out. "If the truth be known, no one in Kansas thought it was strange."

"No nicknames?"

"Again, not until I came East. I guess for the same reason—my schoolmates here could say Strick easier than Carrol."

"I think Carrol is lovely." Her voice thickened and her eyes grew dark. "It's like a song. Something to rejoice and be joyful with. Like your voice, though your eyes always look unhappy. No, uncertain."

"You say you don't like Robin."

She shrugged, pressing down on the rolling pin. Her slim arms are surprisingly muscular. "I used to think I was supposed to hop about with a bright eye turned to the ground. Chirp chirp."

"What do you like to be called? What should I call you?"

"Often." She laughed and turned her mouth down to disparage the joke. "I hate Robbie also. Ditto for Rob. I had a roommate at Vassar who called me that. I'm afraid it's just too egregious. I can't even relate to a masterpiece as you can. My parents must have looked out the window that spring morning when I flew in. So much for the originality in that branch of the family."

"How's the pie making coming?" Cora Endicott called from outside. Strickland was annoyed by the interruption. The glass of water he had left Cora to get in the kitchen still sat on the counter top next to him; a palatable excuse, as it were, to talk with the young woman.

"I better go," he said softly.

"Come back," Robin replied in the same tone.

Cora waved a full-color brochure at him. "Aren't these sweet darlings?" Pictures of Ethiopian children raised a silent chorus in the Connecticut patio. They smiled at the camera as if it had been a stick of candy. "These are some of the kiddies that Rev. Bubba Nelson's Mission is educating. I'm just going to write them a nice, fat check. They are so darling."

"Some sort of school for waiters, is it?" Strickland was still annoyed that he had to rejoin her. He could see Robin's petite silhouette through the screen door, leaning over the counter top. Busy.

"Carrol, you're being very crude." Cora's jaws clamped down hard on the ebony cigarette holder between her teeth, which compacted her terrier face even tighter.

"Well, it seems to me that down in Kentucky or South Carolina or wherever Rev. Bubba's ministry is located there must be all kinds of wonderful little black boys and girls that could use a little know-how."

"I'm just going to pretend you didn't say that. I'm just going to wipe that right off the slate," the invalid said and bent over the large checkbook open on a tray across her lap. "This is just too pretty a day—smell those roses—to hear such ugly things. I know you experienced perfectly dreadful events in the war but . . ."

"Cora, you know nothing of the kind nor can you write out a check for the information. That's one of the ironies of money. No amount of it can get you information if fluency in the language doesn't accompany the transaction. You have the money, but not the fluency." The woman's eyes popped out even more, but she continued her business; sealed the check in the envelope and placed it with the others ready to be mailed.

Strickland felt cheapened by his own outburst, the sound of his rhetoric continued to high-step it through his head. As he sat in this rose garden by this small pool, he recalled how he had walked around in a kind of portable isolation booth because of the language, a straitjacket of Vietnamese macramé woven around him. Or on some days, he would remember it was like living within a large balloon that made everything unintelligible, a chattering space growing larger and higher but never going to burst so that he might be kept within its luminous enigma forever, never to understand—never know the language while trapped inside the din of it.

Not too different from Cora Endicott's dilemma, he told himself. Her fat checkbook forever trying to pay off her infirmities and so he turns back, if not with a new understanding at least with a concord, ready to apologize for his tone of voice. The woman's pug of a face had become rounder, like a balloon itself, and the eyes extended more from their sockets. Her plump torso almost vibrated and then something popped. Her lips had even shaped the tiny explosion that had occurred elsewhere. "Robin, darling," she cried. "I've made potty."

Long after the girl had wheeled her aunt inside the house, the birds in the garden remained silent as if stunned by a blast, as if all the matter in the bricks of the neat paths and the molecules of the clear pool water had gone haywire to combine in some kind of critical mass that obliterated all sound. Strickland did not want to think of what was happening in the pink tile bathroom, of what Robin was doing there; yet his imagination flashed pictures of her long, capable fingers unfastening Cora's garments, of her young hands washing the befouled, slack flesh, and he stood up quickly and took several turns around the elliptical pool. Cardinals found their songs and he felt better.

He considered leaving. He had no stomach for seeing Cora again soon and, in the first place, he had not driven all the distance from Hudson to see Cora but to see her grandniece and now he was embarrassed for the young woman; she might not want to face him right after this mess. The time in the kitchen had been so easy, so intimate that he was angered by Cora's intrusion, by her incontinent claims on Robin's time and—he had to smile at his real frustration— on his own time with the girl.

All this he would come to understand much later; but then, standing in Cora Endicott's rose garden, he had a sudden and terrible longing for Nancy and he turned toward the sundial, which was surrounded by a lush carpet of myrtle; Nancy had stood there years back. It was a summer party, and Strickland could have turned to her and been able to tell her all this, sort out his feelings. Because she had told him everything. That evening the heavy June air had almost splintered, the candles on the small tables around the pool held still, their flames frozen. "These worthless people—can't I ever escape them?"

"What? What is it?" He had rushed to her defense, ignorant of what was being attacked.

"Just kiss me."

"What, here?"

Nancy grabbed him by the arms and took his mouth hungrily. Laughter surrounded them like expensive cutlery being set down on the tables and some one said, one of those sneering, lock-jawed Eastern voices," Ah, those instant-cooking Endicott women."

"Forget it," Nancy had spoken against his lips and she gripped his biceps through the seersucker jacket for his muscles had tensed, pumped up in some kind of instinctual response to do battle. "Let them cook in their own bitterness."

In yesterday's episode, Carrol Strickland, prime-time announcer and suspected secret agent, confronted his wife—the raven-haired and egregious Nancy Endicott Strickland—during a garden party at her cousin Cora's with the news that he might be attracted to another woman, one much younger than he and who he suspected of being something of a . . .

Or another time as the two of them cooled off in the breeze through the bedroom windows, their sweat-varnished flesh prickling in the hot August air, Nancy gave a flattering evaluation. "I mean I didn't put this together until lately. But you got a lot better with me after . . . after I told you about Daddy and me." She had leaned over him and began to kiss his chest. Her lips shaped themselves, almost experimentally, around his left nipple. "I mean you were bolder and that's better. I think there's a connection."

When she had first kissed him this way, suckled him almost, he drew away and then relaxed, taken not so much by the physical sensation as by the feeling of freedom her mouth gave him, a falling away of layers of stuff that was no longer necessary to put on—at least between them. The same kind of openness was unwoven, as it were, the night she told him about her father's use of her. All this was several years after their marriage—yes, Leslie had been born, he remembers the next morning taking the small bundle of her for sled rides up and down the hill beside the house. It was their first winter in Silvernales, they still had the apartment on East Seventy-forth and they had decided to have Christmas in the country—like an old Cary Grant–Irene Dunne movie—and it had been like that, innocent and gay and full of a nostalgia for a warmth and a time neither of them had known and therefore not quite right. In the same way little Leslie's hearty laughter tumbled into the snow—from the first everything about the girl, including her laughter, was oversize—but not even the child's huge glee could fit over the awful details Nancy had told him the night before, could seal them off.

Because all the adolescent fantasies that floated over the study halls to waft hotly under the thin dormitory blankets of Furness Academy had been acted out, and then some, by Everett Hale Endicott and his little girl, and right under their pimply noses. It was almost like a pornographic novel—"The Headmaster and His Daughter." Headmaster—get it? All those tennis games whose rhythmic *twang* and *pop* had sent shivers through the student body turned out to be rather elaborate forms of foreplay, a steady give and take of points and advantages, serves and breaking serves, to when the real game would be played out in the shower afterward; more times than not a final match on the furniture stored in the attic of Doral House, the headmaster's prerevolutionary, pink brick mansion. Even in her bed. My God, Strickland would think of that balanced, perfect facade, how its classic lines had entranced him those first years at Furness, all the homely entry ways of Kansas left behind—the very symmetric proportion of the window casements seemed to embody the ideals of Jefferson, the will of Washington. Yet all that time behind those windows . . . Nancy had sat up suddenly, turned away from him. "Daddy was some kind of a fuck."

For some reason her revelation, made that evening when she was cold sober and, as a matter of fact, as they were dressing to go out, had not really surprised him. She had confirmed his suspicions as she chose her earrings. "What about these? How do these look?" Incest was given about the same importance. He preferred the diamond studs. It was only later that he sensed a change and, as Nancy was to say, he did become more bold with her as if the revelation of her abused past, this criminality she had been forced to share—forced to become a criminal—gave him a license with her that he had never dared before.

Meanwhile, the shadow on the sundial in Cora's garden had lost all definition; the ancient, untrimmed privet and stockade fence around the perimeter blocked the light of the west-going sun. But Strickland could clearly perceive that time past when Nancy picked over her jewelry case, how the fine column of her neck curved, exposed under the dark gloss of ebony hair. She wore her hair short and curled under then. Slim, muscular arms bare and the wide shoulders made so very feminine by the delicate silk strings of an ivory silk camisole. "I'm a leg man," he remembers saying one time, chagrined so by the memory of that stupid boast that he is turned around in this Connecticut garden, suddenly stung by his own self-ridicule. But when he had said that, he had been trying to placate one of Nancy's off-hand laments for her small breasts.

All that, all that he would remember, looking down into the lily pond, all that burned to a black crisp in San Diego. Those legs burned to a crisp, that had folded so gracefully under the small seat before the vanity table, prim-kneed and turned to one side like a parallel drawing of the same perfect line, even the wide, darker band at the top of the stockings duplicating the faultless turn of thigh—this detail stuck in his head with an unshakale perversity—while Nancy had picked over her jewelry and idly told him what he had suspected all along. As she held up some earrings for his opinion, she had also offered him this secret about herself like the one last virginity.

But there would be side effects. Sometimes, as he toiled happily with her toward a joyous release, usually his first night home, the image of Everett Hale Endicott would pass across his consciousness; not scenes from the attic treasury of Endicott family togetherness, which might have been strangely exciting, but the image of the headmaster leaning down to tell him to look up Professor Moon at the university, that Moon would take care of him, and Moon did. "What's the matter?" Nancy would say abruptly. "Here. Can I do something?" But there was nothing to be done and he would try to laugh and shrug away, and she would beat the mattress. "This goddamn war. This goddamn, fucking war." She would be right, partly.

But all of this would happen and come to him after he stands up to stretch in the sun on the banks of the Hudson River, watching the seaman's urine arc over the stern of the *QUEEN CITY COMMAND* and feeling thick with a need to be somewhere and with someone he could just be himself with. The closet full of clothes, the way Robin had swept back the drapery like one of those game show hostesses on TV revealing the grand prize; he knew where he was headed and why.

"I hear voices," Strickland is saying to Robin Endicott. The grounds outside her loft above the old stables drowse in the late afternoon. "My head is like a control room from the old Blue Network—but you don't know about that—and the console has gone crazy."

She sits patiently waiting for him to go on, her face alert and then the expression clouding over as he says nothing more. Between them is a large portfolio. Strickland turns over a drawing and then another. Her work is in pencil and ink and she apparently uses some kind of a brush-like pen, probably Japanese, so that what might have been a simple line, not placed too well in the space, becomes a ragged if no more interesting line, not placed so well. "These are just doodles—ideas only."

"But you work at it. I admire that. I admire that discipline."

"Well . . ." her arms go straight out in that string-doll effect again, "that's what I do. That's all I want to do." Her voice reaches down in a way that stirs him as the professional part of him gives high marks to the technique.

"What I'm saying is that I seem to be out of synch these days while you are all together. Watching you make that pie just now, minding Cora, applying yourself to this." He held up a sketch of a table and chair. "That's what I admire."

"But it's easier for me," Robin says and clasps her hands between her knees. "Look at all you've been through. Has anything been left out? I ask you. No wonder you say you hear voices—you've been trying to say it all, all at once." Something so wistful in her manner almost makes Strickland want to forget the rack of clothes behind the drapery. He glances that way now, half expecting to see movement behind the monks cloth, the guilty secret hiding there ready to give itself away. "It's you I admire."

He feels as if she has given him a cue, he feels that her line delivered so intently and with such seriousness must be part of a script and that it is his turn to say something. Or perhaps the script calls for action, perhaps he is meant to reach for her at this point, take her by the arms as she perches on the sofa next to him, her lips pursed and eyes half closed like the swooning heroine in a Gothic romance. "Where did you get all those clothes?"

"Clothes?" Robin blinks.

"All those clothes in the closet."

"You mean how did I get them?" She seems suddenly weary. "Well, I'm in Hock City, if you want the truth. I just got carried away with the plastics. But I'm paying it off doing chores here." Her nose wrinkles as if a whiff of something disagreeable has just come up through the floorboards. "But I'm not complaining. Now you want to know why?"

"Why?"

"Sure. Why does she need all those clothes?" Her voice had become mechanical, ugly. "Well, one simply cannot walk into galleries and museums for job interviews like a fey creature from Dusty Corners."

"Wait a minute, hold on." Strickland does touch her now and finds he is touching stone almost and though she smiles, the line of her teeth is a sharp warning, like an animal showing its fangs. This sudden transformation amazes him and then her attitude shifts again and she looks penitent, face turned aside, hands together and in her lap.

"Oh, it doesn't matter," she says. "It's just that I'm weary of always explaining myself, of always having to justify myself. I don't ask for much. A place and time to do my work. A place, however humble it may be, which will be mine and genuine. I don't say I deserve anything special, I know I must earn my way, and I am not loathe to tasks that some would find disagreeable . . ." Her half laugh is bitter. "Some?" She rises and walks across the room to stand in the one large window.

Something a little fiendish in Carrol Strickland urges him to stand, to give a standing ovation to this performance and even her silhouetted figure seems to be waiting for the acclaim, but another part of his nature, stronger and not so simply explained, keeps him quiet and his silence makes him a player in the scene. If he were to think of it, he might consider the moment as an audition of sorts and that his reticence was only part of the role he has just successfully read for. But Robin gives him no time for such reflection.

"Please go," she says in a quiet voice, still with her back to him. "No," she answers the startled, half-commiserating sound in his throat. "Please go. I'm all right. Call me later."

"When?" he found himself saying as he stood to exit.

"Oh, tomorrow, the next day. I'll be here . . . minding Cora."

Strickland is still bemused by the young woman's performance as he drives back to Silvernales. She probably wasn't even aware of its stagecraft—her charade was so profoundly a part of her that she could no longer see the daylight on the other side of the footlights, and he could identify with that, as the saying goes, for how many times had he believed, or wanted to believe the lines he read from a prepared broadcast. Actors know that the lines they speak, the scenes they move through are false; sometimes they become addicted to these falsehoods. Wasn't he so addicted, and, like the most miserable junkie, didn't he supply others with the falsehoods they craved to support his own habit? All the lies he had broadcast from Saigon were for a nation of junkies who only wanted a quick fix.

But like an audience with a train to catch and that rises quickly as the curtain falls on the last line, he is now anxious to get back to Silvernales. He wants to check his traps. What if those steel jaws have chomped down on something? What will he do then? Maybe he ought to remove them, discontinue his guerrilla warfare before it gets out of hand, before someone really gets hurt. The narrow, winding Route 7 back to New York from Connecticut is always difficult to make time on and the hearse in front of him only makes the journey more of a nettle. He shifts down, letting the Swedish gearbox of the Volvo roar his impatience.

Blowing your horn at a hearse is somehow sacrilegious if not even pointless, he thinks. Through the rectangular rear window of the vehicle, he can see the curved top of the coffin, rising like one of those bran muffins Georgia sometimes brings to work and warms up in the oven for her lunch. He wonders about the corpse being carried from Connecticut to New York for burial—if it is for burial. Is there some sort of a regulation, like the old Mann Act for example, that prohibits the transportation of corpses across state lines for immural purposes?

Better to pull off the road and eliminate the aggravation, the cause for all bad jokes, and Flo's Kountry Kitchen offers its rutted dirt turn-off at the next curve. He was no stranger to this roadside spa so he knew that Flo had long left the counter and a kitchen, where only three hotplates and a warming oven supplied the specifics of a very select menu. He bought a cola and the afternoon paper that had been trucked over from Hartford, maybe tossed out the back of an earlier hearse, but was unable to read it, only glance at the headlines about North and Poindexter, about files and papers being subpoenaed, which calls him back to his own search through Emerson Caldwell's papers.

All the miles he had driven this day from Albany to Hudson to here and now back, he didn't need that kind of a reminder, which might be only another bad joke. In any event the guy behind the counter, who wasn't Flo, but who had taken over the business when Flo went to Arizona, was talking to him whether he tried to read the newspaper or not. All about sauces again and Strickland couldn't believe that he was in this same conversation about sauces that he had a week back and only a few miles from here in Green River. Almost the same.

"It's the spices. They been irradiated," the current proprietor of

Flo's is saying. "That's why I don't make my own sauces anymore. The spices you buy these days have all been irradiated."

"Oh yeah," Strickland says and turns the page. It seems discourteous to point out that the menu offers no dishes with any sort of sauce, but largely items depending on turkey roll and bologna.

"I been to the VA and they won't do nothing for me. Sure, I can check into the hospital in Albany but I got no compensation, they say, because there's no proof that those tests did it to me."

"You mean the Navy tests. After the war."

"Yeah, after the War. The Big War." He wipes a section of the Formica counter with a dishcloth. "I got to go in for transfusions now. They do that for me but they won't accept the claim. They had us all in these ships and with our backs turned. We wasn't supposed to look at it. And I didn't look at it either. I never even saw it," the owner of Flo's says. He shuffles a couple of menu cards and puts them neatly into a clip rack that holds a sugar dispenser, salt and pepper cellars. "I didn't even see it."

Strickland has just come across an item in the back pages that is more interesting than the front page stories about conspiracies and the misuse of power. He starts to read the whole article, carefully, as the other man continues to talk about radiation and sauces.

TRUCK, DRIVER
LAXATIVE CARGO
ARE MISSING

Chapter

7

"Talis hominum oratio qualis vita."

"What's that, something you saw on a label?" Carrol Strickland asks.

"That's Seneca, my friend," Benny Stone replies. "Four B.C. to sixty-five A.D. A man's oratory should be no better than his life." The agent pauses, looks wisely across his desk top. His eyebrows and my moustache, Strickland thinks, should all be on the same face just for the symmetry of it. The rest of Stone's head resembles a pink egg. "That's you, Strick."

"I don't get it."

"Your life and these dumb voice-overs you've been doing—how the pollywog putzes . . . 'The Norman Rockwell Sketchbook.' What kind of material is that for a talent like yours? I ask you?" The agent looks extremely sad. A curious buffet covers his desk top; plates of meats, vegetables, a slice of watermelon; also a three-layer cake, a grilled rainbow trout, rococo ice cream sundaes. "This General Products account is the original pie in the sky." As if to illustrate his point, Stone picks up a slice of chocolate cream pie and points it toward Strickland.

"Where'd you get that?"

"Isn't this a beaut?" The agent's smile turns him into a baby with Groucho Marx eyebrows. "I spotted this one in the window of a greasy spoon on Canal Street. They hadn't had anything like this on the menu since LaGuardia was mayor. I had to buy it in Spanish. Cost me all of five bucks." He lays the plastic piece down with the others.

"I thought you collected plastic purses," Strickland says. Benny Stone had always been good for him, both for jobs and a few laughs.

"Naw, that was last year. My Joan Crawford period. Everybody's doing purses now. But there's something genuine about these." He lifts a plate of pale orange spaghetti. "You know—food. Basic stuff. I think we're entering a proletarian period. Back to essentials. It's a reactionary time, you read it in the papers. So I'm collecting with the times. Call it harmony." His eyes twinkle over the pastel plastic display.

Strickland cannot hear the sounds of traffic thirty floors below. The agency's building is on Fifth near Forty-second Street, close to the New York Public Library, and the windows have never been open as far as he can remember. "You're saying I should get with it. Get into harmony. But Jesus, Benny—a toilet bowl cleaner? Why can't you get me a Mercedes or even a jeans sponsor?"

"You see, you still don't know what you got, what you sound like. I think that's funny, going around listening to yourself speak but never knowing what you sound like. You can't do stuff like jeans because your voice doesn't fit those tight little tushes wagging back and forth—it's too substantial. And things like luxury cars are poison—they are one shot only. But John Boy is a product you can ride for the rest of your natural life."

"John Boy?"

"That's the name of the product, John Boy. It's basically the usual toilet bowl brush but it's got this extra gizmo on it that sanitizes as it dispenses a perfume. And they got five flavors so far. I think—wait a minute, I got the specs right here somewhere." Stone pushes an earth-colored dish of baked beans to one side and fans out some papers. "Here. They got pine, verbena, magnolia—I hear the magnolia is dynamite—and . . ."

"So, I'm to be the voice of John Boy, is that it?"

"Wait'll you hear." Stone puts up a hand as if to hold back Strickland's enthusiasm. "They got some of Disney's best people to do the animation, and they're trying to sign a superguy for the music. I hear they're talking to Previn."

"Previn?"

"Well, that's what I hear." The agent shrugs and looks out the window. In the windows of the building across the avenue Strickland sees people at desks, talking on telephones, conferring with each other. He wonders what any of them think he and Benny Stone are doing. They could be accountants or lawyers.

"I don't know," he says finally. "I've never done anything quite like this. Been identified with a product. Like this."

"Listen to me," Stone says slowly and in quite a different voice. "It's time you cashed in on some of your credits. I know about you, Strick. I know about what you have gone through. Do I have to spell it out? In your case, your life has been better than your oratorio. I want to address that imbalance. That's my job. Also, I heard about the turndown at PBS."

"It wasn't exactly a turndown."

"Look, I ran into Cindy Block at a function last week. She used that key phrase—mutual benefit. That's what people say in this business. Just as the knife goes in between your ribs they whisper in your ear, 'This is to our mutual benefit.' You're quality, Strickland, and this rig wasn't built for quality." Stone, almost without looking, picks up one of the food displays and holds it toward his client. Strickland stares at the cup of plastic strawberry pudding. The foam whipped cream has yellowed and the maraschino cherry on top has turned purple. "Get the picture?"

"But if I'm quality, why not a Mercedes commercial? A quality product and not this shit stick?"

"That's precisely the point. It's a play-off—your voice against the product. You can play with it, give it humor, give it a dimension it doesn't have. You remember Orson Welles and that two-bit wine? You remember how his voice gave that sardonic twist to the words so you didn't quite believe what he was saying but he was obviously having fun with it so maybe it would be fun to drink the stuff at least once? Jesus, how I had to fight to get that idea across."

"You're responsible for that commercial?"

"I had something to do with it," Stone replies easily and turns to look at the view from his window. The heavy eyebrows level, lie flat. Strickland reads their message: this is serious business. No joke.

Except he was the joke, sitting across from Benny Stone and listening to the sounds of the agency office outside the door, the discrete ting-tings of the special telephones that kept going off like kitchen timers; something was cooking. He felt not only cooked but bleached out like the dry husks of cicada carcasses he used to carefully collect in a jar at the end of August. The Kansas heat had turned them into toast. "If I were a pot," his mother used to say, "I'd be boiled dry." Spring wheat would be about ready for harvesting now, an inland sea of it rippling as far as Colorado where the mountains threw it back. The sweet flavoring of silvery greenness rose suddenly in his memory even as he looks out the window behind Benny Stone, even as he makes out the flat monolith of the Pan Am Building. That was a terrible thing to do, to put that skyscraper up over Grand Central Station.

"Is this mike on?" the agent is saying. He's been looking at Strickland close. "Look, it's not the end of the world, right? Think about it. Let me send you their proposal. Did I tell you the money? I'm asking for a hundred G plus residuals and a refusal on their next in line. And it's nonexclusive. You can still do your birdcalls, if you want. They haven't blinked so far."

"The voice of John Boy."

"It's beautiful, baby. Pussy in the bank. See." Stone stands up, still holding the goblet of fake pudding. "I knew you'd be interested."

Strickland's smile as he prepares to leave has given the agent the idea that he is interested in the deal. He can feel the smile open up his face and he can do nothing about it. He can visualize how he must look, much like the photograph in the shoe shop only a few blocks from here. The broad expanse of large teeth unveiled beneath the thick, dark bar of the moustache, a gleaming signal, like a banner of geniality, fraternity, and collegiality—everything everyone wanted to be. Anyone looking at that picture, at that smile, would know that Carrol Strickland, boy bullfrog, had it all, and they would be envious. Funny, he thinks.

Because he wasn't interested in doing the commercials, and he had only smiled as he left the agency because of the understanding that he would probably do the commercials. He needed the money, he always seemed to need money lately, and this distinction didn't matter to Benny Stone. So Strickland had been smiling about the route that had brought him to this place, irresistably and with all the lines laid down, the turns clearly marked and not the way he could remember his father sometimes twisting the wheel in the middle of a boundless landscape to head the Dodge three-quarter ton off in another direction, maybe south toward Wichita, following a route in his head, not on a map.

Once on the street, on an almost deserted prenoon hour Fifth Avenue (Stone had not offered him lunch either), he half turned toward Forty-sixth Street and the shoe store, and then turns back downtown in the direction of the massage parlor on Second Avenue, and then pulls up short, feeling like some tourist from Minnesota not knowing which way to go.

(*Man's voice, older*) *Well, here we are, Margaret, in the middle of the greatest city in the world.*

(*Wife*) *Land's sakes, Ezra, do you know where you're going?*

(*Announcer*) *GRAND CENTRAL STATION, Where hundreds of real-life DRAMAS are played out daily against the backdrop of the World's Largest Railroad Terminal, CROSSROADS of a NATION and HUMAN DREAMS . . .*

A fever burns in him that he could not identify but which had sometimes found a sort of peace in those two places, and he suddenly remembers the joke about a classmate who, on business trips to New York City, would drop into the Public Library, just three blocks down, and look up his biography in *Who's Who*. Check on it; make sure he was still there, still alive. His sudden laughter turns a couple toward him: he goes to a shoe store for similar reassurance.

The quick pleasure promised in the second direction makes him hesitate at the curb, then something stiffens his shoulders and he strides across the avenue toward Madison instead; to all appearances, a man with an important appointment. What righteousness, he says to himself and laughs again so the cop on the corner briefly looks him over. He'd been lucky so far. He's never picked up the clap or any of the other nasty burrs that the gods put into the honey, and lately he had been giving this some thought—for the first time in a long time—a recall of a kind of purity he associated with Saturday night in downtown Salina where there always seemed to be a contest as to who had the cleanest fingernails, the most earnestly scrubbed ears.

All this because of Robin Endicott. He has been wondering about the other time in her studio over the old stable and what would have happened if he had reached for her as she sifted through the drawings she brought him to see. Showing him her etchings! How old a dodge was that, and they weren't very good drawings at that. Average student work—she must know they were—so why else haul them out but as ruse for her own seduction? He feels dumb.

"You're kind of new in town," he half says to his reflection in the huge plate glass beside him. He looks through the ready-made smile beneath the dark moustache and into the display of the airline ticket office. The large color display is a photograph of a couple running up the beach from a glistening sea. The woman's brief costume displays her youthful body, dazzled by drops of the Caribbean and recontoured by Nautilus. Particularly the belly, where the navel resides like a pirate's cove within the vertical lineae of stomach muscles. Her companion is broad-shouldered and looks manly.

(*Girl, enchanted*) *Oh Carrol, how wonderful to take advantage of Pan-American's off-season package rates.*

(*Man, resourceful*) *And to think that we have this beach to ourselves, except for the discreet guitarists who are out of sight. Shall I ravish you here?*

(*Girl, resisting*) *Wait, we must wait for the test results. I am only a poor cousin, related by marriage it is true, yet still healthy. We must know for sure if you're clean.*

(Man, sensible but disappointed) You're right of course.

(Girl, brightly) Anyway, there are so many wonderful shells to gather. *Donkey rides around the old volcano. Visits to ancient battlements—and the food. Ah, the food.*

(Announcer) AHHH . . . PAN-AMERICAN! *Three-hundred twenty-nine dollars all-inclusive. Double occupancy . . . where medical results permit. (Music—up and out)*

On Madison Avenue Strickland takes a bus uptown, for he is in no hurry to meet with Virginia Caldwell. Her note said she'd be home all day and that he was welcome to come by whenever he wished. She had something interesting for him to see. Some fascinating memento of Emerson's selfless service. A piece of the shining armor, maybe. His favorite chopsticks, presented to him by a grateful people for his contribution to their debauch. Perhaps the Ambassador's personalized tube of KY, which Jack Kennedy had presented to him in the Rose Garden as a part of his portfolio, to be handy whenever the President wished to give it to him up the ass.

"How far are you going?" Nancy asked one time.

"To Seventy-fourth Street," Strickland says aloud.

"Turn down the crapola. How far are you going with these people, these zombies who feel nothing for you?" They had the house to themselves and it was autumn. He remembers the blue haze of that late afternoon. Leslie was spending the night with a school chum who lived nearly twenty miles down the valley and he had just got back from dropping her off. Distance didn't matter. Leslie had trouble making friends at this rural school; maybe this new school chum would be different. Was she happy about it? He couldn't remember now, as he rode uptown on the Madison Avenue bus.

"I'll get some more wood," he said, poking at the fire. The maples had turned golden outside the living room windows to create a luminous effect within the old farmhouse, as if they were held inside a large, clear jewel.

"We don't need more wood. We need some answers. Fix yourself a drink. Fix me another." Strickland sat down on an ottoman next to the fireplace. Nancy crossed her feet on the sofa and rattled the ice in her glass. "Now you're being sulky."

"No."

"You have no idea what you were like, do you." Her voice seemed to come out of darkness, the light in the room gone under something as Strickland let the bus rock him gently into a half doze of remembrance.

So tell me what I was like, he thinks. Rube, they called him at Furness and fortunately the name never caught on. It was Strick after his first year, after he showed them how quickly he could become like them. Then they called him Strick. What's it like out there in Kansas, Rube? Still got Indians and cowboys? Yes, as a matter of fact, and the answer made them silly with laughter. He never knew he could be so funny. Their response surprised him, lay across his wonder like a magician's blindfold to mesmerize him and make him a victim, struck by his own facility but he never saw it coming.

"Oh, I've heard all that," Nancy's voice came from behind him. He almost turned in the bus seat but she had got up to fix her own drink at the dry-sink bar. He remembers that. The yellow leaves outside swept against the window panes, urchins in the wind. You poor child, his mother would say, you've never seen leaves. How beautiful autumn can be. But they had cottonwoods and they had elm, about ten of them planted around the house as screens against the ferocious iron of the sun, but it didn't seem to matter. The heat found its way into the house anyway to press his mother, all the laughter pressed out, leaving only that thin, cold anger that made her almost shiver with scorn. In Vermont in October, she would say, the mountains became God's palette.

"We all have monsters in our lives," Nancy said. He can hear her voice over the guttural sound of the bus engine. "Your mother was of the same genus as Everett Hale, both of them had their way with us."

"I don't get what you're saying."

"I mean she fucked your head over as surely as E.H. fucked me over, making you feel ashamed of yourself. She set you up for the whole East Coast scam. Everett wasn't ashamed either. Well, uneasy, self-conscious then. But you certainly weren't one of those Eastern preppies. That was for sure." You poor darling, his mother would say to him, hugging him to her flannel-covered bosom, the cold winds down from Nebraska raked over the roof shingles, testing, always testing. You poor boy, an orphan to the wind. I'll see to it that you won't be stuck out here in this place. I must stay, I made that decision and it was my choice but you—you had no say in it and I will see to it that you get away. I will do that for you.

"At least I didn't have all that sanctimonious pap," he could hear Nancy say. She would have pulled her legs up on the sofa and covered them with an afghan. "Everett never said much; he just went to it." But sometimes she'd hear her mother's voice rise from the stuporous mash that kept the whole house in a kind of comatose, as if something heavy and thick had spilled out from beneath the door of that bedroom down the stairs to coat everything—the leather wingback chairs, the Chippendale end tables, the bookshelves, even the white, blank-eyed bust of Ralph Waldo Emerson—cover everything with an unnatural silence so that those times, the bedsprings of her own bed (the bunny decals still on the headboard when it had first started, is that too much? Is that detail just a little too much? Well, it was true) so sometimes the bed springs sounded like flocks of geese flying over in early winter. Geese? Yes, she thought of geese then. "I'd think of anything to keep from going crazy," Nancy said, and this little girl she was talking about would say *wait, wait, wait,* but the father would think she was trying to keep him from his mania rather than from the sound it was making. She just wanted it to happen quietly, that was all. "Never said anything." No, never said anything and looked like he was about to explain some fact of history, some detail of algebra; patiently explain it, but sorrowful that such explication was necessary.

"Maybe you better get another log for the fire," she had said, and Strickland looks out the window of the bus for firewood along Fifty-third Street. Delis, florists, newsstand, shoe stores, several art galleries, a pharmacy, but no firewood. Nothing here on the East Side of Manhattan like that? Wood stacked next to that hosiery shop? Why not? It could be a cold winter. Put another stack of oak outside the

Kitchen Kounter Shoppe, like the one he came across this morning when he checked on the traps. Who had cut and stacked that half cord of wood? It had been there for a long time, well seasoned, the dense fiber quietly poised to release the hot gases stored in the grain long before he was born, probably. Strickland wonders if there might be stacks of wood like that in woods everywhere, cut and stacked by someone long cooled down, forgotten. Wasn't there a poem about that, by Frost or someone like that? That sounds like Frost who was Moon's favorite and he thinks of T. D. Moon reciting poems about stone walls and birches to the slant-eyed, brown faces in Saigon, which is how all this got started, wasn't it? Reading poems about New England farms to little brown men still damp from the rice paddies?

And that's how he, Carrol Strickland, confidant of Jack Armstrong, got into the funny business, as Nancy called it while she sat with her graceful, muscular legs wrapped around with the afghan Cora Endicott had given them. The light of the fire showed its warmth on her high-boned cheeks and sparkled on the large, even teeth but the smile was sardonic. "Wasn't that it? Professor T. D. Moon, Fulbright Lecturer at U. of Saigon—when was it, 1960? Laying the ground plan. Wasn't he?"

Whose woods these are, we never knew, but we're going to give these gooks a royal screw. Woods you can walk through and never come to an end, his mother used say, with sweet mosses and cool little brooks like silvery threads coming undone in the earth's bodice. "Oh, save me from that." Nancy lifted the glass again. That would be her third drink, and by dark she'd be loosened up and a little crazy. But that's how his mother talked; the words small, delicious morsels she pushed around on some plate in her head to position here and there with deft, delicate maneuvers of knife and fork but never eaten, never fully tasted. At least not in that high-ceilinged dining room with the big window looking out in the direction of Topeka, east of them, and where on summer mornings the sun appeared so fiercely that the room couldn't be used until way after four o'clock. They still ate supper in the kitchen, which was cooler, and in the winter they continued to eat at the red enameled kitchen table as if they had forgot the use of this middle room, like one of his father's harrows unhitched and left by the stock water trough after some past spring work, left there to rust in its untried utility. Sometimes he'd come on his mother standing in this dining room and looking at the dishes on the plate rail that went around the four walls up near the ceiling—plates she had brought with her from Vermont when she had come out to take that teaching job at Kansas State, plates she now only looked at like someone viewing an exhibit in a museum, wondering at the beauty of these artifacts as well as at their meaning.

"Oh, the lady on the prairie," he could hear Nancy say. "She could have made a fortune posing for Walker Evans. I can see her, standing on the back porch steps, hand over her leathery brow, staring into the horizon." And she rose from the sofa, a little unsteadily, to take up the pose. "Jesus, what suckers those pictures have made out of us. She would have rather sent you to Exeter or St. Paul's instead of Furness, but then I would never have met you. Then I would be really dead."

"You've had enough."

"Not nearly enough," she said and walked with a parody of elegance over to the bar. The fire snapped, crackled and the ice cubes clinked. "You saved my life, Carrol Strickland—you gooney bird with your eyes and your voice too big for the rest of you, an unlikely Lancelot riding in from the West to save me from the stake."

At Sixty-seventh Street the bus becomes fouled in traffic and stops athwart the cross street, Strickland's window has halted precisely at a corner where a couple stand kissing each other. They are young and oblivious to this stranger, only the thickness of glass keeping him from being a participant in their affection. Both wear the kind of dishevelment that has become a feature of perfume ads— though their look seems unstudied, and their lips touch and caress with a happiness that was unrehearsed. Strickland finds himself smiling.

The shy, savored kisses he and Nancy exchanged behind the library at Furness or in the long twilights at Northampton—those evenings were long and dreamlike and rather formal, and not coming undone casually like the couple outside the bus window. It was a time of neatness: cashmere sweaters, polished loafers, pleated skirts—yes, a strand of pearls around the Peter Pan collar. He wore the fitting complement: scuffed buckskins, Windsor knot, Harris tweed by J. Press. They were like something out of Scott Fitzgerald, struck by their own image, unable to get through to the other side of the glass. Or fearful of doing so, of what they might find, because all this time as he took her hand, let his arm encircle her shoulders at the movies, felt her cool lips press against his mouth—all that time she'd be waiting for her father to come kiss her goodnight.

She would hear the footsteps start at the bottom of the stairs, one after another rising like the sounds of a nightmare that had awakened her just to hear those footsteps coming closer, unhurried because there was no need to hurry. She wasn't going anywhere. "Who could I tell? Who would believe me?" Her mother turned in a bath of chemicals. The family was distant, already critical. She had her pride, after all—even at ten, at twelve, at sixteen. This was the sort of thing Cora Endicott—if Strickland ever told Cora Endicott about this, she would personally nail his balls to the mantle; more than that, Nancy felt to blame, and after a while she even enjoyed the secret they shared. They had something on the rest of those asshole Endicotts.

But my God, how did she keep from going crazy? "It was the talk before that was worse than the action that came after. He'd carefully fold his clothes and ask me about school. How was it going? Had I done my homework? He always made sure about that. Didn't want to interfere with the homework. Then he'd discuss current events. The Nuremberg Trials. Truman's amazing defeat of Dewey. Always the educator." Then he would be there, before her. Huge.

"Books." Strickland remembers Nancy's laughter in the shadows of the living room. The fire their only illumination so the whites of her eyes glistened. "All those books in his library—these same books right here." She had raised her arm to include the ones around them. "I kept reading in them—Dickens, Cather, Thackery—I kept reading about the rest of the world, so I knew what was happening to me wasn't the usual way of things. Because if I thought that it was, that if this nightmare I was caught in was the way things were to go, then

I would have killed myself. But I knew from books that there was another world out there somewhere. I just had to find a way of getting to it. Then you rode into town. Just in time."

Me, thinks Strickland, as the bus moves on again. Wearing the new clothes bought at Wolf Brothers in Kansas City—the stores in Topeka not stylish enough—but still looking odd in that roomful of chinos and blazers during the headmaster's reception for new boys that first New England autumn, the first brilliant change of season that was to torture him with its ineffable beauty. Bulky and too thick around the shoulders, the fabric of his new clothes was cut and forced into patterns it had not been woven for, just as he felt forced into that book-lined study, a fire crackling in the hearth—always a fire crackling in the hearth—forced into that school and its unspoken rules that were all the more humiliating when broken because they were unspoken, unknown to him and unknown only to him. He didn't belong there; the rules had a way of showing him that over and over.

But there he was. Uncle Grover was a trustee of Furness Academy, his mother had told him. He'll like it. It will be a good place for him. He will be with boys who become the men that guide the destiny of this country. Oh, sure, Ma. Sure. And she had continued folding the laundry, his new shirts washed out and ironed so they wouldn't appear brand new or bought for the occasion but something he had been wearing all the time, every day, in Salina. He became the boy a place was made for—move over and let Carrol sit down. Even that first Thanksgiving away from home, spent with Uncle Grover's family in that small town near Ossipee, New Hampshire—the pervasive heat from the kitchen's wood stove still tingles his cheeks as he calls up the aromas of cinnamon and mince and apple from the pies that turned crisp in the oven's black iron caverns—even there a place was made for him; he was the odd plate on the corner of the table.

His benefactor would take him down into the village later, to the weekly newspaper he published almost single-handedly, it seemed, with the help of a multiarmed Linotype that swung into action like one of those Hindu gods handling several destinies all at once. Uncle Grover spent the afternoon showing him the intricacies of that machine. "I think it was some sort of a test," he told Nancy. "Like an audition. To see if I had the aptitude for it, because he had no sons—no one to carry on."

"Maybe that was part of the bargain," she said. "He got you into Furness if you were supposed to take over the newspaper."

And maybe that had been the bargain. Looking through the front window of the bus at the noontime congestion ahead on Madison Avenue, Strickland imagines himself as the cagey country editor writing editorials that would please everyone in town, make his readers feel smart about their own unchallenged opinions. He would have married the daughter of the congregational minister; a nice girl who wore plain underwear and felt it was her duty to satisfy his needs. That would be what she called it—his needs. She'd also help put out the paper (maybe she got her degree in journalism), reading proof and managing the classified ads and legal notices, which would be quite lucrative. For holiday they'd spend a week now and then in Las Vegas. Two children, maybe three. Todd, named after her father, would help out after school, addressing subscriptions, cleaning the press rollers. He was a good kid and seemed interested in getting into the business. After Dartmouth, of course. And the girls would be like their mother; earnest and healthy and ready to be wonderful mothers themselves. Homemakers.

(Editor, noble-voiced) Margaret, we must take a stand on this PTA issue. The paper has got to set the standard for the community's conscience.

(Wife, wise and supportive) You will do the right thing as always, Carrol. Yes, we might lose the Dolly Darn Store account, but I am with you as always . . . no matter what you have done. (Music up)

(Announcer) WHAT COULD MARGARET KNOW ABOUT GENIAL, CAGEY COUNTRY EDITOR CARROL STRICKLAND? TUNE IN TOMORROW WHEN *we hear the glamorous Dolly Darn say . . .*

(Woman, sharp and possessive) Carrol, isn't it about time we got this yarn untangled . . . (Music up and out)

But then this toothy tomboy with black bangs came over to him with a cup of fruit punch. "I'm Nancy, the headmaster's daughter." It sounded like part of a limerick or one of those puns passed around behind the gym where the older boys went to smoke cigarettes, and she laughed as if to acknowledge the association, and he no longer felt like he was stuck out in the middle of a field, a target for crows. His stomach had been turning sourly, as if a peculiar umbilical cord had been severed and he had to adjust quickly to a different, unappetizing diet as he had to learn to pronounce such names as Prescott and Whitney and Nathan, many of these followed by numbers, not just Junior, but numbers, like the second or the third! How soft and easy the old names like Wilbur and Homer and Mae were in his mouth. This morning, in the field above Silvernales, Strickland had a whiff of something very like the Clorox and cornmeal mixture that used to come off the clothes hanging in his grade-school cloakroom. Probably decaying matter, leaves and such, sending up a little methane into the atmosphere—his own woods contributing to the cycle no matter how it's going to come out, or run down. What's the word, entropy?

So his clothes were funny looking, was that it? "No, that wasn't it, not all of it," Nancy said and leaned forward to let gold bangles spill from her arms onto the floor by the sofa. She had begun that slow removal of items, jewelry, belt buckles—anything that might bruise the flesh. Though admittedly his jacket did look like something made out of an old army blanket, but that made him more interesting. "You see, by then I had begun to believe that there wasn't any escape. I had been watching the classes come and go—all of them paraded before me in blazers, soccer and football uniforms, all of them the same. Same ones, back and forth, up and down the field, paraded as I stood on the reviewing stand. The headmaster's daughter. The princess." Her laughter unraveled in the dark and she drank with a great thirst from an invisible glass.

"All the same, just junior versions of Everett Hale. I knew all their routines already—before they knew them themselves." Her whole length stretched out on the sofa, tensed, then subsided into the sporadic gloom of the hearth. "So I was saying to myself that there was no point in going on if I was only going to exchange the same partners—all the same. Your voice came on like your clothes. I heard it first and then I saw the clothes and none of you fit. Nothing fit and I thought, hot dog—they're not all the same after all. He's going to get me into that other place I've been reading about. I remember you talked about Kansas and it sounded like China . . . like Shangri-la." She had pronounced the word thoughtfully. "Funny, but all the time I thought you were going to get me out, I was getting you in. Almost like the final push into the pot your mother had cooking for you."

"But you wouldn't have lasted," Strickland says aloud, under his breath. Sherry-Lehmann passes on the right, the store's windows a display of rare wines, dark bottles in uncovered wooden crates, like projectiles. Jesus, did they ever not owe Sherry-Lehmann money? *Uncle Grover, this is Nancy Endicott who wants to be a country editor's wife except she has this account with Sherry-Lehmann;* truck after truck tooling up old Route 1 from New York City all the way to Ossipee, New Hampshire, taking the tight turns slowly in the mountains and past the summer resorts, vacant and closed up for winter. Truck after truck roaring through villages like some effete version of the Red Ball Express, low overhangs of autumnal foliage brushing the tops of the trucks loaded down with Bordeaux and Montrachet and Bombay gin.

(Folksy male) What's that there addition Editor Strickland and his missus is building onto their back porch?

(Old timer, Yankee accent) Why, that's a loading dock for them liquor and wine trucks that come up from New York City.

"You wouldn't have made it," he says to the window. The whole bus is reflected in the liquor store's front glass and he sees himself, a face looking out one of the bus windows all in a row, like one of those faces Renaissance painters would put into their larger canvases to be both witness and participant in whatever was happening in the piazza. He had been one of those; the front half. "But you never gave me a chance to give it a try, to say no," Nancy might have said. She had thought it, he was pretty certain. Silvernales was far enough away; only two hours from the sparkling reservoir of Sherry-Lehmann, and she had still gone cabin crazy.

This morning the village of mobile homes could have been freight cars that had been sided into the small niche of scrub fields, left to rust so their wheel axles had become one with the undercarriage and they were parked there, slowly going back into the earth from which they came while waiting for the ore mines in Hot Ground and Black Rock to reopen—a kind of fracture of the geological and historical cycle.

Strickland had looked down on this scene this morning, quite early so the sun had not yet dried the patina of dew on the sheet-metal roofs and siding of the trailers, so that they looked factory fresh, just wheeled in rather than put there years back—but only for that brief moment at dawn would they look new. He had got up at daybreak as some old settler might have done before the trailers, before the railroad even, to check his traps: he hoped not to be observed as he made his way up through the back fields, spooking rabbits and stilling birds.

All the traps had been sprung. Two had dead branches stuck between their steel jaws, and the third one was clamped down on a metal fence post that had been ripped from the ground, parts of the earthen clods still solid with frost lying around the rupture, so the fury, the blind hatred that had uprooted the steel post, could be assembled from the hard fragments. All at once, he had been grateful and enraged. In his craziest anger, what had he hoped to find—the skeletal remains of a sportsman from New Rochelle? Yet he was sickened—and it was a familiar nausea—by his own foolishness, the recognition of it by him and by others, for surely they had seen him lay the traps. They were probably observing him right then, holding back their operatic, Neapolitan laughter as he stood looking down at the sprung traps, his polished Wellingtons smeared with mud and the material of his twill slacks stuck with dried thistles—wearing all of the clothes he had put on to become the voice of John Boy and at that very moment being looked at from the other side of the broken fence line and laughed at. Call in the 1st Cav. Let's burn those fuckers out!

The shotgun blast had been more like a morning gun signaling the arrival of a new day on some peaceful outpost that still kept the rituals of an orderly camp, still enjoying the luxury of being away from the conflict and so able to follow the manual for such order. None of them had ever seen how quickly chaos can seize a day. Strickland had waited as the report bounced off the wooded hillsides above Silvernales; then, faintly, once again; waited not for more gunfire but for the notes of a bugle saluting the rise of a flag upon a staff, an unfamiliar standard lifting against the sky and more and more triumphant and more and more unjustly so. But the woods lay silent around him. He sat for a moment on the bench of cordwood, cut and stacked so neatly by ancient hands, then—like someone who might have paused in a park to collect his thoughts while en route to an important appointment—he stood up, pulled the belt tight on his trench coat, and walked down off the hill.

Chapter

8

Shapes continue to rise in Strickland's mind like crows flapping up out of corn stubble, but silently, like a film with the sound off, so the images were there cleanly in black and white and he could add whatever sound he wishes. Lately this flock of memories seemed to assemble and wheel above his boyhood, the time before he came East. He rarely spoke of this background anymore or of his family back in Kansas. The reticence had been more of a protective coloration, than a factor of embarrassment; an instinctual play for the covert to protect his unsuitable biography in the hostile territory of the Eastern Frontier.

Sometimes he imagined this earlier identity, or not so much imagined it as he let the outline of it expand in his mind. Another Carrol Strickland had stayed on to run the farm, marry, and set up a life very different from his; had become one of those men he used to see trading talk around the grain silos by the railroad siding, the skin of their arms above the shirt line milk white, and a similar division across their brows where straw Resistols seemed permanently glued. Like those grown men who spend their idle hours fitting together models of something they would never know, Strickland invested his double with meticulous details, accessories and appointments. He would have taken his turn on the school board and been a good member of the Grange. He'd be on the board of directors of the local bank. His name would be one of several dozen lined up in a discreet column on the left border of a U.S. senator's stationery—advisers on farm policy. His bass voice would center the choir of the Christian church every Sunday, and he and three other farmers—no he would make one of them something else, maybe the drugstore owner or the veterinarian; yes, good ol' Doc Somebody—anyway, they would make up a barbershop quartet that would perform at the Lions Club, or even the county fair. In fact, they would win the talent show at the county fair.

People would say that he could have been a Broadway show star if he hadn't loved the soil so much. He could have been a famous television announcer, like Alexander Scourby or Hugh Downs.

He and Sue or Rose or Mae had redone the house, added on a bedroom upstairs in the back so the girls could have separate bedrooms and on the first floor underneath they had put an office for Rose, who did all the bookkeeping for the farm. She had a good head for figures, and remember that big window in the dining room? Well, she had put a drapery all across that one wall—something she learned in Home Demonstration—so the sun was now kept out and the whole place had a kind of elegant look to it, like one of those pictures in the magazines she was always reading. But they still ate most of their meals in the kitchen, at the banquette he had surprised her with one anniversary, and the dining room was saved for special occasions. Then candles would be lit and he'd pretend he was in the wrong house. "Oh Carrol," she'd kid him. "You'll never grow up."

Then Strickland sees these shadows become silhouettes against the illuminated screens of the evening television and the sounds of Kent State and Mylai and Quantri and Watergate and Xuan Loc are lofted across the vespered prairie by the fluencies of Douglas Edwards or Edwin Newman. Walter Cronkite. *And here's a special report from Carrol Strickland.* Pretty special, those reports, and at this point in his modeling Strickland would turn the sound off. None of that went with the scenes he created for his twin; none of it seemed right for that family to hear every evening, sometimes even hear his voice speak of the disaster in terms of national security, though he knew they must have heard and that Salina had had its share of aluminum containers lifted down onto the AT & Santa Fe freight siding near the grain silos. None of that should have started on the playing fields of Furness and St. Paul's and The Hill.

So this reticence about his background was not just part of a suit of manners he had put on to look like the other new boys at Furness Academy but an attempt to preserve something he had left in that background, the possibility for innocence, and this covert behavior was interpreted by the headmaster's daughter as the secret sign put out by a fellow conspirator. Later, of course, he actually would have things to hide, and he sometimes wondered at the innocent origins of this craft, this practice of deception you might say; how the one virtuous charade had been a rehearsal for the other pernicious dissembling. "And all that time you wanted to get in," Nancy had said.

"I want to get out!" He has used his most commanding voice, for the bus has started to pull away from the stop. He has just jumped up and rushed to the exit doors, not knowing what cross street it is but knowing he has to quit the vehicle, get out into the air. The bus driver looks at him tiredly through the large mirror over his station. Another tourist who doesn't know his way around the city. "Stop this bus!" Strickland says in a tone of voice that could be a five-star general's, somebody signing a death warrant. The driver stomps on the brake, the doors hiss and Strickland is ejected on to the sidewalk, stiff-legged and with clubs for feet.

He stands before a fancy lingerie shop near the Whitney Museum, thinking of his daughter. Somewhere in the junction of his thought and its location and what he saw before him at that location lay a synthesis of all that bedeviled him, the coil of disparate mechanisms that had sprung him from the bus and if he could just poke around, Strickland thinks, stir through the layers of devices, he might find the lever that would release him from all his anger and anxiety.

For example, Leslie would never wear any of the lacy garments and harnesses that festoon the window like little explosions from a Mardi Gras float. She was already beginning to look like one of the Schuyler women, hearty matrons who trace their lineage back to the Dutch maidens from Amsterdam, aprons loaded down with pigs' knuckles. Or whatever. Strickland laughs and then laughs again as several women pass behind him. They cast him in the mold of their disapproval—he can feel their scorn harden up around his feet. What would they think of him if they knew he was looking into this window of frou-frou gewgaws and thinking of his daughter?

Well, what kind of underwear *does* Leslie wear? Can't that be an honest speculation a father could ask without incurring a public stoning on Madison Avenue? Indeed, he might make a case for such inquiry. Nothing like these multicolored net constructions, accents of black significantly struck throughout the display, but probably more like the sensible white and pink affairs he remembers from the pages of Montgomery Ward catalogs; pages he would sometimes secretly pour over at night as the winds from Nebraska circled the house like wolves.

"You have this fiction in your head about fresh milk and country ham morals," Nancy once said. "But it's all the same here and besides which, their teeth are rotten. Have you ever looked into one of the locals' mouths when they open them to laugh at you? Green cheese." Remembering Nancy, just then, makes him wince—what was the underwear *her* father preferred? Something very innocent, no doubt.

He feels a little shamed, because Leslie is a good kid. Eager. Earnest. Sensitive. It has been hard on her with Nancy gone. Mothers and daughters have a particular relationship; the bookstores were full of such stories, the idea was everywhere this year. If he could only find something for her, something that would move her out of the house, spring her from this security he had so carefully put around her. Then he would be free too. The house was becoming a burden, financially and emotionally. He could sell it. He could use the money, but more to the point, he wanted to get away. Get away from the stench rising up from the ground.

Stone was right; the agent's hunter nose had caught the whiff of decay in him as well. His voice, something about him was going bad. No question that Antarctica program would have been his a year ago. Now someone like a Cindy Block walked him to the elevator, and without lunch. And she had been right to do so.

But hadn't he been thinking of himself when he'd bought the place in Silvernales and moved them all there? Hadn't he also been trying to construct a safe house for himself, a make-believe to which he could return from the stink of Vietnam—a hobby village modeled along the lines of Salina, Kansas, or at least how he remembered that place?

Nancy had always kidded him about trying to find out-of-the-way places; candlelight on pewter, polished wood and worn leather, a large log slowly turning to embers in the high fireplace of the taproom. The food would be secondary but it would be excellent, of course. None of that existed anymore, not even in Connecticut. She'd laugh. You're thinking of all those movies you saw back in Kansas with Cary Grant and Kathryn Hepburn or one of the Bennett sisters. That was all on a Hollywood back lot. All made out of canvas and plaster and artistically lit. No, not all.

How about the Black Oak Inn, where he had first seen Robin Endicott? Didn't it have that smoked, dim coziness and just the right amount of pewter on the mantles so that you could imagine Alexander Hamilton coming through the door, talking about Federalism? Okay, so the service was pretty poor; not up to the standards for menials established by the Constitutional Convention, but then Robin explained that the regular waitress had been ill that night and that she was only filling in. Her regular duty was to be the charming hostess, swaying to one side in her deferential manner so each guest felt the intimacy of her greeting. Then he reminds himself as he looks into the lingerie shop, after all the pots and pans were polished and hung up, the chef apparently had her perform other tasks.

The bus for a brief time had given him direction. Merely to be on board the vehicle as it swayed and lurched up Madison Avenue, had put him on a bearing that had given him a sense of purpose, a feeling that he was advancing in a slow but somewhat meaningful manner. Now, on the street, he's forced to plot his own course, sort through old and new routes. There must be all sorts of people, he thinks, who get on buses and ride them up and down Manhattan all day long, just to feel they are going somewhere, to feel part of a general movement that's going somewhere.

This is Carrol Strickland speaking to you from Seventy-third Street and Madison where the annual migration of aimless individuals take to the Number Fours, Fives or even an occasional Number Nine and the casual observer of this phenomenon feels that he is observing an organized . . .

—Let's take it again, Carrol, and this time say he or she is observing . . .

—Sorry . . . he or she is observing an organized movement but actually . . .

Actually, the *she* who fits shadowy breasts into these cups of tissue, who lifts a glistening thigh to adjust a satin strap, is the shadow of Robin Endicott. He has been following her image all morning, since daybreak standing in the woods above his house, and all the way up to this corner in Manhattan, he has been pursuing Robin in his imagination as she appeared and disappeared before him like the mist in those woods, like the smoke here in the street, like one of those naiads from the old literature who on hills were always repairing. Or like the girl in *Green Mansions* who kept him company the winter he had scarlet fever, or like one of those seductresses in the French literature, Zola for example, T. D. Moon was always touting who led akward suitors through forests of suspicions, tangles of frenzied fantasies, pursuers vainly tracking the laughter of the pursued and finding nothing more. And why was she laughing? Who—that is to say what he *or* what she was making her laugh so, and how?

Strickland is tempted to go into the store and to try, in his imagination, some of these intimate items of apparel onto the figure of Robin Endicott, an imperfect fitting to be sure but no less interesting because of his lack of specifications. The old joke comes to mind of the young man buying a brassiere for his girlfriend, who responds to the clerk's request for size by sucking on the tips of his fingers to locate a familiar dimension.

Quickly Strickland turns around as if someone might have heard the corny joke run through his head, and goes back to the window with a brush of his moustache. Where does the urge come from to dress women in these bands of silk and lace? To adorn them, tie them up like fancy packages, every adjustment provoking a frisson in the flesh? Perhaps some impulse never permitted as a child and which, ironically, can be fulfilled only as a grown man. Only as a grown man is one allowed to dress and play with dolls. But that has manipulative connotations; the term would be Leslie's—he can hear her use the language—though Robin Endicott's image steps beside the models in the large photographs in the window as if to wait for a fitting. Her eyes are that startlingly blue and contemptuous; no deferential swoon anywhere in her posture now, but challenging. She's no doll to be turned around by some middle-age, pussy-whipped swain.

Men of his age take this pleasure as a form of homage. How's that sound? After all, didn't the ancients adorn statues of their deities with garlands of flowers, scarves of fine silks? Why not a similar worship at these youthful shrines, for to dress and adorn the bodies of young women is to decorate one's desire for immortality—say; someone who has begun to see the dark at the end of the tunnel who might offer a whimsical sacrifice now and then to any scheme for eternity, no matter how rickety it might be.

The mere pursuit of these reflections in the window of the lingerie store gives Strickland a reckoning of sorts, and he turns up the avenue, walking without hesitation, his booted feet placed down one after another in a swagger that seems to grant him the sidewalk. The strollers and the shoppers almost make way for him.

He would say later the whole day had been like that; the review of a stock company in which he took many roles. The bumpkin standing in the woods by his sprung traps. The rube betrayed by the Eastern Establishment. The eternal juvenile. The sad, older lover of young flesh. If the truth be known, Strickland could not locate himself behind any of those masks; yet he knew the lines for each and played all the parts. Even as Virginia Caldwell was to sort through a collection of papers on the Chinese Chippendale table in her apartment, he had sorted through the different personae of this traveling company, this enterprise—the Carrol Strickland Road Show.

These discursions he can now admit with each purposeful stride—were intended to delay the interview with Virginia Caldwell. It was to keep the standard, if you will, well in front of his advance guard and unreachable. That was why he'd got off the bus. He was getting there too fast. All the voices from the past he had been looking at, like a forum in his head, have begun to present the case for nothingness. Nothing was to be learned about Emerson Caldwell's mission to Saigon in 1963 which wasn't already known. His widow would not have come across any memo, no copy of an order to assassinate or not to assassinate the leader of another country because there never was such a memo. The whole thing had been a hoax from the start.

Probably it was Professor Moon's last joke so he could die laughing, and as usual it was the kid from Kansas who played the fool. Strick, take this ball and run that way. And he would run and run, the wind bringing tears to his eyes, all the way, only to learn that everyone else had run the other way or sat down to watch him huff and puff so the tears in his eyes became heavy and stung.

He doesn't want to know, actually. If the truth be known. If he could be so bold as to speculate, he doesn't want to know. "Just what the fuck are you doing," Nancy would say. Look at yourself, standing here on the corner of Madison and what, you don't even know the street, Seventy-sixth Street. Yes—there's the Carlyle. Still following this standard someone holds up. A dead man, a ghost of something. Like some old movie with Ronald Colman; the Lost Legion meeting for drinks with Cary Grant and Katherine Hepburn in the back room of the Black Oak Inn. They see this figure trudging up the road, kicking through the golden harvest of autumn leaves, purposeful, on assignment and faithful to the end.

(Colman adjusts his Foreign Legion headcloth) Who is that intreprid fellow coming our way?

(Grant looks sideways) It's that chap from Salina.

Gosh-all-get-out. (says Kate Hepburn, and they do get out. Strickland enters to find back room empty, only a large log smoldering in the hearth.)

"It's so good to see you once again," Virginia Caldwell says as she guides him through the intricate maze of memorabilia. Strickland pulls himself in, steps carefully—one false move and the whole place might come down in shards, the spoils of Southeast Asia showering East Seventy-ninth Street. Somehow the ambassador's widow moves almost negligently through the scrimshaw and porcelain, rather like a large ocean liner maneuvering through a crowded harbor—a sense of right-of-way casually handling the helm.

"Emerson kept meticulous notes for all of his appoin'ments and I came across some entries which I think might interest you. Of cawse, his journals are even more conclusive . . . he tells all in those." The idea has made her breathless and she has halted their progress under a small crystal chandelier to catch her breath. "You understand, of cawse."

"Understand what?"

"Why I must keep them privy sanctorum for now." Her large, almond-shaped eyes look almost roguish. If he would just say the magic word, she would reveal everything. "I must keep them closed until the right time."

She has led them into the formal dining room of the largish apartment, and Strickland quickly surveys the view outside the draped windows, the blinds are down across the way, and then looks back at the Chinese Chippendale dining table to which Mrs. Caldwell is pointing, like a magician's assistant announcing a trick. Papers and notebooks have been set out on the gleaming surface of the table in preparation for his inspection, though the atmosphere, the precision of their presentation would suggest that more than one perusal was expected, indeed, that a delegation from the United Nations, say, was expected momentarily to ring for entrance and start pouring over the collection. Until then, a porcelain shepherdess from Meissen stands guard in the center of the table.

"As you see, I've done a bit of homework myself," Virginia Caldwell says with a liquid graciousness, the flavor of smoked ham still redolent in her throat. She wants to collaborate, Strickland is thinking as he steps toward the table. She wants her name on something other than her husband's tombstone. Coyness turns in the great moose features. "My expertise is nowhere comparable to yours, Mr. Strickland, but, as you see, I've put the records in chronological order, starting heah, at the head of the table—so to speak."

Where Emerson Caldwell must have sat down to his corn pudding and larks, Strickland thinks as he looks closely at the documents. 1954, May. The meeting in Geneva that ended the fighting between the French and Ho Chi Minh. The 17th parallel was established, dividing the two Vietnams. "My husband had been invited to participate by Eisenhower to promote the bipartisan atmosphere, though Emerson often claimed that he was meant to keep an eye on Mister Dulles." She laughs pleasantly at the memory of those days.

"Why was that?"

"Well, Mister Dulles often had very strong views about things. We called him the Christian Soldier. The year before he had talked about dropping atom bombs on the Vietminh around Dienbienphu and my husband was one of those voices—" she says the word in such a way that it calls up not only the halls of Washington but the ancient, echoing forums of the Roman senate, "raised against the *ideeah*. He had been advising—sotto voce, of course—General Mathew Ridgeway who was then army chief. He wanted nothing to do with any of it."

"Too bad he wasn't listened to," Strickland says and prepares himself for a long afternoon. The table presents a large buffet, a twenty-year repast that he is expected to partake of. "But see heah that most of the important agreements were vocal between Mendes-France and Chou En Lai as my husband's notes," she says and taps the papers respectfully, "will indicate. Only the military agreemunts were written down. A curious war, that, all those French generals naming their forts from their lady friends." Virginia Caldwell smiles with a fond remembrance that seems to go back to cotillion times, crinoline skirts sweeping up the floors of Richmond.

Then, as if the shades had suddenly flown up in the windows across the street, Strickland catches his breath. Had that been what all of it had been about? T. D. Moon, in those last minutes of his life, had said it—*Was it as good as it seemed or was it only just so young looking, childlike.* Could it be that a country was devastated, millions of lives torn apart, a generation or two sent to whimper in the corners of their lives, tons of resources squandered, pissed away—all over pussy? The place reeked of it, he remembers, but maybe that was the way it had been from the beginning. The French had named military installations for their mistresses. They brought in plane loads of the silkiest birds from Marseilles for the delectation of their little yellow brothers. Old Bao Dai, he remembers hearing, had a beautiful blonde number appointed to his cabinet. Minister of Oral Transport. "She's only doing her job," the Emperor was supposed to have told some American Presbyterian, maybe Caldwell. "I'm the whore."

So was that it? He looks around the table at the papers assembled by the diplomat's widow, all the commonplace and cliché-ridden documents that would reveal nothing to him on this fool's errand that Moon had sent him on. None of them contained any mention of the vulva, the various uses to which female flesh could be put on the back alleys off Lam Son Square. *Hey, Yank—thwee way, yank.* Nothing in any of them that might have Henry Kissinger lean over to Le Duc Tho in Geneva and say something like, *Ve must weach some agreement on zee responsible and appropriate realignment of vagina rights.* That's what it had been about?

Virginia Caldwell has moved down the table to the next setting. "Before we leave 1954, it's worthwhile noting my husband's opposition to the Southeast Asia Treaty Organization, which was Mister Dulles's ideah mostly."

"But he never came out against it in public."

"Clearly here." She taps the 1954 pile of papers. "You can read it for yourself. Then, heah is 1955 and Mr. Diem comes into the picture, becoming president of what he called the Republic of Vietnam."

Virginia Caldwell continues like one of those hostesses in a restored mansion, a gracious guide through chambers she might have claimed as her own but for an accident of economy or history. Strickland is placing himself in those rooms as well. In 1955 he and Nancy were trying out the new furniture of their marriage. Leslie about to be born. It was a time of country inns in the chill of autumn and Nancy was the Princess of Hot Chocolate and he had begun to tinker with his success as a professional voice. Wasn't that the American story? Tinkering with a little quirk in something, whether a personal flaw or an apparatus that didn't quite work, so that the bicycle put on wings and flew or the greased parchment talked and conveyed messages? Squawk, squawk—that's Caruso, folks!

Emerson Caldwell had tinkered with his smartness as a history professor and become adviser to Presidents, messenger for the gods. Brought East from Chicago. The academics were tinkering with foreign policy, economic programs—you name it—in those days. Something about their tweed jackets, the patches on the elbows, that made their opinions and their ideas alluring. T. D. Moon, authority on American Literature, invited to discuss Cooper's *The Spy*. In fact, Mrs. Caldwell is saying, "And heah is 1959 when we first met your Professor Moon in Saigon. He was a Fulbright Professor at the University theah. My husband, of course as you know, was advising—heah, heah's an entry which will interest you."

Strickland takes the old memo from her spotted hands. The typing does not have the standard evenness of a pool secretary; obviously something the Ambassador must have knocked off on his own. A communication too important to be risked outside his own purview.

LUNCH WITH DIEM TODAY. TWO AMERICANS, A MAJOR BUIS AND SGT. OVAND KILLED BY INSUR-GENTS NEAR BIENHOA. I THINK THE FISH COURSE HAD GONE BAD.

1959. The two soldiers must have been almost the first to go, Strickland thinks, and the ambassador was kind enough to note their deaths as he reviewed the luncheon. Strickland remembers hearing the first two casualties, had been watching a movie when they were shot dead. But here were their epitaphs wrapped up with spoiled fish. They used to wrap fish in old newspapers, didn't they? "Yes?" he looks up expectantly at the ambassador's widow. Surely she waits to let him in on the answer; what does this memo mean? She is giving him the fraternity house mother look, as if he knows the joke, wonderfully wicked boy that he is, and she's too much of a lady to speak about it directly. *Pussy*, Strickland thinks to himself, and then looks back at the paper quickly, feeling his face grow warm.

"So you can see," she finally says, taking the precious document from Strickland's fingers and putting it back carefully in the pile. He nods. "And heah is 1960 and President Kennedy and that lovely Jacqueline."

Sex again. After decades of FDR and Eleanor, Harry and Bess, Ike and Mamie—the country goes crazy with the idea of two people humping in the White House. In Lincoln's bed, even! "Who is this Emerson Caldwell?" Nancy asked him. It was the 1950s again when so much seemed possible. He had come down to Northampton to see her. They had dated off and on since Furness; quiet walks on the Smith campus, bowls of chowder in town, kisses fragrant with New England. The Princess of Hot Chocolate. Surely she did not have a body beneath the cashmere sweater, limbs to caress within the folds of the pleated, flannel skirt. She couldn't be like other women.

Someone to watch, this Emerson Caldwell, so his English professor, T. D. Moon, had said. A real neat guy, this English professor, he told Nancy. She raised the mug of hot chocolate to her wide mouth. He had been invited to Professor Moon's special get-togethers. Moon served Scotch whisky and they talk about all sorts of stuff. Nancy liked that, liked the idea of him being there with the other fellows. He thought something turned on in her eyes as they sat in the diner in Northampton that weekend. Emerson Caldwell had been contributing pieces to the *Atlantic*, to the *New Republic*, and Professor Moon read them at these informal meetings. Essays on the Cold War.

"Cold War," Nancy said sometimes, turning the phrase over thoughtfully, though she had been thinking something else, apparently. "What a funny expression, Cold War." They were walking down the street, hand in hand. He could visualize how they looked. Like every other couple that weekend, like pairs of mannequins animated by a gentle wizard and turned loose from store windows all over New England. Wound up and set going in tweeds and gray flannel. It was like becoming a member of a new race of beings and it wasn't just the clothes, either. It was those afternoons in Professor Moon's library with the aromas of pipe tobacco and malt whiskey. It was this girl walking beside him, holding his hand and being just so perfect for the afternoon, for the next ten or even twenty years of afternoons and even the nights too. Maybe forever perfect, looking perfect for the part. But she had been saying something all this time, as Strickland remembered his sense of well-being that day long ago. So many possibilities, it seemed, so many ways to go.

She had been saying she didn't have to be in that night. Indeed, she didn't want to go back to her dorm that night. She had signed out for a cousin's house in Connecticut. Old cousin Cora Endicott, who lived near Salisbury in Lakeville. Well, he could drive her there. He had borrowed a car from a friend, another one of Mooney's Boys. Once you were in this special group, everyone took care of each other. She didn't want to go to Connecticut either, Nancy Endicott was saying, a little smile on her like a secret. Let's get in the car and head somewhere, maybe find an atmospheric inn—already the joke was a familiar link between them. Did she mean—somewhere? She had nodded. What if they find out? What if they check her cousin's in Connecticut and she's not there? You've got to be kidding, the Princess of Hot Chocolate said, and pulled him along to the car.

They found a motel near Springfield that Strickland felt was discreet enough and where the lady at the desk didn't even say a word, just handed him the key after he handed her the fifteen dollars so the elaborate narrative he had put together with false identifications remained untested. He felt strangely frustrated. When did such cover-ups become unnecessary? It was a different world all of a sudden.

But that was just the beginning. The room was small and damp and the bathroom had no shower curtain. Nancy had looked it over, shrugged, and wiped off the top of the water closet to put down the zippered plastic bag she had been carrying in her leather purse. Her traveling kit, she said and laughed. Toothbrush, shampoo, deodorant, and diaphragm. A diaphragm, no kidding— he could hardly believe it. All that afternoon as they walked around Northampton, talking about Emerson Caldwell, the fellowship of Mooney's Boys, what movies they had seen, all that time she was carrying around this diaphragm. In her bag. He didn't think anyone at school knew a girl who had a diaphragm. But Nancy Endicott who wore Peter Pan collars and looked like a coed on the cover of *Saturday Evening Post*, she not only had one but knew how to use it. The very idea enthralled him; her ownership of the device gave her an unexpected sexuality he wasn't sure he could handle but which excited him tremendously.

Only for a few moments, as he drove the gritty streets of Springfield's outskirts looking for a liquor store, did he wonder why she owned such an item and for how long. None of that mattered, he quickly decided, and the wisdom of this attitude, this newfound sophistication, pleasantly surprised him, as it seemed to set him apart, if not from every man in the world, certainly from every classmate at school. He had a woman waiting for him, waiting for him and the bottle of Scotch she had sent him out for, she who looked like she came out of an ad for Colgate toothpaste, and who was prepared to go all the way in this motel room off of Route 5.

When he returned with the whiskey, Nancy had already hung up her camel-hair blazer in the closet and had carefully folded her dark green cashmere sweater and gray flannel skirt to place them on the pressed-wood top of the rickety bureau. Her loafers were set neatly, toes lined up, against the wall by the bed, and the knee socks hung over the back of the one chair like some illustration for a Christmas story. Yet, wasn't this a gift of some sort she was about to bestow on him? The headmaster's daughter sat on the end of the bed watching a basketball game on the black-and-white TV as she waited for him, waited for the Scotch. He couldn't get over it, and the certainty of what was going to happen next, pretty soon anyway, stopped him inside the door, the brown paper package in the crook of his elbow. Nancy Endicott waited for him in her underwear.

What? She turned from the TV. The flickering light caught the sterling-silver barrette fastened in her hair. She started to look uncomfortable, a thread of second thoughts sewing up her expression. He had to say something quickly. Just your underwear, he remembers saying randomly, though he would think later, years later, that his response had not been so arbitrary. What about it? She looked down at herself. It's black. Brassiere, half slip, everything was black. When she laughed, her eyes looked back up at him with the same light he remembered that afternoon in her father's library at the smoker for new boys. *Hi,* it said, *you must be the new boy from Kansas.*

Later, they found a Chinese restaurant in Springfield and went to a movie about strategic air command pilots with Rock Hudson. He left the movie feeling very much a part of that world, those courageous, tight-lipped men, and their patient, adoring wives who waited for them on the ground, keeping up bright, Technicolor kitchens (their own form of courageous duty, and who was to say, really, who was the more brave) so that when he handed Nancy into the car after the movie, a tingle, a thrill went through him when he touched her bare arm, not just because of the remembrance of what she had shown him earlier, nor the sense that the same lesson was about to be gone over again, but that the two of them had become a part of something much larger and more wonderful than he could ever have hoped for. That he would try to meet this glorious test he never doubted for a moment as they drove back to the motel. He even silently swore an oath of eternal loyalty to her as she tried to get some music on the car radio.

The road ahead had been empty of traffic and clearly marked. No possibility of making a mistake, taking the wrong route because, he would think later, from that afternoon on there had been only one route possible. Amazingly, a few hours earlier, sipping hot chocolate in the diner in Northampton, the ways he could have gone had been without number.

Chapter

9

"*Nineteen sixty-three,* a pivotal year," Mrs. Emerson Caldwell is saying. She neatens a stack of documents halfway down the table. "Henry Lodge comes to Saigon. A very deah man. A gentleman."

"You knew him?" Strickland moves closer, takes up some of the papers. Maybe this pile, maybe a note in the old history professor's meticulous hand—something about the fish course wasn't quite right but the message was delivered anyway—a culinary review that might free him if he could only find it. He is holding his breath as he sifts through the memoranda, the onion-skin carbons of findings, recommendations, trying to be casual, trying to seem as bored by these papers as he has been by the others.

Virginia Caldwell recites some genealogical connection with the Cabots and the Lodges of Boston, and that was no surprise, for it had been his instruction that they were all related. The Endicotts were in there as well. Smelting the ore from around Silvermines and Salisbury into links and then into anchor rodes for the Continental Navy. Funny how all those lines of iron or hemp laid down still secure the area, tangled and fouled as they are, they still hold the ground.

Strickland flips through the documents that account Caldwell's first meetings with the Boston Brahmin. In June, the first Buddhist monk torched himself in Saigon. Lodge arrived in August. Caldwell shows up in September. Kennedy, interviewed by Cronkite, says that Diem has to make more of an effort in the war against the insurgents or the U.S. will—will what? Well, reconsider. Nhu, Diem's brother, is acting up and should be given a few knuckles. Will anybody remember these names, Strickland wonders?

All those people down below on Madison Avenue, looking in the windows of wine shops, delicatessens, and boutiques, how many could identify any of those names even now? Or, here's another one. Conien. How many remember him? So Caldwell had met with the 'dirty tricks' squad leader himself.

DINNER WITH LUCIEN CONIEN AT A NOISY PLACE ON TU-DO STREET NEAR THE CARAVELLE. A BIG, TALKY MISSOURIAN. HE SAYS SWOPE PARK IN KANSAS CITY HAS CHANGED A LITTLE.

Is that all there is? Strickland looks up. Virginia Caldwell beams. Her expression says everything; she has done her work well. Strickland looks back at the memo. Maybe it was a code of some kind. Swope Park stood for the Diem regime. Swope Park (the Diem government) has (had to be) changed. Could it be that this former history professor, sent by Kennedy, meets the number-one CIA operator in a Saigon nightclub and they talk about the elephants and the camels at the Kansas City zoo? The lions are off their feed? Concern is expressed here about the baboons. Send more pandas.

"This is it?" he asks and she looks confused. "I mean nothing about President Diem and his brother being killed. Nothing about Kennedy's assassination?"

"Why on earth would my husband have anything to do with any of that?" Her right hand has taken its place upon her bosom, as if she were about to swear an oath of some kind. "He was sick, sick at heart over Mister Kennedy. Heah I'm talking and I haven't offered you anything."

Strickland accepts iced tea with fresh mint. Maybe they had drunk mint juleps on the veranda of the embassy. The heavy blanket of the monsoons just lifting, the drone of Saigon like a screen of cicadas around the enclosure. Lodge might stick with martinis, ice blue in crystal. Conien would have bourbon with Caldwell as they discussed knocking off Diem and Nhu. Did it ever happen?

Washington needs some straight answers? CONFERENCE WITH LODGE AND COL. CONIEN. *What about these generals? Which ones can we rely upon?*

Conien might shake his head. (Music gradually fades in.)

Deplorable, perfectly deplorable, Lodge would say, crossing Ichabod Crane legs. AMBASSADOR LODGE WEARS THIN SILK ANKLETS. *Diem will not talk about any of the questions the President asked me to raise. He just looks at the ceiling and talks about the wisdom of Confuscius. Absolutely deplorable.* JACK DANIELS BOURBON.

The generals have set no timetable, not that I know of, Conien might say. (Drawl of Missouri accent colored by years in France.)

I should tell you (Caldwell's professor tone speaks to inattentive students) that Washington is coming apart over this issue. It must be resolved.

Fine. Let me resolve it, Lodge nods, agrees to his own suggestion.

Washington (Caldwell patiently makes his point) wants some clear answers. The President's brother is suggesting we pull out now. Completely.

That runt, snorts Lodge. (Street sounds.)

Robert Kennedy often sends up trial balloons for the President. Also, he's not the only one. Many think this is the time to get out. Paul Kattenburg is giving the same sermon.

Oh yes, Kattenburg—he stresses the berg *in the foreign service officer's name—was just here, Lodge says and pulls on his nose.* THE ULTIMATE SNEER WHEN LODGE ELEVATES THAT NOSE OF HIS. *The message you have brought me from the President gives me complete discretion in this matter.* JFK'S MESSAGE READ AND COPIED.

Yes, I understand that—Caldwell coming to the edge of his seat in the twilight—but is the coup on or is it off? Washington has no sense of what's happening.

The Colonel knows this better than I—Lodge turning to Conien, that

peculiar patronizing shift of his head on his neck—what about it, Colonel?
(Music abruptly stops.)

    Conien doesn't say anything but drinks from his glass. CONIEN A
BIG MAN, WELL PUT TOGETHER WITH A FRANK, BROAD
FACE. *He resembles the popular English teacher who also doubles as an
assistant football coach.—Well, what about it, Emerson Caldwell finally
asks.*

    *Well, I went to the dentist today, Conien finally says with that peculiar
drawl.*

    *The dentist? Caldwell looks at Lodge quickly. He didn't leave Virginia
and come thousands of miles to talk about such things.*

    *Ho-ho-ho, goes Lodge. Maybe he might have slapped at his knee. He's
in on the joke, of course. That's where the Colonel meets his contact, the
Ambassador would explain to a confounded Caldwell.*

    *I guess I must have just about the cleanest teeth in Southeast Asia,
Conien would say. Well, as to your question, the feeling is that the right ones
are about ready to go. The concern is that the monks might set fire to more than
themselves. There's a lot of tinder lying around and the worry is that the
wrong bunch may start something too soon. So, all I can say is that the time
is getting close. But I have no specific hour or day for you.* GENERAL
CONFUSION AS TO GENERALS PLANS. <u>CANNED</u> PINEAPPLE
FOR DESSERT.

    *By the bye, Lodge might say, do give my very best affection to Virginia.
As a girl, she often visited my sister at Newport——LODGE SENDS
REGARDS TO VIRGINIA. She was splendid at badminton, death at the
net. (Music up and out.)*

    "You see Mister Lodge's kind remembrance of me," Virginia
Caldwell is saying. "He was one of the last gentlemen."

    Sure, Strickland thinks, continuing his own private movie of
those halcyon days. Brother Henry, in his white flannels, gallantly
retrieving the shuttle cock his sister's friend had whacked into the
rhododendrons. Meanwhile and ahead in 1963, Diem and his brother
Nhu catch several dozen rounds of automatic fire as they sit in the
back of an armored personnel carrier. This last of the gentlemen then
cabled JFK that the prospects for a shorter war had been vastly

improved. He threw a party for the generals at the embassy; champagne and, this time, maybe fresh pineapple. Probably one of the last messages Kennedy was to get on the war. He flew to Dallas, thinking—This thing is under control, at last. *So when we get back to Washington, Jacqueline, I want to try out the Dolly Madison love seat in the Blue Room.* Everyone celebrating in Saigon too. Nightclubs full blast. Like a big fraternity party. And there were only 15,000 American GI's in Vietnam by the end of the year. Only 15,000; just advisers.

"You were related?" Strickland asks the ambassador's widow. How mournful the horns of stalled traffic sound to him. Nothing moving below on Madison Avenue.

"Well," she says and nearly bundles up in the question, "very distant. What we call kissin' cousins."

"You'd think he would have held it against Kennedy for beating him. Beating him twice, actually. First for the Senate and then in the Presidential when Lodge was Nixon's running mate." Anyone down there in their cars, trucks, massaging horn buttons and enjoying themselves in that curious urban anger—any of them remember any of this?

"That was the furthest thing from his mind," she says. "He was a true sportsman."

Sure, Strickland is thinking like all of those true sportsmen he had encountered at Furness Academy, those golden boys from Exeter and St. Paul's who would kick you in the balls and then put out a hand. *Deplorable conduct,* they'd say. *I am so sorry. Deplorable,* Lodge would say, *but I'm going to screw you over, you Mick—you and that runt of a brother.*

Strickland looks again at the copy of the typed message he holds in his hand. LODGE SENDS REGARDS TO VIRGINIA. He looks at it again. A code for sure, not about assassination—but recognition. She has called him down this day to see this particular dispatch, this communication that has been kept top secret, under wraps, until now. It was about her. Henry Cabot Lodge had sent his regards to her. Strickland figures a similar reference could be found in each of the piles of documents arranged around the large dining table. The

following year, say—the year of the Tonkin Gulf resolution—
probably a note from Dean Rusk, a fine Southern "gentulman" at
that. MY DEEPEST AFFECTION TO VIRGINIA. And on around
the table, year by year. Strickland's fancy picks a year at random.
1968. Over a half million men in Vietnam now. The butchery of
Hue. Westmoreland takes over. North Vietnam bombed by B-52s.
What would the secret and valuable document in this file reveal?
MURIEL AND I THANK YOU FOR THAT SUMPTUOUS RE-
PAST. YOU MAKE SOUTHERN COOKING ALL THAT IT
SHOULD BE. EVER, HUBERT.

Strickland looks down at the paper in his hand once more.
Perhaps if he turned it upside down it might give up its secret. Put
it in the microwave and the message in invisible ink would appear?
JFK'S MESSAGE READ AND COPIED. Nothing more. Surely this
review should have revealed more. Surely the documents contained
something more than a thankyou note from a vice-president for some
grits and fried chicken? Surely this historical review was arranged to
illustrate something more, something he could slip into his pocket—
the incriminating evidence—and throw into the next waste bin.
Okay, T.D. Moon—mission accomplished.

He thinks about leaving this archive above the mannered clamor
of the Upper East Side, getting down to street level where the noise
is more authentic, and then coming to one of those steel-mesh baskets
the city puts out on some corners of the borough. There, as if he were
only cleaning out his pockets of mint wrappers, old receipts, lint, he
would casually drop in the message from Kennedy to Lodge that
would nail it down: the President of the U.S.A. had ordered the
assassination of the leader of another government. He would casually
drop this directive into the basket, not even bother to tear it up? Even
if it were discovered and read—one of the city's garbage men, a
hard-working guy from Queens, maybe a Vietnam vet—the person
would not understand what it meant. One last misunderstanding.
TAKE HIM OUT. OR: PROMOTE THE GENERALS. Or simply:
OK, JFK. No one would understand the message. In any event, there
was no such message. Maybe never.

"I've found what I want." Mrs. Caldwell looks a little put out.

"But you haven't looked through the rest," she says. "Heah's 1969 when Mister Kissinger is secretly meeting in Paris with the North Vietnamese. My husband accompanied him and made some valuable observations." Her large, once-elegant hands go out to invite him closer to the table and its display. To invite him to the year as well, he can feel her gesture drawing him back toward 1969, toward that other junction where so many roads were possible and where he had turned down one of them, T.D. Moon's arm around his shoulders. "Hey, Bub, you sounded great on the Godfrey show the other day. I want to put you in touch with some guys, you remember Zeke and Toby and old Skip? They have a sweet deal for you."

This is Carrol Strickland for the Voice of America.

"I've found what I need," he hears himself say once more to Virginia Caldwell's disappointment, but it had only been an excuse to leave. This morning, standing in the woods by the sprung traps; he felt stupid and snared in an endeavor that had been both wrong and unsuccessful. He feels the same way now. Pragmatism, that made in America philosophy, might live with one of those determinations but not with both, and Strickland had been educated to see little difference between them anyway.

What he did see, now on the street and waving down a taxi, were the reflections of himself in different windows, the same images he had looked through all day long; but their thin print of innocence not seen through by him, not even now. Just poses that look a little ridiculous and which were untenable, to use some of the old jargon. What he had said to Mrs. Caldwell was true and not just an excuse to quit her little shop of antique conspiracies. He had found not what he wanted, but what he needed. Moon, directing him on this fruitless search, had shown him something unexpected. As he gives the cabbie directions to the parking garage, he wonders if that may have been the old professor's intention all along; a last exercise for the kid from Kansas, a final lesson.

The Volvo took the turns of the Taconic Parkway as if they were the bends in the Monte Carlo. He could almost drive the road blindfolded, and he keeps his foot down on the accelerator, scouting the familiar territory ahead, knowing the different locations where state troopers usually park with radar. It is a good omen, a concordance with his new sense of purpose, that no cops are on station. He thinks of Leslie, of how to tell her of the new job. John Boy. He'll make a pile. They'll sell the house at Silvernales and go west. Go to California, maybe she'll like that. A lot of opportunities for her out there. The whole atmosphere of Southern California, the beaches, the emphasis on physical fitness. It will be good for her.

Then he would take care of Robin Endicott. All of her poses and attitudes, those demure moues put on for his inspection; what were they but reflections of a woman that no longer stood before reality? He would strip away these false self-impressions, these delusions, as he had erased his own, so she could be herself and the two of them could be straight with each other. Start again. Together they could make a haven; they would become fellow conspirators. It is a mystery, Strickland thinks as he glances down at the speedometer; the suddenness with which a person can become so all-important to your life, a mystery at once frightening and exhilarating. He speeds through the intersection at Hopewell Junction.

"Take it easy," Nancy had said. They were driving down with Leslie to see *Nutcracker*. A very cold winter with little snow and the Taconic was clear and wide open. His mind was full of other views, sounds; he had only been home for a week. Around Hopewell Junction they hit a patch of ice and he felt the wheels go out of control. He wrestled the Ford LTD wagon, completely reversing the wheel right to left, left to right, trying to keep the car on the highway. Then the road leveled out, flat fields on either side, no fences, no trees. He let the car go and it bumped over the shoulder and into the frost-crusted field where its wheels gradually took hold, slowly becoming dependent on the car's mechanics once again and responsive to his hands on the wheel. They stopped. "Where in hell were you?" Nancy asked. Leslie peeked up from the back seat. *Wow.*

He had been going back to hell, drifting down the beautiful Taconic Parkway—FDR's gift as governor to his Dutchess County friends. Americans were killing Americans at that very moment.

"Fragging," it was called. Some young shavetail out from the States, still earnest about bringing democracy to the slants. The grunts knew better and if he couldn't be reeducated then he'd find a live grenade in his pack. *Hello, Sir, here's an apple from the teacher.* Whole units coked silly. Blacks and whites taking shots at each other. Men slept with their guns cocked but not because of the Vietcong. Because of the good ol' boy from Birmingham in the next hooch over. Saigon had become like a huge pudding, rich and so flavored with high caloric evil that the senses became clogged, addicted. As visions of sugar plums danced in little Leslie's head, Strickland was thinking he didn't want to go back; yet he couldn't wait to get back. He was an addict—not to the obvious licenses, the mayhem, but to the falsehood of it. The pointlessness. The total silliness. What had the point been to any of it? Had it ever had a point? *This is Carrol Strickland with the point.* Then the wheels went funny.

"Look out," Nancy was suddenly saying. "Jesus, look out! Get down, Leslie." And all that happening right here. Strickland looks across the median at the field next to the southbound lanes. Actually, Nancy had about seven or eight more years among the living right then. And he had almost taken them all out that morning in December. Strickland rolls up the window next to him, as if the April breeze had become chilled. But not yet dead. "You're not bringing back some cruddy disease, are you?" Later that night, safe at home, after Leslie had fallen asleep over a glossy program of slim ballerinas, Nancy had paused to look close at his penis.

No, never. At least not that sort of disease. He was so safe he was a walking Boy Scout manual. One of the perks of the business—free penicillin, morning-after pills, the works. Safe, so far, in that field back there—safe home he had thought, sitting behind the wheel of the station wagon that cold morning, the motor ticking over innocently, as if it had not almost pulled them into eternity. He remembered thinking of all he had been near in Vietnam, and then to have almost chucked it over on this December morning in Dutchess County, New York, with all the sweet perks of that life around him. Safe home. Where had Robin Endicott been that morning in December? Had she been safe in a field somewhere, her own disaster idling momentarily? Maybe going to see *Nutcracker* too, but by train down from Hartford? He coasts through the Poughkeepsie interchange, continuing north. Silvernales is twenty minutes away.

She is about the same age as Leslie, he figures. A few years older. He knows little about her but he imagines a similar morning—she and her family going somewhere. Something almost happened. She would not be swaying, head turned down and to one side, a figure that had become familiar in all the rooms of his imagination. And that's the mystery of it, he thinks. Was this other person always "there," beside your life, carrying on her own agenda in completely different rooms, perhaps spinning out of control sometimes but coming to rest safe in an alter field and then through a chance turn, you come face to face? The two of them like spheres in different orbits, self-contained in their particular cosmos, Strickland thinks, and then through a freakish shift of the atmospheric current, the orbits intersect.

But first he has some housekeeping to do. He cannot leave those traps in the woods. The whole ridiculous folly of that enterprise makes him laugh as he grips the steering wheel. What kind of crazy game had he been playing? Some kind of paranoia leftover from 1975? Some of the guys had booby-trapped their liquor cabinets at the Hotel Duc, before they left. He shifts down for the driveway and turns off the pavement, through the open gate and up into the pasture behind the house. When Leslie was little, the three of them used to drive up into the fields to pick apples in an abandoned orchard far back. The first couple of years in Silvernales they thought this orchard belonged to them, was part of their property. Boundary lines were only casually observed in those days and no one worried about trespassing. Neighbors were neighbors, even if you were from the city and showed up on the Johnny Carson Show. *The missus and me saw you onto that television program the other evening.*

Then another city couple bought the orchard, bulldozed a road into it and put up a weekend cottage. Sometimes, back from the war, Strickland would put on an old pair of boots and walk over to the high ground above that orchard to spend whole mornings observing that cottage, imagining what it must be like inside. He shifts the Volvo down once again, feels the wheels slide, take hold, and the car jerks forward, up the rise of the corn lot. The ground is wet with the spring thaw, and Schuyler has fertilized the field as well—the smell of manure comes up through the floorboards, through the seams of steel—not even Swedish craftsmanship can keep the odor out. Beyond, he sees the line of woods, the large sycamore with the hawk's nest in its top branches. He almost expects the windshield to splatter with the star shapes of enemy fire. But there is no gunfire. They are watching the red Volvo approach. He's sure of it. Watching and waiting.

The car becomes stuck, mired down in a sinkhole of wetness, the mud and slime churned up by the wheels as the rear end sinks deeper and deeper and the dark brown concoction is thrown up inside the fender wells and the underbody, an undercoating of offal. He leaves the car. He can get Schuyler to come over with one of his tractors to pull him out. *Now that we're alone, Mister Strickland, I'd like to ask for the hand of your daughter. Or maybe you can just get that fancy foreign car of yours pulled out of the shit by someone else.* Maybe he'll call the garage over in Green River.

As the ground becomes higher it becomes drier, and Strickland cleans off his boots as well as he can with a handful of dead weeds. His fingers become stained with the stuff. The woods are still. At the base of the sycamore he sees only the debris of last autumn. The traps are gone.

Could he have made a mistake? No, here's the fresh wound in the tree's root where he had screwed the eye of the trap's chain. He starts to trash the area, then stops, carefully looking before each step. They could have moved them, set them up anywhere. His own woods, his own property is now off limits. He has become a trespasser on his own land, and the offense would be instantly punished by the cold snap of steel jaws. Strickland stops, chilled in the shade of the woods but afraid to walk toward the sunlight of the open field below.

The sound of a motor turns him toward the far fields in the direction where the old orchard lies. Three fields over, one of Schuyler's new Chevrolet pickups comes up over a knoll, turns around by a crumbling stone wall and stops. From where he stands the truck has a toylike appearance, but then Leslie gets out and then young Schuyler. The farmer takes her hand and they walk slowly toward a small stand of birch just coming into leaf, the sunlight washing the yellowish green leaves with brilliance. Strickland shouts but they cannot hear. If he runs to warn them, he might hit a trap—if he steps cautiously he will not catch them in time. In time for what, to stop what? Even now, their two figures have moved behind the shimmering tapestry of the birches. The young man has put his arm around her waist. Strickland wants to warn them of the danger. One step and her foot would be crushed. They'd have to amputate on the spot to get her out of the woods. She would cry *Daddy, it hurts. It hurts.*

PART
II

PART

II

Chapter

I

Affection was a burden Robin Endicott did not wish to carry. She could do without desire. The smaller expressions still bothered her; the courtesies Carrol Strickland was always doing like opening doors, standing up when she left or returned to a restaurant table—pleasantries that seemed to draw attention to her in an unwanted manner, unduly, that made her turn her head away, a kind of slow shrug that disclaimed such attention and which, perversely, made someone like Strickland want to bestow even more upon her. "You don't have to do that," she often said. Part of her felt such considerations had to be earned, were in any event like an unwanted gift, so when these tokens of respect dropped on her, they only rattled her composure, actually made her feel a little angry sometimes, as if a joke was being played on her.

"Why do you do that?" she'd say to some guy over from Yale. Dumbfounded—they always got that stricken ox look on their faces—and this one stood there with her parka clutched in his hands, all of his training in good manners and decorum being challenged, and she would take the jacket from him and slip her arms into its sleeves by herself. The whole weekend down the drain because he had held her coat out for her; she could read these calculations of dismay in his face—so much for this, this amount for that and the Bib Lit. assignment put aside besides. Oh c'mon, she'd say and pull him out of the place and to whatever motel room he had rented to fuck her in, a rush in her veins already because of his expression changing, because she had controlled that change. She had done that to him, like a fairy princess, with a wave of her hand that had almost made his zits pop out. So she had had her pleasure before they even got to the place.

"Robin is her own best friend," her mother would say. "She gets that from my family." She liked this distinction between herself and the Endicotts, even though she bore the name. Their manner put her off. Even family members like her father who were not in the direct line to the real power but played at being vice-presidents in the rope business outside of Hartford; she could remember him walking around like a snooty butler in an old movie, carrying a tray of credentials that weren't his.

So she had got this reputation of being independent, and later a feminist, though that was undeserved, for she came to the understanding early on that she would always be dependent on men. Men reached for her to pet and cosset her. Always a hand reaching out, not because she was especially pretty nor, as she matured, did she fulfill the requirements of the current desirability. For example, she thought her nose was a horror; long and thin, with a slight hook at the bridge that she could foresee becoming witchlike as she got older. Definitely not the compact, retroussé snout of a Endicott, and she would study it before her bedroom mirror, her gaze drawn to it from the frightening appearances of her new breasts, and lament this one distinction from her father's family. She would be a crone before her time. Then, after many such afternoons before the mirror, certain poses and attitudes began to assert themselves and a kind of persona appeared that she liked. A lift and turn of the head and the nose enforced the independent Robin. Look down and away, and the innocent Robin made her entrance, not entirely sure of herself but with a hint of courage. So hands, men's hands, reached for her to harness this independence; they reached to stroke the innocence.

She thought about this a lot; long afternoons going into

dusk—her favorite time of day—in which she might sit unmoving, staring at a flower in a vase, or the contour of a distant field, mesmerized by the beauty as her mind distilled everything, even desire; a purification that left her like the clearest spring water, like the serenity years ago in Hartford when Julien would jab her butt with a load of smack.

Yesterday afternoon Carrol had trouble getting it up though he wanted her, but his desire was frozen in his head by a climate of worries—about his daughter, about hunters trespassing his property—he talked about these things with a disarming frankness, but if he really had had desire, she thought, all those worries would have been melted down and recast, hardened into something he could use, so he would have reached for her like all the others.

"It's this rubber," he had complained.

"We are really strangers. All of your experiences in Vietnam. You know nothing about me. Who I may have been with." She sat up primly and refastened her hair atop her head, looking down and away slightly, knowing how she appeared, knowing what her uplifted arms did to her pretty breasts, and that it would be difficult for him to believe, just then, that she had ever been with anyone. But none of that had affected him. He lay on the day couch like something that should have a label: PUNCH DELI KEY.

Then she had jounced off the studio pull-out humming merrily like a school girl, slipped on a pair of high-heeled clogs, and only those, and clomped behind the drapery drawn across the primitive kitchen of the loft. "Let's have some tea." His sigh thrilled and amused her.

A temporary disfunction, the books would call it, and it seemed to her that this mechanical design gave women a particular edge over men. Men required desire or affection or curiosity or—remembering the rage in Max's face at the restaurant—even anger sometimes, but women need only lie and lie there. Didn't this disparity explain some of the fury in the feminist rhetoric? The awful irony of the design, the differences in the design that permitted men to use women against their wills—wasn't this proof enough that God was male?

But if the truth be known, to use Carrol's own language,

couldn't this accessibility built into women, this perpetual open season, as it would seem, be turned to a woman's advantage? Men had no way of hiding their feelings—they either stuck out there or not—whereas women's feelings one way or the other did not have to accompany their usage. One way or the other. And there was something else.

"What's that?" she had asked Julien long ago.

"When these old guys show you their dicks, it's supposed to turn you on, okay? You drop the school books and get to work, okay?"

"I don't know I can do this." But how had she been able to do any of it? The walls and ceiling around her; a cell blotched like bad skin, wooden laths showing in places. The hall outside of his room smelled of urine and kerosene. The mattress on the floor was sour. She always carefully folded her clothes and put them in a paper bag she brought with her. Sometimes as Julien fucked her, she watched roaches tippy-toe along the edge of the baseboard, like a TV cartoon, comically they went back and forth. Sometimes it made her giggle, which annoyed Julien and he would take forever to come, going on and on. Oddly, the heroin never bothered him that way.

Like in a dream or a hokey novel, she could review those two years, watch this other girl move through those rooms smelling of plastic and old coffee grounds and pine disinfectant; somehow never touched by anything that happened in them. In the end she had felt sorry for Julien—all of his fearsome regalia falling away so, actually he was like all other men, but would she ever forget how he looked leaning up against the huge Harley-Davidson parked in the driveway. *Julien is outside,* some one said over the beat of the music. She thought of a saint. His name, Julien. He never joined the party in the house, older than the rest and out of school. Standing outside of things. She had gone outside to where he was, right away feeling better listening to Television and the screaming laughter from a distance. Being apart from it, as she had been apart from it all along but only realized it right then, going through the motions until Julien gave her that perspective, the distance that had been inside of her from the beginning. He brought her out, as he kept telling her proudly, as if she were a racehorse or an athlete and the idea tickled her at first, then took another meaning one evening, looking across the dining-room table at her father and mother eating Mrs. Somebody's Chicken Pot Pies off of Great Aunt Cora's Haviland china—nor had her father been given the complete set, her mother often reminded her. It was like looking at them from outer space, a view enhanced by the needles Julien talked her into just to join him, to be one with him, something to share as they looked in from the outside.

A calmness had spread through her like the ointment Cora had applied to a sunburn that one summer, all of her on fire but for where the straps of her new sun dress had crossed. Her blistered flesh a warning that she had toddled into a garden she was not supposed to be in, that was off limits to her branch of the family, but then the fabulous peace of Cora's magic cream, a mixture of herbs and the jelly from millions of bees, a smell like sweet grease slightly powdered, like something brought up from the depths of an old purse. Money smelled like that.

So it was all one. Robin was convinced that she had been prepared for Julien; that the instantaneous relief of Cora's luxurious cream was the same as the calm Julien injected into her after the first, tiny bee sting of the needle. If she had not got that fierce sunburn, if her parents had not parked her with Cora that summer—her life was full of *ifs* and there was no point in reviewing them. But the calm of him as she saw him that first time, leaning up against the motorcycle in the driveway of the party house. He could make her feel so easy, so calm. St. Julien. He even looked like one of those old warrior saints, someone who had done all the violent things a person could do, cleansed his blood of all the rage possible for a human and was now ready to live a life of peace and sanctity.

Even as he shifted up against the saddle of the hog, he creaked and made metallic noises as if he wore armor; though the most endearing little tings also, so he wasn't really frightening; like the sounds of a gift shop door, opening and closing as customers came and went, which was in fact happening as she stood there. People approached from the noise of the party to do their whispered business with Julien, who responded with a crink of leather, a brush against chrome like a cymbal being lightly tapped—everything put together himself, she instantly recognized. Nothing inherited in any of his gestures, in his pose, but everything earned, everything original and with weight. He had three, maybe more dimensions to him that were all his own. She had stood there watching as his voice slipped from the corner of his mouth and he looked sideways at the figures in the shadows, and then without warning he was looking straight into her. Right into her. "What are you looking for?"

Peace. She had been looking for peace but hadn't known it until he had asked her, hadn't known it until he offered it, carefully prepared it for her as she had watched him cook it in the spoon with a fleur-de-lis on its handle, part of a service he had burgled from a house in New Britain. Already his smallish cock would be hard, as if the very act of preparing the heroin, pulling it into the syringe, were some kind of foreplay, and, thinking back, the sexual act had been redundant, a poor substitute for what he had already done to her. Years after, when she had walked out of all those foul rooms, somehow closed the doors and walked away, she had come across a novel by Faulkner about a girl taken and raped with a corncob and she identified with Temple Drake. Desire might be a constant but it was also odorless, colorless, only the implement used made the difference, gave it a form.

"No, you don't have to do this," Julien had said, patiently holding the spoon over the flame. "But this stuff has gone out of sight. You're going to have to split the bill, you know? Your baby's got a big appetite."

"How did that happen, I wonder?"

"Hey, kiddie, this is Julien, remember? You had the deck. Did I presume upon you? Did I? Did I tell you what card to play?"

"No." He held the hypodermic up and away from her line of vision as she lay on her stomach. She felt cold sweat push through her flesh. "But . . ."

"Sure, you can do without it maybe. They got places you can go. Your people can afford it. But then your ritzy family will find out you're a fucking needle queen."

"They're not ritzy."

"Hey, this is Julien, I been to your house, remember? All them Chinese gongs and big dishes on the tables with marble eggs. I seen them, okay?"

"So who are they? What do they want? These men."

"They're old guys. You see them sitting around the park. No one will know you. You don't even have to take your clothes off, okay. They just want a blow job. Put your hair in braids and tell them you're twelve or fourteen."

"I'm sixteen."

"That's too old. They want something younger. You got to look like it's the first dick you've seen, okay? Every time, you act like that. It's like being in the movies. Like it makes you hot just to see it, okay?"

"Hot?" The word made her giggle.

"This is business. Nothing funny about how much this shit costs. You come here like you own the fucking deal. You think you're some kind of fucking royalty or something? So, you want this? You going to contribute? You going to share?" One of his hands rested on her left buttock, squeezed it, pulled it.

"Okay. Yes. Yes . . ." She pressed her face against her arms, breathed in the air filtered through the cruddy mattress as if it were a sea breeze and let her desire reach out, assume the shape of its release.

If she were a man, she thought yesterday as she fixed some herbal tea for Carrol Strickland, she wouldn't care what the woman felt. Even those senior citizens back in Hartford who knew why that girl in braids and knee socks showed up at their doors, even they insisted that she deceive them with a forgery of desire. So she had been able to invent a kind of freedom within the tyranny that had taken her over. Peculiar that men need such deception, but a woman's facility to invent it reverses the roles, Robin figured. At least evens things out a little.

"Robin, honey, don't you have homework?" her mom would say.

"I did it already." And she had. Four algebra problems and an essay for history—"The Congregational Church in Connecticut"—

had been pretty much worked out in her head as she took care of three old guys that afternoon. *Hey, you're a nice girl,* they'd say. *How old you say you are? Twelve? Only twelve? You're a hot number.* Yes, she was hot, she'd say and continue.

"That's a terrible story," Carrol Strickland said and sipped the tea.

"But with a happy ending," Robin said. "My grades went up and I managed to get into Vassar on a scholarship. I got away." Her voice took on that mournful quality of self-mockery, and of course she hadn't told him everything. Yet she had guessed right. His interest in her was directly proportional to her life's adversity—up to a point.

"But you came through it," he said. "You got out of it." She knelt beside him on the low bed, and she could tell by his expression that Strickland could not yet believe that this slim young woman was perched beside him and naked. It was a familiar mixture of amazement and reverence, not unlike the expressions that had greeted her in Hartford, when doors opened on the smells of cabbage and the waxed dirts of linoleum and she would be standing there on the landing with her book bag slung over one shoulder.

That may have been the problem yesterday afternoon. The unexpected jut of her breasts, the sharp angle at her waist and swell of hip; the very ingredients that should have inspired Strickland's desire somehow made a powerful antidote to neutralize it. Free for his taking and he could not take; perhaps because it was free.

"Let's get this old thing off, shall we?" she said, putting down her tea mug and pulling at the prophylactic.

"Listen, I'll get a blood test," Strickland said. He looked very naked, she thought, stretched out with only his thick moustache. "We can both get tested. I know a doctor who will keep his mouth shut."

Robin continued to peel off the rubber. She smiled. "What's this? What's going on here?"

"So, the old warrior is not without honor." He had this quaint way of speaking that amused her, a way of disclaiming himself she recognized, so he was different from others that way. But his eyes had that familiar plea in them, begging for release. In college, she had drawn cartoons that featured a traffic jam of men pushing huge erections before them on wheelbarrows. They all had that same look on their faces. Women figures chatted at café tables, paying no attention.

"My goodness," she said, "look what I have." She shifted her position so she could caress herself. His half-mocking language had given her an idea. "Do you mind if I do this?" she spoke to his look. "Doing this makes me very hot."

"Hot," he said and his head turned back on the cushion, a funny smile beneath the moustache. He looked almost boyish. "What a word. Where did you get that word? That's an old expression."

"Hot?" She could feel his excitement surge. "That word? hot?"

"Yes, that word. Yes," he said, and began to buck and moan. His heavy voice seemed to vibrate in her fingers as if she were holding a tuning fork. She shivered slightly and Strickland may have thought that she had also come, but an idea had just taken Robin Endicott with almost the same suddenness as an orgasm. A brilliance broke within her like the sun coming through the afternoon's overcast outside the window. Such things were good signs for her; she had read her future in such configurations before.

The tea leaves stuck to the cups from yesterday, and she sees herself and her mother dressing to go shopping—even white lace gloves in summer—but they'd go past the stores and drive to West Hartford and the frame house off of Farmington Avenue, near Harriet Beecher Stowe's house, where the reader sat behind beaded curtains, ample and confident and with a smile like Aunt Jemima's pancakes, a sibyl wrapped in electric blue silk and a white turban. So very formal and always on time for their appointment, though Robin sometimes wondered if it mattered when they arrived; that is, maybe they were the only clients, the only ones who still believed in this mumbo-jumbo that Miss Stowe's famous book was supposed to have dispersed along with other superstitions and spurious rituals. The careful preparation of the cards, the paisely cloth on the table smoothed and aligned just right, their breaths—her mother's and hers—syncopated as the reader took her time, sometimes pausing, cruelly holding up the careful placement of the pasteboards to speak loudly over her shoulder to someone in the kitchen behind her, a command for the person there to be patient, to wait until she was finished with her professional duties, though Robin could never remember any voice from within asking for attention. Sometimes a canary chirped in the back rooms.

A very promising display. The black face would look down the table with pleased wonder, always mildly surprised by the gift in her own small hands that had turned over this promise of good fortune, card by card. Yes, promising. Her mother's spine rose straight off the ladder back chair, stiff with anticipation. Here, they'd be directed. And here, did they see this card and in this particular order? Oh yes, full of promise. Hope. A good thing they came this particular afternoon because the elements were specially lined up in a felicitous manner. The woman pronounced the word *felicitous* as if it were a rare ornament she had taken from a jewel box, perhaps located in the back room where the bird sang in its cage, maybe a bedroom rather than a kitchen where another person waited for her to give the immediate future a design, a shape of good things to come.

Her mother was always so relaxed when they drove away, her skirt pulled high up on her legs like a girl on a lark, driving her dad's car, and they usually went to the Baskin and Robbins at the Avon Mall for milkshakes and then to Saks and Bonwit Teller and sometimes Macy's where the sales staff didn't seem to mind how many things you tried on. *Poor baby,* her mother would say, *that's adorable on you but* dehors question *price wise.* Between outfits Robin would be left alone with all of herselves in the mirrors of the changing booth, a stranger to all of them, imagining Julien's silent laughter at her in panty hose, slip, and low-heeled pumps. Maybe she ought to dress like this sometime to make the rounds of her clients. How would they react? Changing her image would only give her a different attraction—present them with another fantasy. *Hey, you a rich kid, huh, but you like sucking cock, huh?*

Try this one. Her mother pushed another outfit toward her. They ought to go, Robin said. She'd had enough. How many things had she tried on and this was Bonwit's and a sales clerk had begun to come by, look in expectantly. Just this one and then there's a *très chic* navy blue with a fitted waist and pleated skirt that would be darling on her. She sometimes seemed a prisoner, no escape from the booth, her images in the mirror, her mother's diversion with her. Only later, after a course at Vassar, could she put into words what she perceived that afternoon in the Designer's Corner at Bonwit Teller. She could not escape those who wished to manipulate her by a change of style, a shift of image. Indeed, such alterations would only attract more usage. Instinctively she knew this was a mistake. One more outfit, her mother promised. Then home for dinner, something picked up at a deli, with her flesh still feeling the weight of the afternoon's apparel; the rasp of crinoline, the warm slickness of silk, and the smug embrace of jersey, all the clothes teased her with an unbearable itch.

"I have to speak with you," her mother said that afternoon. Robin had just noticed the car slowing down as it turned into an emergency area. Her breast pounded and she looked down quickly to see if the disturbance was making her blouse quiver. "I wasn't prying, Robin, but I needed a Kleenex and looked in your purse and I saw those cigarettes. How long have you been smoking cigarettes?"

"About a year, maybe a little more." She heard herself as if from a great distance. The early rush-hour traffic drummed around them like surf. Her mother was very angry with her for smoking cigarettes. Not only was it bad for her—hadn't she seen the reports on television, it could give her cancer—but it also was a filthy habit. Despite all the commercials about women coming into their own. Those were models, anyway, her mother continued; she doubted if any of *them* smoked! She wanted her to promise that she would quit. Promise? Robin recalled her mother's mint-flavored breath puffing about her face, seeing close-up the earnest expression and seeing, not for the first time, nothing behind it. The expression of a missionary, Robin would think later, who knew nothing about the natives, nor cared if any of them understood the sermons. Promise? When she nodded, her mother presented the cigarettes to her and she took them and, as she guessed she was expected to do, dropped them out the window. But she made her own promise to herself.

The old telegraph unit fixed to the lapstrake wall buzzes and the angry sound snaps Robin from her reverie. "You can just wait," she says aloud and carefully puts the teacup in the wooden drying rack above the sink. Precious china, delicate and exquisitely painted with bouquets of violets, ribbons of siena and crimson. "You have such beautiful things," Strickland said yesterday. Not many. She cashed in his compliment for a currency of her own. She had promised herself, she told him, that she would rather have few belongings—only two of these teacups and saucers, for example—that were genuine, than a cabinet full of stamped-out glitz. He had listened to her thoughtfully, impressed.

The buzzer razzes once again and she reaches up, almost angrily slaps at the brass lever that cancels the white tin flag behind the glass face. The same care and workmanship that had fitted the wood and stone of the stable together had also been lavished on this small mahogany box that was to summon a groom and, later, the chauffeur. Robin often studied the neat mortises of the corners, the curlicues tooled into the wood by a craftsman's awl. The gold border on the glass was still, in places, as fresh-looking as when a small brush had applied the paint. All of this expertise to fashion a device to call a servant. A wire went to the house, where it terminated in small, round bell buttons throughout the house, not unlike some of those she used to press years ago in Hartford. Tiny tits, she used to think and stick her finger out, push against the nipple.

But what awaited her this morning? Apparently, Cora was up and about, not lying unconscious in her own vomit. Maybe the mail has come. She looks at the brass carriage clock on the pine shoemaker's bench. It's early. Perhaps the old girl wanted her back rubbed or some books returned to the library, or some new ones checked out.

"Yes, yes, yes," Robin says and steps briskly to the drapery that hangs across the end of the room. She already wore her sweatsuit but no shoes. As always, she felt a rash of prickliness when she pulled back the curtain. Her clothes. Everything neatly arranged, and all hers. It must be how a miser feels upon entering his vault. She has an urge to push her arms through the hanging coats and dresses, to enfold them and immerse herself in their textures and softnesses that become an aromatic surf. But there's no time and she pulls a shoe box out from a file of shoe boxes, a little pleased with her self-denial, this sign of confidence-building will power, and snaps it open. The Adidas sneakers are royal blue, matching her sweats, and after lacing them tight she makes a few jaunty skips before the large wardrobe mirror, turning to view herself over one shoulder. "Pretty woman," she hums and laughs.

But it is a funny thing about mirrors, she thinks as she goes down into the courtyard and turns into the garden. The day is warm and bright. What if mirrors kept the images of all they had mutely witnessed, kept all the shapes and shadows and highlights somewhere between the glass and the mercury backing and these remained, only waiting for some new chemical process to develop them? Wouldn't that be some panorama?

The secrecy and solitude of her life had made Robin Endicott's memory into a mirror where she tried on the different ensembles of her history; it was a cheap but engaging form of entertainment, so the idea that mirrors might have some kind of a memory did not seem all that far-fetched to her. After all, were not all human inventions, however banal, some kind of imitation, an outward representation of an inner human aspiration or process? Even as she walked through the garden, probably following the electric line buried under her feet that has just summoned her, she called up images of herself from her own past. For example there—by the sundial—is the little girl in a frilly, white sun dress whose bare arms and shoulders were turning crimson with an inflammation that can never, it turns out, be soothed.

"Oh, I was so worried," Cora Endicott says when Robin comes through the kitchen door. Her great aunt maneuvered the wheelchair around the center island and toward the corner counter where several appliances were plugged in. Coffee has already been turned on, Robin had preset this last night, and she could smell bread toasting in the small electric oven. Cigarette smoke was also in the air. Cora had probably already smoked several.

"Why were you worried?"

"Well, you didn't answer when I buzzed you."

"I'm here, aren't I?"

"Now you mustn't be angry with me, Robin. You're all I have."

"Well, your worry is sometimes a burden. Do you want marmalade on your toast?"

"Lovely, thank you."

"What did you want?" The young woman puts down the jar of marmalade at the place setting on the kitchen table. The jonquil she had put into the crystal bud vase last night looked deliciously edible as well.

"What?"

"You rang the call box. What did you want?" She stares into the withered blankness of Cora Endicott's face. Her great-aunt's expression is that of someone hearing music from another world. "While you remember, I'll get the mail."

The mailbox was at roadside, on the other side of the high privet that masks much of the house from travelers who take this way into Lakeville. The privet also screens out random traffic, sometimes heavy during autumn when the trees turn color, so even if her great aunt had wheeled to the front windows to watch her, she could not have seen Robin look through the mail and take out a a couple of the envelopes and slip them into the elastic waistband of her sweatpants. But of course Cora was still in the kitchen, wheeled up to the table and vigorously chewing up whole bran toast.

"Well, what do we have?" she asks eagerly. Her small, misshapen form vibrates within the silk kimono like an engine out of adjustment.

"Looks like Rev. Sammy Jack Blaine. The Friends of Freedom, and here's something from Nigerian Relief."

"Oh good, we haven't heard from them in a long time."

"The usual Pro-Life brochure, and—this is a new one, isn't it—The Cortez Institute? Something about freedom in Central

America." She puts the stack of mail next to Cora's coffee cup. "I'm going running. Do you need anything?"

"No, thank you, dear. Oh, Robin, I remember why I called you just now." The older woman's face has become sly, like a terrier's. "We've had an invitation to dinner."

Already hot, the morning takes a humid shape around a new sun that lifts vapors from the rain-dashed pavement of the back roads Robin Endicott smartly tracks—one foot after the other, one-two, one-two, one-two—the sounds stapling the blue-clad runner to the road, the road to the lush greenness of spring, this part of Connecticut to the cloudless canopy above. All one, she thinks, and she's part of it too. She is breathing deeply, her even respiration countering the quick tap-tap of her sneakers on the macadam.

More than just part of it, she is the source of this unity. She can feel it go out from her like wavelengths of energy to encompass everything, everyone, and the sense of it—she can almost visualize the aura—gives her workout a snap, her feet cracking down on the road surface just so, her thick hair pulled back in a ponytail and switching back and forth as her head turns right to left and back again. Just like a pony, in fact, a cute pony doing tricks in the center ring with the rose- and cinnamon-colored lights on her. Lift this foot and then the other. *Turn over,* Strickland said yesterday, *like this,* like a little pony, but that didn't work for him either—maybe if she had tossed her hair around like a mane, whinnied or done something cute like that, he would have got a hard-on. Funny men, funny men— funny-funny, men-men.

Dancing about her, she had picked up on him early, dancing about her—even that dinner when he talked about the hunters, meeting with the mafia types up in the woods—even then she could feel his attention like a warm hand placed on a crease of her, a familiar sensation and why, she had always wondered. Why her? Nothing special about her. The tightness in her legs creeps down the tendons behind her knees and not special legs, either, nothing special about the knees, in fact a little bony, but trim. Everything trim. She pictures everything trim; flexing, pulling within the blue sweats. One-two, one-two.

Strickland didn't remember her from the restaurant, not at first. What a night. Max furious. The waitress calling in sick. The power had gone off earlier, a storm knocked down lines, so the prep was delayed. How could he cook like this, Max said, smashing saucepans. He was getting weird then, too. *Just don't hurt me,* she said. She was so flexible, he said. She didn't mind, actually. *Show time,* as Julien would say. Max tying her up like one of his *poulet rôti,* and it was almost restful being helpless. Not responsible. Secure. But why, why her? Flexible, loose. Stay loose. Her arms ache, her thighs feel ready to burst apart. Hang in there, this stage will pass. The blood starts pumping into the muscles, warming, loosening them up. Be a doll, a rag doll. *Be like a doll,* Julien told her. You can't carry a doll but be like one—loose, flexible. Think flexible when you move so they get the idea they can do anything. Anything. Anything. One-two, one-two. That's better. Her legs are warming up, the muscles like corn syrup. Sweet.

There's the problem yesterday. Yesterday with Carrol. He never got a chance to feel that way. *Okay,* she said, *you want this, here 'tis.* Here 'tis, here 'tis. One-two, one-two. He was a courtier. She should have tagged him early. He had expected to win her slowly, bit by bit. First this. Then that. Should have known. That night in the restaurant, the way he came on as he ordered. Lah-dee-dah-dah-dah. One of those courtiers. A gray seducer. Except he wasn't very gray. But like that history professor at Vassar. You inspire me, she told him. No kidding, he said and looked around his office. For what? Some other identity among his credentials? Framed letters from the Guggenheims? Award from the National Endowment for the Humanities? *Mrs. Reagan joins me in congratulating you . . .* No kidding, he said inspire you? Yes. Yes. Yes. Left-right, left-right. He wanted to believe it, believe that fucking her on his desktop was part of his intellectual inspiration. If those other two professors had been men she might have graduated, but she couldn't do that. She had thought about it, but it would have been too obvious.

Yeah team! Team! Team! Her arms are like stones as she raises them over her head, on the last turn now before the gentle rise between hay fields bounded by stone walls built a hundred years back, maybe by someone going off or just back from the Revolution. Alone, the blue figure takes the center of the empty back road like a counter in a board game being advanced along the path of the play by some unseen hand, a throw of the dice way back in those times when the odd-shaped pieces of limestone and quartz were fitted together, and which had set this figure running all the way to the end where the prize was to be collected.

But it is Julien who waits at the intersection a mile off. Robin can barely make out the black dot of him in the greens and blues of the countryside, like something to be connected to other black dots, so that this gentle, venerable landscape would have another, quite different pattern superimposed upon it, something grim but more truthful because it was so black and white, so pitiless in its diagram of how things really worked. Strickland's stories about Vietnam, told to impress her, she supposed, with his feeling of guilt and remorse; therefore what a likable fellow he was to be with—actually they only enforced what Julien had taught her back in Hartford. Carrol misinterpreted her attention; he wasn't showing her anything about himself, but only giving proof to an old lesson she already knew by heart. It was all like that and the rest was make-believe.

The thin pad of envelopes stuck in the waistband of her warm-up pants begins to kiss and pick at her skin as the sweat works its way down her torso to collect around them, to moisten the paper of them so it stuck to her like that handbill pasted there to the pavement— Bazaar and Auction—glued to the pavement by the morning wetness so that the printing might be transferred to the hard macadam much like those decals at Easter time for eggs. One morning she was dying eggs for Easter and the next night she had met Julien. Putting Donald Duck and Minnie Mouse on their smooth sides, she had felt too old to be standing at the kitchen sink in Hartford decorating Easter eggs but didn't quite know why, though looking back, it was a kind of rite of passage toward him, he who waited ahead for her in that driveway at the party as he now waits at the intersection like a black knight out of King Arthur, ready to claim a trophy, a toll.

But who's in charge, who's in charge? I'm in charge, I'm in charge. Yeah team. Here she comes, he's thinking, feeling full and sure of himself, never thinking he's the runner. He's the runner, he's the runner. Max showed her that. Max, the sober Boy Scout leader, so serious with his knots and little ribbons, never knowing that he showed her who's in charge. Really, really who's in charge. I'm in charge. Those times with him, like a zany package, all wrapped up and going no place, if she had crossed her eyes or stuck her tongue out, made a silly face, she would have blown the scene apart. Control, control. Poor Max, he was so helpless when he made her helpless.

Big finish coming up the rise. No. She'd stop a little ways and walk the distance to where he sits on his new hog, the chrome a little worse for wear, one saddlebag a little out of line, let her muscles slowly loosen up as she gently cools down, let him watch her walk slowly toward him, taking her time, the envelopes pressing against her belly like lithographs transferring their glossy illustrations through the sweat-soaked paper onto her flesh. Sexy navel, Strickland said yesterday, his lips moving across her skin to pause, then press against the dimple, a prelude, a practice for things to come. Who's in charge? I'm in charge. Here she stops running, one step coming slowly after the next until she walks purposefully toward the black figure leaning against a black motorcycle parked beside a broken-down stone wall. Crows, the color of him, cry their fierce alarms and rise to dominate the sky.

Chapter

2

The night of Strickland's dinner, Cora will insist that they go by way of Irondale. She wants to stop at the old general store that was made into the centerpiece of the old mining town by a developer some years back, a restoration to promote his real-estate business.

"He just brought in a crew of painters and repainted the whole town overnight, all different colors," the old woman says. She hugs herself. "We'll just find something amusing at the general store to take Carrol as a little gift," she'll say to Robin, who actually didn't mind the diversion, the long way around, because she enjoyed wheeling the huge Buick convertible over the gentle rises and curves of the topography in this part of New York, feeling like a riverboat queen in one of those trashy novels she would bring to her great-aunt from the Lakeville Library. She has to perch on the edge of the seat to grip the large wheel in both hands, as much to hang on as to steer, while trying once more, and failing once more, to imagine the shrunken, podlike woman sitting behind this same steering wheel forty years before when the car was new. Cora Endicott with the top down, on a mad dash to a party, a tennis game—a lover? The idea was ludicrous, of course.

"Isn't this charming," the old woman would say as they coasted down the grade and into the village, as if the air were suddenly purer at this lower elevation, as if they had come into an atmosphere that renewed the act of breathing.

"Yes, it is," Robin will agree. She is pleased with how she looks. She has chosen a summery, cotton dress with a full skirt flounced over a petticoat. As she stops the car, puts on the brake, and climbs the three wooden steps up to the store, she sees herself—this other Robin in this pretty dress moving spritelike against the raspberry-colored siding of the country store. She can picture her bare legs looking slimmer and more bare as she steps nimbly into the fragrant interior; the clip-clop of her low-heeled sandals will draw the pleased attention of the girl in a calico gown and apron standing behind the curved glass belly of display counter. Her own flouncy white dress with blue inserts makes her look just right, Robin thinks to herself; she could be part of a magazine picture or a TV commercial—something smart and a little carefree. "Ooh," she will say, straining one leg out to bend over an old pickle barrel now filled with stuffed dolls. They are dressed in calico gowns and aprons and with the most precious bonnets on their little wooden heads.

She has done more than fit the picture, Robin will think; she has made the picture, that is, made it complete; her presence a perfect contrast to the shelves of rustic delicacies, the sparkling jars of candy and long licorice sticks and items made of wood. The girl behind the counter also seems to feel this way, something in her expression tells Robin that her appearance, just her coming through the door, has made the whole thing perfect. "Isn't this adorable," Robin says, holding up something from a counter of small items made in Korea, but somehow she has included herself as well.

"I'm sorry about the smell," the salesclerk says.

"Smell?" says Robin, putting down the article. Only then will she get a whiff of a sourness filtering through the lavendar and vanilla scents, the packaged sachets.

"It's the laundromat," the girl says. "They had to close it down because the drainage went bad. The town is sitting onto a shelf of rock, seems like. I was getting soapsuds out of my kitchen faucet."

"How dreadful," Robin replies. The more she looks through the merchandise, the less interesting it becomes and the more difficult to choose something that would be "amusing" for Strickland. He is difficult to amuse at the start, so full of the grief he holds for himself, for his dead wife, for his daughter. Even his laughter sounds a sad recognition of its own powerlessness against the winterlike melancholy, so it is no wonder that Aunt Cora wants to give this gloom a start, but where in this mass of reproduced nostalgia such a thing can be found is beyond her. "Oh, here," Robin will say, grabbing up an item quickly, almost at random. "This is just too egregious." She laughs. "What is it?"

"It's a back scratcher." The girl demonstrates, reaching the long wooden wand over one shoulder to maneuver a small carved hand up and down between her shoulder blades.

"Perfect," says Robin and hands over the money.

"Perfect," Cora Endicott will agree hacking through a lungful of cigarette smoke as Robin steers the old convertible through the intersection. "He'll love it. What every loner needs. Something to scratch your back with."

"He still mourns Nancy," Robin will say. The dead woman's name is pronounced with an odd familiarity, as if they had been contemporary.

"Sweethearts since high school. I expect they told each other everything."

"Everything about what?" Robin will say, thinking the old woman's language curious.

"Well, everything there was to tell," Cora says and pulls out the ashtray from the automobile's console. Her fingers are the same color as the Bakelite knobs on the dashboard and Robin imagines how the knobs might have been manipulated by slim fingers with lacquered nails. She pictures a young Cora pulling off a wide straw hat in an outrageous blue or yellow and throwing it on the leather seat beside her as she drove furiously to a lover.

Cora will have continued to recount Carrol and Nancy Strickland's history, much of which Robin already knew or had guessed at. The yokel from Kansas running off with the Eastern Establishment princess, she makes it sound like an old movie—something with Jimmy Stewart and originally made in black and white but through the technique of Cora's reminiscence, tinted with an unnatural romance. How much of this falsification was Carrol's, Robin wonders as she operates the gear shift on the steering column—they would be coming up the last hill just before Silvernales—and how much was her aunt's revision would be hard to separate. Mostly him, she thinks, shifting down. She had recognized the traits of his dependency almost at first sight—the signs of a man who asked to be lied to.

At the top of the grade, just as she works the old manual lever back into high gear, Robin must quickly brake the car to avoid a tractor that swings out suddenly from a side road. The tractor pulls the long, coffinlike shape of a manure spreader and the wheels of this machinery throw out a spray of the stuff, like beaters being pulled from a pudding mix. The farmer high on the tractor's seat, will turn and wave and smile at them, though whether it is a friendly gesture or one of scorn is impossible for Robin to tell. Aunt Cora has quickly rolled up the window beside her but the acrid odor comes through the Buick's grill, the floorboards.

"Typical," the old woman will say and curl up tight on the seat. "It's so different over here, across the border. You can see it in the farms. They look so different, scraggly, run-down. They look stolen, don't they?"

"Stolen?"

"And they were stolen from the Livingstons and the van Rensselaers. All of it still part of the old manors, even after the Revolution. Almost to the Civil War. Everyone over here tenant farmers. They couldn't own the land they worked on. Not like on our side, in Connecticut, free men owning their own property from the beginning. So the scrubs just took it over, this land. A rebellion against the Livingstons and the rest. Just stole it. It looks stolen." Cora Endicott peers out the window at the fields under cultivation, and then they will pass across the small bridge over a creek and the first trailer home which marks the village line of Silvernales.

"That's true." Carrol Strickland will take up the history lesson at the table. "This very house was part of the Livingston manor and the people who lived in it could not buy it even if they had the money."

"But that's almost slavery," Robin says and lifts a fork of heavy silver. All the details of this dining room thrill her. The very mold of the house casts an image of Nancy Strickland, and Robin seeks an intimacy with the dead woman. After all, she has already shared her husband. She feels a kinship, a sudden warmth, and spears a morsel of barbecued chicken with a casual maneuver of the antique fork that is both elegant and nonchalant. "Some revolution," she says and laughs.

"Right," Strickland says and slumps to one side of his chair. "You see the Livingstons and the van Rensselaers had the good wisdom to support the rebels against the British—the Livingstons, for example turned out cannon balls for the Continental Army in their foundry just up the road." His heavy voice will spoon out the history of the place, and Robin can see by his daughter's posture that it is a familiar serving. Leslie sits pulled in beside Aunt Cora, a little younger than herself yet somehow of a different generation, and Robin will try to study her—amiability fixed in her expression should Leslie catch her eye—to find traces of the mother in her face.

". . . so to reward this loyalty to the cause," Strickland continues, "the Continental Congress allowed these manor families to keep their holdings and maintain the same feudal system that they took over from the Dutch in the seventeen-hundreds." He pauses to sip some wine. Leslie drinks iced tea and seems to rattle the ice in her glass a little too much.

"Quite different on our side," Cora will say, and it almost sounds as if she makes a distinction not only between her family and the Livingstons but between herself and Carrol Strickland, the apparent heir of those Livingston tenants, because he is quick to take the challenge, pathetically quick, Robin will think.

"And mine too," he will say. "My people were free-soilers who left this kind of indentured service and trekked across the wilderness to Kansas. Free men—and women, of course."

"I don't know that women were so free," Leslie will say, pushing her plate away. She's not eaten much.

"Well, I mean in terms of the land." Strickland's voice booms as if a volume control within him has gone haywire. Robin tries to think of some pleasantry to get them through. She hates for this lovely atmosphere to be marred by harsh words. The corner cabinet with its collection of silver and fine crystal, the luster of polished woods; all the appointments that have been giving her such comfort. But Leslie is already speaking.

"In fact, the case can be made that women are still tenants, unable to sell or buy property, paying for the use of the property by the rental of their bodies."

"Oh, my," Aunt Cora will say and rapidly fix a cigarette into the ebony holder.

"We will live under a feudal system." Leslie turns toward Robin as if to enlist her agreement, then turns away sharply, another idea suddenly joining her argument. But Robin will remember the gesture, and its sudden withdrawal. "Something else—all this business with Central America, Nicaragua, Guatemala—what are they but tenants? Isn't this the same kind of bullshit. Wasn't that the deal in Vietnam? We made them tenants on their own land."

"That's a little over-simplified." Strickland will smile and push back to cross his legs. The heavy emphasis of his dark moustache seems to highlight his teeth. The long twilight is closing in, Robin notices through the windows, and the candle flames before them seem to lengthen, aspire to a new brilliance. "The situation in Central America is a reflection of the military's frustration with the way things turned out in Vietnam."

"That ignores the history, Pop." His daughter's voice is firm. "Maybe what you say is there but only as an extra ingredient to an attitude that's been there for fifty years or more. I mean what the hell is the Monroe Doctrine all about anyway? Doesn't that say this is our manor and these are our tenants, so everybody else stay out."

"I've been in contact with some rather knowledgeable experts," Cora Endicott says, tapping her cigarette holder against a silver ashtray in the shape of a clam shell. "The evidence of the Russians moving in is quite conclusive." She smiles benignly upon Leslie Strickland, who shrugs and throws her napkin on the table.

"How marvelous," Robin will blurt, bending forward, one hand at her throat. She's managed to interrupt. "You people have these geopolitical seminars every night?" She hopes her laugh with engage Leslie because she's taken a liking to her, wants to retrieve an elfin smile—some of her mother's mischievous quality probably—from the sober slough of the girl's expression. At the same time, Robin will have a flash review, a comparison with the table talk of her parents in Hartford; the continuous ledger of debts, of slights and oversights.

"You folks want dessert in the library?" The housekeeper, Georgia, will have appeared in the shadows by the kitchen doorway.

"Case in point," Leslie says and stands up, almost knocking over her chair.

But only Cora goes to the library, bundling herself through the rooms with Georgia's help, like a child holding in her excitement for the promised treat. Leslie will have gone upstairs and Robin follows Strickland out through the kitchen and to the patio behind the house where he closes down the charcoal grill. Over the darkened corn lot that rises up toward the woods, the western sky has become purple, marbled with veins of crimson, and Robin will let her feelings lift into this spectacular display, the beauty of it, like a lovely gown to be put on. *Raiment.* She thinks of a word. The sky is a lovely raiment. Tree frogs begin to croon in the dusk and a northerly breeze carries a faint whiff of rotted manure off the field above them.

Strickland's head lifts as if to inhale the aroma. "Listen."

"What?"

"Not a sound up there. The woods are silent. They used to be like that all the time when we first moved here. Day or night."

"Your chicken was scrumptious," she will say after a little. "Did I detect lemon thyme in the sauce? Where in the world would you get fresh thyme this early?"

"I'm beginning to understand this country," Carrol Strickland will say, scraping the metal grill. He sounds as if he's been carrying on another conversation someplace else. "I tell you I know it. We're all on the surface. Nothing sinks in except garbage." Expertly, he scrapes and slaps the spatula against the barbecue. The grease flares against the hot coals, quickly illuminating his face and expression.

Robin will be startled by a hardness in his face, an anger that seems alien to his usual jolly self.

"The whole thing about Central America," he will continue, "is the loss of Cuba, Havana. I used to run into old guys who would talk about the old days in Havana, pre-Castro. It was a wide-open town. You could get anything down there, do anything, see anything. Do anything. Any color. You know what I mean?"

"Of course."

"Now all you have is Las Vegas or Atlantic City. Pale imitations—or should I say pale-face imitations. But there's a bunch that have never come to terms with losing Havana. So all this about Nicaragua and El Salvador, it's just a way to get back at Cuba."

"Surely not to overthrow Castro. That's impossible."

"It's like a heat in them. Reason, historical possibility or impossibility, none of that counts. Like Vietnam. They have the hots for this idea, to get back the old days where anything went. Nothing else matters." He closes down the grill's canopy, eliminating the minimal glow of the embers, so it will have become totally dark. He takes her by surprise, turning around so that the whole side of him was all at once up against her, like the wall of something there in the dark.

"Speaking of that," his voice will deepen. "The results from my blood test came back and guess what?"

"What?"

"I'm negative all the way." His hands grip her shoulders and she can feel him through the thin material of her dress. His excitement burns her a little, the fact that she can do this to him, has this effect upon him.

"We should go in. Cora and Leslie."

"Cora is rolling in the chocolate mousse and Leslie is upstairs pouting, still angry with me for announcing the fall of Saigon." He will be kissing her, his moustache lightly brushing against her neck before he takes her lips. Robin will let herself go limp, allow him to press her against his hardness—she lets herself moan as this happens—and she will try to picture how they look, how her back arches in such a way over the bar of his forearm.

"We can't. Now is not the time," she will say against his eager mouth, yet lifting herself ever so slightly up against him. What was that statue of Leda and the swan, the woman lifting one hip off the ground to maximize the bird's final thrust? She remembers this from art history and must still have the textbook. She will look up the artist's name.

"Why not?" Strickland rumbles with urgency. "No, not here. But my car. Or in the barn? Don't you see, I'm desperate for you."

"That frightens me," Robin will say, pushing him away and then turning, taking one, two steps. Lights have come on from above, probably Leslie in her room, and the patio is illuminated like a stage. "Yes, that frightens me," she will repeat, liking the sound of it. "I can't be that responsible, don't you see? Commitments terrify me."

"Yes, well, all right. Okay. No commitments. I understand." Strickland speaks over her shoulder. "I'll be careful. I won't burden you." But his arms will encircle her from behind and he moves into her.

"Can't we be more . . ."

"Tasteful? Or maybe organized, you mean? Better planned. Yes, I should have planned it better. So I'm left with the back scratcher, is that it? Solitary gratification?"

"Well," Robin will laugh and look about them. The rush is over and she feels in charge of the moment. "This little frock by Laura Ashley would never quite be the same after being wiped over these damp bricks. I mean I do like the spontaneous but the cost must be reckoned." She almost takes a few steps on the brick, a clattery dance of sorts, for Strickland's long face is a wonderful content of desire and frustration, wonder and disbelief. His suffering quickens her pulse, yet his pain—a pain she is a little pleased with—also calls up a genuine sympathy for him. The contradiction startles her briefly, then will fascinate her, and then, almost all in one, will suffuse her with a strange and strong feeling for Carrol Strickland; not because he is the cause of this clash of opposite poles but because he is their object, turning in their field.

So, with a tenderness and desire that Robin Endicott can only believe to be sincere, she will turn and kiss him fully on the mouth.

"Come tomorrow afternoon," she says, "and we will do everything."

"Should I bring the back scratcher?" Strickland will reply, hooting and thoroughly spoiling the mood she has so carefully put together.

Chocolate is a substitute for sex. Robin will remember reading that somewhere as she spoons the thick, rich dessert between her lips. Or is it aphrodisiacal, or maybe both? Old movies she's seen on television sometimes had bored, unattended ladies in white satin reaching into boxes of chocolate bonbons set at bedside, so true or not, the idea had a currency. On the other hand, take her great-aunt, hunched down in the corner of the library's sofa, a trace of the mousse still on the hairs of her upper lip. She gives no suggestion of lust, repressed or rampant. Her eyes have become a little glazed but this is because of the heady fumes of the brandy snifter, Robin will figure, and the thought of a frisson sending shivers of desire through the gnome-like Cora is just too irresistible for laughter.

"This mousse is totally yummy," Robin will say.

"One of Nancy's recipes," Strickland replies from the corner where he has been fiddling with the radio.

"I'm fixing to go," a voice announces from the hall outside the room.

". . . and Georgia makes it perfectly," Strickland turns, directs their attention to the darkened hallway.

"The texture is just perfect, Georgia," Robin will address the doorway.

"Thank you," the voice replies. "Well, I guess I'll go on, Mistuh Strickland."

"Okay and thanks again, Georgia. Everything was perfect."

"That's all right. I'll be seeing you, then." Over the faint strains of a piano sonata—something impressionistic—the wheeze of night sounds rises. Cora clears her throat and carefully inserts a fresh cigarette into the ebony holder. "You be all right, hear?"

Cora makes another adjustment in her throat. "Pay the woman, Carrol," she almost snaps. "Georgia would like some money."

"Oh, of course. How dumb of me. I'm sorry, Georgia." Strickland goes through the doorway, one hand reaching into his hip pocket.

"That's all right," the genial voice says once again. A chuckling also seems to forgive him but Robin notes the complex nature of a laugh that contains no humor.

But what will puzzle her more, takes up her attention even as she gathers the last of the creamy dessert on her spoon, even as she hears the crisp snap of bills being unfolded in the dark hallway, is this feeling for Strickland that overtook her a few minutes earlier as they stood behind the house. She sorts through the thesaurus of her emotions to find one that will do, for Robin Endicott has never liked combinations of anything because the result is always so mixed up, never one thing or another.

So the inexactness of this emotion disturbs her as its sudden infusion made her slightly tipsy, almost nauseated, her pulse gone out of kilter. The thrill of commanding his desire for her—that was a familiar sensation, but it was blended with other, strange feelings. Pathos might be one of them, she will think, though this announcer, this expert of the disembodied voice, has nothing of classical stature about him and she remembered that the old Greeks always made a big deal of pathos. And she likes the word anyway. It suits him, she thinks. Also he evoked a kind of nurturing in her—and that is very weird, she thinks, but his appetite for falsehood calls up an urge to take pity on him. No, she will not like this feeling; not like its confusion, not find its sick-making agreeable, but there it is. Just like that, she will think, and puts the empty dish on the floor beside her as Carrol Strickland returns to sprawl at the other end of the sofa.

"What's all this?" Robin will point to stacks of folders, manila envelopes, papers arranged graph-like before the vacuumed hearth.

"Those are the unpublished memoirs of one Emerson Caldwell," Strickland replies. "He was a minor figure in the Kennedy state department."

"Oh, yes—you told me about him."

"He also made a try for President before that," Cora tells her grand-niece. "A liberal." Her pug-dog face turns toward Strickland as if they share some secret.

"I'm supposed to be doing a biography of him," he will

continue, looking at the material on the floor. "The Bellweather Foundation is funding it."

"Really?" Cora Endicott takes another look at him, a closer look. "I know them. I just sent them a check." Something funny about that starts her laughing and coughing, and Robin notices that Strickland seems to know the joke as well for he has blushed a little and glances away.

"Are you?" she asked.

"Doing the biography?" Their eyes meet and he will stare at her with an intensity that stirs up the miscellany within her even more. "No, I don't think I am," he finally says and looks back at the papers. It sounds as if he has only made the decision.

"Of course, I don't know why you let yourself get mixed up in all that in the first place." Cora Endicott shifts a little in the sofa so she can almost face him. Her feet do not touch the floor. "He had wonderful opportunities. Johnny Carson was ready to hire him."

"No, that's not true."

"Well, if not him, one of those big shows; I remember Nancy talking about it." Cora Endicott turns to her grand-niece, a laugh croaking deep in her throat. "He certainly wasn't going to be drafted. But off he goes to that mess, leaving wife and child behind, leaving all sorts of jobs."

"It wasn't like that, exactly."

"Why did you do it? Go to Vietnam?" Robin envies his posture, the easy way he lolls in the sofa. His possession of comfort strikes her as something to be envied for the very reason it could be scorned. He makes her feels uncomfortable as she sits almost primly on the low footstool, like a commoner in the presence of royalty and fake royalty at that.

Strickland rests his head on the sofa back, his eyes scanning the library ceiling as if for an answer. "This will sound silly. Fatuous."

"Well, what?" Cora finally says because the man will have said nothing more and except for his open eyes, appears to have drifted off to sleep.

"My first year at Furness, I went out for soccer—that was the in sport there. I'd never played and I wasn't very good. But I ran like hell, did all I could and worked hard at it. When I put on that jersey, the shorts, and the cleats, boy, I felt I was something. Then they started taking pictures for the yearbook. They took two pictures of the soccer team; one with all of us in it and another with just the first string—for the coach they said. But that's the picture they used in the yearbook. You'd never know how hard and fast I ran all that spring, and I wasn't in the picture.

"So, I guess," he says as he sits up, one hand going to his face to smooth the moustache with the back of his thumb, "I guess with Vietnam, it was a question of wanting to get into the picture. It seemed important. It just seemed important."

While Strickland has been talking, Robin hears a sound in the hallway and imagines Georgia has returned, maybe even counted up the money Strickland has given her and decided it was not enough. But then, just before he sits up, concludes his reasoning, his daughter steps into the doorway.

Leslie has changed her clothes and wears jeans and a man's shirt loose over her hips. She carries a dark blue sweater. She must have crept down the stairs, Robin thinks, or else Strickland's speech was more fascinating than she thought. Or perhaps she had spelled herself into a kind of deafness, his words striking one more key in her sensibility, a similar note in her own history that turned her on to him even more. "I'm off," Leslie says. "Nice to see all of you." Her manner was pleasant. If she heard her father it is not obvious or perhaps what he said did not matter.

But what Robin Endicott did not recognize in herself, this element that she has been trying to identify that seems to be pulling her toward Carrol Strickland, was the show of a kind of innocence, like a mirror image, and not too much different from the processed innocence of the country store in Irondale. In all of them the play of innocence was performed long after the time for it was past.

"Well, we must get on the road too," she shakes her head and stands up. "It's nearly midnight." And she goes to help Cora to her feet, to smile over clenched teeth as the dry weight of the old woman's hand presses down on her arm. It is a sad thing, all of this, Robin will think matching her steps with her great-aunt's faltering pace. She is a little sorry about Julien and about her part in his plans but there is nothing to be done.

Chapter

3

The crows, suddenly gone like bandits, leave the day's silence pure, as if in their flight they have robbed all sound from these fields, the state of Connecticut, even the whole world emptied of noise so that her next step is clearly articulated. Robin hears the gravel gnash beneath her sneaker, can almost count the different grains of sand grinding under her foot. In a similar manner, the birds' piercing disappearance has also wiped the glass of morning spotless, so she perceives Julien in every detail, in every hard-edged outline of button and zipper and machinery fitting.

"Hey there, Robbie." Even Julien's voice is neutral, washed of the liquorish resonance that used to burn her senses like something too rich going down the throat, like eating too much chocolate, though his lemon-gray eyes watched her with the old fascination, the light within them like the reflection of a sky over some other planet, and which, here on this back road in Connecticut and years after, still called forth something in her that had once walked on that other planet, so that her stride shifts momentarily to that old way of walking, pelvis slanted forward and hips lazy, and all to the accompaniment of an arrogant jangle and stamp of foot. "Looking good, baby."

"So what's this about?" Robin says. Her posture has redefined itself, almost military.

"Get on." Julien starts to swing onto the motorcycle. It's a Yamaha these days. "We'll get someplace to talk."

"Talk here. I have to get back." She almost laughs at his quick response, the abrupt halt her words effect. Laughs at herself for ever seeing this poor copy of an old movie cliché as some dark angel sent to deliver her from the commonplace—what had there been about the flitting light in that driveway years ago to stun her? Yet she owed him a little something, just enough to make her listen to him when he telephoned a month before, enough to bring her to this country intersection in the Litchfield hills—out of nowhere the phone ringing, and his almost-forgotten voice like a tongue in her ear as Cora fell asleep over her lunch. Guess who?

"Well, okay then," Julien shifts against the leather bowl of the bike's saddle. He begins to tell her his idea, the plans he has made thus far to carry out the idea, and she listens, hands at ease beside the white seams of her blue sweatpants, seeing a pink boil behind his left ear as he turns away from her as if suddenly shy of her, the confidence in his idea shaken by her cool manner.

Like a poison, anger had circulated inside of her, making her listless by day and grinding her teeth in a viselike brux at night, then Julien had appeared to bring it to the surface, to bring it to a head like that angry-looking postule on his neck and to lance it, as it were, with his magic needles, so that the fever, never identified until then, had been cured with its diagnosis. A dangerous cure, for it had been similar to some old practice like bleeding which many had died from, but she had been one of the few lucky ones who had not only survived but had been cured by it. The fever had been broken. Julien had drawn out all of her anger and, at the same time, this risky therapy had somehow satisfied its own terrible need. It had been like throwing away that pack of cigarettes as her mother watched. Almost that easy.

"You're not listening to me," he says.

"I hear you," Robin replies. "The truck has been stolen in New Jersey. But can't it be traced?"

"Naw. We had it repainted. Different plates—from Pennsylvania. Wait 'til you see the sides of it. Guess what's on the sides?" He waits for her to join the game, his eyelids closing once, twice over the light-colored stare. "Guess what we painted?" Robin only shrugs. "Enterprise Movers—Long Distance Specialists." His hands print the words in the air and she notes the delicacy of the fingers, the whiteness of his hands appearing from the black-leather sleeves of the jacket like magician's tricks.

"You have the wrong idea about my aunt. She stays to herself. She knows none of the summer people around here. I can't be of any help to you."

"Come off it, baby. I know you. You've got that snooty nose right up the Hershey route." Robin winces not so much from his description as his reference to her nose. "This is old Julien. I know about you. Pretty things turn you on. You know where to find them. You must have heard something. Just that."

"So what if I do know. Then what?"

"All you do then is show me the way. We have this guy in Baltimore who flies these antiques all over, even California."

"Why should I do this?" Robin watches the flight of crows lift from a distance field and then fall back again, like the dark sparks from a peculiar fireworks geyser. Julien continues to elaborate on his theory as to why she will help him with the burglaries, his thin mouth twisted to one side in some sort of attempt at a sardonic expression, but which only makes him look stupid. He's like something you see in a museum. "I'll have to think about this," she says, turning away from him so she'll look as if she *is* thinking about it, his silly threat to blackmail her; actually she's afraid her face might not be on straight enough.

The muscles in her thighs have begun to tighten up and she shivers slightly in the warm sun. She has come this far to meet him only because he could be an annoyance—she'd say he was someone from her Hartford days who still had a crush on her, Aunt Cora would relish the story—but she couldn't be bothered. At roadside, she bends to pick a wildflower from the tall grasses growing there. "No one will know anything," he is saying, implying that everyone *could* know everything also, but wouldn't that be easy to handle? Aunt Cora signs about two dozen checks every week to cover the cost of saving souls and shaky regimes, and here is a juicy one right under her roof. Her own grand-niece! Wouldn't she just thrill down to her little shrunken bone marrow if she heard some of that story? Just some of it. How her niece had overcome bad habits to make such delicious desserts. She can hear herself give the testimonial now, on her knees in the sunporch and by the TV, where Aunt Cora watched similar confessions daily.

Moreover, she blows on the blossom in her fingers, she had come this far away from Hartford, away from all the places of failure, and then to have Julien show up out of one of those places like some character in a story, well, it was all too outrageous. However, Robin looked for meanings in such occurrences, reading in their random samplings some lucky pattern for herself, and so Julien might be useful.

"Give me a little time," she says. "I'm getting chilled also. Let me jog down there and back. Do you have to be somewhere?" A silly question.

"Take all the time you want, baby." Julien stretches in the sun, the sounds of him like an old ship under sail, and he smiles thinly as he thrusts out his pelvis so the pod of his genitals push against the tight jeans. Robin recognizes the gesture, this waving, as it were, of the proletariat dick under her nose that was supposed to bring her to her knees. Another sort of testimonial—she smiles at the pun—and just as spurious as those Aunt Cora watches so avidly on television. The same game to be played—here's where he was so stupid—that Julien had shown her how to play yet here he was, leaning on his bike in the middle of nowhere, caught up in the charade like all the others.

As she trots away from him, her legs aching a little from the strain and then loosening up, her mind also eases back from the focus on Julien. Released is more like it. Maid Marian, Strickland had called her the other day, when she showed him the picture of herself at camp, taken just before the arrow's release. Twelve that summer and the long bow as tall as she was, the feathered arrow pulled tight up to her ear and her bare legs almost bent backward with the tension pulling up from her spine, pulled up from and into the fierce concentration in her eyes. Taking aim, Strickland said and leaned over the photo album between them to kiss her naked breasts. She feels like that now, just before the release of the arrow, everything pulled to one point, toward a target, a single mark.

But by the time she reaches a lone oak growing at roadside, all tightness has slipped away and the arrow, as she thought of it, was on its way. She couldn't call it back even if she wished to do so. She slows her pace and turns back, looking up into the cloudless canopy above as if to catch the last flash of a feathered shaft, but only the errant flight of a sparrow cleaves the air. Julien has pulled a cloth from a saddlebag and is wiping the chrome-and-lacquered surfaces of the motorcycle—something in his manner of the hired driver waiting for his fare to continue the journey as he polishes the vehicle for that journey. Indeed, the perception is accompanied by her own role and Robin finishes the lap with a couple of springy leaps. He is hers to command in almost any direction.

"I want some money," she says.

"Hey, baby, the sugar bowl is empty."

"Now listen to me," she says. "I can probably find some places for you. After all, my family has been in these parts for . . ."

"Cut the shit, Robin." Some of the darkness that used to suck the light from around her has come into his face. She has to be more careful.

"I need around three thousand dollars—right away."

"What have you been up to, little pussy?"

"Look, do you want me to help you or not?"

"Okay, okay. Cool down, lady. You saw my place. Did you see all that money stacked up on the table? I mean I'm just rolling in dough, right?" His laugh is high, almost feminine in timbre, which makes him an unlikely accomplice, and Robin turns away, thinking she might reconsider. But he had always laughed like that, she remembers, as if he might be kicking at something caught on one boot.

The house he and his girlfriend and her brother rented was an ugly, asbestos-shingled aberration on the beautiful Connecticut landscape that somehow had been overlooked by Cora Endicott's Founding Fathers and their descendants when they zoned everything for their own proper usage. The split-level with two dogs chained to the patio, where a half dozen wooden lawn ornaments turned in the breeze, appeared to have popped up like a mushroom after a rain, an unsightly fungus. He had dragged Robin out there once and she had gone, curious only to see how this part of her past was doing and gratified to find it doing poorly. The girl offered her a hit on the bong that was cooking on top of an orange crate. Mattresses on the floor—always mattresses on the floor, she remembers thinking—and some kind of noodle concoction dried hard in a pan on the sink.

But did she have any choice now, wasn't the arrow already in flight? Only the heedless flight of a bird might intersect its trajectory. Moreover—her breath caught a little, wasn't this one of those occasions that had always marked her life, a turning, an opportunity rising just as the need for such an opportunity pressed down upon her? Hadn't her instincts served her well? So, despite Julien's scraggly arrogance, his comical conception of himself as a death's head at her feast, might he not be, in fact, the unknowing agent of her reprieve?

"What's funny?" he's asking, looking even more innocent, or stupid—she can't make up her mind.

"Do you have someone who will buy stuff from you right now?"

"Like what?"

"Silver, jewelry. Someone in Hartford, maybe."

"Sure, I guess so." He leans back against the Yamaha and crosses his arms. The lemon-gray eyes slide sideways. "What are you saying?"

"Day after tomorrow, my aunt and I will be going out to dinner. We'll be going over to Silvernales, across the border into New York, so it will be a long evening. I can keep her out until midnight." Julien whistles and sticks a finger into one ear, rotates it, then looks at it closely. Robin continues. "She has most of the family silver. Plates and service by John Flaxman. One of the finest collections of Sanderson and Hull." Her voice rises, uncontrollably lofted on the thermals of the pedigrees she intones.

"Those names don't mean shit," Julien replies. "Silver is silver."

"Well, there's lots of it," Robin says quickly. "Also a large emerald ring, several diamond pins, strands of pearls. Earrings, bracelets. A quantity of rather good jewelry. Everything in a Chinese box in her bedroom."

"You're something else. This is your aunt?" Julien looks at her close and his eyes have their old intensity, like the colorless, smokeless jets of acetylene torches, but Robin returns the look and crosses her arms.

"She's my great-aunt. What about it?"

"Two nights from now?"

"I'll leave the garden door open."

"No, don't do that. Let me break in. Any alarms?"

"No," she says nodding. That would have been a mistake, leaving the door open. His catching her up makes her feel a little better about using him. "So how long will this take? To get the money, I mean?"

"What little pet are you feeding now?" Julien says, smiling in a way that she can tell he believes to be wise. "Well, okay, maybe a week, maybe a little longer. If the stuff is as good as you say, it should move fast."

"You can have the rest. All I want is three thousand."

Julien has straddled the bike, his booted feet toeing the pavement on either side of the massive machinery. "Man, you are out of sight." He shakes his head and looks at her with something approaching admiration and she is amused to accept it. "Sure you wouldn't come out to my place? We could party. Celebrate the partnership."

"No, thank you," and she has to laugh, join his sardonic leer, for her nose did rise in the air, automatically and without her thinking about his invitation. Though what did he expect? What did he have in mind—a little threesome with girlfriend or getting it on with her brother? She remembers this boy said nothing the whole time and glowered at her from the corner.

Then Julien rises high in the air, grips the steering bar of the motorcycle, and comes crashing down on the kick starter, energizing the power between his legs this way rather than by turning the electric starter, and Robin, for a moment, feels herself drawn into that roar and sudden heat. She visualizes his surprising thinness within the thick black leather, the boots and coarse accoutrements of his ensemble, and sees him as one of those naked youths painted on ancient vases, holding the horns of the bull over which they somersaulted, perpetually held above the animal and not falling down into the roaring power of it, or, as she further remembers him, rising above her, holding her arms down for leverage, then plunging into her with a scream she was not always sure came from him. But only for a moment does she think about this.

The sound of him pulls away toward the horizon behind her as she runs toward the low hills that crest above Lakeville. Gradually the other sounds of morning return as the drone of the motorcycle grinds itself down to a null point, articulations rising about her from the fields like crisp notes from gigantic speakers and some of these are, in fact, bird song though she cannot identify them. Not meadowlarks, because Strickland told her meadowlarks only sang in those fields he had left behind him. None of them around here, but he would sometimes hear their trebling calls in his sleep, he told her and wake.

"My agent says I'm out of synch," he said. He had sat on the edge of the Brauer reproduction, holding a sock in his hand. She appreciates the depth of his chest and width of shoulders and his rather slim ankles—feet almost too finely shaped for a man. "I keep hearing voices; old programs played over and over. We had matches in Vietnam that were especially made for the weather. It rained all the time. Everything wet. On the cover it said something like—these matches are especially designed for wet climate. Then on the inside of the cover a warning was printed. 'Matches may not light after long exposure to damp air.' That's me. I may have been exposed to the damp air too long."

Robin had raised a perfunctory disagreement, a sociable gesture on the level of what one might make when a stranger apologizes for a sudden sneeze, for her thinking had already turned the page of the particular account book she kept in her own head. Even as she washed up at the sink, took a rinsed sponge to her breasts and thighs to wipe away the crystalline stains of their impromptu caress, she had been going over the possibilities the man getting dressed behind her might provide. And at the same time, she was conscious of his eyes upon her as she stood bending over the basin, looking very much like a Bonnard, she imagined. One of those luscious nudes in purples and greens and rose, whose frank, unglamorized nakedness suggested intimacy as well as it inspired an appetite for such intimacy. The envy, as always, was stronger than the desire.

Yet it is Julien who has met her at this crossroad, almost carrying the solution to her dilemma in one of those saddlebags of his black Yamaha. She continues to run away from the finely ground noise of him until the extreme point of his disappearance meets the swelling ellipse around her—the racket of a milk truck shifting down in the distance, the buzz and hustle of the woods almost at her elbows—so that when she follows the bend of the road, it's as though she crosses a border of some kind, has run back not only just into Lakeville but into something more. Also, if Julien had stopped to look back at her from a distance, he would not be able to see her.

So she slows her pace and then stops, and then half sits against a large gray hunk of limestone. She pulls the envelopes out from her waistband. Her sweat has almost glued them together. The total of the charges is a figure that has controlled her for too long, made her a listless prisoner ready to bargain with any turnkey for release. Like Strickland yesterday, but even better now was Julien. The opportunity he has just presented to her, and that he did it with such arrogance; that old manner which used to excite her as it now angered her for he still believed he could bend her to his will—well, it just made everything more delectable.

Give or take a few dollars for interest on the overdue accounts, the bills add up to pretty much what she knew they would; yet she reads through them avidly as if they might have been rescinded, like a condemned person still hoping to find a pardon in the wording of the final death warrant. A letter accompanies the Saks' bill, addressed to Cora Endicott, sternly advising her great-aunt that the matter would be handed over to a collection agency if the account was not settled within thirty days. Of course the charge card would also be canceled.

Robin continues her way, walking slowly as she folds and returns the bills to their envelopes. The day has turned cold and dark though the sun is even stronger, and her shadow is sharply etched against the road surface. She feels drained and weak and a little sick—a feeling familiar for this time of the month but having nothing to do with her own cycles but these awful rhythms outside of her which rule her even more and which ensnarl and diminish her. So unfair. She is reduced to nothing. She is more than something to be added up by a computer. Her taste, her sense of quality cannot be added up into a quantity that is then turned over with interest. This was the worst sort of usury, a usury of the soul, and she was made ill by it every month; every month these tabulations of her worthlessness, her lack of value and her powerlessness arrived by mail.

"Well, look at you!" The little chipmunk clings to part of the fallen tree at roadside, the merest vibration along his spine and through his tail acknowledges her. Robin bends over, hands on her knees, to greet him, to savor the genuine delight she has in this meeting. Another being as small and as defenseless as she sometimes feels, so courageous and so cute. Robin begins to feel a little better, and, as she resumes her walk, she reckons that the figure she gave Julien leaves about a three-hundred-dollar surplus beyond the total of the bills she carries against her belly. Like an unused credit, almost. She could take the Bonwit card and go to the mall outside of Great Barrington. She would get some gorgeous lingerie. Old Strickland would probably go in for lacy items but that wasn't really important—what he might like. She starts to run again, her stride like a panther's (she can see herself: graceful and powerful), as she feels her face being polished by the sun and the light, feeling herself being pulled toward Lakeville and what was sure to be a lovely afternoon at the mall.

PART

III

Chapter

I

"I read something in the paper the other day," Strickland says to Benny Stone, who has just brought him a paper cup of coffee. The two men relax in a corner of the darkened studio. "It's about somewhere in the Midwest, Wisconsin I think, where a whole cargo of Milk of Magnesia has been hijacked. A big semi full of the stuff disappeared. They're a little worried it might get into the water supply."

"And?" As the agent lowers his mouth to the coffee, the polished dome of his head reflects the tiny lights in the control room above them and, for a moment, Strickland could believe he's observing one of those planetarium displays depicting the movements in a distant cosmos. The studio lights have been dimmed so that the monitor screens are more distinct.

He waves the two-page manuscript like a fan. "Well, I was thinking the geniuses that created this script," he waves the two pages fan-like, "might have incorporated something like that in here just to give it a contemporary sense. Maybe even a little humor, though maybe the American sensibility is not yet ready to mix humor with taking a dump. On the other hand there's that whole literature of jokes that . . ."

"What the hell is this?" Stone's voice rasped like a file. "You're a professional. I'm getting you top dollar for this gig. This is into-the-sunset money. What it says or doesn't say here," he brushes the script with the back of his hand, "is not important. How it is said and who says it; that's important. Why should I have to tell you this? What's going on with you?"

"FIVE MINUTES, STRICK."

The youngish voice filtered through the speakers like the incorporeal voice of a spirit at a seance but calmly, as if everything were going all right on the other side. Strickland could see that everything was going all right on the other side of the large window of the control room. The figures moved among the blinking lights, the silhouettes of electronic consoles, at ease in the situation. He can see heads turning back and forth, one even went back as if in laughter, so at least something was funny inside there. Ad reps, sound men, tape technicians, continuity editors, directors—they were all professionals, just like him. Well, much younger, but just as professional. Maybe more so.

"What's up with you?" Stone looks at him closely, as if the low light has somehow made his client unfamiliar. He sees something and grins. "Hey, I know what you need—a little R and R. There's a new place in the Eighties with Korean chicks. What they do with fruit salad, you wouldn't believe. It'll be my treat."

Strickland gets up and moves to the podium set up before a monitor. He puts the script on the stand. The coffee is thin, an imitation flavor of a flavor of a flavor. Stone's offer has not offended him, for ordinarily he might have been interested, but something sprung him from the seat, almost made him jump up and away from the agent. He busies himself with the script, all six lines of it.

"CAN WE HAVE A VOICE LEVEL, STRICK?"

"This is Carrol Strickland speaking to you from the banks of the Mississippi River just above the town of Red Wing, Wisconsin, famed for its sturdy work boots and moccasins, but which may now take on an entirely new identity because of what people in this area call the Big Shit Spill. It has not been calculated how many thousands of gallons of Milk of Magnesia have found their way into this historic waterway, this great divide of American history, lore and literature—which Mark Twain once navigated, and Sakagewea led Lewis and Clark across and into the territory, but the effects of this spill have been felt, passed on, it might be said, in an ever-increasing cycle of pollution which has left the resources of municipalities both strained and weakened and the average citizen very sore. The federal government has . . ."

With an oath, Benny Stone angrily left the studio; swept up and slammed through the heavy swing door. Strickland has watched as his shadow reappears in the control room, arms waving and the round ball of his head stuck out on its stubby neck. But the rest of the crew ignore him, lean forward and are obviously enthralled by the monologue. A couple bend over to hold in their laughter.

". . . even as I speak to you now, with the banks of Iowa in sight, where the mysterious outlines of bears and serpents were left carved in the earth by a race of people who disappeared long before the first American Indian fished these waters, help is on the way in the form of John Boy sanitary kits. By Presidential order, the first flight of Army C-130 cargo planes have touched down at Lewis Air Force Base loaded with John Boy. Experts believe this new product will leave the entire Mississippi basin fresh and sweet smelling . . ."

"STRICK . . . STRICK . . . GIVE US A BREAK WILL YA . . . WE GOT IT ON TAPE. IT'S A COLLECTOR'S ITEM. YOU'RE SOMETHING ELSE . . . BUT WE GOT TO EARN OUR PAY THIS MORNING. SO LET'S TRY IT ONCE FROM THE TOP. THE TAPE IS RUNNING . . . ON THE NUMBERS . . ."

The small screen to his left flickers and the animation appears. He's alone in the darkened, echoless studio. The cartoon had been artfully done—the little toilet-bowl mop puts on a manfully determined expression as skinny arms strike an akimbo pose. Strickland takes his cue and starts to read from the script. Later Benny Stone will still be angry with him, even that he had done the commercials in one take seems to make the agent more incensed with his playing around, as he calls it.

"Oh, sure they thought you were real funny," he fumes. "But

keep doing that and after a while people will start saying you're not very professional. You—the Ace. Jesus—all in one!"

"It wasn't all that difficult," Strickland says and looks out the window of the cab. They have stopped at Broadway and Twenty-third; the studio was a new one, far downtown. The cabbie has a small transistor radio hanging from the rearview mirror and it plays a music in which melody seems to have been replaced by a prolonged exhalation. For the few minutes of his own reproduction of certain sounds, Strickland figures the thousands and thousands of dollars he's made, less Stone's percentage. Maybe *made* is not the right word, he thinks. "Anyway, I wasn't doing it for the control booth."

"You're a pro. But the gods are jealous of such gifts as you have." Stone kicks against the back of the partition that crams them against the seat. "Misuse your talent, mock it, and the gods will seek a terrible revenge."

"I wasn't aware you were so religious, Benny," Strickland says.

"Okay, funny—ha ha. But this is a gold strike, Strickland. Jesus Christ!"

"Another faith heard from . . ."

"Okay, listen to me. Don't you understand, I'm trying to make you independent, free you from the likes of Cynthia Block and her hoity-toity public television. Listen buddy, I've seen bimboes like that come and go. They fuck their way into the business for a couple of years, meanwhile dumping on a pro like you simply because they don't like the way you comb your hair. Or you remind them of their fathers or the guys who took their cherries. So they play havoc for a few years and then end up marrying successful dentists and move to Englewood, New Jersey, come back to the city once a week to get laid and visit their shrinks—maybe all in the same office. Sort of a One Stop Screwing. But in the meantime they've left talents like yours smoking at the roadside. Don't you see, whatever you think of the material it's going to set you up. Make you independent. Put you on a different level."

Strickland gives his agent credit, at least, for touching on the unhealed wound left from his interview with the television producer earlier in the spring. He disagrees with Stone's assessment of Cynthia

Block; though the alternative is no more to his liking. Back at the studio, Stone had said that the material wasn't important, only the way it was presented, but hadn't that been the case in Vietnam? What's said isn't so important as the sincerity with which it is said. His voice had been used to sell phony history like the copy for a toilet bowl cleaner. What was the difference?

"The whole thing should burn," he says after a minute.

"You know, you scare me sometimes." Stone's thick eyebrows check up and down, a process perhaps meant to print the words as he pronounced them. "I wouldn't want you on the other side. I bet you did a lot more over there than just read the news. Didn't you?"

At any other time Strickland might have been amused by Stone's eager expression, someone about to hear a mystery revealed, a secret already guessed. Verification. Even his silence contributes to the other's suspicions; the truth was not to be believed—even Benny Stone preferred lies and Strickland does finally laugh.

"I knew it," Stone says, sitting back and kicking his glossy black loafers against the partition. "I knew it. You son of a bitch. You son of a bitch, you."

"That's not it," Strickland says. But he can say nothing more, for to deny Stone's version would only increase its credibility. He switches the subject. "I have this old cousin, actually she is Nancy's cousin, but a couple of weeks ago her house was broken into and the whole place was turned upside down. She lives in a little town called Lakeville."

"Sure, I know, Lakeville. Connecticut."

"Right—but it's so far from the city, it came as a shock that anything like that could happen there."

Stone studies his client as the cab passes Thirty-eighth Street, then makes a dash for an open lane of traffic on Sixth Avenue. He waits as if Strickland is about to explain something. "And so?"

"So it's everywhere. Like I said back at the studio, maybe it's got into the water supply."

"You should have been a poet," Stone says. "You make as much sense sometimes." The cab driver, a small figure hunched over the wheel, takes advantage of the clear avenue temporarily opened up ahead. His foot has pressed to the floor and the taxi lurches forward at ever-increasing speed, throwing them against the ceiling and against the sides of the interior like pilots in a dog fight. The cross streets clip by in a blur, and the music on the small radio howls an exhortation or a dirge, maybe both. "Hey, stop a minute! Hey, pull over," Benny Stone yells through the glass partition, and tries to hold on to the metal cup of the ashtray fixed into the seat in front of them. His street is long past.

He continues to rap the glass fiercely as the taxi careens up the avenue. "Hey you, driver! Stop! Stop!" With obvious regret—he might have made it all the way to Central Park—the driver at last pulls over to the curb and stops. "Jesus, you have to speak six languages to talk to a cabbie these days. What's this city coming to?" Strickland waves away the money Stone offers as he works his way over the boxes and files of the Caldwell papers and then over Strickland's feet and finally out of the passenger compartment. "Now do me a favor, okay?" The agent speaks from the sidewalk. "And this is for yourself as well. Stop playing games. Clowns are for circuses. On the street, they're out of place."

More wisdom from Chairman Stone's black book, Strickland laughs to himself as the cab continues its route up Sixth Avenue, its drive chain clunking and whining. The day is warm and the sidewalks and courts around the glass walls of the magnificent buildings in this part of town are thronged with an early lunch crowd. Strickland checks over the younger women, comparing them with Robin Endicott, feeling intimate with all of them having been so with one. That is to say, he feels a kind of ease with himself now, now that he has come to terms with this affair with a woman so much younger than himself.

He had flipped through the different versions of himself already, and he had decided it didn't matter. The older man and the younger woman. The sugar daddy. The pussy-whipped male in midlife crisis. He was all of these and none, and so what? Who invented that term, anyway? Midlife crisis. One of those middle-class censures leveled by certain women's magazines, which at the same time print articles on how to handle older men?

Robin touched him with her pretensions, her desire for beauty and a serene life that lay far beyond the limits of her own aptitude. Her iron-willed aspiration for these things moved him. Her drawings—and she had also pulled out some canvases to show him—are at the same level of student work and nothing more. Yet she had this awful urge for beauty. She was like the bud vase on the low white table of her studio, flawed and only able to hold a perfection she herself could not be. This perception of her—he's especially taken by the image of the bud vase—is what draws him to her.

And he must give her great credit, he thinks as the cab passes into Central Park, for the way she handled the burglary. Poor Cora had been nearly done in by the loss, by the violation of the break-in. Robin had been so caring, so mindful of the old woman's feelings. When he had arrived at the house in Lakeville surrounded by state police cars, Robin had already prepared a list of the items stolen for the investigators. He remembers how she protected the old woman from the insensitive questioning of the more aggressive cops while deftly bringing her a clean ashtray, a fresh glass of soda water with just a slice of lemon. In the same efficient manner she served the police coffee, and her inconspicuous yet visible service reminded him of the stage hands in Kabuki plays who, in full view, arrange and rearrange the stage yet are not seen. She was somehow—Strickland tries to find the word as they pass joggers in the park—somehow organic to his life, and the idea bursts within him with an unexpected combustion. "Well, at least we have the Meissen left," she had said, pointing to the fancy sugar and creamer on the tray with the coffeepot. Her matter-of-fact humor had brightened the scene of the pillage; even Cora had rolled her head back to laugh a little. The cops had smiled indulgently as Robin, in a no-nonsensical fashion, continued to put back cushions, sweep up broken glass, generally clean up the mess the thieves had made. All that time humming to herself.

The driver has just said something, gesturing with his right hand. If he spoke in English it still sounded like his native language. "What?" Strickland leans forward and the driver says something more, and waves his fingers again, pointing to a pack of joggers jouncing down the lane beside the roadway. The women's bodies move explicitly within sweatsuits, or shorts and T-shirts. "Yes," Strickland says and the driver replies with a phrase that is just as unintelligible, though now clear in its meaning.

Strickland is not at all sure he likes being made akin to the driver's appreciation of American womanhood on the move, and he turns away with a kind of jingoism that gives him pause. For wouldn't Benny Stone see only a universal truth here, a brotherhood joining arms in appreciation? What difference did it ever made to him on Tu Do Street, anyway? Wasn't it all the same and wasn't there enough—too much, in fact, to make the idea of possession not only archaic but senseless? No, there was something else, he tells himself.

For just a second, he had placed Robin running in that group of women now left behind the taxi's progress. After the last time they made love, she had put on her running clothes as he dressed, to do her six miles, she said, and it was as if the one activity led to the other or there was some causal relationship between the two. Her discipline, her rigorous division of pleasure and exercise—something almost classical about it and he thinks of T.D. Moon describing Sparta, the battle of Thermopylae. So what he actually resents is this small brown gnarl of a driver smacking his lips over a group of women, one of whom could have easily been Robin Endicott.

When they emerge from the park at Fifth Avenue and Seventy-ninth Street, Strickland eases back in the seat and into himself, one arm resting on a box of Emerson Caldwell's papers, to enjoy the spectacle of New York. Coming out of the woods, out of Central Park, into this sophisticated settlement along the broad thoroughfare of Fifth Avenue has always given him a particular excitement. Something like coming out of the wilderness to find—not the rude huts and log cabins of the first settlers, but the stone mansions and elaborate townhouses of several generations hence, as if a time lapse had speeded up history. Or even better, maybe these palaces *were* the first dwellings put up by the pioneers, but rich pioneers, and carved out of the hardships of others or delivered at the point of a gun, like the Frick mansion and gallery down the street to the right. Turning machine guns on steelworkers in Pittsburgh had somehow preserved a notable collection of the world's art, still maintained that collection on this frontier of Fifth Avenue. Perhaps in this topsy-turvy history the rude huts are yet to come, Strickland thinks, and he, the new Goodman Brown, has emerged from the woods with a vision of that truth.

But the taxi crosses the avenue easily, almost unnoticed, and slips into the side streets of the Upper East Side. He feels a little sorry that this will be his last meeting with Virginia Caldwell, sorry to anticipate the disappointment in her face when he returns her husband's papers and journals. Her husband's reference in history, whatever part of a footnote it might be, was also a reference to her, a validation of her own existence and worth. Strickland regrets a little what he must say to her. He'll cloak the message in a caddy of language that will not offend her, but she'll be hurt anyway. Your husband was used, Mrs. Caldwell as you and I have been used; as all those people walking their dogs, going to lunch, shopping, buying drugs, choosing baby rattles, getting fired or hired, browsing in bookstores, running to lovers or leaving whores, trying on dresses, getting prescriptions filled, picking their noses or looking up at the sky between buildings—all of us thinking the lesson for the day is the same for all of us, that it comes from the same book, which actually the priests in charge are running an entirely different ceremony.

Hawthorne was right, Strickland laughs to himself. What a great T-shirt that would make! He could run up several hundred and make a quick profit before the fad consumed itself. "Just a minute." He jumps toward the partition. "Where are you going?" The driver raises both hands, a supplication to Heaven, and mutters what sounds like curses over the continual whine of the radio's music. But whether his oaths are directed at the noon-hour traffic, his ignorance with this part of the city or the fates that have miraculously lifted him up out of his own familiar ghetto and put him down into this strange one, does not concern Strickland. Patiently but firmly, he directs the man through the maze of congestion at Second Avenue and Seventy-sixth Street and then south, like Natty Bumppo explaining the way out of the forest to a befuddled Chingachook.

On the other hand, Strickland will think later, whose woods were they? Even if he could have pronounced the driver's name (would Mark Twain have called him Chicago?), it was Carrol Strickland who was the stranger in these parts. He would feel outnumbered in the old neighborhoods, somehow no longer a citizen and transformed into a trespasser on his own land by a swarm of new citizens who had only recently been trespassers themselves. Perhaps this was the turn of history the capo of those hunters in the woods north of his house was patiently explaining to him that morning, patiently bringing the ringed hands together as if in prayer to tell him in a kindly way that he, Strickland, was on foreign soil—not hostile, just foreign. If anything it was the driver, whatever his name was, who was showing him the way, however wrong it might be.

But this would be later, and for now, Virginia Caldwell with a poise leftover from the surrender at Appomattox, perhaps, has made it easier for Strickland so he wheels the Volvo north on the Taconic Parkway, with some California fusion on the radio and an urgency in his loins to seek out Robin Endicott. The diplomat's widow had almost apologized when he'd returned the materials, as if it had been her idea in the first place. She had invited him to tea, and wouldn't he take this small elephant carved of ivory? As a memento of their relationship?

"Emer-ra-son and I found this place in Singapore." Then, as if to hold him just a bit longer, she said, "You were with Professor Moon when he died?"

"Yes."

"A complex person, and not altogether there."

"There?"

"I mean," she put a hand on her throat, "I don't think Professor Moon showed us everything. He kept most of his cards face down."

Indeed, he did, Strickland agrees as he eases up on the accelerator. Sometimes state police stake out a radar unit here at Croton. The sensual, rowdy sounds of the jazz perfectly accompany his mood, his sense of release, as if he were only just now quitting the professor's death bed. But wasn't that the case? Whatever Moon had

had in mind for him, whether a last joke or a last mission, Strickland felt he has done the chore, played the straight man, and now he is free. If such a memo existed, it must be squirreled away in the bottom of the trunk the diplomat's widow keeps locked up in a closet, and it would have to be uncovered or destroyed by some future biographer. Dull stuff, he thinks. Dull and predictable and banal. *Call off the dogs. JFK.* Some note like that, maybe, and no more startling than a few more stains on the White House linen.

Strickland checks the rearview mirror for police who might be overtaking him, or maybe he would spot Moon in his hospital bed, cranked up and steering the bed with a maniacal look in his eye—that last, intense beam of mockery before the light went out. The road is empty. Strickland takes a deep breath. The death bed has been left behind. Maybe at Hawthorne Circle; the old professor going round and round and round, unable to find an exit as the charts, IV tubes, and catheters whirl and clatter.

Maybe to join other hospital beds, like wing mates peeling off in an old movie about flying, Moon's bed and the others Strickland had left behind—himself as much a victim as the still and silent wounded lined up like so many torn-up cartons, the litter of a huge, mad picnic. *This is Carrol Strickland speaking to you from the Third Field Hospital just outside of Saigon where the last of American casualties in this war are being* . . . strung out along the Taconic Parkway, the mountain laurel and dogwood losing their blooms but still lovely. He quickly checks the rearview mirror once again. No familiar white head pursuing him, holding onto the hospital-tight counterpane and diving down on him from out of the sun. But that wasn't her style. She had other maneuvers.

"That really was my granny?" Leslie had asked. They were following the Missouri River east from Kansas City, the road leading them out of the town of Lexington where he had gone with his father once to buy mules. Leslie must have been about nine. A small white plastic purse dangled on a chain from her left wrist and she pressed a delicate handkerchief, from time to time, to the sides of her round nose, against her baby-soft temples.

"It's so good of you to come visit. I'm sorry I cannot offer you much in the way of refreshment." His mother had looked around the small room of the nursing home. Then her eyes, as if their review of her familiar surroundings had only been a playful preliminary, fixed upon her granddaughter. Leslie's shiny Mary Janes turned inward under the stare.

"Nancy's taking a break, doing some tennis," Strickland told his mother, still holding the bones that were her hand. "I thought I'd show Leslie some of the old territory."

His mother laughed, something scraped harshly against the back of her throat. "What little's left of it," she said. "No point going out to Salina, there's nothing left there. There was never much to begin with."

"No," Strickland replied, putting an arm around Leslie to squeeze her quiet should she start to say something about driving through Salina cut in half now by Route 70. West of town the house stood vacant, in the middle of a limitless wheat field, like a derelict ship one might encounter adrift in the middle of the ocean. Something out of a story by Conrad or Crane, Strickland thought, as he leaned over the wheel of the station wagon. One cottonwood remained, the rest cut down. Was that your house, Leslie had asked politely? Yes, he said, and that was my room, up there on the right, the second floor. The dining room was just beneath. He knew what happened to the plates. Brought down from the rail near the ceiling and sent back East.

"What are these?" Nancy had said, unwrapping several editions of the *Kansas City Star* from around the china and holding the plates out from her as if they might harm her, offend her in some way. Explode in her hands. And there had been no use trying to explain their history, how they had gone West with a determined young woman, not unlike herself, to be placed high above everyone in that house, to remind everyone in that house that looked out on all four quadrants of an intemperate compass that she was somehow finer, of better stock. Returned East—he knew the plates had been sent back East not so much as a tribute to their marriage, a gift, but to save them from being thrown on the ash heaps of the cultural wasteland she had been trapped in. Like returning bodies for burial to their place of origin, Strickland had thought; those fifty thousand bodies lifted back and reset in their native soil. So he had said nothing as Nancy stacked them in the bottom shelf of the dining room's corner cupboard, never to take them out.

Yet as he held his mother's skeletal hand, it had occurred to him that her own body meant less to her than those plates, a funny kind of humility about herself that set off the great pride she had in the small but select dowry she had brought to her own marriage; some sheets and pillowcases and the odd assortment of Wedgewood china. What these items represented. She had never asked him to bring her to Silvernales, or any place nearby, and without any fuss or bother had put herself into this Quaker establishment, the last proceeds from the farm signed over for their good works.

All this history Strickland remembers being told once more, one last time, as he held the old hand. The hand had pushed at him as it had pushed him out of the kitchen, out the door of Kansas and into the preppy ken of Furness Academy. Little Leslie had already begun to inspect the room, embarrassed by this new grandmother's harsh tone of voice; confused and bored by the unfamiliar cast of characters in the old woman's bitter saga. The only grandmother she was to know had turned out to be a witch. He could see the idea, not altogether unappealing, pass through her nine-year-old consideration.

"Then he went and lost it all to the seed company. All those years down to a few lines, small print on a contract. He wouldn't sell when I told him to. No, he had to hang onto it. Like a dog with an old bone, until it was chewed up dry. Then it was just down and down while the seed company waited for the right time, waited until they had worked the last sweat out of his back and his arms." His mother's laughter was dry, unforgiving. Then: "Oh, his arms." She had looked about the room as if there might be some new feature, an article that had appeared since her last review. "I expect the house has fallen down by now."

She waited for him to confirm or deny it. She knew, of course, that he had been there. He had the same sentimental streak as his father, that same stubbornness of sentiment that ultimately destroyed her garden of wildflowers she kept so long against the furnace blast of August. All that withered and blown away and lost by that weakness, as she called it, and the son would have been swayed by it, she knew, to go there and sniff about the old yard. It was almost comical—she might have laughed if the pain hadn't been so bad. The ransom of the other's failure had been dug up and reburied so many times over that it was worthless.

Strickland said nothing, not to confess his deficiency, but she had turned her head on the pillow anyway, a sound of confirmation in her throat and almost a shrug of her withered shoulders as if the latent image of the old farm on his mind had been transmitted into hers, its very bleakness powerful enough to make the transfer. Why is it empty, Leslie had asked him, looking over his shoulder? The station wagon's engine idled. Her child's sense of rightness was challenged by this perfectly good house standing unused; its windows broken and the door frame whopper-jawed, but still livable.

Sometimes at night, he told her, he'd go to the bathroom, which was on the second floor, on the other side from where they had stopped to look. On the north side of the house. A window poked out there through a dormer in the roof just over the bathtub. Sometimes, looking out that window he's see a prairie storm light up the sky, way far away, maybe as far as Nebraska because there was no sound—only the flash of lightning, the sudden projection of a cumulus cloud on the black screen of the night. Isn't it funny, he said to her, that there are clouds at night too, but they can't be seen except by lightning? Then nothingness again, all silent. Maybe the sound came when he went back to bed, Leslie said helpfully. When he had gone back to sleep. Maybe so, he said, turning to nuzzle the damp plumpness of her neck. Well, Leslie said cheerfully as she settled herself back on the car seat, that storm must have been in Canada.

"Now, mother, now, don't distress yourself." *Don't upset Leslie,* he had wanted to say. This one and only meeting with your only grandchild, and you are giving her material for bad dreams. Is he sure Emily Strickland is not behind him now, following him up the Taconic? Strickland glances at the mirror of the Volvo. Only a nondescript sedan trails him and not a hospital bed. She might be waiting for him at this crossroads, this turn-off for Fishkill, say, all the bitterness and bile of her energies revved up and ready to slip the clutch.

"You've done very well." Was this her approval of his driving seventy miles an hour, so far eluding speed traps on the parkway, or for siring the pretty child who had waited with a mannered patience for the sick-room interview to conclude? Which was it? Or was it something else? "Yes." His mother had looked at him, a curious smile on the age-pruned mouth, as if it were a joke between them. "You've done well." *In spite of everything,* he had wanted to add for her. In spite of being a little dense, a little thick. In spite of all the handicaps that came from being born and raised in Kansas, fathered by a failure, reading the words of others, announcing a history he never made. That's what she meant. Thank you, mother. Yes, he had done well.

"Does Granny love you as Mummy loves me?" Leslie had asked. The meadows around Lexington rolled away from either side of the road. This part of Missouri always reminded him of Virginia.

"Yes."

"I'm happy we are making this trip," she continued, chatting with a maturity that amused and moved him at once. "I think it is useful to know where a person comes from. Also, I am very happy to have my Daddy back, especially while Mummy is gone for her tennis camp."

"Thank you."

"Do you want to know why?"

"Why?"

"Can we stop somewhere soon?"

"How about Boonville? It's about fifteen minutes up the road. Can you wait that long?"

"Well, of course," Leslie said, sounding, for the moment, remarkably like Nancy.

"Why?"

"Well, why . . . I do love Georgia and we enjoy each other's company considerably." She seemed to have saved up a lot of new words just to use on the trip. "But I got to thinking, what if something should happen to me? Say I cut my finger or I fell down and broke my arm on something. Now would Georgia be able to take care of me? I am not sure about that. But you would know what to do. You would fix me up." She hugged herself, satisfied with her reasoning and its conclusion. "Now what about this Boonville place?"

"Not far. Is this an emergency?"

"Not quite yet," she said darkly. "Like in Daniel Boone?"

"No, it's spelled differently—without the *e*. Probably from when the French were around here. *Bonne ville*. Pretty town. Somehow the word got changed, after we took over." The road signs of Boonville's commercial establishments began to appear with increasing frequency.

"The Louisiana Purchase," she said and sighed wearily, as if she had been part of Jefferson's bargaining team.

"Yes, I think so. You know a lot about this, don't you?"

"Well, not for nothing am I in the top percentile of my class."

"Good going." She had done well, he almost added.

"Have you ever been to Boonville?"

Yes, he had told her, one time with his father. They had business in Lexington and then instead of turning around and heading back west they had continued on because the senior Strickland had promised his son a genuine hotel breakfast and he knew of a place in Boonville—in fact it was the Boonville Hotel. The coffee shop that adjoined the small lobby was no disappointment. Strickland can call up its aromas even on the heady parkway in New York. The smells of sausage, biscuits, and gravy, and the sweetness of maple syrup and fresh butter and the smooth, addictive pungency of strong coffee, cream—all of it had made up an essence in Strickland's head that he thought of as Boonville No. 5. That first breath of it, following his father through the heavy swing door into the place, the older man looking back over his shoulder with a kid-like smile on his sunbaked face, anticipating the look on his son's face as he breathed in that first draught—something he could do for him at last, something that was fun that he could do for young Carrol at last. Breakfast at the Boonville Hotel.

Yes, he told his daughter, he had been to Boonville once before, but that was all he said. Putting the rest into words, speaking it, would never do the place justice and it would dissipate the fragrance he held of it. In a similar, less-savory context, his images—the smells and outlines of Vietnam—could never be put into their proper language. Especially was this true of the feeling, the palship, he had with his father that morning, the pleasantness and the simple joy of sitting down together in this hotel coffee shop far off their actual route. To do something different with his father, that no one else would do, was like playing hooky from school almost, and to see his father doing something that wasn't connected with Salina, to see him happy—no, he hadn't even tried to put it into words. In fact, he didn't even try to locate the Boonville Hotel but stopped at a McDonald's. While Leslie used the toilet, he ordered her a soft drink and coffee for himself, stirring in the dairy substitute with a plastic straw.

So by the time he pulls off the parkway at Jackson Corners, only two hours from New York, Strickland feels he had driven the whole way from Kansas City once again. All across Missouri and the Mississippi River and the flats of Indiana, Ohio, and then into the length of Pennsylvania, up over the Allegheny Plateau; turning left on the Appalachian Trail, going north and into the Catskills, then down and across the Hudson at Kingston. A backward pilgrimage, a crazy, wrong-way Corrigan of a pioneer and he felt exhausted and chagrined by his journey—the one just made in his mind and its ever-present wrongness, pointed out to him by that specter left behind in that nursing home in Kansas City but always in pursuit.

The Hotel Boonville; he can hear her laughter over it. You had to stop at the Hotel Boonville! You had to go into that sentimental dive once again with its greasy food and the rank coffee—you're just like him. You poor dear, someday I'll take you to Locke Obers in Boston and then you'll see what a real restaurant is like. Ah, dear mother, it wasn't the food, he had always meant to say, it was the company.

Chapter

2

So in that same distance of one hundred miles from New York City that he had driven so often he could almost do it without looking, as if he had become a part of the automobile and the automobile had become a part of the distance itself and all were one: pavement, trees, him behind the wheel, intersections, radar traps, the velvet folds of the Harlem Valley—in this length of travel, Strickland has shifted his attention as well. He had left the city fantasizing of Robin Endicott, but when he turns off the parkway wondering where Leslie might be.

The manicured fragrant route of the Taconic gives way to the unruly flukes and weed-scragged twists of the road around Jackson Corners. It was like passing from the well-tended conscience of a FDR, like traveling through that good and benevolent manor lord's mentality that gave us the WPA and the New Deal, back into the scrub acres of the tenants who were to be pacified by those programs and kept at a distance by this parkway. At least on their side of it.

To help clear his head even more, the fields on either side of the county road give up the astringent proof of their recent fertilization, which Strickland breathes in, takes great gulps of now—even rolling down the window on the passenger side to allow more of the stuff to be sucked into the car and his lungs, perhaps even deeper than that; he would not guess. *This is Carrol Strickland speaking to you from Prairie du Chien, just above the fork where the Wisconsin River joins the mighty Mississippi and where the white sludge of Milk of Magnesia, like a great ice floe, a veritable glacier of laxative, is making its inexorable way down the mythical colon of this Republic.*

The new urgency to locate Leslie pushed his foot down on the accelerator and the car responds, eager to prove its engineering features on this back road after the unchallenging uniformity of the parkway. What if something had happened to her and he was not there? He hears her voice, her nine-year-old voice, confidently assuming that he would be nearby if she needed him. They should have more time together. Like that trip back to Kansas. Sometimes he would put together long dialogues between them, discussions based on the day's news or on a current novel or on a recent scientific discovery. Or about Nancy, whom they rarely talked about anymore. He would imagine Leslie listening to him, carefully considering his opinions and then responding with her own. They would employ a classic form of argument—an inquiry into the truth of the matter. Socratic, almost. He could even visualize her, as the colloquy continues, rise and move about the room, with her head down as she weighs a point he's making, perhaps picks up a peach and neatly skins it, halves the fruit for them both, as she evaluates his thesis. She would be slimmer and moves gracefully as she hands him his portion of the peach.

But in fact he was always tongue-tied. When they encounter each other, all the eloquence which entertained him in these solitudes would dry up like a farm pond in August. Each of them looked aside in different directions, with Leslie holding herself in, putting up a shield of discontent to ward off his conversation. And what dumb conversation it was? Not the effect of Jesse Jackson. Not the moral consequences of genetic design. But where was she going? Where had she been? What was she going to do with her life?

Strickland takes it as a good sign that the farm ponds about here are full with spring waters. Herds of dairy cows gather around them like matrons taking a spa. The fields stretch out, become less cramped and more cultivated the closer he gets to Silvernales, so by the time he comes to the last, familiar rise of this much-traveled route, the landscape unrolls like fine wool in a tailor's window, an endless bolt of a soft tweed in green. Just below him, the blue skyline of the Schuylers' many silos rises from the center of this panorama, as if the glass-lined cylinders had been pushed up from the earth by the thrust of the young corn around them—and that isn't far from the truth, he thinks. Just beyond the Schuyler place is the wooded knoll of the forest that overlooks his own house. He cannot hear it, but he can imagine the gunfire in those woods that shatters this bright afternoon light, that perforates shadows and shreds life.

From this distance he can plainly see the barns and equipment stalls of the dairy farm, all of it miniaturized and looking like the neat illustration in a children's book, without odors or flies or the palling cries of animals. "We Visit Our Country Cousins," or some such title. Where was Leslie's car? She was not visiting young farmer Schuyler; her green Chevette is not among the vehicles pulled into the outer barnyard. Yet when he coasts down the hill toward the complex, he turns into the driveway of the large house set back from the highway across from the barns. The main house must have been built around the early part of the century, the last of a series of homesteads the Schuyler family had put up to replace those destroyed by fire or storm or which had just worn out in the several hundred years since their forebears had been brought here by Queen Anne to make tar and turpentine for the British navy.

> *The history of this valley is inexorably linked to the history of the Palantine War (1702–13), during which Queen Anne rescued those of the Protestant faith from persecution by Spanish Catholics and brought them to the colonies, and among these were the members of the von Schuyler family, who still cultivate the same fields they cleared and planted in 1726.*

The prose style of Henrietta Schuyler, town historian and wife to Gus Schuyler who naps on the plastic cushions of a chaise longue on the front porch, was the least of her recommendations to the town board for the job. The nuptial connection with her husband's family gave her access, it had been reasoned, to an archive of unique information pertaining to the history of Silvernales. Not to employ her would be to allow that history, maybe even the town's identity, to slip under the wake of the flotillas of mobile homes that had anchored in the unrestricted holding ground of Silvernales's poorer soil districts.

Something that bothered the town fathers, men with names similar to *Schuyler* and who seemed to conduct more business at the Sportsman Cafe than at the old schoolhouse used as a town hall, was the great number of children those trailers seemed to produce at the school bus stops every morning. It seemed like some process other than the usual one, something unknown or never practiced by their Palantine forebears—was switched on each night within the thin, sheet-metal walls of those trailers to continuously crank out scads of new scholars who pushed school budgets sky-high. Local taxes could not keep up. The state's resources were limited.

The town board petitioned the corporation that employed most of these newcomers to contribute something to the town budget, but the dye-and-ink plant was located in neighboring Hammertown, on the site of an old Livingston mill in fact, and was already paying out considerable sums to support the value of real estate there. However, the board of directors of the I.B. Stern Company did not turn a completely deaf ear to citizens of Silvernales.

The Silvernales Memorial Park, dedicated to those sons of our community who have served in the wars of freedom, from the Great War of 1918 to the recent struggle against the forces of repression in Vietnam, was a gift of the I.B. Stern Company, producers of textile dyes and inks, and officially opened on July 4, 1982, in a gala ceremony attended by many important state and local leaders including the Assistant Secretary of State of New York, August B. Walker. As the picture shows, the flagpole is mounted in a bed of perpetual greenery and the small but distinguished marker is of native stone.

* * *

Certainly the flagpole, maybe even the flag, had been part of the gift. The stone was contributed by a local farmer who had dug it out of a new field. The company paid for the bronze plaque bolted to its rough surface and, now and then, sent down some of the maintenance crew from the plant in Hammertown to mow and trim the perpetual greenery. The job might take all of ten minutes, Strickland would guess, for the park was only about three strides in length and two across, having been transformed from the triangle laid down by the three county roads that intersected at that point. On one side of the isosceles was the Sportsman Cafe and on the other was the fire station.

I.B. Stern had persuaded someone in the county bureaucracy to tear up this small part of downtown Silvernales and to fill it with topsoil, but the flagpole had to be replaced almost annually, Strickland remembers, because milk trucks racing over to the cheese factory in Connecticut sometimes drove right across the park when barreling through the intersection. Nancy used to call it the Silvernales Commons.

How long Gus Schuyler has been observing him, Strickland cannot figure. His mind has been making such long journeys within brief perimeters, not unlike the park he has just been thinking about, that he could no longer be sure the usual sequence of time had not slipped away completely. In any event the farmer must have been roused from his afternoon siesta by the sound of the Volvo's engine in the driveway, and he has sat up on the edge of the couch, a geniality composed of curiosity and an affection as offhand as it was indiscriminate. Strickland could just as easily be one of Schuyler's holsteins, who had somehow backed out of her milking brace and wandered across from the barn to stand on the lawn. He received the same benevolent recognition.

"Mr. Strickland." Schuyler nods and smiles. "I was just getting up." The man's natural noblesse oblige, perhaps put into his genes by whatever ancestor served the court of Lower Saxony, had plainly anticipated the apology for disturbing his pre-milking rest. But

Strickland was thinking that Nancy should be here to see the farmer's teeth. What a fine set of choppers the man's smile reveals—milk fed and milk white and strong as a bull's pizzle in May. Nothing rotten in that mouth.

But why is he there? Leslie's car is not in evidence. The farmer waits for him to explain his visit; a pleasant, expectant expression on his sun-browned face. Strickland seems stuck on the second step of the stairs leading to the porch. He can visualize the whole scene, like a tableau prepared by Henrietta, wife and town historian; a playlet to be entered in the Home Demonstration contest at the County Fair. "Our Changing Times—City Man Meets Farmer."

Just then, as if to supply the reason, several sharp gun reports echo off the hillside behind the house. Two more blast the afternoon, giving sound and action to the pantomime. "Hear that?" Strickland says. "We have to do something about that." Schuyler's eyebrows have begun to work on his bald, sun-browned face, but he continues to look pleased by something. "Doesn't that bother you at all, Gus? Day after day those guys are up there shooting everything on sight. I wouldn't be surprised if they don't start popping a couple of your cows."

"Haven't yet," the farmer laughs and shrugs. When he stands up, he seems shorter than he should be, his height mostly in his torso.

"But Jesus, Gus." Strickland likes to use the man's given name. "It's not right, is it? I mean those guys disturbing the peace like that."

"Well, it's their land. They can do what they want, I guess." His manner and tone of voice were those of someone referring to ancient law tablets; obviously written and in force long before Carrol Strickland came on the scene.

"But you sold it to them," Strickland says, recognizing the speciousness of his argument as he speaks it.

"That's true," Schuyler says, pulling his neck up from his shirt collar. "But when you bought your place from old man Hicks, nothing in that deed that says you couldn't put up anything you want onto it. A roller coaster, anything you want. Same thing with those fellas." Not only had he probably checked the deed, Strickland thinks, but he's still a little miffed that he didn't get to Hicks first and has to rent the acreage from him.

"But Gus, they are coming across into my property. They're shooting birds and animals on my side of the line. And they have to cut through your back field to get into my back fields. Do you give them permission to do that?"

"Well now, that's quite a different kettle," Schuyler says juidiciously, and comes down the steps and past Strickland so the latter has to turn and follow him. The farmer takes up a stand, arms folded, by a bed of flowers set into the lawn. "We need to get proof that they're doing that. That's only fair, isn't it. We can get Van Deusen to keep an eye on them and if he catches them doing that, then you can bet the law will handle it."

"Oh, I've been through that. Van Deusen can't even get close to them. They spot him coming a mile away."

"Well, there you have it," Gus Schuyler says and looks off into the distance behind his barns where several young heifers nudge a fence line. His attitude is not necessarily one of dismissal, but more like an accountant returning to his ledger, though the effect is the same. "It's a free country," he says at last, as he looks over the holsteins.

Thinking of his father most of the drive back from New York had put Strickland in a sympathy for Gus Schuyler. The ardors of dawn-to-dusk labor, the uncertainty of weather and marketplace, all these elements in the farmer's life were familiar to Strickland. He had seen them harden his father so that the flesh and the sinews had become like parts of the machinery that was always breaking down and that, ulitimately and irreparably, did break down.

Nancy would make some crack about this identification with the local farmers, his romance with the "noble savage" as she called it, but he could remember and give countenance to his own father's deep silences, dug into the soil, as it were, to tap some reservoir of eloquence that ran too far down to be brought to the surface. So, he stands behind Gus Schuyler and waited for the dairy farmer to say something more. Feeling at the same time anger at the probable truth of Nancy's clear-sightedness, feeling once more—and how many more times need it be demonstrated—that he was a player in a game that others never took seriously, that he followed a set of rules long ago abandoned.

"So, what's to be done?" he finally says, not expecting an answer. "I could sell out, I suppose. Move away. That's one solution."

"Well now, you could do that," Gus Schuyler replies. "But those fields of yours have got a little run down of late. You got that drainage problem up there onto the old orchard, which has taken away quite a few acres of topsoil, and then there's the run-off of that western meadow, don't you know. I expect that doesn't have the topsoil on it that it had when you bought it."

Strickland can see the older man making a careful, thoughtful analysis of the back fields, of how the property has gone down in value under his ownership—and under Schuyler's lease and cultivation of them as well, Strickland thinks, but no matter—and if he were to offer the property for sale; say, offer the property to Schuyler, he is sure that the farmer has a figure ready to give him; a price that had been added up as he worked over the teats of his herd, a "fair" price put together as he tilled the back fields on his high-wheeled John Deere and casually assessed the property across the way. Strickland would have to understand that it would be a little less than what they had paid for the place originally, because it had run down.

Strickland's laughter, more of a heavy clearing of his throat, turns Schuyler around with a puzzled, slightly offended manner. Then the man smiles good-naturedly. Probably has the money on him, Strickland thinks. Carrying around the offer in his bib overalls, just waiting for the opportunity. Like now.

"How much time would you give us to get out?" He asks Schuyler, who isn't on the same thought and frowns. Rapid fire from the woods makes them both turn in that direction. "Listen to that." The other shrugs. "By the way, has Leslie been around?" And he is sorry for the question; he only wanted to change the subject.

Schuyler shook his head, saying that the last he had seen of "them"—the farmer's sly look was not lost on Strickland—the couple had been headed off to the mall at Great Barrington. Strickland feels chagrined by the sudden bond between them that his question just created. Fathers-in-law together. He imagines Schuyler's short, burly figure squeezed into a rented morning coat and striped pants, standing in the foyer of the Irondale Presbyterian Church. Or were they Lutherans? Something in frosted blue, perhaps. The farmer would be like one of Rip Van Winkle's bowlers pulling his neck up out of a starched wing collar and taking aim on the ninepins.

More than that, he would think as he turned into his own driveway, he had been a little ashamed to have his concern for Leslie caught out in the presence of the likes of Gus Schuyler; his affection for his daughter—freshly burnished on the Taconic Parkway—was too rare an intimacy to be exposed in such rude surroundings.

But for now, he swings the Volvo up and around the graveled road, his back pressed against the seat by the force of the acceleration and the attitude of the roadway, eager to get into his house where a note might wait on the kitchen table. *Daddy—see you at supper. Love and kisses, Leslie.* At the top of the drive several cars come into view. It is Van Deusen, the game warden, he thinks—come to announce a strategy to get those Italian gunners. But the official blazons and the roof lights on the automobiles identify them as state police cruisers, one from Connecticut and the other from New York.

Even with all of his years at the elbow of power, what he considers to be a blameless record of service and good citizenship, Strickland is no different that the rest of us in that this sudden appearance of uniformed authority calls up a quick inventory of guilty possibilities. Ignored and long forgotten, the scrap of a misdeed, even the omission of a parking fine, has at last been tracked down and not just by the law officers from one state but from two. Both cops casually lean against one of the cruisers, admiring the perpetrator's view.

He drives past them and up to where Georgia's sagging Cadillac is parked by the barn. An instant fear for Leslie grips him. Could his thinking about her all afternoon have been a foreshadowing of some awful accident? *Would you know the driver of a green Chevette, a young female approximately twenty-eight years of age and weighing approximately 150 pounds? We're sorry to inform you . . .*

"I'm guilty!" Strickland shouts at the police officers as he walks toward them. "I'm coming out. Don't shoot." But his joke passes into the air like stale smoke. What happens to their sense of humor when they put on their badges and their magnums?

"Good morning, Mr. Strickland." The New York trooper makes the introductions and, for a moment, a near-comical sequence of hand-shakings and exchange of names takes place, like a Marx Brothers routine. Strickland even takes the Connecticut policeman's hand a second time before they get down to business.

Well, this is just a routine call, they tell him; *an advisory courtesy,* they call it and nod agreeably, their expressions now becoming unfrozen in the warmth of their shared jargon. Seems that a house-breaking gang has moved into the area; summer homes have been broken into and looted—this outfit uses a truck, scouts out the area and the houses and really cleans them out. Backs up the truck and takes everything. Like movers. The officers speak with no little admiration of the jobs done. Most of the burglaries are in Connecticut but over the weekend, they had one in Hammertown which showed a similar MO. Yes, they nod pleasantly to each other, the same MO.

"We're making this canvas of homes in the vicinity," the New York cop says, "that have these particular characteristics. Places set off the main road and isolated."

"Yes, isolated." The trooper from Connecticut nods. "Set back, you know?"

"Houses that might be closed up for some reason or not always occupied. Your occupation takes you to New York City for long periods of time. You're on TV a lot, aren't you?"

"No kidding," the Connecticut cop says. "You're on TV?"

Strickland says nothing but looks intently at the New York officer, who continues. "So we're just making an advisory tour, don't you know."

"Big houses," the other cop says and looks toward the old farmhouse as if to calculate not only its dimensions but all that it might contain. About the same sort of look on the face of the thief, Strickland guesses, who has probably already made a similar evaluation.

"Just an advisory," the first policeman continues. "Do you have any sort of alarm system? It's warm weather now, but you might consider locking up your windows when you leave for extended periods of time."

"It won't stop them, of course," his partner says as he picks up his part of the presentation, "but it will slow them down. Make it difficult for them and maybe give us enough time to apprehend them."

"Yes, the best defense in all this is not us, you understand, but the steps the property owner takes. Alarm systems. Double locks. Dogs are good."

"Yes, dogs. Do you have a dog? You don't have a dog?" The officer looks incredulously at the property owner.

"We had a dog once," Strickland offers, hoping past ownership might count. Old Jack, a mutt picked up at the animal shelter to be a companion for Leslie when she was about six. The dog is buried next to the apple tree behind the barn. "Just never got another one," he says.

"You understand this is just a precautionary measure," the New York cop says. "These gangs come and go. They may be off somewhere else by now. Or they may never see your place, never know about it."

"Sure, you're set back here—funny, as much as a protection for you, this isolation, as it might be a problem. You know?"

"I know," replies Strickland.

BANG . . . BANG . . . WHAM . . . TAT-TAT-TAT-BLAT . . .

The policemen spin around, hands to their pistol grips in the best John Wayne tradition. More gunfire cracks from the woods above the house like a stage effect, empty of real threat and the officers relax though they look at each other. "Sounds like a M-16 up there."

This was the trooper from Connecticut, and Strickland notices, for the first time, that he is the younger of the two. He'd be too young for the Mekong firefights, so his recognition of the weapon must come from another source. Briefly he explains the gunfire. "Maybe while you're in the neighborhood, you could go up and have a talk with them," he concludes.

"Just not our jurisdiction, I'm afraid," the New York trooper says and shakes his head.

"And I'm from Connecticut." The other shrugs.

"Game laws are enforced by the Conservation Department. Now the guy to get down here on this matter is Van Deusen, the game warden for this area. Want me to call him in?" He makes a motion through the open window of his cruiser, toward the microphone of his radio. "I'll be glad to put out a call for you. Maybe he could authorize us—well, me anyway—" (the one from Connecticut has looked away apologetically), "to go up and take a look while he gets down here. He might be out on call somewhere, of course. Those guys in Conservation have even a busier schedule than we do."

"That's for sure," his companion agrees and slaps the wide leather of his gunbelt. "You can say that again," and he slaps the leather again.

"Forget it," Strickland says. "He's been here and can do nothing."

"Yeah, well, it's a free country," the Connecticut cop says and walks to his cruiser. It's like the finale of a *pas de trois*. The other policeman also turns and goes to his car. Strickland stands between them, ready to partner either. The first trooper starts his engine and then the second car motor turns over. The cop from Connecticut slowly backs up and then goes forward and, with all the majesty of the Nutmeg State, disappears down the driveway. The second one pulls out slowly; then stops beside Strickland.

"We'll try to keep your place, and all the others like it, under surveillance," the New York trooper says to Strickland. "But that was good advice he gave you."

"What's that?"

"About getting a dog."

"I hear you," Strickland says and waves good-bye.

Inside, at the dining-room table, Georgia Wilson sits polishing silver. Strickland is astounded by the coincidence; that she would choose this day, this day of caution about the defense of personal property, to spread out the large collection of plates, pitchers, servers, and covered bowls that had been partly Nancy's dowry and partly wedding gifts. The convex surfaces of the different vessels seemed to absorb the light and then return it, intensity increased, like the lenses of coastal watch towers—though in some of these pitchers and bowls, dark, ambiguous blurs color the silver. The reflection of Georgia's face filters the radiance.

"They come right up to the door," she is saying to Strickland. "Just like that and I say nobody home and they say they wait. But I don't let them in so they go back down to their cars and then you come on up."

"Did you have all this stuff out on the table?"

"That's right," she replies, giving a vigorous buffing to a creamer. "Why's that?"

"Nothing," he says but wonders if the cops, getting an eyeful of the loot, might not put a hit on the place themselves. When it comes to the allocation of wealth, Strickland learned in Vietnam, only a thin and fragile line separated those who were hired to maintain the division and those who wish to reach across to steal it. He is overwhelmed all at once, standing within the graceful proportion of this dining room, by the savage sounds of April in Saigon a dozen years back—the rip and tear of looters, the crash of rain. He changes the subject. "Have you seen Leslie? Do you know where she's gone?"

"She up at the mall in Great Barrington with her project."

"Her project?"

"Uh-huh, her project." Georgia has finished the creamer and carefully sets it on the silver tray beside its mated sugarer. He can't ever remember them using this set, nor very little of the rest. Nancy only brought out a few dishes, sometimes on holidays, but kept the collection closed up in the corner cabinet—closed up as if she were ashamed of the stuff—and actually only brought it out to be polished, to give Georgia something to do, as it were.

"What's this project about? Cancer or the Heart Fund?"

"Outer space," Georgia says and starts to laugh.

"Outer space?"

"That's what she say, outer space." She laughs deeply and picks up a large water pitcher. Robin would probably recognize the design, know the silversmith's name. Georgia has started a vigorous polishing of the vessel, pausing now and then to look intently at its surface, perhaps to inspect her reflection or maybe to see if her image still remained upon it. Either would do, Strickland thinks. "She got rockets in her car and a whole bunch of things."

"Rockets?"

"What you doing with all those rockets, I say to her. Georgia, she says, we have to protect outer space. The Russians are putting things into outer space that's contaminating the milk and ruining the water supply. What next, I say. Seems like we no sooner get out of one predicament and we get right back into another one." She's become agitated, her handling of the pitcher is clumsy, jerky. The act has gone from a pleasurable occupation to a trivial chore, as the world goes to pieces.

"Relax, Georgia. I don't know what this is about, but believe me none of this is true. The Russians aren't putting anything in our milk." Strickland feels foolish even saying it.

"Oh yeah. Is that right?" Georgia eyes him over the rim of the silver pitcher. Suspicion and a strange jolliness imbue her large, expressive eyes. *Who's this naive number,* her look asks.

"You can believe me. I don't know what Leslie is saying to you, what she's up to, but believe me, there's nothing coming down from outer space."

"Well, how come the health department closed down two wells out on Greentree Road? They say the water's gone bad."

"That's something else. I don't know what that is, but it's something else. Probably runoff from the fields. Nitrate fertilizers. In fact I've been wondering about whether we should get our well water tested."

"Is that right?" Georgia says pleasantly, but he knows she's a little alarmed. She drinks a lot of water. She was always standing at the kitchen sink, a tumbler held to her lips, mop handle or dust cloth or utensil held in the other hand. "Anyways, that's what she says and that's where she's at." She sets down the pitcher and picks up another piece of silver.

A great weariness falls upon Strickland like a heavy garment thrown over his shoulders. The weight presses down along his arms.

This must be what a heart attack is like, he thinks, and in truth his heart is attacked by feelings of the utmost futility. Nothing has changed, he is thinking. All the good and bad deeds, the innocent and the guilty, the foolish and the wise—none of that has made any difference. Some prepunched program continues to play out the roll regardless. The memorials should be changed, even the simple one at the intersection in Silvernales. *They will have xxxx died in vain.* The negative chiseled off the bronze tablets. Isn't that the honest truth of it?

So what's to be done but have a bit of fun? The payment for his few minutes as spokesman for John Boy was in the tube, as good as in his pocket. He and Nancy used to call it fuck money. That is, like found money, payment for something done with the left hand or even the left foot, while the more serious work, the more earnest and worthy endeavor was performed with the right, therefore the proceeds not of the same value and meant to be squandered frivolously. As he walks through the house toward the telephone in the library, a weekend in Paris comes to mind. They had flown over to blow one of these checks at the Ritz and mostly at the bar. What that had been for he couldn't remember. Some voice-over for a network promo, when he'd begun to do those. What had they done with Leslie? Georgia must have stayed with her. And who had stayed with Georgia's children? Was that before Roger Wilson had wandered off into the thick glue of the Vietnam jungle or was it after?

"Oh, hello. I've been thinking of you." She sounds half in reverie.

"Have you?" He feels himself giving way, loosening, sinking into a warm bath of his earlier fantasy.

"How did it go?"

"No sweat. Listen Robin, how would you like to go somewhere?"

"Go somewhere?" Her voice becomes alert.

"I mean what if I came over there right now, swept you away to some little country inn in the Berkshires where I would hold you hostage for a few hours?"

"What a charming idea." Her laughter takes on a darkness that belies the propriety of her words. "But what of Cora?"

"Fuck Cora."

"Goodness, you are desperate—poor dear." She laughs again but this time in a different register, a harsher, more common sound that excites him even as he wonders at its origins.

"I need to see you," he says finally.

The silence between New York and Connecticut stretches out to continent length and he wonders how she looks, what she is wearing, what she might be doing as she considers his declaration. And just for a moment Strickland has a sharper image of himself—the older man imposing upon the younger woman, using all the trappings given him as a man to impose his will on her, and just for a moment he thinks of how defenseless her neck must look as she lowers her head to one side in that fashion that moves him—and just for a moment, he feels ashamed and foolish and contrite. But then she answers him.

"Give me an hour." Her voice changes once more, becomes fragile in his ear. "What would you like me to wear?"

Chapter

3

In his heart of hearts, Carrol Strickland knew the young woman beside him was rather ordinary, a copy of an ideal to be found on the glossy pages of a magazine and, further, he knew in his heart that he took advantage of her aspiration for that ideal, the aspiration for beauty or for a success that would grant her, if not independence at least some temporary distinction from the commonplace. What was this advantage?

Some of it came with the package, as it were, part of the original equipment that presently lolled against one thigh, cooling and moist and pleasurably stinging from the most recent demonstration of its unfair power, this unequal friction. Dozing in the chintz-hung bower where they had spent most of the early evening, this achievement like all others appeared questionable; money to be squandered and a profile of confidence that was beyond Robin, who had been trained— perhaps generations of instruction; he could not guess how many— yes, trained to stand to one side, face turned away and slightly down.

For example the mystique of his voice being reproduced almost everywhere at once, really only a trick of technology, seemed to affect her like a stimulant she was powerless to resist, though she gave the impression that part of her might wish to do so. "Your voice," she had said earlier. "I can't help myself. The vibration of your voice thrills me. I feel your voice rather then hear it, feel it vibrate in my mouth. Talk to me." Or was this all an act?

Later, when he thought back on this time, such language would make him laugh for she often used the heightened speech of a soap opera. She and Cora watched several every day. Particularly during sex Robin would talk like that, as if the genteel rhetoric was to clothe lust, create an aura about it like the frilly canopy over the bed where they lay dozing, only to make the nakedness beneath more erotic. Could he believe her? "I wish to do this for you, give you what I have never given anyone before," she had said earlier and she still lay face down, her hips raised on a kind of altar they had made of pillows.

The dim light sifted through the velvet drapes to dust her flanks and the deep, articulated vale of her back, the sudden rise of her behind. Strickland was afraid to touch her when he paused in the long story he had been telling her, his narrative interrupted by the thought that she had been making up a passion to accompany her language, that the sacrifice might be a rather commonplace one for her. He didn't mind. Nor did he question the truth of her "total surrender," to use her soap-opera language. Indeed, beyond soap opera, to something out of Victorian pornography and this idea made him smile in the room's dusk. Nor did he mind that they seemed to have fallen into a cliché as they had fallen into this reproduction of a four-poster bed in this New England inn—the old warrior soothing the young female with tales of his adventures in the lull following his usage of her. A hack scenario, but the charade had enveloped him with its own powerful make-believe. Then Robin spoke. "Go on."

So it was his history that overpowered her as well and put a political twist to his advantage, because it was a history that had been available only to him, as a male. Simply that. Like telling a child a bedtime story, something made up on the spot with fragments of actual events to overwhelm her disbelief. Only a male wizard would possess such stories and this made them foreign and curious for her, not unlike other stories she may have heard, he would guess, but his variations had held her a hostage in this four-poster bed in this small room with a view of the Housatonic River. She lay face down, one arm hanging over the side of the bed. "Go on," she asks.

"For some reason, I've been thinking of that time a lot today." He stretches out beside her and gently tests the small of her back with his hand. "The sound of the big choppers coming in. Then the rain. It was a rainy April. Heavy, heavy rain. You can't imagine how wet it could get. The sky opened up and water and noise came pouring down. The choppers started coming, landing on roofs all over the city—embassies, wherever. Everyone getting out. It was a total hemorrhage, everything running out, rain, people, shame, time. Everything. Thousands a day being lifted out. The North Vietnamese were just outside the city, waiting for what no one knew. Waiting for the troublemakers to get out so they wouldn't have to deal with them, feed them; could start fresh. That was one theory.

"But the dining room at the Hotel Continental was still serving marvelous food. Most journalists hung out there, where I ended up." He turned to cuddle her, one arm across her shoulders, and kissed the fine muscle over the blade bone. "Business as usual but not exactly. At the studio, the idea was to play 'White Christmas' when the time came. That was the signal for all of us to get out. Get to the roof and wait for the chopper, whistling 'White Christmas.'"

"'I'm Dreaming of a White Christmas.' Bing Crosby? I remember that. My mother would play it as we decorated the tree." Her voice was muffled against the comforter. She bent her right leg back, raising it to arch one elegant foot in midair. Strickland recovered a twinge of desire. A short time earlier, this foot and its companion had similarly raised together to batter against his butt, to spur him on and goad his furious riding of her. Now the delicately boned foot lofted with a lyrical insouciance. Her head turned, the thick dark hair splayed on the pillow and she faced him, almost peevishly, as if to summon this childhood memory of Christmas in Hartford into the room was just a little too much to ask.

"Yes, that one," he said. "In April, 'White Christmas.' And everyone knew. Secrets poured out and ran in the gutters like the rain, swept away by the rain. Everything gushed. Looting. The world gushed with looting day and night. It became a business. Anything that could be lifted and carried was lifted and carried. Furniture. Strange items. Electric fans. Air conditioners of course. Framed pictures. Stuffed animals. I remember one guy carrying card displays of watch bands. Dozens of them. And all over the streets were letters, copies of letters, millions of copies littered the streets. Like an explosion of bureaucracy. How many days and months and years of secretaries carefully preparing the carbons of those letters, carefully filing them away. *Dear Mr. Duc Ho, Your request has been received by this office and further action is being taken by the Bureau of Bureaus, etc., etc.* Archives of trivial shit like snow on the streets, spilling on everyone, people slipping on sheets of paper that turned into pulp in the rain as they tried to get out. That was the worst."

"Getting out?" She had taken the next move toward rejoining them. Her head rested on his chest, her left arm thrown across his waist. Her lips pressed his left nipple as if his next words were to be found there. "Go on. Getting out."

"It was crazy. Like all those forms and letters and applications and requests and approvals—all those copies had become a glue in the rain that fastened people to a fate we had told them would never happen. We had promised them in all those words, typed neatly with standard margins and real signatures at the bottom, that none of this was ever going to happen. Didn't they believe in Disneyland? Tinkerbell? The years of betrayal, the years of glut and waste and treachery, all the typed messages, all the decoded for-your-eyes-only findings had been cooked down in the wet heat of that monsoon, sticking people in their tracks, helpless and waiting to be run over by Charlie coming down the old boulevards in his T-5s, cruising down the boulevards to run them over like so many groundhogs stuck in hot tar.

"So they'd come to you," Strickland continued after a moment. "They'd bring money, jewelry, their women. Anything. Worst of all they'd bring the IOUs. They'd say, their eyes would say, here's so many years of trust. Look how the interest has accumulated, how my faith and belief in Tinkerbell has compounded. Surely we can cash these in now. And you'd have to say, only so much room in the boat, pal. Those certificates have no value anymore. You'd say take your clothes off and go native, you'll look like everybody else. It's your country at last. You'd see on street corners, in doorways, once in the back seat of a taxi—yes, the taxis were still running—I saw a complete uniform. Boots, tunic, pants, blouse—everything that had made a major in the Army of the Republic of South Vietnam, all of his ID, like he had been beamed up by Scotty and just left his clothes behind. I still wonder about the guy who got into that taxi, an officer if not so much a gentleman, who got out across town, near the Pizzeria, what used to be a nightclub anyhow . . . I can see this taxi pull up, and this little Vietnamese gets out in shorts, sandals, T-shirt, and sunglasses to become a cyclo-driver. A pedaler, face down on the bars, hoping no one will recognize him. No one call him sir. No more. No more salutes."

"Then Bing Crosby."

"If they played it I never heard it, but somehow the word got around that the last train out of Tombstone was on track nine." He had told Nancy some of this, but never with the same feeling—she might have laughed or turned away a little scornfully at such emotion. Robin's age perhaps was the difference, another mark to his advantage. He could elaborate, wallow in his recollections and, in fact, he pushed himself deeper into the softness of the bed's comforter and pulled her closer to him.

"You sound like you miss it."

She had caught him off guard, so he shifted, started telling her about Mrs. Caldwell, the Ambassador's papers—she would remember those for she had asked about them that night in the moonlight, just before she squatted down to adjust his pants over his boot top. Did she remember that? Was that only four months ago? Did she remember suddenly dropping to the ground that first night they met to pull his one pants leg up over his boot?

"Well, I don't keep a record of all those incidents, but your pants do have that fetching way of getting snarled up over your boot tops. And you know how I can't stand to see things out of line." She had raised up to look at him, her smile luminous in the room's dim light. "So tell me about the Ambassador's papers." Her head used his chest for a pillow once more.

So it is another fairy tale, Strickland thought, peopled with knights and sorcerers named Kennedy and Lodge and Ngo Dinh Diem, names she had only learned in school but never grew up with, that mystified her and cast a spell around her because he spoke of them casually, almost like people he had known. But as he recounted the history, this narrative that had become an entrapment for her as it had been for him, something nicked him. Could he identify it, search it out even as he spoke? *I'm doing you a favor,* T.D. Moon had said. A favor, sending him on this chase through the banal notes made on napkins by a broken-down gunsel of the Eastern Establishment?

"You have to remember," he murmured into Robin's soft hair, "that in the beginning, the feeling was genuine. Somehow democracy could be given to our little brown brothers—and sisters. We really believed that. We believed that the North was only after the rice bowls south of the Demilitarized Zone. Only that." He heard his voice give the lesson. He rarely spoke of Vietnam so as to avoid arguments or dead silences. Also with Nancy, a kind of disgust had finally closed her up entirely, as if when he had returned from there a smell about him made her turn away.

Moreover, in the telling, all the events somehow became sanitized, so why bother? He never could figure out why this was so but that had been the problem from the beginning. It wasn't the censorship, the deliberate word-mongering by the desk chiefs, but even if he had been allowed to write his own reports, the broadcasts he made from that airless studio would have been just as bland, no closer to the truth. The air conditioners were running backward and had filtered out all of the purities. Somehow you couldn't tell the truth of that war even if you tried. All of Saigon was like that; one big air-conditioned fraud.

And yes, he did miss it. Her question had tagged him out. All those years he had missed it without recognizing the loss; kept going back to the memory he kept in his head like a dog going back after a bone buried somewhere, some last luscious bite of rotted meat to be savored and swallowed and tongue-whipped. "It was like playing out Tom Sawyer and Huckleberry Finn to their utmost, to their logical conclusions. Vietnam *was* the territory, where we could do anything we wanted, free of all the Aunt Sallies that endeavored to make us civilized."

Was it all that terrific? Moon had asked him, that cartoon of a face straining up from the hospital bed. Talking about those doll-like women with their eyes slowly rolling, swimming in American sperm. But was he talking about that, about them? Strickland was no longer sure.

"This is funny," Robin had been saying. "You seem nostalgic for a way of life, a chaos that I want to escape. I want to get away too. Let's go up on the roof of this place. The Yankee Tinker Inn indeed." She laughed and gave his penis a playful tug. "Tinky-tinker. Let's go up on the roof and wait for the helicopters."

"Where would we go?"

"We could escape to Vermont."

"That's where the invasion is coming from. We'd be flying right into enemy hands. The Bennington VCs, treacherous and skilled at night fighting." She looked at him for a moment as if he might be serious. She was sitting up on her knees beside him and reached up to locate a hairpin still left in the rumpled mass of her hair. Quickly she swept up the left side and pinned it, exposing the small shell of an ear to give her countenance a domino effect; one side exposed and childlike, the other half that of a sultry *amoureuse*. Strickland reached up and softly touched both.

"No more of that," she said and slipped away, off the bed. "You're going to have to feed me now." She winced a little as her feet hit the floor. One hand reached around to touch herself. "Brute," she said.

"You asked for it. Are you okay?"

"Oh sure. Oh sure, I asked for it," she said and laughed dryly. She turned toward the mirror of an antique bureau.

She leaned forward to inspect her face, take a brush to her hair. Strickland lay back against the pillows. Something about her figure from this rear view, perhaps the foreshortening effect at this angle, turned his feeling for her into a kind of tenderness. Her hips seemed a little heavy, her legs too short—none of the small, classic proportion of the female she presented from the front, and he would think of this anomaly as endearing. A little of the peasant showing up, some gene from her mother's Huguenot ancestry maybe, though Strickland instinctively knew that to voice this allusion would make the rest of his evening a sorry and lonely vigil. So he was content to watch her vigorous strokes with the hairbrush vibrate the firm cones of her breasts. Her sturdy legs and thighs tensed and relaxed, then tensed once more as if she were pushing the whole dimension of herself into the flat mirror image, and the images of peasant women in Vietnam squeezed into his mind; how they leaned against carts loaded down with all their possessions, their generations, their future, clattering and banging like so many pots and pans. So there it was again.

"What's the matter?" She had caught his restive movement in the mirror.

"I was just admiring your pretty ass. No, that isn't it," he added quickly, for her face had gone dead, the expression slid coldly from the glass. Strickland felt he knew her moods a little, so he thought his remark, this objectification of her, if you will, was not what had angered her. Something else. She knew he had been hiding behind his comment about how she looked and so had used her without permission. This had irritated her.

"Okay. I'm sorry." He swung around and sat on the edge of the bed. Robin continued to inspect her face. Looking for what, he wondered? Sometimes he would catch a look in her eye, a kind of *click*, that would be a self-revelation of some sort, he was sure of that, some kind of an epiphany, to use Professor Moon's language, had happened right then but about what he didn't know. But these moments of self-recognition, the times he noted it happening, had begun to make her precious to him and he had been moved more than once to take her in his arms though she would struggle away almost angrily, but angry with herself, he felt, for letting down, for showing a moment's doubt. But he could not be sure.

"Okay. Let me try again. Last chance, right? For the last couple of months I've been on a wild chase. I told you about it. The ambassador's papers. And there's Moon. The old guy who got me into this business said he was doing me a favor. All he did was put me back into the whole mess again."

"But you have never left it. That's all you talk about, even when you're not talking."

Strickland shrugged. "All the time I was looking for a piece of paper, so I thought. I was supposed to find it. I was supposed to destroy it to keep the record straight, to keep the history pure. But there was no paper. Not that I could find. I don't think there ever was, and he knew it. That's what I'm thinking. Moon knew it."

"This old professor of yours knew it." Robin had finished with her hair and she sat down on the chaise with her feet flat on the floor, legs apart, head resting in one hand, arm on a thigh. All the ingredients were there; flesh, muscle, bone, hair, texture, but she was no longer sexual. She resembled an illustration in an anatomy book. An illustration for art students—the human figure, female. Nothing erotic about this body.

"Why would he do that?" she asked. "You're saying he tricked you? What I don't understand is why you don't do something." She had paused, waited for a better word than *something* but when he said nothing, she took the first ordinary expression at hand. She even threw out her right hand. "Get mad!"

And Strickland began to laugh, remembering how Nancy would say such a thing, his laughter tightening his eyes around the tears her sudden presence had provoked. Oh, no, not again, poor little Carrol, just a boy off the plains being made a fool of by the city slickers. The pathos is wearing off and the stupid is showing through. The loss of Nancy, the whole crazy, arbitrary loss of her came down on him as he sat in that quiet room with this young woman. Not so much mad, he thought, but a sobbing in the heart. What would anger serve?

It was probably wrong to be here in this room with Robin, but it didn't matter. For a moment he felt like some kind of a geneaological baboon, swinging from one branch to another in the family tree and now hanging onto one of the younger limbs. How old Robin was he wasn't sure. He had never quite believed her when she'd told him her age, for she seemed much older sometimes, but she was certainly little more than half his age, and sometimes she showed a maturity that almost made him her junior.

"I know how the so-called other woman must feel. Nancy still has a claim on you, I can tell when your mind, even your body turns to her. This hurts me." Robin had got up and came to stand before him. Her hands go to his face to model his features for some future reference when she might only have a sense of touch.

So at dinner they played at having a last meal in a city under siege, a Massachusetts village about to fall into the hands of insurgents from Bennington. The prim rusticity of the inn's dining room went with the scenario they created over the Yankee Tinker's plain fare. Robin hugged herself, anticipating some good treat, and he could imagine the rest of her, knees pressed together, toes lined up beneath the linen of the table, ready to spring into the pleasures of the menu. "Oh, dear." She looked up, her lips twisted. "The menu seems to lean heavily on prepackaged, frozen entrées."

"You can recognize that?"

"I've been in the business, remember?"

"Well, I expect they are down to their last Birdseye. The city has been surrounded for months."

"Of course. I forgot." She laughed, and color rose in her face. Her eyes were as blue as corn flowers and luminous.

"But the champagne should be okay." He had already ordered some wine and the waitress, a sedate lady of some years, had expressed surprise that his selection was on the menu. She had even taken the wine list from him and studied it closely to be sure, then returned to their table somewhat triumphantly to tell him that they did indeed have the Dom Perignon 1978. Did he still want it? Behind her he spied the bartender, a man who might be her husband or brother, looking out in wonder from the dark emptiness of the paneled taproom. Yes, he told her astonishment, and one bottle would not be nearly enough. Please be sure another was on ice.

"To take to the roof with us," he told Robin after the waitress had gumshoed away. "To toast the surrender. Our escape."

"Champagne forgives almost everything." Robin leaned toward him, placed a hand over his. "What is it? What are you thinking?"

"I was thinking of how lovely you look tonight."

"Oh, just a little paint and some magic dust."

"The basic model is classy to begin with." She looked away and down, again that pose so familiar that he had begun to wonder how rehearsed it might be, though she blushed. She wore a fitted dress of dark blue with small white polka dots, that was cut deep at the bosom but rose high around her neck in a Regency-like collar. The design flattered her; as the line and openness revealed her throat and upper chest—*gorge* would be the right expression, as the French always seemed to have the right expression, Strickland thought. Her jewelry was silver, two slim bracelets and earrings, and the blue of the dress intensified the faience quality of her eyes.

Earlier that afternoon, on the phone, she had asked him what she should wear and he had said something simple. "Oh, we're into role playing, are we?" Her voice had been metallic but humorous. "Am I to be the doctor's receptionist or the professor's favorite student?" No, nothing like that, he had said laughing, though her suggestions had set off a fuse laid down into a storehouse of such fantasies. So she had walked into the Yankee Tinker with him dressed like the new vice-president of a small bank; tastefully conservative, all business, and obviously prepared to set forth the agenda of the seminar on the trade deficit that she and her colleague had mistakenly thought was taking place in this Berkshire backwater. But not to worry, no time was to be lost, for once in the room she went right to the chaise longue and sat down on the edge of it. "Take it out," she had instructed, her eyes gone dark and fixed on his belt buckle. "I've been thinking about it all the way up here. Take it out and let me have it."

That clothes were her obsession was no surprise to Strickland, but that her pleasure in putting them on, trying this or that garment, fastening or unpinning or rearranging a particular fold of material was the important dynamic of this obsession was something he learned only that evening at the Yankee Tinker. The reverse was the usual case, or at least the case Strickland had known, but for Robin Endicott dressing up had the same erotic significance as the removal of clothes had for others.

Strickland had tried to remember, as he watched her dress for dinner, the name of the burlesque dancer whose routine was similar to the one Robin presented for him; selecting underclothing, holding up a strap of something silky, then fitting and fastening these items upon a nudity freshly pink from the bath, layer by layer until she was fully clothed. That he was to observe this ritual had been a tacit understanding, her poses were too artfully taken not to be meant for an audience, though he wondered about this also. There was an air of self-infatuation about her movements, for example when she looked over her shoulder at the mirror image of herself, that suggested her pleasure did not entirely require his presence. But at least she shared this urgency with him.

Then, just as he opened their room's door, she pulled up her dress, ostensibly to check her hose, then to inspect the garter clasp fastened to the darker band at the top, while exposing all the frivolous finery nearby as if to sum up the performance or to give him a quick review, as it were, of all that had gone before.

"Scrumptious." Robin had taken another sip of the champagne. She licked her lips. "This lady adores the stuff, but don't let me drink too much. I get positively wild on champagne."

"How much more wild can this lady get?" The words made Strickland almost gag, but he had said them. They had the dining room to themselves save for a couple in a corner table. He figured them to be a little older than he. The man was bald and his belly collapsed over the waistband of his powder-blue slacks.

"You are unlike any man I have ever known. I would do anything for you." She had become serious, her voice taking on that melodramatic finish that he wanted to believe.

"Yes." Briefly he wondered how many men she had known.

"It will take time. You must be patient with me. I carry a lot of baggage, some of which I wish to open for you, some of which I may never have the courage to show you."

"Okay." He looked around the table almost for his part in the script she seemed to be reading from. He broke off a piece of a roll and chewed it.

"You know very little about me," Robin said, leaning forward. Perfume lifted from her throat. "I can be very determined once I set my mind on something." She paused and her eyes closed slightly as if she looked into a breeze, a zephyr coming over his left shoulder. "I want to be good for you."

Strickland thought it appropriate at that moment to lift his champagne in a toast. "Here's looking at you, kid."

"Here's to our escape," she replied and touched her glass to his. Her eyes over the rim had grown large, trusting. "Where would we go?"

"Across the wide Missouri." Where had The Great Laxative spill got to by now? As far as Hannibal? Maybe, rounding the bend above St. Louis, the whiteness of it turning the brown majesty of ol' Miss into a milky serum, poisonous as cobra juice, tasty as chalk. *Oh, turn on the taps. Plug up the sink. Mammy's little baby, gonna make a great big stink.* "I'm sorry," he said to Robin's confusion. "My mind had slipped off."

She took his hand in both of hers. "Carrol, don't be sorry. I can't possibly know everything about you either, what you have been through. But it's part of you and you have to go there sometimes. I go back to rooms myself, that I closed the door on long ago. Or so I thought. It's just that . . . that . . . ."

"What?" he said, leaning toward her.

"Oh, only that when you go away like that, you make me realize how alone I am. Knowing you has made me aware of how alone I have been."

The moment obviously called for more champagne and as Strickland refilled their glasses, he noted that the man across the way had been staring at them. His wife ate her salad at a ferocious rate. "Here," he said and put his hand under Robin's jaw. He kissed her lightly on the lips, mouth open.

"You make me . . ." She paused, looked away.

"What?"

"Whole," she continued, facing him once more and sitting back. Their supper was being served. "Oh, goodie—taters!"

Their waitress took up an amiable stance. "Our chef does them himself. They're very popular." The woman seemed prepared to observe them eat the entire meal. Strickland felt adopted. They ate silently with delicate passes of silverware, Robin holding hers in the

European manner, knife poised in the right hand, fork in the left. "Well I guess I'll go see what those folks want," the waitress said at last.

They continued their meal without speaking, as if they were now unable to break the silence forced upon them by the waitress who had joined the other diners. Her presence was welcomed at this table, for the couple acted as if they had wanted some one to talk to. The conversation turned to antiques and the waitress recommended different shops nearby. Once Strickland caught the man looking around the waitress's haunch at Robin and then at him. Just then Robin crossed her legs, sending up a wispy cry of nylon against nylon.

So press down hard on the stereotype key. Why was he here with this young woman, young enough to be his daughter? That was the question he could read in the man's face. He had already asked it himself. Was his mourning for Nancy so profound that he would not lift it with someone closer to his own age, who might truly replace her? Was he fated to sniff about young women like Robin because they offered no real challenge to Nancy's memory?

But perhaps Robin did actually satisfy more than a need—and less of a sexual itch that could, after all, be scratched on demand and with far less bother elsewhere. Something was wrong about her, he couldn't quite figure out what it was, but it was that wrongness that fascinated him. All those clothes hanging in her closet, for example, and the strange gaps showing in her history, talked over quickly and in generalities like passing over thin ice. He was willing to accept almost any explanation.

Her affectations also got to him, even though he knew them to be put on like the clothes. So much of her seemed to be made up on the spot and lately just for him, as if she recognized that he had to be played with, to be fooled even. It was a habit formed long ago but she had discerned his habit, a dependency begun in the dry heat of a Kansas summer when a half dozen plates were taken down and polished, then taken down again and wiped and put back on display—as if that routine employment multiplied their value.

They had begun to talk. She had been telling him about Cora, how resilient she was, how well she had taken the losses of the robbery. The police investigation was still going on. Cora's wasn't the only place that had been robbed, he told her. She stopped eating to listen. He told her of his visit from the state police. A place near him? She asked questions. What did they say, the police? Any clues? They think it's a gang?

"Oh, how I'd love to get away from here," she said suddenly. She had raised and stretched her arms above her head.

"But we will." Strickland poured them more champagne and tried to get the waitress's attention. They needed the other bottle. "Drink up, it's almost time." He begun to hum the melody of "White Christmas" but his heavy voice made the tune ominous. The group in the corner turned toward them and he held up the empty bottle, waved it. The waitress slowly comprehended. "That helicopter is on its way."

"I mean really get out," Robin said almost to herself. She looked smaller in the chair, like a child shrinking away from a hated food.

"Robin, what do you want? Say this is our last night. Say we are taking off tomorrow, never looking back. Say you had a wish?"

She caught her breath. "One wish." She became grave, almost plain. "I would like to do something—one thing that is truly beautiful."

Strickland waited for more, for her to define it. "Only one?"

"Just one. Well, truth is beauty and all that rot." She shrugged and laughed.

"Wait a minute. You mean your art? One beautiful painting, one drawing?"

She leaned forward, struggled with her meaning. He could almost see the different thoughts tumbling behind her eyes, all of them shapeless and indiscriminate, and he was sorry to have put her on the spot. She took his hand once more in hers and pressed it and looked at him intently. It was like an oath was being taken. "My art. You've seen my art." She shook her head. "No, it doesn't matter. I just want to do one perfect thing, be part of one beautiful act. It could be anything, a perfect anything. Anything. See a perfect sunset, experience a perfect moment. How that would release me. I would do anything for that."

But if he were able to cut her loose from this tangle of genteel distortions that she had wound around herself, would she not be terrified by her own weightlessness? Strickland looked at her more closely as she finished her food. For to be weightless in any atmosphere is to risk a kind of euphoria known only to saints in that last delirium of their martyrdom. That look, helplessness before perfection, would be in Leslie's expression when he came upon her the next day at the Great Barrington Mall. Robin will be trying on clothes at a place called Bonnie's Boutique, where she seems to be known, and Strickland will be wandering the corridors of the mall, one more time the traveler puttering about the tubular framed airlocks of this consumers' colony set down on the moonscape of western Massachusetts.

He sees Leslie behind an aluminum picnic table set up in a foyer; young Schuyler stands nearby talking to another couple. They talk to each other, going over something seriously. Strickland dodges into the entranceway of a shoe store to watch Leslie, a different Leslie, talk.

CLEAN-UP SPACE
STOP THE WORLD POLLUTERS

The large banner is taped across the front of the table his daughter oversees. Piles of booklets and leaflets are before her, and several cardboard rockets tower above her head, like sumac, Strickland thinks, springing up wildly like weeds through a stand of plastic palm trees that are part of the mall's cultivation. Schuyler and two other men seem to hawk the cause, breaking apart to attach themselves to bemused shoppers, a man in coveralls, a couple with a small child. Single women with children don't pause long enough to be engaged. As he watches, the pattern of their routine becomes evident. The three men present the argument, deliver the thesis, and cite the evidence. They look like college kids selling tickets to something, maybe the spring frolic. He hears some of the discourse from where he stands. The Russians are filling space with waste materials. America is doing the same. Newspapers are withholding the true facts. Stillbirths are up. Cancer rates continue to climb. And now here's AIDS. Where did that come from all of a sudden?

When the subjects begin to nod, whether in agreement or in an attempt to agreeably slip away, they are led to the table like believers to the mourner's bench, where Leslie takes over. Her mother's smile coaxes, firmly holds their attention, sustains their newfound cause. A petition is pushed forward, a pen is held out, and another signature is added to the list. Right then Leslie gives up that look of infinite fervor, like the face of a saint in a Renaissance fresco. Her eyes lift up, the pupils rise like moons above the rolled-back whites, glowing.

Right then all of her heaviness seems to fall away and he sees how very pretty she is. She looks the same as when she was a little girl; reaching up to him, like light coming into his hands, when he would bathe her at bedtime. Nancy turned in a stupor on the sofa downstairs. The white shell of the tub gave up her plump pinkness, echoed her happy singsong as she made herself adorable to divert them both, distract him really, from the sadness on the sofa downstairs. Not until he watches her in the mall does he realize her child's strategy of years before—the memory of the moment coming at the same time as his understanding of it, and he will want to come forward, to sign up with the others in belated gratitude and thanks for the gift her small hands had reached to him. Her eyes turn and lift up toward the tops of the tubbed palm trees set about this peculiar oasis.

Last night Robin had looked up at him similarly, her eyes rolled back in her head, just before she retched and threw up into the toilet. Champagne had made her sick, not wild. She folded over his arm held across her middle and spewed out the wine and the meal and the crème caramel. Perhaps the whole afternoon coming up, everything had been too rich for her. Maybe it was to be his fate, Strickland thought, to assist such slobbery devotions, to bathe and put to bed a soiled innocence that could hold neither its champagne nor its deviations. Not only to bathe but undress as well, for as he unhooked and released the different fastenings that had been put together so artfully before dinner, he was struck by the irony of his practical occupation. These buttons and clasps designed to delay the moment, tease the anticipation, in the end had only teased his clumsiness, had delayed tumbling Robin's unconscious nakedness into bed where she had greedily reached out for sleep.

When he was sure she rested comfortably, even pulled the feather tick up over her shoulder and kissed her on the cheek, Strickland went downstairs to the taproom. The bartender had been talking to a customer at the end of the bar who turned out to be the man in the powder-blue slacks. Both men looked up at him, startled, and he guessed by the way they regarded him that they may have been talking about him and Robin; this guy with the young girl who must be having a helluva good time of it as they sat there talking about the Celtics going to the play-offs. Then he showed up. They looked a little disappointed.

"Nightcap?" the bartender asked him and squinted. He was working hard at being clever.

"Just some soda," Strickland said. He still stood. He wasn't going to stay long or even give the sense that he wanted to talk.

"The little woman's into antiques," the fellow at the end said. He even winked and looked apologetic.

Strickland recognized the opener, a bid that confidences were to be exchanged, and for half a moment he wondered at the response if he said something like *My little woman's into butt fucking.* Though another glance at the man told him something like that might already have boiled over inside his cooked countenance. Moreover, Strickland was instantly shamed by his thought, even unspoken. Smart ass, he thought. It wasn't a joke. To even think of saying something like that to amuse his own vanity, for whatever reason, was a betrayal of some kind.

"Hey, lots of them around here," the bartender took up the slack. "Lots of antiques. But you got to move fast to beat the city people to them. You know—the people from the city." He looked around quickly, at Strickland, at the dark emptiness of the taproom, then back toward the other. "Jews."

"Lots of them around, eh?" the man said.

"Oh, sure. Summer, you know. About now they start coming up." The bartender put a foot up on the bar sink and stroked his raised thigh as he spoke. It gave him the look of an athletic coach talking to his team, man to man.

"Like birds migrating."

"Yeah, birds. That's for sure, birds. Another?"

"Sure, what the hell. There's no kind of action for me tonight, speaking of antiques." They both chuckled in a knowing fellowship.

Strickland continued to look at the fixtures behind the bar. Ice fell into a glass. Liquid poured and soda fizzed. A figure in breeches and a tricorn on his head, presumably the Yankee tinker, was carved into a medallion over the bar's mirror. The plaque was flanked by the illuminated heraldry of beer blazons. The tinker's face looked startled, about to say something perhaps but interrupted by a sudden Tory spell that had struck him dumb in wooden bas relief. Like the sudden spell of coughing that had stiffened Professor Moon's face and interrupted his last assignment.

He had been doing him a favor. Strickland went back for the umpteenth time. Moon had sent him back to a place he had never left, never escaped from, to look for a marker that had never existed. That was the favor? No, the ticket was the favor. It was the other half of the round-trip ticket he had never used, never got to use on that helicopter lifting off the embassy's roof. He was getting out for good. "Was it all that terrific?" Soda water was all he had, but Strickland raised the glass and the tinker looked amused.

Maybe he had been struck by the first traveling-salesman joke, the original of the genre created right here where Strickland stood, but in—he looks again at the relief—in 1771. Or maybe it was the same joke, just now told at the end of the bar. The joke goes with the place, told over and over. No wonder the tinker looks peculiar. His amusement is frozen stiff, he's heard it all before.

"That's a good one." The man in the powder-blue slacks laughed, sipped his drink. The glass went down on the bar like a gavel. "You Nam?"

Despite himself, Strickland finds his head turning.

"Thought so. I said to the wife at dinner—that there honcho has Nam writ all over him." He smiles broadly and raises his glass. "I'm Korea. Second infantry. Old Baldy." He paused for recognition, then added, "Arrowhead." The names had a familiar sound to Strickland, something he may have read. "But I guess we never learn our lesson. Old Matt Ridgeway tried to tell us, but we wouldn't listen."

"How's that?" the bartender finally said. Obviously Strickland wasn't playing his part. For a second time that evening, he felt as though he couldn't find his place in a script.

"He said never get in a ground war with the gooks. Never get caught with your pants down in their rice paddies. We should have dropped the bomb on those goddamn slants."

"Yeah."

"They had that plan to use it on Hanoi."

"Is that a fact?" The bartender's foot went up on the sink once more and he caressed his underthigh, smoothed down the pants leg to his sock.

"Sure, I read about it in one of those memoirs they put out. In *Reader's Digest*, I think. She gets the *Reader's Digest*, you know, and sometimes they have good things in them."

"To be sure." The bartender leaned forward.

"Anyhow, one of them talked about how Nixon was thinking about using the A-bomb on Hanoi and someone talked him out it. But that would have made it easier for you, wouldn't it? Cleaned it up fast. Where were you?"

"Mostly Saigon," Strickland replied.

"Command, right? Sure, command. I'm just an old grunt but I can spot headquarters from way off. Well hell, we're all the same. Like the man says, we all have to sit down to take a dump. Right? No hard feelings about that. But I tell you one thing, we got our hands full of it south of the border. Now that is our territory and we got to clean it up."

"That's for sure."

"When you think of the expertise we got in this country, of the professional meanness we got trained in the last few years, you'd think we could clean up that mess down there. I tell you that's where the party's going to be and if I was only just a few years younger," he paused and Strickland felt the man's regard like a steady bead drawn on him. He continued to stare at the stuff behind the bar. "Like I say, if I was just a few years younger I'd be down there right now, getting ready for the party. Hell, they owe us billions of dollars, we might as well go in and collect. What's your business?"

"Waste disposal," Strickland replied. More speculation struggled for a footing on the rungs of the man's frown, which climbed into a slick baldness. Strickland, out of the corner of his eye, could see the questions shakily putting themselves together. Been married long? Who's the girl? What's she to you? Strickland finished his soda water and turned to leave.

"Hey, I'm buying," the man in powder-blue slacks said.

"No, thanks. It's been a long day. We drove up from the city."

"Yeah. Well, like they say, no hard feelings." The man's eyes almost glowed in the dimness. "Maybe another time. You know, south of the border?"

The inn's large lobby seemed to have been decorated out of one of those catalogs Nancy was forever getting and which still regularly arrived in the mail addressed to her. Wicker furniture, chintz at the windows, well-thumbed magazines on the tops of the pine tables, prints of hunting scenes and old mills on the walls, all of it must have come out of a warehouse where such stuff was stored, rented out even. But the large fieldstone fireplace looked authentic and, in fact, a marker ought to have been fixed to its face where he and Robin had stood before dinner to have an aperitif. Some record should be made of that historical occasion. All of their moments, the way stations of this peculiar journey, had assumed an importance for him that ought to be recorded. He had begun to think of them as a couple, to think that they left an impression of themselves, their outlines still hanging in the air, after they had left a room. What was Robin Endicott to him? Muffled laughter in the taproom accompanied an interpretation of that very question, he was sure.

Through the archway, he looked into the darkness of the dining room and recalled her luminous face at dinner, by turns serious and roguish, and then the sadness that overcame that bright expression as she leaned forward, eyes partially closed against the doubt his question had raised—what did she want if she could have one wish? It was like one of those clouds that had passed over the brilliant green of the Berkshires they had driven through, she silly and gay beside him; as if one of those clouds had raced ahead of their car to cast its shadow over her in the dining room of the inn. He saw in that flicker a recognition of her helplessness before her own limitations, and he had been struck by the sadness that had briefly sobered her.

To be made privy to this knowledge about herself gave him the ultimate advantage over her. It was like coming across a revelation in someone's secret journal that was both prosaic and awful, and to be conscious of this edge he had on Robin somehow made her closer to him, made her more valuable to him. A sensation with all the disturbing heartbeats of love shook him. Perhaps, Strickland thought, love was composed of these advantages one person might have over another and that was why some ran from it. As he climbed the wide, creaky stairs to their floor, he thought of that chipped bud vase on the table in her apartment over Cora's garage.

When he let himself into their room, Robin lay under the coverlet as he had left her, breathing evenly and deeply. The night air was raucous with the sounds of peepers and crickets; a larger population, it seemed, than what surrounded his house, south of here in Silvernales, and this was strange. One would think abundancy increased going south and that numbers became fewer going north. Why would he think that, Strickland asked himself as he quietly undressed? The moment his head touched the pillow, Robin suddenly sprang up as if she had been slyly waiting for him all that time.

"Oh, where have you been?" she cried.

"Downstairs. What's the matter?"

She flung herself upon him, embraced him with a strength that surprised him. All of her bone, flesh, and hair pressed against him. "I had the most terrible dream," she said into his neck.

"What about?" But she had fallen back asleep. Her breathing was smooth, childlike. Strickland held her to him, somehow reassured by her weight upon him.

Then, as if to be companionable, as if a remembrance of good manners had pulled her from sleep, she started to smack her lips, tasting the question before it was asked. "What's happening? What's new?"

"Nothing. Nothing's new," Strickland replied, eventually letting the heavy undertow of her sleep pull him under.

Chapter

4

All at once, Carrol Strickland stepped from the foyer of the women's shoe store. He had begun to feel strange staring through the display cases at Leslie and her crew, for to anyone observing him, the object of his contemplation might have been the high-heeled pumps, the exaggerated arches of leather or the elaborate laced boots inside the store's window. He was upon Leslie almost before she saw him.

"Daddy!"

"Where do I sign?" Strickland said. He already had his pen out.

"Wait a minute," she said, standing up. She looked pleased and alarmed all at once, and he could see that a faint line of perspiration had broken out along her upper lip. "Do you know what this is about?"

"Yes, I've been listening," he said and bent over, pen in hand.

"Wait, wait," she said and pulled the petition away from him. Her face showed a special concern: that he was only doing this because it was her project. Strickland instantly identified her doubt, referred it to all the other times of her school years when his too quick response, his facile agreement to an opinion had discouraged her; when his approval had become without value.

"I'm on your side," he said. "The crew of the Nautilus must stick together."

"This is serious," Leslie said. Her face grew red.

"Hi there, Mr. Strickland." Young Schuyler had come up to them and stood at his elbow. The young man seemed to take after his mother, Strickland was relieved to note. If offspring came of this activism, they might not have the squat, sauerkraut look of the boy's father. "Can I tell you about this?"

"You certainly can." He put on his most serious manner, hoping Leslie would believe him sincere. "It's about the water and the air. Right?"

"We live in an envelope," the young man began." Some would call it a divine envelope. I won't go that far—"

"No," Strickland agreed but saw Leslie's quick irritation out of the corner of his eye. He shut up, determined to be a passive audience.

"—not that far, but it is a good way of explaining just how fragile the circumstances are for life on this planet. Think of us as a space ship. We are a space ship. Aren't we already in space? We are self-contained with our own ways of generating the atmosphere we need to live. Now look what is happening. The Russians have been sending rockets into this atmosphere for years that penetrate the membrane around us, that defile the special life support systems that have been working so perfectly for millions of years.

"And what do these rockets carry?" Without looking, the young man reached down and took a pamphlet off the table. "Here's what they spew into our system." He opened the folder with elaborate care and held it up between them so they might both read together, like sharing a hymnal, Strickland thought. "Agents that create the craving for drugs and alcohol. Organisms that pollute the groundwater supply. Chemicals such as mercury and lead that become part of the food chain for fish—you've read about the problem with the bass in the Hudson River?" He paused and looked at Strickland.

"Uh-huh." The young farmer's vocabulary and his persuasive charm were impressive; he would be a success in any sphere of salesmanship, Strickland thought.

"Well," Schuyler snapped the paper with a finger and smiled wisely. "The air we breathe has been littered with poisonous debris from these rockets—sometimes when the light is right, you can almost see the stuff floating in the air. Have you noticed?"

Several lines of questions had come to Strickland's mind, not to challenge Schuyler but to offer companionable counterpoints to his discourse but even these, he sensed, might only ignite Leslie's suspicions. So he chose to ask the question that was begging.

"What can we do about this?" His voice sounded a depth of seriousness. It was a question written into almost every script he had ever read. He had asked it recently in a program on the wild horses that raced in and out of western canyons. What's to be done? He had asked the question about the destruction of the rain forests. He had asked it recently, about stained toilet bowls. What can we as sensitive, caring, concerned, right-thinking and clean-living citizens and animal lovers do about all this crap? Just now, as when he read from those scripts, his voice carried all the freight.

"We can petition our government to reestablish the program for the rocket defense system—the so-called Star Wars idea. This will present a shield against these unlawful entries into our atmosphere. We can tell the Soviet Union that we will break off all relations unless they stop this pollution of our space. Economic blockades are not out of the question."

"No."

"Then, and foremost, we can support the advocacy of Dr. Marvin Bullard." Schuyler pulled out another document from the pile on the table. Strickland had seen the face, the pamphlets were strewn all about, but he had not really looked close, his attention drawn completely to Leslie. She stood behind the table, her face aglow. Something melted inside of him. He wanted to pick her up and hold her close. The idea made him smile.

"What's funny?" she asked darkly.

"Bullard has a moustache too, just like mine almost." The picture on the pamphlet looked like a composite, one of those likenesses of a criminal suspect put together by a police artist; even the heavy, horn-rim glasses seemed to be drawn on the face. "But first and foremost, we can support Dr. Bullard's advocacy." He used young Schuyler's words and they came easily to his lips. Too easily, which made him take another, longer look at the young man.

Something of a pious smugness about him, a deliberate importance given only to certain religious converts or, as Strickland remembered from college, majors in cognitive psychology. Successful salesmen. As he continued to speak, Schuyler's sharp profile cut the air like a hatchet. His style was not convincing as it was a relentless attack on his listener's patience. Like clearing brush in one of his father's back pastures. Finally one was pared down, ready to surrender all doubts only to stop the endless chop-chop. From time to time Strickland glanced at Leslie. She looked pleased, almost proud of Schuyler, as if he had been her discovery, something she had turned up on her own in the long season of her solitude. Perhaps it was his decisive manner that attracted her, Strickland thought.

The young farmer—could he even be called that anymore?—had been talking about lobby groups, representation in Washington, the full-time staff Dr. Bullard maintained; specialists in environment science, agronomics, interplanetary dynamics, not to mention demographic statisticians (yes, it was a think tank of sorts; he laughed politely at Strickland's term). For a moment Leslie had tensed up a little but now all was okay.

"But this organization only underlays and supports the interventions Dr. Bullard creates with members of Congress. Even the President. His opinion and advice is sought at all levels and he's had regular briefing with the Joint Chiefs of Staff. Just to show you." Schuyler drew a large folder from his pocket, apparently a document so rare that it must be kept in his possession at all times. He unfolded it like a triptych, and its photographs showed Bullard sitting opposite Reagan before a fireplace, turning toward several senators at a table messy with coffee cups and the remnants of a meal, standing with generals near a launch pad at Cape Canaveral. In several pictures Bullard was alone; usually the shot was taken from below and he was posed on the steps of a government building or a natural promontory and the angle suggested, despite the double-breasted suit and the regimental tie, that some last Ascension was about to occur into the very space that was the good doctor's worry.

"You see?" Schuyler asked.

"Yes, I see," Strickland replied noticing once again the strangeness of the pictures, particularly the group shots. Eye contact between Bullard and President Reagan or between him and the senators was not quite right, as if one of them were looking elsewhere, speaking to someone not in the picture. The forgeries were so obvious Strickland felt a little insulted on behalf of the local people. Was the same crude display held out everywhere? Or were different brochures composed for different locales; say something more artfully designed for the White Plains shopping center and maybe the slickest fabrication reserved for the byways of Rodeo Drive in Beverly Hills.

Meanwhile Schuyler had determined that Strickland had seen enough. The folder was closed up and put back into his jacket pocket. Now he was to sign, now he had been fully prepared to sign the petition. It was like joining something, Strickland felt; like settling an account. Schuyler, his pitch successful, had disappeared. As Strickland recapped his pen, looked up, he was staggered by Leslie's look of affection. She hadn't looked like that at him since, he couldn't remember when. That's all it had taken—signing spurious documents. Bring them on, then, let him stand here all day and put his name to fabrications and paste-ups. But hadn't he always done that, hadn't that been his profession? Put his name and his voice to falsifications, lent them credence?

"So, what are you doing here?" Leslie asked as he put away his pen. The old suspicion had begun to play around her face once more.

"I came with Robin Endicott. You remember Robin. She wanted to get some clothes."

"Oh," Leslie said and then, "Oh," again. Something changed in her eyes. "That's funny,"

"What?"

"I thought you might have been checking up on me when actually you're here with someone."

"Leslie, I wish we could sit down sometime and just talk. We haven't had a good talk since that time we drove out to Kansas."

"Yeah, there was a captive audience."

"I thought you had a good time on that trip?"

"Oh, sure," she replied as she handed out a brochure to a shopper passing near. "Protect our space. Put the lid on the Russians." She turned back. "What do you want to talk about?"

"Nothing special. Well, yes, maybe special."

"Like what?"

Strickland looked around the lobby. Schuyler and his aides had homed in on a family of five. No one else was nearby. He took a breath. "Just now, when I signed your petition, I felt like I was closing a deal, signing a contract. And I have, I think, come to an understanding about myself, about this country."

"That's great." Her voice had no inflection, but she shifted her position. Her arms were at her sides; not folded across her bosom. "This country. You and this country." Her laugh was forced.

"Yes," Strickland kept going. "All this time I've been looking for something that's supposed to have been hidden, that's just beneath the surface, underneath certain papers, in a file somewhere which would explain a lot of history—maybe even tell me why I behave the way I do. Back and forth, I've been going through miles of history; my history, the country's history, and it's a trip that comes back here. Right here in this place. To you."

"To me?" She took a little step back.

"Yes, to you. Because what I've discovered is that nothing is hidden. There's no secret lost in the files. It's all right out here in plain sight. It has been all along. It's like the 'Purloined Letter'—the secret has been lying here in the open all along. Me and your mother and you. Now there's just you and me. We share this space. Real space and there's nothing hidden in it. We're right on the surface, in broad daylight. I want to connect with you, Leslie. In the space we have." He had stopped speaking suddenly. Leslie looked transfixed, astonished. "This hasn't been easy for me." Strickland buttoned and then unbuttoned his jacket. "There's no footing in space, is there? We have to learn to hold on without holding down. Without looking down."

"Boy," Leslie finally said.

"What?"

"You nearly had me. That fucking voice of yours nearly had me. What a performance."

"What do you mean?"

"I mean you come on here like some dumb-shit commercial for deodorant pads and I nearly bought it. Tell me about Mama, why don't you?"

"About Nancy?"

"Yeah, tell me about Mama and why she drank like that. Why you cut her off so that she drank like that and then she cut me off. Like a chain letter. She cut me off. I'd say Mama, and she couldn't even answer me. Tell me about that space, why don't you. Get your goddamn foot into that, why don't you?"

"Oh, Leslie, your mother's problem had nothing to do with me or with you. It went way back to something that happened long before us."

"And look at me." She had begun to cry; her body shook and he could tell it was with anger. She cried as she had as a little girl, like a flash flood, her cheeks suddenly wet and the tears almost jetting from her eyes. "Look at me, Daddy." As if to indicate she wanted him to look not just at her heaviness but to look away from it, she spread her arms out to encompass the table before her. The gesture acknowledged the material, seemed to confess to its fraudulence and that she knew of it. "Just look," she sobbed.

"What's the trouble, Babe?" Schuyler quickly came over. He looked at Strickland.

"Oh, just family stuff," she said. "I'm okay." She held a handkerchief to her eyes, wiped her cheeks and shrugged. "I'm okay." She looked at the young farmer with a pleasant expression that carried a total comprehension of the man, of her destiny with him and of the inescapable call of that destiny. Strickland recognized the look; Nancy had directed the same upon him more than once.

"Yes, we're just having it out," Strickland kept his voice down, trying to be casual. "To be truthful, something you'll have to get used to with us Stricklands." He calls her Babe, he thought. Already he's renamed her.

"Let me go pick up Robin and we'll have lunch somewhere," though where, Strickland continued the thought, would be a mystery. The cavern of the mall was redolent with the aromas of overheated grease and molasses.

"That's one solution," Leslie cracked.

"Well, you give one."

"Thanks, Mr. Strickland, but we have a working lunch with one of the group leaders who's come out from Washington." Young Schuyler had that evangelical look about him again, as if he had just swallowed the secret of Creation. He had come to stand beside Leslie behind the desk, the two of them together facing him down. When had all of this happened? How long had this been going on? Was this some kind of Palantine Conspiracy to take his land over *per vaginem*?

"Well, some other time," he said. "Well," he said again, "Leslie, what about a kiss?" Her distrust was swept away by the same look of affection that had blessed him when he had signed the petition.

"Oh, sure." She bent forward over the table, a little awkwardly, her arms open. For a moment it seemed she might lose her balance and topple into the Bullard literature. Schuyler even put a hand out as if to steady her, though how effective a counterweight he would be was problematical.

"Well, good luck," Strickland then said as he gestured to the table and its contents. Leslie and Schuyler almost nodded in unison, like a couple. They were a couple, he had to admit; like a photograph in some series in *Life* magazine—*farm couple manning protest booth*. She had even begun to look like the women he'd encountered at the Safeway in Green River, hugging themselves in the checkout line with a hearty self-satisfaction.

His own contentment surprised him as well. Once again at the entrance to the shoe store, he looked back at the group around the tables set up beneath the plastic palm trees. His daughter turned happily within the circumference of their cause, and he recognized that, however dubious the ministry might be, its zeal promoted a community she had joined, that had accepted her. Something of value he had not given her, and she had found this oasis on her own, he reminded himself, which pleased him even more.

Strickland turned away and worked his way back through the mall toward Bonnie's Boutique; one more community to which he could never belong. Here, young women sorted through racks of clothes and the scrape of shifting hangers made for a sort of counterpoint to the rock music that drilled through the walls of the place. The women made a casual brush of metal on metal, now quick, now slowly drawn out, as if the unrhythmic cadence of their shopping was to reject the steady bass beat that had been programmed for them and the store. Earlier Robin had gone into one of the changing booths at the rear, arms full of clothes and with a single-minded determination, leaving him alone with the rest.

The women moved about him, almost swam around him with quick, deft maneuvers; not entirely ignoring him, only a little curious about him, eyes fixed and faced flushed. The pursuit of a blouse took on a sexual tension that made him feel superfluous and silly. He had stood in the center of all this like the interloper in the seralgio, a tissue of feminine mystique woven around him by the strands of perfumes and light voices. His part in this scene had amused him.

He had felt slightly illicit, but perhaps he did belong there after all. The figure of the older man standing in the middle of such luxuriance, a happy dumbness on his face, was as much a part of the fittings as the music or the whippet-like salesgirls who emerged suddenly from the displays to keep up the tempo like chic cheerleaders. He was a cliché, and the term made him laugh a little. In shops and boutiques like this all over, a figure like Carrol Strickland stood by the size sixes or tens, lounged in a chair by the negligees, or leaned against the sweater counter, a gallant out of the *fin-de-siècle*. And if he had not accompanied Robin this morning, the store probably had a substitute ready; one of those life-size plastic dolls that can be blown up and arranged in different positions, complete with rep tie and blazer, urbane and slightly graying at the temples.

Just then, he had looked out through the boutique's open doorway to meet the quizzical gaze of a woman his age, maybe older. She was not interested in these frisky styles, her own was proof of this, but she had been studying him, and her broad, country face showed a kind of droll surprise to find him there like coming on strange dog sniffing around the peonies. Then she moved on, around the bend of the passageway. It was then that Strickland had started to explore the mall, just strolling out of the boutique in a casual way, and had come upon Leslie and Schuyler and their booth.

"Frightfully solipsisic, wouldn't you say," Robin had said on the drive to Great Barrington that morning and reached out to finger the hair falling over his shirt collar. He had used back roads; the day sparkled and Robin chattered gaily beside him without the slightest hangover and fully refreshed. The air was soft and fragrant on their faces. Strickland kept his eyes on the winding road and wondered if she meant sophistic—she sometimes confused words.

But both might be appropriate. They had been talking about clothes and fashion, how self-centered it was, to which she freely confessed, and how shallow a pursuit it could be, which darkened her expression. "But what do you feel about fashion?" he asked. "What do all these clothes mean to you? Dressing up? Playing roles? What?"

"I'm such a vagrant," she said. "That's why you're attracted to me, isn't it? I'm an orphan like yourself—we've been kicked out just as we see the goodies on the table."

"Noses pressed to the window." They passed a road sign. Danger—Antiquers Crossing. He looked for the couple from last night, perhaps ready to dart out from the bushes and into the path of the Volvo. No hard feelings, the man would say, as he slipped beneath the wheels.

"I mean it." She switched her position, sat straight in the seat, face forward. Her dress was crisp cotton, a yoke collar and in a tone of mauve that turned her eyes to dark lavender. "How I hated that life in Hartford. The pretensions of it. Then one summer they left me with Aunt Cora. My father was trying to find a better job, something not in the family, and they had to travel. I remember I got a terrible sunburn and Cora put this cream on me. It was special. Made from millions of bees. Oh, and the feel of her sheets, the pillows. I had never slept on pillows like that—so soft, so many of them. I used to crouch in her closet for hours where it was cool and feel the silk fall on me, on my bare arms and face, like rivulets of cool water. A magic cave, and I would imagine that when I stepped out of it I would be transformed. But at the end of summer I went back to Hartford. The same old life, unchanged."

"You'd seen how the other half lives."

"Was that all there was to it?" She had asked herself really. He glanced toward her. She looked through the windshield. "Like Bovary, I'd had that one taste of opulence and then the dish was pulled away. Is that what you're saying?"

"A classy allusion." Strickland chuckled, feeling an extra pleasure with Robin—that she could speak of such things as well as enact them seemed to give their affair an extra dimension. Value.

"I'm a classy kid with a classy habit. You've found me out and I don't care." She had almost sung the last words, her arms thrown out and her head back. "Dress me up and you can take me almost anywhere. Take me," she had said more soberly. Her hand rested on his thigh. So he had taken her to the mall in Great Barrington and to Bonnie's Boutique.

When he left Leslie and got back to the shop, all the sales girls turned their pasteled faces toward him. They looked like pretty raccoons caught in a beam of light. "Here he is," one of them cried. And another took up the alarm. "He's here!" One or two customers looked up at him with a forgiving amusement, then burrowed back, elbow deep, into the hanging garments. "Robin's been asking for you," the first one said. "She's in the back."

"I want your opinion," Robin said when he came to the dressing booth. "Now look at this." She pulled a dress over her head. Her underwear this morning was plain, functional, and suitable for this occasion. "What do you think?"

"I think you are lovely."

"The dress, dolt. The dress."

"The dress is okay."

"Well look at this one." The garment was pulled up over her head and another was slipped back down. She took a pose and waited for his response. Her eyes had become deep, as if she looked at him from a great distance. She really did want his opinion, he saw that.

"That looks better."

"Well, what about this?" and again another change. A kind of frenzy had come over her, but in slow motion and governed by the narrow dimensions of the booth and by her care with the clothing. Each piece was neatly returned to its hanger before another was prudently undone; yet he could feel the excitement surge through her, all the more keen because it was so tightly hemmed in and when, at one point, she turned and embraced him, held herself close to him with an unspoken but clear exasperation that there was no other way to show her feelings, he could feel her heart running wildly. She nearly panted. "This is wonderful. Wonderful."

"Take them all," Strickland told her.

"All?" She looked stunned. "All these?"

"Sure, why not?" Her expression made him laugh. Something of the guilty child caught with her hand in the cookie jar, who's rewarded with the whole bunch.

"But . . . well . . . you just don't," she flapped her hands, helpless and inarticulate. She blushed deeply. "Well, you just don't take everything." She looked about seventeen all of a sudden, maybe because of the utilitarian underwear, Strickland thought, but also this unexpected fluster gave her a dash of defenselessness.

"Why not?"

"No." She shook her head. "No. You mustn't do that, even offer." A severity had come over her which instantly reversed the previous aging process. Near-naked as she was, it seemed another garment had slipped over her, invisible but heavy and fashioned in a cheerless salon. The weight of it made her grave, and Strickland realized he preferred her this way, something in him reached out to her when she looked like this and whatever it was she was thinking, whatever memory of some awful time past cut into her, the result gladdened him. He even opened his arms to her.

"Oh, get out. You're no help at all." Her perky manner had returned. "Go out and wait. I'm going to pick out three things. Is that all right?"

"Take four."

"No, three," she said with a seriousness that would entertain no more persuasion, and she drew the drapery across the booth's opening, blocking his view.

So Strickland once again took up his station at the small counter, chatting sometimes with the sales help who offered him coffee or a coke. The atmosphere, the easy intimacies of the young women who staffed the place, the jolly camaraderie they seemed to have with each other, their casual yet professional amiability with him, made him think of other establishments that also had booths in the rear but where a different sort of fashion was tried on. The unexpected allusion made him grind his teeth in a kind of chastisement.

Robin had emerged, her arms laden down with dresses and clothing, her face still flushed but her walk businesslike. She had worn her hair up this morning, and she looked to Strickland like one of those pretty laundresses French artists at the turn of the century were so fond of painting. Or was this an image he may have picked up in one of T.D. Moon's literature courses, say in Proust—but why did he have to fit any sort of reference around her at all? He went to help her.

"All right. These three will have to do," she said and laughed with an outrageous glee. Then, to his embarrassment, she showed him the three price tags, one after the other; right in front of the others. "Okay?" Her violet eyes studied him seriously.

"Of course," he replied and reached for his checkbook.

Cora Endicott's very large checkbook lay open across the metal arms of the wheelchair that had moved her and then anchored her, as it were, to the center of her living room where Strickland came upon her later that day. The scraps of folders, torn envelopes and crumpled letters rose around the wheels of the conveyance like debris in the surf after a storm.

"Robin has gone back around to her place," he told the old woman. "She'll be back directly."

"And about time." Cora bit down on the cigarette holder, then switched it to the opposite corner of her mouth. She tore a check from the page of checks, slipped it into an envelope and ran her tongue along the gummed flap. Strickland noticed that some ash from her cigarette fell into the envelope just as she sealed it as if to season the donation, make the contribution even more palatable to the cause. "I don't understand why she had to go to Hartford."

"Something about her father's estate," he said and looked out the window. The garden was luminous with the long, slanting light of early evening, stage lighting almost, that fell across the facade of the carriage house making everything look a little false and melancholy, like the final scene of a play by Phillip Barry. He imagined Robin upstairs, opening the boxes and hanging the new clothes in her closet. Maybe she might be trying them on once more, unexpectedly seized by that peculiar mania he had witnessed earlier, but just then, she emerged from around the corner of the building. Her sober expression and no-nonsense stride dusted off his frivolous idea—she even seemed to wash her hands of the idea as she came through the garden. The rip of another check behind him separated Strickland from his thoughts.

"Father's estate, indeed. But why did she have to spend the night in Hartford?" Cora muttered.

"That was my fault." He turned back to her. "My business in Providence kept me over there. But I made sure of the place she stayed in Hartford—was safe." Robin's heels clattered on the terrazzo floor of the garden entrance and he swung around. "I was just telling Cora that I made sure you were safe and well taken care of last night."

"Oh, he did. How are you, you old darling," Robin said as she embraced the woman and stood by the wheelchair. The shriveled face turned against her blouse as if to nuzzle the firm breasts within. Strickland looked away.

"I hate it when you leave me like that," Cora whined. "You are all I have."

"Well, wasn't Mrs. Dixon good to you?"

"Oh, that woman," Cora made a contemptuous grimace. She took up her correspondence, sealed and threw another envelope onto the collection at her feet. "She drives me nuts with her chatty-chat."

"But I left you a lovely supper, all ready to be put into the microwave. Didn't you like the *veau sylvie?*"

"Ahh, the *veau sylvie.*" Cora remembered the dish with a liquid lusciousness.

". . . and those dear little *timbale aux épinards* you enjoy?"

"The *timbales* were indescribably delicious." The old woman's head had gone back, eyes half closed, a sort of ecstasy on her withered face that might have been obscene, Strickland thought, were it not so ludicrous.

"And what about the pear *clafoutis?*" Robin demanded. Her pose was that of a parent with a naughty child. He half expected her to tap a foot impatiently. "Wasn't that a nice dessert I made for you?"

"Oh it was lovely, dear Robin. Don't be angry with me, I just hate it when you're not here. What would I do without her?" She asked Strickland directly.

"I think we could all do with a cup of tea," Robin said, walking toward the kitchen. She had taken charge completely. They could hear her humming as she closed and opened cabinet doors.

Cora lit another cigarette—the crystal ashtray on the floor was overflowing—and returned to her funding. Strickland wanted to leave. But he also wanted to hold Robin close in his arms once more, to demonstrate, if nothing else, his protection of her so that she might feel freed, if only for that little while, from the servitude he had just witnessed. It would not occur to him that this gesture, with all its good intentions, might suffocate her as well. So he became lost in a reverie of his own nobleness (the two of them embraced, standing together) and did not hear all that Cora Endicott had been saying. "I'm sorry."

"I said that I understand, know her better than you do, Carrol." She was not even bothering to look up at him as she talked. "She will be with me until I die. She likes it here. I know what makes her run, what she wants." Now she looked up from her checkbook, her glance in no way softened by the veil of smoke it pierced. "She's an Endicott."

The old woman, confined to her wheelchair and consigned to spurious business, had been quickly transformed into something quite startling. Her image was no longer pathetic nor even formidable but somehow powerful with all of its ugliness—the figure of her sitting in the shreds of her correspondence called up a loathsomeness in Strickland's mind, as if he had come upon a rodent-like creature that had just been spontaneously born of the debris of its own nest.

＊　＊　＊

That afternoon, Strickland had taken a different route back from Great Barrington, an old route originally laid down for the wagons that transported heavy chunks of iron ore like small meteorites up over these hills in Connecticut and down into the Harlem Valley and the smelting mills around Irondale and Hammertown in New York. Tons and tons of the stuff laboriously pulled along by teams of oxen to be melted down and made into scythes and chains and cannon balls and stoves, and then later into rail lines and steam locomotives that were able, in turn, to pull even heavier loads of ore from the earth and into the furnaces—a kind of industrial tautology, a man-made cycle.

Here he was now, Strickland mused, wheeling this Volvo made of Swedish steel up and down the same grades, transporting boxes in the back seat full of delicate finery turned out in Milan or Manilla, and the whole arrangement empowered by yet another mineral from the earth that reproduced the sun's energy drop by drop. How much longer could this exchange go on? How much farther could he carry the heaviness within him, this rocklike substance that could not be melted by all the power exploded routinely within the Volvo's engine, and that threatened to pull him and Robin, the car, all of her new dresses, this historic road, and the picture-book landscape on either side of it—pull the whole panorama into the infinite and immeasurable gravity of his anger?

"I suppose this makes me your mistress," Robin said at just that point. She lolled on the seat beside him, something worn around her eyes, a weariness in her manner that suggested an exhausted pleasure, and the quaint innocence of her remark, whether feigned or not, freed him with the flash of a solar flare, burned away all of his heaviness. "Why are you stopping?"

"To thank you, to thank you." He quickly braked the car on the shoulder and took her in his arms and kissed her.

"Well, my goodness." She sounded genuinely surprised but pleased. Then pulled back to look at him, her eyes gone soft and speculative. "No," she said after a moment. "Don't say it." She even placed a finger against his lips.

In a little while they stopped for a snack at a country tavern in the village of Stout Falls. The place was built of huge round stones so that it looked like a full-scale version of one of those fanciful castles made for fish tanks. They sat outside at one of a half dozen tables placed at the end of the building beneath a bare arbor of two-by-fours which adjoined a weed-grown patch. It might have been a baseball field at one time, for the splintered square of a scoreboard gawked at them from sumac and briars. As they sat in the open sunlight, a chill breeze occasionally came around the building's corner to seek them out and to make Robin press her knees together, vigorously rub up the circulation in her bare arms.

"Cold?" Strickland asked.

"Oh no—it's just the Endicott circulation. We're mammals, you see, and warm-blooded. Unlike that midwestern, reptilian heritage of yours. But I prefer the outside to the inside. Did you see the way those people in there looked at us?"

"It's just a simple place. They don't get people like us every day. We're strangers."

"You have a penchant for these out-of-the-way places, don't you? Atmospheric inns." Her laughter was on the hard side of sarcasm.

"You're saying the Yankee Tinker was not up to your standards?"

"Those potatoes last night had been basted in old grease. That's what made me sick. By the way, thank you for that. For taking care of me." Just as she reached across to take his hand, their hamburgers were brought out by the bartender. The man's bare arms looked raw, scrubbed through the first layer of skin, as if frying their hamburgers had interrupted some kind of crude surgery in the back room. A cigarette smoked in the corner of his mouth. "Oh, look—lettuce!" Robin exclaimed.

"Something to drink?" the man asked. "Catsup? Mustard?"

"Not catsup," she said, "but perhaps a cup of tea."

"No tea. Soda. Beer. Coffee."

"Diet Coke, then."

"We got Pepsi."

"Very well," she said and laughed. "Pepsi." She continued to chuckle after he left, and poked at the hamburger, removing the top of its bun.

"Looks okay," Strickland said hopefully.

"Looks cooked, for sure." With a delicacy that seemed to him just a little exaggerated, Robin cut the sandwich apart with the plastic knife and fork and took a small portion between her teeth. So he looked away from her, out at the field.

This holiday, this splurge, had become something different from the senseless extravaganza he had intended. With all of her taunts and flippant manner, Robin struck a resonance in him that was somber, so low in register as to be silent and unheard by any ear but his, because it was the same note that sounded within himself. Though the years between them put the two of them into separate envelopes, as it were, and made for a disparity that seemed permanently rent, each of them carried the same message. Like strange Valentines, he thought.

He and Nancy had shared a similar inner harmony though their histories had been so different and now here was Robin, striking the same sort of chord, as profoundly sad as it was so familiar to him. He had been about to say something like this to her when he had pulled off the road a few miles back. He had been ready to use the word *love* to sum up his feelings, economically if not inappropriately, but she had stopped him.

"Hey, Penseroso. What are you thinking?" With the edge of the paper napkin she wiped hamburger grease from around her lips.

"I was thinking of the national pastime."

"Oh boy! This place rents rooms too?"

"No, I mean baseball. Out there." He gestured toward the field beyond them. "The games played out there. Small towns like this used to have baseball leagues. Teams sponsored by local businesses—probably this tavern had a team."

"When was this?" She leaned forward. Some of her hair fell loose and she reached up to repin it.

"Oh, not too long ago. Maybe before television."

"That's a long time back." She winked at his response. "Okay, so recent times. And?"

"I'm always trying to put different histories together. Like putting transparencies one over the other to get a single picture that would tell everything."

"Well, of course," Robin said. She hugged herself in the chilly sunlight. "A history like yours is so fractured, it's no wonder you're always trying to find the one version."

Strickland turned toward her quickly, almost to verify the source of this insight, but she had looked away and down at the Formica top of the table—again the pliant pose, as if suddenly made shy by her own perception. "So, you . . . you . . . you," she stuttered to get the conversation back into the groove. "You were saying baseball."

"Oh, I was thinking of the games played here—not just here but all over. Everywhere in this country, and the people sitting here watching them, country people like those sitting inside and elsewhere. Not mean or vicious but trying to be honest, mostly, trying to be fair, observing most of the rules. Accepting the umpire's decision. Making hamburgers the best way they can. Right? Then I thought of pictures of the men who had killed Medgar Evers—" Robin raised an eyebrow, so Strickland chewed and swallowed a last bite of sandwich.

"Medgar Evers was a black civil-rights leader in Mississippi in the sixties. He was gunned down on his front porch by some whites, a couple of them deputy sheriffs, I think."

"After Martin Luther King?"

"Before King. Before Jack Kennedy even. Our bearings were found by the sights of assassins. Evers was the first that made headlines. We take it for granted now. Few remember his name. It upset me, made me very angry. But I just thought of the guys who killed him. Pictures of them sitting in court, arms crossed, arrogant and proud of what they had done. Sure they would get off—and they did. Well, I can see them sitting here, right here at this field, comfortable in the summer sun, having a beer and enjoying the local boys loading up the bases. How can that be, Robin?

"I mean baseball is just a beautiful game. It's not violent. It's not dependent on war strategies. It's grace and intellect and skill. It's civilized. It's a civilized sport and how come goons like that can play it, can enjoy it? Even here, not just Mississippi. I mean the whole structure—not just baseball, but the whole game. You see what I'm saying? I mean the country—everything. Think of that design. Think of the arguments, the checks and balances so-called, all the guarantees for this or that liberty, this or that freedom. All those elaborate preambles about inalienable rights and happy pursuits—all that is trashed by the players themselves. It was a fraud from the beginning. It looked great on paper and I memorized all of it at Horace Leonard grade school in Salina but then I found out that it only applied to certain people. Medgar Evers showed me that. Vietnam was my final exam. But I still don't get it. I mean, god damn Tom Jefferson and Jack Kennedy. God damn them both.

"It shouldn't have happened the way it did. The people who like baseball shouldn't be the same ones who blow some guy's head off because he's a different color or talks too much. Or looks through slanted eyes. Maybe the game, the idea, is beyond the players and only tolerated by the spectators. It's always been that way; like one of those dreams the ancients used to sketch; imitations of birds. The thing was never able to fly. If so, no one could operate it. No one really wanted to fly it. Maybe that's it. But I am angry."

Some insects had set up a wheeze in the weeds of the old outfield. The day had turned warmer, almost pleasant, and the distant rumble of passing vehicles further lulled the moment. Stout Falls had once been on the main road that ran north to Boston Corners and then on into Massachusetts. But a larger, four-lane highway had been built parallel to this route some years back to bypass the village and, in an odd way, turn back its clock, restoring to the hamlet a somnolence from the early part of the century. The town road that passed before the tavern was scarcely traveled.

"Well," Robin finally said. "You do have a way with metaphors." She laughed nervously and seemed uncertain.

"Look, putting words together was never my forte. Okay? I'm only hired to pronounce them. That's my job, okay? I perform the script. That's what I do."

"Oh, Carrol." Her hand was gentle against his face.

The screen door slapped shut and the bartender came out with her soft drink. "Sorry I was so long. We had an emergency in the kitchen."

"The anvil blew a fuse," Robin said under her breath as she smiled up at him. "Thank you. Just in time, in fact." She drank thirstily and put the soda can on the table, patted her lips dry. Sometimes she used a gesture, like that precise daub with the paper napkin, which was the manner of a much older woman; say the stereotypical old-maid librarian. Strickland would ascribe this to all the time she spent alone, had lived alone.

"Did you see the moon last night?" she asked suddenly. "No? It must have risen late. Quite large. I guess around three o'clock. I woke up and the room was flooded with light. The light of it woke me. What's funny?"

"Just that truck that went through. See it?" She turned to face the road. "No, it's through the intersection now. It was a moving van but the company's name was misspelled. Or maybe they meant it to be a pun. Enterprize Movers. With a z. Get it? Enter prize." He laughed and felt a little pleased with his conception.

But Robin faced him and her eyes were slightly lidded, as if she looked into something stronger than moonlight. He recalled Leslie as a little girl being posed for a photograph, maybe at some point in their trip to Kansas—a visit to the birthplace of James Whitcomb Riley, say—looking like that. The squint, come to think of it, was not so much a shield against bright light as it was a signal of a distrust with the photographer, a suspicion as to the use to which the photograph would be put. In fact, he remembered just then a picture Robin had shown him of herself at about nine or ten, standing in her driveway in Hartford and holding a long bow with an arrow fitted to the string. She had looked out at the photographer, her mother probably, with the same wary look she gave him as they sat outside this tavern by the old ball field. "I'm sorry," he said. "I interrupted you. What about the moonlight?"

"Oh, just that it was so bright." Now she almost slouched in her chair. Her eyes slipped to one side, humorously. "I was thinking how beautiful it was—as always, caught up in the stage effects. How much romance, how many poems had been inspired by that silvery illumination. Then I got up and went to the bathroom. Really all the moonlight was doing was helping me find my way to the can without breaking my neck. Really."

Chapter

5

The birdcall pierced Carrol Strickland's sleep to bring him fully awake. He lay in bed trying to identify the bird by its song. Was it more than one bird? The sounds were so various and of such different chord structures that it seemed like several in chorus. All the mornings he and Nancy had lain in this bed, slowly or abruptly awakened by such sounds, and he could not yet tell a robin from a blue jay or a cardinal. Now, meadowlarks were something different and he could still hear their lyric spiral, even in his sleep, but meadowlarks sang a thousand miles or more from Silvernales, which spoke to a sort of disloyalty to this place that had received them when they'd moved from the city.

The bird challenged him once more, the sounds round and juicy like the berries it must have already breakfasted on, and it was singing right outside the bedroom windows, perhaps perched on one of the dormer peaks. Strickland reviewed his limited knowledge. The Strickland Album of Familiar Birdcalls. He and Nancy and Leslie had not been like the other émigrés who seemed to arrive from the city with little helpful books already in hand; small volumes entitled *Songbirds of the Northeast* or *The Flora and Fauna of the Harlem Valley.*

groundwater had lost their original composition? The soil had been made into something completely different. Plastic. When had Leslie understood that the atmosphere of her house reverberated with the sounds of falsehoods, the odor of deceptions and denial that floated in the air only faintly disturbed by the tings of the Terry clock in the library?

But in the meantime, he was alone in the house—now totally alone. If not the first man on earth listening to an unnamed tweet tweet, maybe the last. First Nancy had evaporated in that fireball in San Diego. Now Leslie had gone. Even the hunters seemed to have disappeared, and all these absences, taken together as he stood looking out the window over the bathroom sink, threw him off balance, like the unexpected release of an Oriental wrestling maneuver, so he felt himself being thrown headlong and out of control by the force of his own anger.

He would take *his* leave. The idea did not so much come to him as it was uncovered, like the arrowheads turned up by Schuyler's tillage of the corn lots. This morning a silvery net of early dew sparkled on the narrow band of meadow grasses that bordered the cultivated fields back of his house—"fairy tents," Leslie used to call them—and Strickland made his way along these isthmuses of virgin soil toward the line of woods at the top.

Already the early sun was hot on the back of his neck and his boots gleamed with the wetness of the high grass. It was the only shine the old, cracked leather could still take, for these boots went two generations back but were of the same style made for him by the Palloucci brothers on West Forty-sixth Street, and only suitable now for tramping about the back fields and the woodlots of his property.

Even in Saigon, where footwear took on a polished uniqueness, Strickland's boots had set him apart. These Wellingtons could not be found just anywhere, their speciality was clear in the way the dark, tanned leather folded at the instep and ankle like thick velvet, the perfect placement of the brass buckle. Also, Angelo always made them a certain height; not too tall, yet of a generous dimension, so that a pants cuff—sometimes both—would catch on the tops to give the wearer a cavalier look and if someone new in Saigon saw

Strickland stroll into the bar at the Caravelle, the question would be asked, "Who's that?" That's Golden Throat, the stranger would be told—the voice of America.

As he rounded the top edge of this field and strode through the spare scrub that grew from a shale shelf, Strickland admired once again the craftmanship that had fashioned the leather, shaped it to his foot and permanently formed it to that shape. Even this pair of boots, as cracked and as worn as they were, could be recognized for their handmade quality, easy to see, and this whim of his, this indulgent vanity for footgear was nurtured a long time back by that kid riding his bike through Salina, dreaming of a pair of boots that would forever set him apart from the ranchers and the grain men who high-hipped it into pickups parked downtown. Different even from his father's wonderfully smelly Monkey Ward work boots. Some of his pals from the early days in New York, guys from Brooklyn or Cleveland, Italian or Jewish, took the paycheck from that first commercial and headed for Brooks Brothers to buy a tie or a tweed jacket. Strickland had walked into the boot makers on Forty-sixth Street.

At the top of the field lay a fallen tree, the casualty of a late spring blizzard that had softly layered the sycamore's broad leaves with tons of snow, toppling the whole thing over. The shale deposit was not deep enough for the roots, Strickland figured, and the huge reef of the tree made a natural hermitage for rabbit and pheasants and other small creatures when it had fallen parallel with his line, the edge of the forest. He sat down, his back to these woods, and looked down the Harlem Valley.

A hawk screeched. Strickland recognized that sound. The other bird that had wakened him had been left behind, perhaps too timid to fly over this open hawk territory, and its song had vanished into the air as though his own song had also vanished. His profession was sound, the making and transmission of pleasant, soothing sounds, which upon their hearing formed a kind of community, a ken. He sometimes went for days without speaking, without opening his mouth to shape the vowels and dentals that represent intelligence as we know it, and he would invent a skit in which he had forgot how to talk—not that he had been struck mute, but that he had just forgot the technique, lost the know-how for speaking. So he had to practice, painfully reworking the sounds.

Hell-lo . . . my . . . name . . . is . . . Carrol . . . Strick . . . land.

The most basic sounds can make or unmake a society. Good morning, good morning. That exchange forms an instant community. A basic fellowship is quickly established. Fatuous to even suggest that to say more is where the trouble begins, for the words are to be chosen. That bird outside his window this morning was sending messages similar to the ones he had pronounced. *These berries are good. This territory is mine.* Clear and beautiful, the bird's song more than decorated the morning; the sounds had given the colorless air substance, meaning. He was paid for making similar sounds that carried similar messages, but their content had been corrupted; the communion of their hearing, perverted. But he was paid very well, as all perversions are paid well, he reminded himself, and he reached forward to caress several stalks of Queen Anne's Lace that grew at his feet.

He figured that he could wrap up the whole John Boy series in a week or two, and get his accounts settled after that. He still had some network commitments, promos for a cops-and-robbers series due in the fall, but he could get them done as well. Over with. Stone would have a fit. He could hear the agent's exasperation, see his eyes become both saddened and bellicose, when he heard the news. Here I get you a whole new career, he'd say, a hand up the ass of the original goose with the golden egg and you give it up? Can you give me a reason? Try me with a reason? You mean this little twit has you by the hairs? What she's got that's so different? Is she that hot? What?

She talks to me, he would say, and, sitting at the top of the corn lot, Strickland laughed out loud as he imagined Stone's expression. The short bark of a laugh, like a report, caused a frantic stir in the weeds behind the fallen tree. Robin talked to him, and, more important, he could tell her everything, anything. Whether or not she was so open with him, he was not so sure; he sensed there were parts of her past, he'd had glimpses, that she had not been all that frank about. He was sure she had even lied about some things but that was okay because he knew she was lying and he even enjoyed it. He was a little aroused, sitting in this open field, by the image of her, the turn her face took when she was lying. In time, she might tell him everything because he would not be judgmental. A special intimacy had taken hold between them; he had felt the lure of it the night she and Cora had come to dinner, and it went beyond sexual heat though it was not unlike that freedom, that sort of energy.

The two of them formed a unit. He was drawn to her because he felt comfortable with her. That wrongness in Robin was like a birdsong or a meadow flower he kept coming across but couldn't identify, yet it matched something in him. Nancy's wise-cracking critiques of his behavior or his motives or his drifting on the surface of things, on the flow of his voice, had eventually cut through to sting him into silence, kept him on guard. But he shared a unique communion with Robin. Her desire for a beauty always just beyond her grasp was not so very different from the truth that always escaped him, that always lay just beyond the range of his own voice. Her penchant for wearing clothes that didn't always belong to her was not all that different from the words he put into his mouth that didn't belong to him. Or look at Leslie trying on causes. "I will be good for you," Robin had said the other evening and though her specific reference was unclear (the soap-opera generic begging the specific— good in what way?) he sensed in her melodramatic pledge an oath sworn to this mutual conspiracy. She believed at that moment, when she said it. Who could ask for more?

Strickland had plucked one of weeds near his feet and twirled the white parasol of the Queen Anne's blossom between his fingers. He felt protected and free all at once beneath the canopy of her tolerance. Wasn't this the appeal of confession? To say anything, to reveal all the details of the week's orgy of falsehood and deceit and brutish behavior—unbridled honesty canceling out unbridled acts. Forgiveness was not necessary, just an audience—another human who would listen to the most outrageous secrets and say nothing. Do nothing. No, Stone would not know what he was talking about; the agent even took a percentage of his own transgressions.

Bit by bit, Strickland realized that he was being observed, some old sense still functioning deep in the primordial spine picked up signals behind him. He held up the white blossom before his face as though it might be a mirror that would reflect the view over his shoulder, and he studied the tiny flowerets, seeing them as the faces peering at him from across his fence line. In fact, when he stood up and slowly turned around, his observers looked much the same as their reflections in the weed.

Though these faces were somber and there were four of them this time and they carried no guns. The one with the hawk feathers in his hatband stood slightly ahead of the rest, resting one hand on the top strand of the barbed wire that made the boundary line. Very slowly, as if to show nothing was up his sleeve, he raised his other hand to wave. The gesture signaled a sadness, perhaps a farewell waved from the fantail of a ship pulling out of Palermo harbor. The rest did not move, looked steadily down at him. Strickland returned the wave.

"Buon giorno." He hoped his pronunciation was adequate, and apparently it was okay because four bands of very white teeth quickly flashed in the wood's gloom.

"Ah, Signore Streeken-lan. Comé sta? Ce tempo bello." And the man became effusive, stringing together vowel-laden sounds at a rapid rate so Strickland was again overwhelmed by sounds he could not identify and that set him apart. The others looked like a backup trio of a pop group; moving, turning, clapping shoulders, enacting each phrase. When he got to the fence line they were still doing their act. All were freshly shaven and their safari garb looked pressed to suggest a kind of discipline in the group that surprised him. The leader regarded him with such equanimity, a beaming fellowship, that Strickland was even more sorry he was not fluent in the man's language.

"Look here," he began. The group became quickly sober, intensely attentive. *The Great White Father greets your people with many hatchets and blankets.* "Look," he began again. "I'm looking for some traps that I . . . well, by mistake—mistake. I make a big mistake and . . ."

"Comé?"

"Traps." The strain in the man's face was almost hurtful. His companions formed a a semicircle around him to support his concentration. Strickland took a deep breath—should he act it out, raise his foot, step into something and howl with pain? He took a chance. "Trap-ola."

The result was instantaneous and amazing "*Ah, si—trapoli!*" Smiles broke out again and their talk became animated and cheerful. The guy with the hawk feathers faced his friends and Strickland almost expected them to break into song. Had he really got the word right? Italian must be an easy language to learn. Then the fellow was speaking to him, quickly and no doubt eloquently, with sharp moves of the hands and shoulders. Wisdom and jurisprudence were present in every nuance, his companions appreciated his elegance; then his eyes squinted, a roguish look twisted his dark face, and he wagged one finger at Strickland. Everyone laughed.

Strickland joined their good humor though he sensed he had just been lectured on some arcane segment of ancient Sicilian law and that a verdict had been handed down, not too stiff a one and only a little embarrassing perhaps. As if on a silent command, the hunters formed in a line as their leader came toward the fence and swept off his hat in the style of a courtier. Or maybe the judgment *was* a stiff one.

"*Per favore, signor . . . per favore . . .* please, you go with?" The man pressed down the top strand of wire with one foot. That was his barbed wire the guy was pushing around, Strickland thought, and he was doing it with a black-and-white sports oxford, at that. But there seemed to be little choice and a clear discussion was out of the question, so he carefully stepped over the wire and onto their side of the boundary line.

Boys and girls, you remember in yesterday's episode, Jack Armstrong and Billy found themselves captured by a band of mysterious warriors as they looked for Betty and Uncle Jim who were trapped in the depths of the Aztec Temple, where they had gone to witness secret rites and scurrilous practices. As we open today's chapter, we hear Jack say to Billy,

"About those traps, trapolas. They were for . . ." Strickland could not come up with a lie good enough, even in a language they would understand. Not even lies could be understood anymore. But it did not seem to matter. His guard of honor laughed, each passing his amusement back over his shoulder to the man behind as they walked single file through the forest. He heard the word *trapoli* once or twice.

They could be bringing him to some sort of rude court of justice set up on the clearing and presided over by the courtly *patron* with the heavy rings. No doubt one of them would be assigned to defend him but the firing squad would be methodically cleaning their weapons already. Or perhaps the traps would be returned to him in a ceremony similar to the illustrations in his history book at Horace Leonard Grade School: *Grateful natives welcome Columbus with an exchange of gifts.* A mistake had been made, they'd say. Someone had put these dangerous devices on his land but they had removed them. They knew he would approve. And here, Signor Streeken-land, they are for him to dispose of as he wishes. *My government tenders its most profound appreciation to your people for their resolute defense of freedom and so forth and so on . . . and so crapola.*

Or he could simply cut and run. Two marched in front of him, two behind, and they were not armed. He could cut to the right and be gone before they knew it. He smiled as he imagined their over-tooled wingtips, more suitable for the sidewalks of New Rochelle, slipping and catching on the rough terrain, the thick ropes of wild grape. But hadn't he stepped over the fence on his own volition? Wouldn't it be somehow graceless for him to flee their invitation now? Besides, they had just passed a wooden platform built into a large oak about fifteen feet from the ground—a deer blind—from where two men in battle garb looked down at them as they passed beneath it. These guards shifted automatic weapons from one shoulder to the other, a form of salute almost, and Strickland sensed that they had just passed the outward perimeter of the camp. He had no choice but to continue.

But hadn't he been contemplating just this sort of flight all morning, some kind of turning off from the hard and fast lines into an unmarked wilderness? Even before this morning, hadn't the theme of these last several months been escape? Hadn't he been following an old, overgrown route all along; driven, if not guided, by a compulsion to take that route—a desire that came with the territory almost, something like a fever caught in its lowlands? From east to west, from Salem to St. Jo to Oregon, the thirst for the natural springs, the hunger for the natural spirit had pushed them all through the wilderness and they had contaminated the springs and slaughtered the spirit as they went. These woods, Strickland was thinking, had become the very horror he hoped to leave behind. Just then a switch of wild hawthorn slashed across his face, cutting him severely.

"Ah, signor, mi scusi, apologii millione." The fellow in front of him whipped off the neckerchief from around his neck and started to attend the bleeding scratches. But he was shoved aside and dressed down with rapid, staccato phrases by the leader in the Alpine hat. Even in Sicily, the leader seemed to be saying, the most naive bandito knew enough to hold branches aside until the man coming behind could handle them safely. The fellow rolled his eyes with operatic remorse, even held out his hands toward Strickland as if to beg his intercession along with his forgiveness. One thing, they did not wish to harm him—the leader's anger with the accident indicated they wanted him whole. Or perhaps some ancient ritual passed down from the Crusades required that the body's envelope be intact save for the neat wound through the heart.

The lacerations were not so deep and were easily taken care of by another member of the patrol, supervised by the man in the Alpine hat. Much discussion and congratulations were passed around with the joyfulness of a wineskin. Then, before starting up again, handshakes also went around. Strickland felt he had just been inducted into some kind of a fraternity, and if he were to escape them now it would not matter. That secret grip would give him away as well as accommodate him wherever he went.

But Robin would have to be with him. He took a branch of chokeberry carefully handed back to him, this time, and passed it on to the man behind him. He considered the steps he had made toward his leave taking, which, without him recognizing the fact, had included her. His reasoning was closer to justification, but what was the difference? Their special communication, their two wrongs making a right, their mutual nakedness which somehow made for a strange innocence; these were the different items of his case. And there was something else.

A week ago at the mall in Great Barrington, he had come to an understanding about Leslie, a divestiture if anything. She had somehow, certainly without his help, come out of the shell that had protected her as it enclosed her. She had broken through, found a purpose, a cause. Not so with Robin. Her future was uncertain, even threatened by the very apparition of beauty that drew her gaze and made her blind to the ground at her feet. Her excitement over new clothes, over luxury, could be the snare that would hold her in a terrible wilderness of her own making. Cora Endicott's deer park.

Or Strickland could imagine her marrying a successful accountant someday, and living in the barren elegance of a suburb just to have fresh flowers on Thursday, just to have a new wardrobe each season. He saw her as the charming chairperson of the local arts festival. Her presidency of the library board, enthusiastic as it was comprehensive, would enrich the community. He could see her moving ever so gracefully among the illuminated tapers of the buffet she would hostess for the visiting choral director. She'd already have auditioned the fellow in her own special way. But all the while something would be bleeding inside of her, some monstrous dream, its term come and gone, would turn within her, atrophied and unaborted. No, he could not leave Robin to that.

Suddenly the thick embrace of the woods gave way like the abrupt ebbing of a tide, and they emerged into the clearing. The place seemed very familiar to Strickland, far more than his one, earlier visit might support. He looked for certain features and found them. Tents, several trailers, the sharp aroma of brewed coffee rising on the lacy smoke of camp fires, the whole area hyphenated by the stumps of trees; and, looking up, he found the dome of the sky still fitted in place like a lid. All he remembered of it, as he might have seen it in a recurring dream.

Yet it was also different. The place was deserted, empty of hunters as the woods had been empty of their gunfire this morning. The game rack was gone, and no trophy, not even the smallest carcass of a sparrow, turned in the breeze coming down from the Berkshires.

If a wild and wooded place could be scrubbed, the job had been done here. Strickland even stopped to look more closely for some scrap of habitation, a mess of civilized droppings, but the camp had been scrupulously picked up. The last of the camp fires turned to darkening embers within the stone circles of their hearths and these hearths already looked vacated, only to be frequented, as the flat rocks cooled, by a curious squirrel or vagrant deer. If, Strickland reminded himself, any were left alive in the environs.

His honor guard had also stopped to inspect the site, and they nodded with approving sounds, self-congratulatory, expansive gestures. Yes, they seemed to say to each other, we are leaving this place very well cleaned up. Now, why did he think they were leaving as well? Some of his own intention thrust upon them, in his usual way? For a moment he was embarrassed by the idea, and he glanced at their expectant faces as if to apologize for his presumption, but of course he had no words to accompany his look.

They had formed themselves into pairs, two in front and two behind, and recommenced the march. They passed the aluminum trailer, the site of his curious interview with their leader. The trailer looked closed up as well—the two lawn chairs had been folded and leaned against the trailer's side by the door. Brilliant geraniums in scarlet and pink bloomed in six pots neatly aligned along the edge of the small cement patio. Strickland took his gait from the leader—a slow, dipping walk, and his boots were harmlessly slashed by the stems of milkwort and dutchmen's breeches. They had left the clearing and pushed through underbrush once again. It amused him to think that after his execution, one of them might take his boots and recognize in the workmanship, in the joining of upper to sole, the hand of Angelo Palloucci. They would recognize Strickland's value by his boots, upgrade the importance of their morning's target.

But the ceremony he was led to was of a different nature, though death was at its center. The corpse lay uncovered in a simple coffin of pine boards, and this rude box had already been lowered into the open pit. The deceased was as dignified in death as he had been that morning months before, when he patiently explained to Strickland the traditional code that permitted them free access to his land, unlicensed jurisdiction to kill anything that moved or flew over it. If anything the man seemed more grave, Strickland thought and forced down a smile as he noted that the white shirt, open at the collar, almost sent up a light from below. The long, patrician hands were crossed at the breast and held a crucifix but were naked of the heavy rings. In an instant Strickland knew that these heavy jewels, the size of the agates he had shot in the school yard in Salina, decorated the hands of one of those gathered at the grave; more than decorated, enhanced and empowered.

Yet it was not the man in the Alpine hat who had been chosen; he seemed destined to be always the aide-de-camp, the adviser and interpreter to the throne. This fellow had halted and swept aside a place for Strickland to stand at the head of the burial. No heavy rings adorned his hands. The hunters standing at the grave site had made way for them, something in their manner suggesting that they had been waiting for him and his escorts; the ceremony had waited on his attendance. More than that, it turned out.

With a gesture worthy of Marc Antony, the guy with the Alpine hat stepped back and began to talk. The rest turned, almost as one, to regard Strickland. The man's rhetoric was fluid and varied, the sounds lifted into the forest like the lingering notes of an aria. Strickland could recognize memorable moments when the speaker broke the rhythm of his speech to fashion language in a particularly graceful manner, pass an allusion or even—his voice soaring on a zephyr of eloquence—make a point. The mournful band around the grave nodded at the appropriate moments, some to join a sibilant chorus of "*Si, veramente . . .*" They looked upon Strickland with both curiosity and respect. He began to get the idea that he had been brought here as a rival *signore* to honor an old adversary, that a truce had been declared for this amenity, and that he, as a rival chief, was expected to deliver the final and proper eulogy.

All of this Strickland heard in the man's address though he couldn't understand a word of it. Moreover something about the atmosphere, the meticulous appearance of the camp site for example, suggested these valedictory remarks embraced more than the corpse at the bottom of the grave. They were bidding farewell to this part of the forest. They were leaving too! Did their patron's death force the decision, or had his last breath coincided with the final flutter of the last wing shot? Nothing more to shoot at, so they would vacate the premises. Maybe his death was the signal that they were to move on, to some new glen, yet wild and bountiful, where birds and little animals cavorted in a fatuous ignorance of what was coming to them. But first they would bury the spirit who had guided their counsels here, led them in their peculiar rituals. The new high priest, one of those standing respectfully with hands clasped behind his back, would lead them to another locale, preside over their daily volleys of gunfire, and sanctify the torn and bleeding results of that gunfire.

Strickland turned away to look over their heads and through the trees at the profile of the distant hills to the west of the Harlem Valley, fully expecting to see a flag raised, a guidon already marking the site of the new camp. Through his concentration, he heard the silence around him. The man had stopped speaking. They all looked to him. Now it was his turn.

Later he would say that it was like giving a voice level for the audio engineer, that the words had spilled out of the storehouse he kept of such stuff and that this "filler," as he called it, was only meant to take up the right space in the script until the actual lines could be written and the whole scene shot again. Meanwhile the extras went through their paces, moved as one and leaned into the sound of his voice, even though his words were incomprehensible to them. Strickland stepped forward and raised his arms.

"From the shores of Gimme-goochy to the sands of Tripoli, our founding fathers brought forth on this nation a New Deal, born in liberty and destined to perish, but which guaranteed a chicken in every pot and two cars in every garage. We are not honorable men and never meant to be, but under one flag, whose broad stripes and bright stars signal the battle is not o'er, we rededicate ourselves to this one principle: that all men are too much with us, Horatio.

"Today, our young republic faces its most serious threat. A great white sludge of Milk of Magnesia has passed through the very core of our destiny, threatening to weaken resources, soil our ideals and sap the very fiber that have made this nation great. We shall be overcome.

We will sit on this pot if it takes all summer. But as good neighbors, we must cast our eyes south of the border, where the waters are never very clear and where this white scourge that knows no boundaries has gone to the seat of their problems. The toilet bowls of this hemisphere must be kept fresh and clean or we will lie face-down in the consequences.

"We gather here today to do honor to one who spoke of these unsanitary consequences. But along came Bill, just an ordinary guy, and by the very substance of his eye, you'd know him well. A simple everyman, a proud and noble brow and for every movement there was a meaning. We who stand as brothers will sit down like men and, yes—like women too. The rest is the stuff that dreams are . . ."

Only as he took the road back to his house, the magnificent tone of his gibberish still soaring in his mind, does he remember the bear traps. In the sentimental majesty of the ceremony (afterward each man had actually filed by to shake his hand at the grave site), there had been no place for such an ordinary concern. Even if he could have made himself understood, to pursue the missing devices at that time would have been the act of an insensitive lout; moreover, the power of his rhetoric had overwhelmed the reason for that morning's mission along the property line—he had simply forgot the traps—and even now, as he walks back down the hill by way of this dirt road, they seem unimportant. Let them rust wherever they lay, their jaws frozen open, astonished by their own corrosion and powerlessness. Let them stay in the woods, like the painful promise of the land itself to punish all future trespassers of that land.

A farmer had cut this road out of the side of the hill some time back to get to pastures at the top, but those fields had long returned to burdock and birch, and the quartz stone walls of their division tumbled and spilled by the irresolute turning of the earth. When they had first moved to Silvernales from the city they sometimes walked up this road to the abandoned meadows, coming on them like unexpected sunlight in the midst of a summer storm. Leslie would run ahead of them when she saw the old fields, as if released from the taut string of their disaffection, into the tall grasses, the daisies and wild chicory that came up to her waist. Sometimes they would picnic, other times pick wildflowers or just admire the different views, but always Strickland would be restless, eager to quit the place, ready to move on once the experience had been registered, filed away.

He is sorry about that vagrancy now—that wayward state of mind—though he might not yet understand the reason for it, and he could feel Nancy's hand in his, pressing his fingers, pressing his stay with the rural idyll he had brought mother and daughter to only to flee from it impatiently himself. Then she had let go.

The road follows the woods on his right that belong to the Italians, posted at the proper intervals, he wryly notes, with No Hunting signs that claim the preserve for the "ABC Sportsmen Assn." Farther down the road his property begins, and to his left the hillside falls away so the soft slopes of the Harlem Valley stretch into the distance, their greenness so intense almost to be blue, and he is reminded of hillsides in Vietnam, how beautiful they were and very similar to these. Alike, also, in that he did not know that landscape well either, and that he left those hillsides strange and foreign as he was about to leave these in ignorance as well. A single hawk circles above him.

Afterword

One image of Robin Endicott, above all others, will always remain with Carrol Strickland. Early in their time together (had they even become lovers, yet? He couldn't remember.), he had driven over to Lakeville to see her one morning. Actually, an irresistible obsession had driven him to Lakeville to observe her, to spy on her. So he had pulled up the Volvo on a side road near Cora Endicott's place and tramped through some woods to a knoll that gave him a view of the entire compound. The day had been warm for April, and the new leaves of the miniature pear trees in the back garden were glossy with dew. Crocuses popped up like candies along the outside of the high stockade fence and fountains of wisteria sprayed against the stone walls of the carriage house where Robin's apartment was located on the second floor. A room over a garage and loaned to her, he thought. Even that.

Strickland had squatted down and made himself comfortable on a coverlet of moss. For what? He had no idea but for a desultory surveillance that seemed to have no cause, not even curiosity. The main house, where Cora probably still lay abed, looked freshly painted, looked like a picture in a paint catalog featuring the colors of Colonial America. The carriage house seemed empty too, unlived in, and he thought of Robin inside still sleeping, her dark hair veiling her face or perhaps fixing herself some tea, some toast—or perhaps bending over to fix herself onto someone sharing the futon. No car was parked in the back—more specifically, no black motorcycle. That was the vehicle of suspicion that had driven him that morning.

Sometimes he had spied on his own house this way. Taking up a position at the top of the hill to look down at the roof line and the smoke rising from the middle of the three chimneys, as a log slowly warmed Nancy's reading by the living-room fireplace, or simply keeping track of Leslie's miniaturized back and forths. All this before the hunters took over the woods. Usually there'd be no sign of activity at all. Peaceful. An empty house, he would imagine. That house used to be Carrol Strickland's, he would think, but no one lives there now. They have all gone.

As a boy he had done much the same thing in Salina, setting up a post in the hay barn to look back at the frame house so exposed to the vast prairie stretched out behind it but for the stand of cottonwoods. He would be apart from the scene yet still be a part of it, and the attraction of this curious ambivalence had stayed with him. It was a way of following the scene, he figured out later, of not being involved in the causes and effects of that scene yet feeling that all the events within it were under his care. He shied away from thinking the word *supervision.* It was much like those grown men who played with elaborate train sets, fashioning landscapes and communities of plaster and pasteboard where tiny trains started up and stopped, always on schedule.

So he had come that morning only to observe, to find out something about Robin Endicott he did not already know. He had no idea what this might be; some innocent, ordinary pursuit he might watch, catching her off guard and therefore seeing her close up, though from a distance. True, his pulse throbbed in his throat as he took up his surveillance, for he half feared to see a black motorcycle parked on the gravel bay at the rear of the carriage house. He had only just followed that couple out of Green River and into the back lots of Connecticut and he considered that some awful urge might have driven him to confirm what he did not want to know; that it might have been Robin who had pressed herself against the black-leather back of the Yamaha's operator. So he felt a little foolish, even saddened to be caught up by this incipient jealousy, this classic fear of an older lover.

When Robin did appear, her task humbled him even more. He did not see her at first, only the slap of the back door screen turned him toward the house. A high hedge and a tulip tree in full bloom hid her passage through the garden so that when she did kick open the door of the tall fence, the surprise of her hit him full force. She was taking out the garbage.

Bags and bags of refuse, neatly packaged in plastic, were carefully set down in a row along the fence for the weekly pickup. He watched her come and go a half dozen times at least. Once she even used a small dolly to wheel out a large carton that came above her head (Cora had got a new refrigerator), and Strickland admired the forceful way Robin maneuvered this awkward shape through the gateway, the wheels of the dolly sinking into the soft ground so the whole rig had to be pushed around with two well-placed kicks. She wore the high-heeled clogs, he remembered, blue shorts, and a loose T-shirt. Her bare legs were slim and pale.

What in the world had the two of them accumulated; what had they consumed to generate such a large amount of trash? It looked like an attic cleared out, a basement as well. She had gone back into the house with the empty dolly for more boxes. Perhaps what he saw was the weekly accumulation of brochures and circulars, bales of letters and appeals for money, all those causes and political crusades that stroked the Endicott conscience and brought the old Puritan gleam into Cora's faded eyes. Robin's task became ironic to Strickland. So enamored of material things, so desirous of the finely made, she was taking out the husks of this curious consumption. It was like some sort of awful destiny, unfair and outrageous as most destinies tend to be. Egregious, she might say.

The no-nonsense manner with which she performed this morning chore—once or twice dusting her hands together after placing a load of stuff at the road's edge—combined with that loose-kneed lope he had grown to love, made for a powerful appeal. The longer he watched the matter-of-fact way she gave herself to the task, the more her manner suggested a kind of courage and, as he was to learn later, it was indeed a sign of this strength in her.

When he thought about that morning, about her carrying out the garbage, he came to understand that she had never had any hope at all, not even from the beginning had she any hope that she could escape her destiny. All those elegant inflations, some worded not quite right, had been no more than wishes that her fate might be different, like someone not wanting to believe the bad hand dealt to her and talking over the cards face-up on the table. She would pretend it to be otherwise. So what he had seen that morning in Lakeville when he had come to spy on her had been a mundane foreshadowing of the valor she was to demonstrate later.

They would be together from here on, like two prisoners en route to where they would serve their sentences for the same protracted innocence, an offense they shared as well, and with this intuition he felt as if all the deferments in his life, all the incidents and reflections, all the pleas of ignorance he had saved up to be talked about at some later time had at last found their place in a quirky narrative. And then what happened, she would ask? She seemed to hold up the sounds of his voice, then put them away carefully in her mind as he had seen her put clothes away, so that what had become a seamless, unending narration for him—the sound of his own voice—was made particular and unique by her selection.

Good morning, Laredo. Here's Rogue Radio from across the Rio Brava and this is old Strick telling you that the river runs milky thick with nutrients this morning. Dip your toes in its goodness, littl' darlin's, and your troubles are over. Baldness cured and the angst of PMS rinsed away. Oh, are you washed in the blues of this land? Hey, here's the new sound from the Boss!

Their last day in Washington had been particularly uncomfortable, the air saturated and close and Robin had seemed to wilt, her whole weight on his arm because she had not completely healed, got all her strength. Is that all, is that the last, she would ask when he had stopped talking. That's the last, he said and they got into the

Volvo and started driving west. Already Strickland had begun a voice level in his head. He listened to the changing inflections of disc jockeys all across the country, a kind of linkage forged as they went along. *Let's pull up, pardners, for a traffic check of the streets of Laredo.*

They crossed the Shenandoah and came down the western slope of the Blue Ridge Mountains looking for a place to spend that night. A week of days and nights in the late-summer pressure cooker of Washington made the evening air in the Shenandoah Valley sweet as sherbert, and they rolled down the windows, the air conditioning turned off, to take large breaths of it. *Strickland reporting to you from this valley where Stonewall Jackson completely derailed McClellan's advance on Richmond . . .*

Then what happened? Her face was turned away from him, into the fresh breeze and toward the darkening countryside, but her expression would be unreadable anyway. The round, blank sema-phores of the large sunglasses covered nearly the whole top half of her face to give her a chic that had drawn the attention of more than one tourist. Both of them had stood out; unique and obviously not the usual kind of visitors at the capital's sites. Were they celebrities who could not be readily identified? They had looked famous—this older man arm in arm with the young woman. Clearly not father and daughter. People had looked at them and then looked at each other. Go on, she said, tell me again. She put her hand on the dashboard and leaned forward to listen.

She remembered that time in Stout Falls where they ate hamburgers and that truck had driven through. Enterprize Movers. Did she remember that? Well, those were the housebreakers. They were the same ones who had robbed Cora and they had been breaking into summer homes—pulling up to the back door of a place and just cleaning it out from top to bottom. Cora had been lucky, they had left her her furniture and her clothes, only took the jewelry. Anyway, a half dozen houses or so all over that part of the county had been robbed.

All over, Robin repeated. Yes, Strickland replied and started to laugh at the picture of it, the zany sort of logistics the Enterprize

Movers must have employed, and Robin apparently got the same picture, some sort of transmission from his head to hers, because she giggled and hugged herself. How many were they, she asked? She wanted to hear the answer again, like a child verifying a particular fact in a familiar fairy tale. Two, three—maybe more, the cops aren't sure. They found the house they rented in Connecticut. One of them was a woman. They found a box of Tampax in the bathroom. Oh wonderful, she said sarcastically and he felt a little silly supplying this detail. Maybe they had guests, she said in a small voice.

In the end the truck was found abandoned at the town dump in Irondale. Robin sat up primly now in the seat beside him, as if to bring all of her attention to this part of the story, for they had laughed and speculated about this circumstance, its significance. Strickland had glanced at her. In the dusky light he could see the long line of her jaw and how it had set in her concentration. He could imagine the rest, from memory, the delicate tracing of the vein in her throat that made its way behind her ear to disappear into her thick and silky hair. His lips had followed that path with wonder and delight so many times. Go on.

The thieves had been using the refuse dumps of the different towns in the area to dispose of the stolen goods that they couldn't hock right away. No one had noticed anything strange about the loads of household items they pushed over into the different landfills. The attendant at the Hammertown dump said it looked like the same sort of stuff always being disposed of. There were two of them, he told the cops, and they told him they were helping with some historical restorations in the area. Say that again, Robin laughed, and Strickland did. Historical restorations. The guard said the movers were very friendly and they all had a drink together.

So house owners who had been robbed had to go to these dumps—even one up near Great Barrington, across the Massachusetts line—to sort through the garbage and debris for their belongings, to try to identify furniture, pictures and bric-a-brac. How many dumps? Oh, at least five or six, Strickland said, seeing lights of a town up ahead. Unfortunately the dump in Irondale had already been bulldozed, everything plowed under and the gravel smoothed over so that the goods of at least one household had become part of the geological history of the county. Robin bounced on the seat. I love it, she said, I love it.

Then they were gone, satisfied with what they had robbed or smart enough to know the cops were closing in, it didn't matter which; they had just gone. They had been like a pack of wild dogs that had run through the area, appearing out of nowhere, disappearing the same way; or like a virulent strain of flu that came and went just as the ground started to soften up in the spring. Even now, Robin said, they could be on the road, finding someplace new to rip off, which made Strickland quickly look in the rearview mirror. The road behind them was dark. She became inertly silent and he sensed this silence was a kind of review—all the various details gone over as if to check this latest version of the story with its original copy, that first report he had given her in the hospital. Yes, she nodded, everything pretty much the same. But he would have to repeat the story tomorrow and the next day and so on down to Texas and into Mexico.

That night they ate their supper at the Blue Ridge Best Western just outside of Buena Vista, Virginia. When Strickland came back with pizza and the soft drinks, the room was still dark but he only turned on the radio between the two king-size beds. They had no need of light. A local station was playing Jim Croce, and they listened to the gentle ballads of remorse and loss as they ate. They might make Memphis the next day where Martin Luther King was shot down, and he would say to her, now we are crossing the Mississippi, and she would ask him to describe everything to her, his voice making it clear and visible.

Still later, on this night in Virginia, she would make love to him, her lips and fingers identifying him in the darkness, tracing his features with a casual recognition. He listened to the radio, let the accent of the announcer imprint itself on the tape of his memory so that he could reproduce the sound exactly. He would practice voices all the way down to Texas, play them back in his head, trying them out on her so she would laugh and clap her hands. He wanted to sound like everybody else, so that he would be ready to announce the new history, truly report whatever would happen.

Then, it was her turn at the narrative, what would become a sharing of storytelling, almost, and because she had been given a share of this narrative passed back and forth, some power of it, she was no longer subject to him, if not altogether equal. What happened next, Strickland now asked and took her in his arms. The rise and fall of traffic outside on Route 81 made him think of the ocean, and he looked forward to becoming a part of this channeled energy in the morning. They would plug into the network, as it were, traveling down Route 81 to Route 40 and then onto 30 and finally south on 35 all the way to the border. He had mapped it out only once but their route was blazed in his mind with a fateful simplicity that allowed no deviation. He thought of his father in his pickup truck making his own turns over the open prairie and how he had laughed like a kid and slapped his knee next to the gearshift, like a kid who had come on the truth of something eternal for the first time. Or maybe it was he, the son, who had just done that.

Robin shifted against him and her lips tasted the words she was about to pronounce. She had gone running. If Cora had tried to buzz her on the old telegraph, she hadn't been there to hear it. All the times she had answered that call but not this time. But why was she jogging at night? It had been so hot that day, and the night was lovely and cool. But jogging in the dark? He asked the proper questions, his part of the dialogue they had fashioned, rehearsed a couple of times already. They switched the roles of narrator and listener back and forth, like children playing dress-up.

Yes, it was dark, but there was a moon. Some of that same moon that had so gloriously flooded their room at the Yankee Tinker. He would remember that moon? He did. Well, there was still some of it left, just enough to illuminate the back roads. Also—Robin sat up in bed, as if to alert him to a new detail, for like all good storytellers, she would add something different each time so the fabric would be enriched, the content freshened—also, she remembered him telling her about driving back from parties with Nancy, driving by moonlight with the car lights off and the whole landscape spectral. Is that the right word? Yes, spectral, Strickland replied and stroked the smoothness where her back flared into her hip. Yes, that was the right word.

So, coming back, when she jogged around the last curve, it first looked like Cora had brought all the lamps in the house into her bedroom to better see her correspondence. The bedroom window looked out on the night with an angry eye. The place was on fire. Robin had yet to tell him everything; he doubted if he would ever hear the whole story but no amount of new material would change the ending. Cora Endicott consumed in the flaming rubbish of her charities. Robin had wrestled with her, dragging the old woman out of her chair. No, she hadn't thought of pushing her out. The metal framework seared the flesh of her hands when she touched it. The brake of the wheelchair was set. She must have panicked. The torn envelopes, the mess of circulars and brochures had been the tinder that had set the whole room going. The slick plastic finishes of the proposals gave off a blue-green flame, like a gas Robin said, and then as she pulled and wrestled with the hot, dead weight of her aunt, the brandy had been knocked over. It was orange and magenta, she said. Like a glorious sunset, and it was to be the last color she would see. Another fire, Strickland had thought.

Everyone agreed she had shown a lot of courage. The village fire company found the two women on the flagstone front foyer, one of them already dead, the other screaming. The living room was already an inferno. Strangely, the young woman had gone back again and again into the smoke and blaze of the bedroom—she must have felt her way—to pull out smoldering old furs, clothes, shoes scattered around, everything piled up like a levee against the flames. She must have gone back and forth several times. Horses did that in barn fires, someone said.

Strickland could imagine the volunteers shaking their heads, good townsmen all. First the robbery and now this fire. But it gave them a chance to see inside the Endicott house, what was left of it; probably something they had been wanting to do all their lives. One or two may have had older relatives who had worked on the place in the old days, in the kitchen or stables. They said you laughed in the ambulance. Is that what they called it, Robin snorted. I guess it may have sounded like laughter, but nothing funny, you know. Once again her fingers traced the features of his face. Her touch transformed his image, gave it more substance than it might possess in daylight. I've known that moustache everywhere, she laughed.

Strickland leaned up to kiss her, but, in the dark, his lips touched the slick texture of the scar tissue and Robin pulled back quickly, not yet ready to share this part of the fate that she had only just accepted. Or perhaps, he would wonder, she had anticipated it all along and that was why she had laughed or not laughed in the ambulance. She handled this accident, this worst of bad luck, with the same kind of stoic proficiency he had seen before. Whether taking out the garbage, making a pie, or pleasuring him, she handled all these endeavors as easily as she had handled the pizza earlier. Did she make any distinctions, he wondered?

So, the next morning as they dressed in silence, she said, turning away from him—you're looking. But he hadn't been looking, he told her, and this was only a partial lie. Actually, he had caught her image accidentally in the mirror of the motel room, a ricochet reflection of her naked face with that look of curious attentiveness that had been fixed on it by the fire in Lakeville. She seemed to be listening to something he could never hear. Well okay, she finally said. Tell me. What does it look like?

Like a beautiful pink mask, he told her. Something for a masquerade, a fairy-tale ball, she asked, or like a gorgeous, an egregiously gorgeous butterfly was resting there. He would not describe her eyes, like two penciled slits drawn in as an afterthought, but if the rest was like a mask then he became something out of a legend, never able to remove that mask, never to look upon her directly again without it. A mask, she repeated and laughed. Well, we're too late for Mardi Gras. Or maybe we're too early. Which? She turned on the sound he made and reached out for him, finding her way onto his lap to embrace him with all the strength in her arms. She asked him for the names of the places they would drive through that day, and this strategy got them over the crevice that had abruptly opened up beneath them, as it had helped her through the agony before. He had come to the hospital and leaned close to her ear on the pillow as if to keep the place names confidential, so that it sounded to anyone else, say a nurse coming in the room, like a litany of some kind. Monongahela. Allegheny. Missouri. Ohio. The sounds seemed to soothe the burning in her flesh as much as the drug the nurse had brought to inject into that flesh.

For Strickland it was like telling a story to Leslie when she was a child. Robin's face became very attentive; tuned in, as it were, to every syllable ·and every syllable turned over in her hearing like a physical object to be handled, assessed and given a new value within the nautilus of her ear. The one sense had not been taken away so much as it had been added to the other, so that a kind of rapture would take her expression, and this had also made the other tourists in Washington take a second look at them, especially as they stood, her hand on his arm, before the long gray wall that stretches like a permanent scar across the perfection of that green vista.

For a whole week this couple would appear so that by the second or third day the Vietnam vets standing their self-appointed duty before the memorial became used to them but wondered who they might be. The couple's slow traverse along the length of the wall differed from the perfunctory prowl of most tourists. Something formal about them also. The young woman was carefully dressed, her hand always in the bend of the man's arm, and the large rounds of dark glasses gave her face an aloofness a little like that of a bride being walked through a very long reception line.

And, in fact, the man—a bit older than her—was pronouncing the names chiseled into the stone like he was introducing her to each one. Like it was some kind of a thing he was doing for them both, one of the vets said. He spoke the names out loud, starting with the first guys, DALE BUIS . . . CHESTER OVNAND, shot while watching a movie starring an actress named Jeanne Crain, a vet told them. Long before *Deep Throat*, he joked and then backed off a little, shamed a little by the way they went on as if they hadn't heard him. Other tourists always laughed. The guy spoke each name for the girl, sometimes leaning down a bit so as not to speak too loud but his voice carried. People turned and stopped to take a closer look at the wall, like they might have missed something, say the name of someone famous right there: EDWARD SMITH, RALPH G. SMITH, FRANKLYN R. SMITH. He spoke low and only to her but you couldn't help hearing him.

JIMMY JOE JONES, RICHARD JONES III, JULES F. KINGMAN. The guy went through the entire roll call, all 54,000 of them he read to her. It took a whole week almost. ELMER WIGHTMAN, JACOB WEINSTEIN, ROGER WILSON. Each name was pronounced with the same deliberate care. Some of the vets began to stand next to them, almost like an informal honor guard to accompany their slow advance along the wall, not knowing the meaning or reason for this ceremony but recognizing it to be a ceremony of some kind, and one which deserved its own quiet space. ALBERT C. KAHN, SAMUEL KANE, GEORGE LOVE, JR., WILFRED CYRUS LUCKMAN.

The veterans would talk about this couple for a long time, wondering who they were and what became of them. They would remember the man's resonant voice as it had printed every one of the names into the air with a resiliency second only to that of the stone; perhaps, to raise another memorial, invisible but no less grand.

And, they would talk about the young woman who never said anything, who sometimes raised her face to the sky as she listened to the names, so the dark glasses caught and threw back the light. They would remember the smile, how it would pass across her mouth almost timidly, as if she saw something so incredibly beautiful that the words to describe it had yet to be conceived.